Also by Tim Murphy

The Breeders Box
Getting Off Clean

CHRISTODORA

In this vivid and compelling novel, Tim Murphy follows a diverse set of characters whose fates intertwine in an iconic building in Manhattan's East Village, the Christodora. The Christodora is home to Milly and Jared, a privileged young couple with artistic ambitions. Their neighbour, Hector, a Puerto Rican gay man who was once a celebrated AIDS activist but is now a lonely addict, becomes connected to Milly and Jared's life in ways none of them can anticipate. Meanwhile, Milly and Jared's adopted son Mateo grows to appreciate the opportunities for both self-realization and oblivion that New York offers.

As the junkies and protestors of the 1980s give way to the hipsters of the 2000s and they, in turn, to the wealthy residents of the crowded, glass-towered city of the 2020s, enormous changes rock the personal lives of Milly and Jared and the constellation of people around them. Moving kaleidoscopically from the Tompkins Square Riots and attempts by activists to galvanize a response to the AIDS epidemic to the New York City of the future, *Christodora* recounts the heartbreak wrought by AIDS, illustrates the allure and destructive power of hard drugs, and brings to life the ever-changing city itself.

Tim Murphy is a journalist who has written for, amongst others, the *New York Times*, *New York* magazine, *Details*, *Condé Nast Traveler*, *WSJ.* magazine, *Out* and *The Advocate*. His July 2014 *New York* magazine cover story on the new HIV prevention pill and its impact on New York City gay men was nominated for a GLAAD Media Award for Outstanding Magazine Journalism. He lives in Brooklyn and in the Hudson Valley.

TIM MURPHY

CHRISTODORA

PICADOR

First published 2016 by Grove Atlantic

First published in the UK in paperback 2016 by Picador

This edition first published 2017 by Picador
an imprint of Pan Macmillan
20 New Wharf Road, London N1 9RR
Associated companies throughout the world
www.panmacmillan.com

ISBN 978-1-5098-1859-4

3 5 7 9 8 6 4 2

A CIP catalogue record for this book is available from the British Library.

Printed and bound by CPI Group (UK) Ltd, Croydon, CR0 4YY

Visit **www.picador.com** to read more about all our books
and to buy them. You will also find features, author interviews and
news of any author events, and you can sign up for e-newsletters
so that you're always first to hear about our new releases.

For Cathay, Clint, James, Maria, and Mark.

And for survivors.

Pull up the shades so I can see New York.
I don't want to go home in the dark.

—O. Henry

CHRISTODORA

PART I

URBAN DWELLERS
1981–2010

ONE

NEIGHBORS AND THEIR DOGS
(2001)

By the time the Christodora House settlement erected its handsomely simple new sixteen-story brick tower on the corner of Avenue B and Ninth Street in 1928—an edifice that loomed over Tompkins Square Park and the surrounding blocks of humble tenements—the Traums had long left the Lower East Side. They were part of that first wave of worldly German Jews who had come to New York City in the early or mid-nineteenth century. Those sedate, self-conscious Jews had slowly migrated uptown as the old neighborhood became crowded with their dirt-poor eastern European cousins, Jews who spoke Yiddish and held to embarrassing old traditions, such as separating men and women at temple. Around the time that WASPs were raising money to fund the new Christodora building, which aimed to civilize these shtetl children and their equally wild-haired Catholic immigrant peers, Felix Traum, an investment banker, was already playing a leading role in the building of the new Temple Emanu-El on Fifth Avenue in midtown, a limestone Romanesque pile that would become the most prestigious synagogue in America. Accordingly, Felix had moved his family to the Upper East Side, where they lived in a not-opulent but still very capacious apartment not far from the Ochses of the *New York Times*.

Felix's son Steven, not interested in the bald pursuit of money, became an urban planner who, in his quiet way, helped hold back some of the worst excesses of Robert Moses, whose neighborhood-crushing projects stopped short of running a ten-lane expressway across lower Manhattan. Steven was part of that 1960s–1970s generation of planners who were much taken with Jane Jacobs's *The Death and Life of Great American Cities* and her idea that the best neighborhoods were small, intimate, and dense. On weekends, Steven would find himself taking his wife, Deanna, also an academic, and their two small children, Stephanie and Jared, down from the Upper East Side to the old neighborhood where his family had first landed in America, inside the humble, semi-derelict synagogues and then to Katz's Deli for pastrami on rye.

The neighborhood was almost completely Puerto Rican now, full of junkies and homeless people. Half the buildings were abandoned, including the Christodora, which had fallen on hard times. Decades ago, it had become the property of the city, which used it for various municipal purposes until it sold the building in 1975 for about $60,000. Nearly fifty years prior, it had cost $1 million to build. Such were the depths to which the Christodora, which means the "gift of Christ" in Greek had fallen. In that time the country was poised to take a rightward swing under Reagan. But that did not stop Steven Traum from standing before the Christodora's facade, with its beguiling and eerie neo-Gothic frieze of angels, demons, and goblins set over the door. Steven held the hand of each of his privileged children on either side and dreamed about reviving the old neighborhood.

In the 1980s, the old neighborhood was rebranded the "East Village," at least above Houston Street. Throughout the decade, the Christodora, still derelict and disused, had changed hands several times, each time for more money, until, in 1986, its destroyed inner plumbing and wiring was properly gutted and renewed and it became a condo conversion—a shocking development that *New York* magazine, on its cover, heralded as the inevitable triumph of gentrification in a neighborhood long thought of as a sanctuary for wayward bohemians. The Christodora offered rooms with massive ceilings and windows looking out beyond the drug-scarred mayhem of the neighborhood onto the vistas of Manhattan. Steven, friends with a social worker and a journalist who bought in immediately, could not resist and, for the trifling sum of $90,000, purchased a two-bedroom, 1,400-square-foot corner unit on the sixth floor, suffused with light and overlooking the park, which in the evenings became an encampment for homeless people and heroin shooters, its black square of land dotted with ragtag tents and bonfires.

Steven began using the apartment as an office. Deanna thought he was crazy, but Steven was delighted to spend his days down in the old neighborhood, and most afternoons you could find him getting his lunch at Katz's, or walking back to the Christodora with smoked salmon on a bagel from Russ and Daughters. Sometimes he would turn the corner on Houston onto Norfolk Street and poke his head inside the ornate old Anshe Slonim Synagogue, whose peak-roofed beauty filled his eyes with tears. In time, he met the Spanish artist Angel Orensanz, who had just bought the abandoned old building to use as a studio. Eventually, Orensanz would turn it into a great arts center, keeping its opulence intact and signaling the rebirth of the neighborhood. Such a rebirth moved Steven to a very fine tremble of excitement.

Steven's daughter, Stephanie, went to college in California and never moved back, but Jared, a handsome, pale-skinned boy who had a mop of curly honey-colored hair and brown eyes that could flash both warmly amused and arrogantly entitled, went to college not far from New York. Even before he graduated, Jared was shacking up during breaks and summers at the Christodora, cultivating a love of the neighborhood that became a quiet bond between him and his father. Jared wanted to move back to New York City and continue making the kind of industrial sculpture he'd started making in college until he was considered the next Richard Serra, so it wasn't surprising that he became the de facto resident of the apartment at the Christodora, rising some mornings after nights of heavy drinking with friends only when the sound of his father's key in the lock woke him around eleven o'clock. Father, arriving with two large coffees in hand, got right to work, while son stumbled to the shower and then, clutching his own coffee, pondered just how he should apply the day toward his goal of being a famous artist. Should he go for an MFA immediately? Find some already renowned artist to apprentice with?

"Russ?" he'd call out to his father in the other room, looking up from the *New York Times* where, in the Arts section, he read with a furrowed brow about the people he wanted to supplant someday.

"Russ," Steven would call back. "Twenty minutes."

And in twenty minutes father and son would take the elevator down to the Christodora's lobby, which was handsome yet very simple, like the Christodora generally, and walk across Tompkins Square Park. It was early 1991, in that short window of time between the 1988 summer riots in the park—in which its longtime homeless denizens and the NYPD phalanxes had faced off amid an atmosphere of increasing rage over gentrification—and the coming May, when the park riots would flare up again briefly and the city would shut the park for renovations until the following year.

Jared had been in the apartment at the Christodora that August night when the riots first broke out. It was 1988, the summer before his freshman year in college. He was drinking and smoking pot with some high school friends, rhapsodizing about the brilliance of the Pixies' *Surfer Rosa*, which they were listening to, all of them trying to stay cool amid the heat by hanging out near the open window looking down on the park, which was a scene of mayhem. Police lights whirled in the humid night sky and sirens wailed, crowds of shirtless skinheads massed and surged, indistinct voices projected over loudspeakers and young people charged around with bedsheet signs decrying gentrification. Most of the heavy action was concentrated on the other side of the park, on Avenue A, so Jared and his friends followed the proceedings on the street below as a kind of diversion, a channel they switched back to occasionally amid their own stoned pronunciations about art and politics. Inwardly, Jared glowed with pride that his family was cool enough to own an apartment amid the loud grit of the East Village, far from the Upper East and West Sides where he and all his friends had grown up. But of course he wouldn't say this to anyone.

"It's so fucking crazy," said Asa Heath, Jared's best and oldest friend, whose hair was as glossily straight and floppy as Jared's was curly. "What do they want? It's supposed to be a park—it's not a homeless camp."

Jared's stoned eyes flashed with righteous indignation. "It's public land, dude, it's public space!" he cried. He had read *A People's History of the United States* just that spring in his final semester of high school, and he was getting hip to much of the passionate populist rhetoric that had animated his father for so many years, often to the indulgent boredom of the rest of the dinner table. "If people want to live there—"

"Dude, you think they *want* to live there?" interjected Charlie Leung.

"Need, I mean," continued Jared. "If people need to live there, if that's the best use of public land in this neighborhood, what right does the state have to intervene?"

"Yeah but it's a *park*," Asa plowed forward, notching his voice higher than Jared's. "It's supposed to be *nice*, like, for kids. Would you want to take your kids in there with, like, dirty AIDS needles all over the ground and stuff?"

Jared paused on that for a moment; he loved Asa like the brother he didn't have, but he'd always thought he was a bit dumb, which was probably why he'd ended up at a safety school in Vermont where skiing was the primary passion. "I like the park the way it is because that's what it is," he finally said. "My dad and I walk through there together. It's what it needs to be and my dad knew what he was getting into when he bought down here."

This earned affectionate jeers from his friends. "You and your dad are the fucking *problem*, man!" Asa bellowed. "You're the reason they're all fucking *down* there!"

Jared thought this was ridiculous. "We didn't kick anyone out to move in here. This building was fucking municipal offices before we moved in. This building is, like, half artists and professors like my dad and, like"—he gestured down at the teeming streets below—"community activists! We're the ones trying to keep the neighborhood real."

"Real!" howled Charlie. "You are *so real*."

And Jared cracked a ridiculous grin, because even he knew, amid his very pleasurable pot haze, how ludicrous he was starting to sound.

Somewhere around three A.M., they all passed out on the couches, but a din directly beneath the still-open windows woke them. Jared stumbled to the window, then his eyes widened. A big chunk of the crowd had somehow made its way across the police-sealed park and were massing in front of the Christodora, their eyes trained on the building's front facade, flashing with animus. *What* were they chanting? *"Die yuppie scum! Die yuppie scum!"* And approximately half the crowd was skinny, messy-haired young white men like himself. They looked absolutely enraged, stark raving mad. *"Come out, you fucking Christodora scum!"* A queasiness bloomed in Jared's gut. *"Oh my fucking God,"* he whispered to himself, fingers to his parted lips, standing back half a step from the window, suddenly terrified of being spotted. He watched with increasing horror as a dozen of the guys in the crowd picked up a wooden, blue-painted police barricade and charged it toward the building's glass-paned front doors like a battering ram. He heard glass shatter amid an eruption of cheers.

Then he felt a light hand on his shoulder. Asa had joined him at the window. "My fucking God, man," Jared said. "They are breaking into my fucking *building*!" The two young men heard another crash. Now the protesters were throwing bottles and bricks at the facade.

"We better step back," Asa whispered. So the two men did, just as Charlie was coming to on the couch, rubbing his eyes.

"They're breaking into the fucking building," Asa told him. "Is the apartment door locked?"

But Jared suddenly felt revulsion at the idea of cowering in the apartment while mobs marauded the hallways. "This is fucking ridiculous," he finally said, looking around for his Nikes. "I'm gonna go down and talk to them and tell them we are not the problem."

Asa looked terrified. "You are fucking *not*! They'll kill you!"

But Jared was messily tying his laces. "Be pussies then," he said.

Asa and Charlie traded flummoxed looks. "Okay," Asa said. "We'll come."

They took the stairs, which gave onto the back right corner of the lobby—where, Jared saw, much to his relief, cops were already pushing people back out onto the sidewalk. Someone had upended one of the lobby's large planters, leaving a mess of ficus branches, black soil, and terra-cotta shards. A light fixture also hung, broken, from the wall. Ardit, the square-headed Albanian doorman, spied the three young men and hurried to them.

"Go back upstairs!" he ordered. "All residents stay in their apartments. It's under control. The police are here."

"But why the fuck are they doing this?" demanded Jared, who was loath to simply retreat. And at that moment, he caught the eye of one of the messy-haired young white men who looked so much like himself—a young man who was being steadily but forcefully pushed back out onto the sidewalk by a burly cop.

"Shame on you! Shame on you!" the young man screamed directly at Jared, jabbing a finger over the cop's shoulder toward him. "Get out of the neighborhood!"

This brought Jared to a new level of rage. "You're fucking crazy!" he screamed back, advancing into the lobby, which earned Ardit's hand on his elbow, aiming to pull him back. "I support the homeless in the park! *We* are not the fucking problem!"

The young man's face lit up with a kind of malevolent amusement. "You *are* the fucking problem. You! Yes, you, you fucking idiot!"

Jared wanted to charge at him. But he felt paralyzed by something. It was the fact that the guy was laughing at him so frankly. That, and because the guy looked so much like him.

"You!" the guy continued to cackle, looking straight at Jared, as the cops pushed him and his compatriots farther and farther back. "You, you, you!"

"Fuck you!" Jared called back, once, for good measure. But he suddenly felt a little halfhearted about it.

"Come on, guys, go back upstairs," Ardit said again.

And as he and Asa and Charlie climbed the six flights to the apartment, Jared entertained a monologue in his head, which basically went:

Okay so fine, they think we're the fucking problem. Which is pretty ridiculous because half this building went to the meetings and spoke out against the curfew. But I guess if we're up in this tower and we bought apartments in here, then they're going to see us as the problem, and what can we do about it? Just that we're not. And just that it's so sad that they think we are. I mean, if we're *the problem, good luck with the fucking real problem!*

"You know," he turned and said to Asa, "if *we're* the fucking problem, then good luck with the fucking *real* problem, right?"

"I'm just glad they didn't really get in," Asa said.

But of course, all that had been three-and-a-half years ago, and now, during the 1991–92 winter break of Jared's final year in college, he and his father walked through the park toward Russ and Daughters on Houston Street, father to get his lunch and son to get his breakfast, and neither had to say what they both happily felt, which was: *We are back where it all began.* And also, in the intervening years, a major dream of Jared's had come true. For several years, he'd been in love with Millicent Heyman, a beautiful painter with dark curls and worriedly beseeching eyes, a heart-shaped face, a husky voice, and a dancer's body she covered with paint-splattered T-shirts from her dad, sometimes tied at the waist, and high-waisted, equally paint-splattered old jeans, often cut off and rolled to just above the knees to make shorts. They'd known each other vaguely all their lives, going to separate private schools uptown, but when they wound up at the same college, in the same art classes, Jared realized in short order that he was in love. He was rendered inwardly dopey by Milly's beauty and by the way that sardonic cynicism and wide-eyed wonderment seemed to coexist so amicably in her. His cock twitched uncomfortably in his jeans whenever they talked, and he would exhaust and befuddle himself trying to remain glib and breezy with her and not collapse into a state of ardent, babbling animal lust. He was not used to this loss of inner control, and on one hand, he did not like the feeling at all and worried that it was not a useful one for him, but on the other hand, he lived in a state of delectable anticipation between such episodes.

And as for Millicent, the short answer to a complicated question would be to say that she loved Jared, too. And that is how she came to live in the Christodora with him after college, when Jared's father fully ceded the apartment to them, and also how, in a matter of about seven years, in a series of extremely random events that somehow all tied together, she and Jared ended up adopting an orphan boy named Mateo, which led to the three of them all living in the Christodora together.

There, as they all slept, Milly would often dream she was flying. She could feel it coming, a stirring, a vibration in her body. It was certainly the world's greatest feeling, slipping off earthly weights. She rose up in the bed, stretched out her arms, and soon it was as though the bedroom were a body of water and she was swimming around in it with a delicious, slow ease of movement, Jared snoring on the bed five or six feet below her. She somersaulted languorously in the air, and then she sailed out the open window, six stories high, and into the warm city night. She watched their apartment building recede as she breaststroked her way higher and higher, until the Manhattan grid emerged below her and she was gently maneuvering her way around the corners of buildings fifteen, twenty stories high. Through windows, she saw neighbors sleeping, turning fitfully—so drearily earthbound! Up here, above the city lights, the stars emerged. She stretched out her arms and wiggled her bare toes, her nightshirt flapping around her thighs, her black curls whipping across her eyes.

The city twinkled beneath her, late-night cabs crisscrossing the grid—*Like dumb toys!* she thought. The Chrysler Building loomed before her, the chevrons atop its crown glowing like white thorns. It was fascinating to spy the crown so close, as she drew a broad arc around it in the air from the southeast. She treaded night air—*so warm! almost steamy! and slightly opaque, a bit milky*—to cut a clear path away from it. But—*oh, good Lord.* She seemed to be caught in a wind tunnel. Against her will, she sailed ever closer to those white-hot chevrons. And she was sailing much faster than she'd like. Oh, this was not good. She'd lost the freedom she'd savored a moment ago; it had all gone wrong. She was seconds away from the chevrons, trying to push back against the current with all her might. How bad would the impact hurt? Terror caught in her throat.

"Oh my God, help!"

She bolted upright in bed, her heart pounding. *Oh thank God*, she thought, gasping for breath, *I'm alive. It was a dream.*

Jared stirred beside her. He reached out—a repulsive and reassuring mass of warm nighttime body smells, foul breath, and oniony underarms—and pulled her close as her breathing slowed. "Were you flying again?" he muttered.

"Uh-huh. I flew into the Chrysler Building."

He laughed in his half-sleep. "Fancy."

That made her laugh a little, too. "It looked amazing up close," she said.

He ran a hand through her hair. "Go back to sleep now, Millipede. It's okay. I love you."

"I love you, too."

Predictably, Jared was snoring again in fourteen seconds. The jarring memory of the dream alone was enough to keep her awake, but now there was that. Milly took comfort under Jared's arm a few more seconds, then wriggled and turned away. A stripe of light from a streetlamp outside fell across her night table, where a photo of her, Jared, and Mateo on the beach last month in Montauk sat in a new frame. She always had trouble getting back to sleep after these dreams; she stayed awake trying to remember the weightless arabesques of floating and flying and trying to shake off the horror of the inevitable crash.

She reached for her cell phone, charging on the nightstand. It was 4:07 A.M. She crept from the bed, padded barefoot into the bathroom, pulled down her panties, and sat to pee. There, taped to the bathroom door, was a drawing of a dinosaur that Mateo had done last Thursday, his first week back in school. She thought idly about the accuracy and sophistication in Mateo's lines, especially in the tricky area around the dinosaur's haunches and feet. When she finished in the bathroom, she poked her head into Mateo's room, resisting the urge to step inside and watch him while he slept, lest she wake him. *Tomorrow*, she thought, *it's our morning together!*

She sat in the kitchen, mulling over the crossword puzzle. Through the half-open window, she saw, on the sidewalk alongside Tompkins Square Park, which several years before had been bulldozed and land-scaped into a treasure of velvety green knolls and winding pathways, some loud drunk kids stumbling forward. She thought about nights in the East Village—oh, eight, nine years ago, well before the unexpected arrival of Mateo—when it might have been her and Jared stumbling home at four in the morning. How radically their lives had changed in almost four years! Everyone else their age she knew were only now just having babies. And certainly nobody had adopted.

Milly sighed amid the gloom of the kitchen. Too often, she found herself sitting at this table in the middle of the night while the men in her life, as she thought of them, slept deeply. What did she need to get back to sleep? she asked herself. What? She must be strong and not go downstairs to the bodega and buy cigarettes. She'd gone nine days without a cigarette and she wouldn't do that. But certainly she could go downstairs and buy, say, a juice? A banana-strawberry Tropicana. Noise-lessly, she pulled shorts and a T-shirt out of the bedroom, pulled her hair back with an elastic, grabbed the keys, and slipped into flip-flops. In the hallway, the fluorescent lamps—those horrible lamps the co-op board needed to vote on to replace—buzzed lightly. Milly shuddered a bit at the rogue thrill of popping out in the middle of the night. She pressed for the elevator.

When it arrived, to her surprise and then mild alarm, there was a young man in it. He, too, seemed alarmed to see someone at the late hour and shrank back into the corner, his hands thrust into the pockets of his tight jeans. His short, spiky hair was gelled, his eyes were obscured by tinted Ray-Bans, his leanly muscled body was constrained only by a tank top, and one high-top sneaker was crossed over the other. He had one of those crown-of-thorns tattoos around his biceps that gay men everywhere suddenly seemed to have. He was clutching a cell phone in one hand, worrying it like a lucky stone.

She hesitated to get in the elevator. She'd never seen him in the building before. But he seemed to be shrinking away from her. Wordlessly, she got in and pressed the button to hasten the descent. She stood in the far corner from him, smelling his cologne and cigarette smoke and noting in the corner of her eye that he rapidly tapped his right foot.

Halfway down, she surmised that he was probably a trick of Hector's. This was something that was starting to become a murmur in the Christodora, where everyone talked, that for the past year or so Hector had been having a parade of guys in and out of his apartment on the ninth floor at all hours of the day and night. When the elevator reached the lobby, the spiky-haired guy scurried from the elevator and across the lobby out into the night, hands thrust deep into his pockets.

Bora was on duty in the lobby, slouched behind the desk with his tiny TV on low, set to a soccer-game broadcast in a foreign language. Albanian, Milly figured. Bora was the college-aged son of Ardit, the super, and he had some accounting textbooks and a laptop spread out before him. Milly saw how he watched the tank-top guy exit the lobby with heavy-lidded, suspicious eyes.

"I'm just going to the deli to get some juice," she told him. She felt the need to explain why she was up so late. "Do you want anything?"

"Will you get me a coffee?"

"Of course. How do you want it?"

"Milk and sugar. Will you get me a cookie, too?"

She grinned slightly. "Of course. Late-night sweet tooth?"

"Thank you." Bora smiled sleepily. "You saw him?" He nodded toward the front door.

"We were just in the elevator together. I've never seen him before."

"Ninth floor," Bora said. "Guys in and out, in and out, all the time."

Milly merely raised her eyebrows and made a face as though to say, *Hmm*. She didn't know what to say about Hector. She felt hurt by him, mainly. Four years before, she had intervened, at her mother's urging, to get Hector into the building. She thought it would be lovely to have a longtime colleague and friend of her mother's in the Christodora—one who, like her mother, had done so much in the fight against AIDS in the city. And once Hector moved in, she'd invited him down to dinner several times. But he rebuffed the offer repeatedly, mumbling excuses. In fact, when they saw each other coming in or out, he seemed as though he barely wanted to talk to her. He'd hurry away, murmuring a hello, his eyes averted, buried in his cell phone. Eventually, Milly started avoiding him, too.

"Drugs," said Bora.

Milly nodded her head. "I've heard that."

She stepped outside. The air was mild and had that delicious, mysterious moisture that the night holds in its wee hours. She walked a few blocks to the deli, passing along the way one of the regular neighborhood addicts—"the rockers," as she thought of them—crouching in a doorway, blissfully comatose. She felt a bit wild, being out alone so late—an echo of the untethered thrill she'd felt in her flying dream. Arabic music met her in the bodega, its plaintive wail.

Omar, like Bora, sat behind the counter watching a soccer game on a tiny TV. He looked up when she came in. "Hello, pretty lady," he said. He'd called her this for at least three years now. Milly couldn't even remember when it had begun.

"Hi, Omar." She asked him to fix Bora's coffee, fetched her juice from the refrigerator, and picked up a black-and-white cookie for Bora.

"You can't sleep again tonight?" he asked, handing back her change.

She rolled her eyes. "You know me too well. I just had a dream where I flew into the Chrysler Building and then I couldn't get back to sleep."

"In Egypt, we say *allah ysallimik*. You know what that means?"

Milly smiled. "No."

"May God protect you."

Milly said the phrase. Omar corrected her and she said it again.

"That's closer," he said. "There, so you don't fly into any more buildings." He smiled at her, an eyebrow raised flirtatiously.

She laughed. She could have stayed chatting with Omar, who had a kind face and darkly handsome eyes, but she felt it would be unseemly—not because it was too intimate, but because what sad soul visited with the bodega man at four A.M. because she couldn't sleep?

"That's sweet," she said. "Thank you for the blessing. I'm gonna hold you to it!"

"Watch, you'll see." He wagged a finger after her. "It will work."

Back in the lobby, she refused Bora's offer to pay for the coffee and cookie. "I'm going to take my insomniac self back up to bed," she said, as though by saying it she could make it happen.

She took exactly two sips of her juice in the elevator. She reentered her apartment with a slight sense of wonder, as though she were actually seeing it for the first time in a long time. She looked at the jumble of hats, coats, and shoes on the rack in the hallway—hers and Jared's mixed in with Mateo's tiny miniature additions, the windbreaker, the Nikes, the Yankees cap. In the living room, she considered her own color-field canvas hanging over the sofa, a small metal sculpture of Jared's on a table nearby. Mateo's pictures and crayons covered the coffee table. She had the feeling that she'd fled her home, this source of familiarity and love, out into the night because of some mild panic, but before anything bad could happen, she'd returned, slipped back into her life, and was relieved and grateful to find it the same, undisturbed. She stepped out of her shorts and laced her arm around Jared back in bed. *How exactly did you say that blessing that Omar had said?* she thought. Salaam alaikum? *No, that wasn't quite it.* But before she could muse on it further, she drifted into sleep.

When she woke, shortly after nine, she found the sky blue and the bed empty, which was not alarming, as Jared woke early on Saturdays to walk across the bridge to Williamsburg, where he had a large studio in an old warehouse where he could drag huge pieces of metal across the floor and weld them. She sat up in bed, a morning shadow passing over her mind, and she remembered the episode of the night before: the exhilarating and then terrifying dream, the strange encounter in the elevator, the brief foray into the night, Omar, the hasty return. It *all* felt like a dream to her now, not just the dream itself—a memory of shadowy corridors with dread around one corner, then comfort around the next.

In the living room, she found Mateo on the floor in front of the TV, watching his new favorite cartoon, *The Fairly OddParents*, and eating dry Cheerios out of a plastic cup. He was still in his SpongeBob SquarePants pajamas, lying on his stomach and absently kicking his butt with his bare feet, his mop of curly black hair pushed up by one little fist, plus a throw pillow. A pile of his drawings and crayons were splayed out in front of him.

"Hi, buddy," Milly called from the kitchen, pouring herself coffee that Jared had made. "Did you see Dad leave?"

"Yep," he called, not twisting around. "He went over the bridge."

She brought her coffee and the Saturday *New York Times* over to the couch by the TV. She ran her hand through his hair, which, with the exception of mixing paints and running into the water at Montauk the first time every summer, was just about her favorite thing in the world. "Do I get a morning kiss?"

"Yep." He smooched loudly toward the TV to suggest it was for her.

"I meant for real." She bent down and nuzzled his face and planted a kiss on his chubby cheek, which made him giggle and squirm and vaguely smile.

"Squinch over on the floor so there's some room for my feet," she said. He did so.

She curled up on the couch, her coffee on its armrest, and watched him absently, the newspaper ignored beside her. Later in the day, they would switch roles: Jared would take Mateo and she would go to her (considerably smaller) studio space in Chinatown and paint until she brought home a pizza for dinner. But for now, she was alone with the little boy who'd become her son, the initial hard years of adjustment over. She felt contented. They'd found a groove, the three of them.

"What are you looking at?" he asked her, not averting his eyes from the TV.

"Nothing." She paused. "Shouldn't we go for a haircut today?"

This was enough to break his gaze. "I don't wanna haircut! I like my hair."

"Because it's so skater boy?" she teased him. He wanted to be a skater boy. It was inevitable. It was impossible to walk around with him in the neighborhood without him seeing the skater boys, so cool with their flat-brimmed baseball caps and baggy jeans and high-tops, and not hear him say, "That's cool, I wanna do that."

"You'll break your neck if you do that," Milly would say to him, tightening her grip on his hand as they walked through the park.

"No, I won't," he'd reply, his valor wounded. "You're not cool."

Now it was she who was wounded. "A lot of people think I'm cool," she'd say. "My students think I'm cool. You don't need to ride a skateboard to be cool."

"I'm not saying I *need* to ride a skateboard to be cool," he'd reply slowly, as though he were talking to an idiot. "I'm saying I *want* to, because it's cool."

"Well, thank you for that clarification," Milly would say. "I think this is definitely an issue we can table until you turn twelve."

"We can what?"

"We can table," she said. "Meaning we can just put on the table and deal with it later."

He said nothing for several seconds. "That's weird," he finally said.

"It's not weird," she'd say. "I think eight is too young for you to be out on a skateboard."

"No, using that word like that," he'd say. "A table is a noun."

"Some nouns you can also use as verbs."

And on and on they'd go like that, and amid it, Milly would realize that she was pretty much happier than she'd ever been in her life, that at this moment, right here—as the old guys who played chess at the stone chess tables in the park's southwest corner looked up and said, "Heeeey, Mateeeo, how you doin' today, little man?" and as Mateo waved back to them—she felt no trace of the doubt and anxiety that usually nagged at the edges of her mind. Sometimes, very quietly, in a whisper even to herself, she'd think, *I made the right decision four years ago, I did the right thing. This was the right choice for us, this little guy needed us.*

"You're very popular with the chess crowd," she'd remark as they exited the park and made their way to, say, the Belgian fries stand, which, along with clusters of skateboarders and paper and crayons, was a bliss-trigger for Mateo. After she said it, Milly would glance down at Mateo to see his face beaming with smug pride at his park popularity, and she'd pull him toward her in a smothery sort of hug while they walked. And when he stayed there for just one moment of surrender before tugging himself away as any eight-year-old boy would do from his mother, she'd again think, *I did the right thing.*

So this morning, before the TV cartoons, she said, "Okay, well, I guess no haircut then."

"No haircut," he repeated sternly, his eyes still fixed on the screen.

"So should we see if Elysa and Kenji want to come out with us? It's beautiful outside. We can all take Kenji to the dog run together."

"Yeahhhh!" he exploded, his feet suddenly kicking his butt rapidly. "Kenji, Kenji, Kenji!"

"Go get dressed," she said.

Twenty minutes later, they were standing in front of the Christodora in T-shirts, shorts, and flip-flops. Kenji, a manic boy-puppy pit-shepherd mix, tore out of the lobby, dragging behind him on a leash Elysa, who wore kneesocks, Converse low-tops, and a cotton plaid minidress, her red curls corkscrewing in all directions. She was a thirty-three-year-old off-Broadway actress who sent everyone in the building AOL e-mail invites to her plays.

Mateo and Kenji lunged at each other. "Kenji, Kenji, Kenji, Kenji, I love you, Kenji, Kenji, Kenji!" Mateo laughed hysterically while the dog licked his face shiny wet.

"It looks like the two guys missed each other," noted Elysa, who often spoke in the knowing, indulgent tones of a much older woman.

"Indeed it does," said Milly, giving a kiss hello to Elysa, her best friend in the Christodora. "A reunion long overdue."

"Kenji, down!" commanded Elysa, aiming to put some bass in her voice and sound authoritative. Kenji obeyed her for about two seconds before resuming his love assault on Mateo, who screamed again in delight.

"Kenji, you're crazy today!" Mateo exclaimed.

An explosion of barking came from the lobby. A fully grown, glossy-black pit-shepherd mix scrambled out the door, followed on a massive leather leash by Hector, shaven headed, with a leather vest fitted snugly over a shaven, muscled brown chest. The leather vest melted into tight black jeans and construction boots. His eyes were obscured by massive black wraparound sunglasses. A lit cigarette dangled between his full lips.

Instantly, Kenji and the other dog were lunging ferociously at each other, their growls so menacing that the boys playing basketball across the street in the park stopped and turned to stare. Elysa and Hector held their dogs apart.

Hector fumbled to take the cigarette from his mouth. "Sonya!" he barked. "Shut the fuck up! Back the fuck down!"

Mateo, whom Milly had scurried to and pulled back from the fracas behind her right arm, watched the proceedings, rapt. "He just said the F-word, Mom," Mateo noted.

"I know," muttered Milly, not amused. She hadn't seen Hector in a few weeks and was dumbstruck by his dishevelment.

By this point, both Elysa and Hector had reeled in their dogs and crouched down to grip them in a soothing embrace. Hector let his smoldering cigarette fall to the sidewalk. "You've got to really curb your dog, Hector," Elysa said, an angry edge in her voice. "She's enormous and she's rough."

"She's a crazy girl," Hector said. He put the wild-eyed dog in a headlock. "Aren't you, you crazy bitch? Aren't you, *puta*?"

Milly cringed at the explosion of profanity in front of Mateo. Elysa spoke for her: "Hector, you're in front of a kid!"

Hector didn't seem to register the comment. "I gotta walk her bad," he said. He picked up the cigarette and put it back in his mouth. "She's full of crazy energy today." He stood up and yanked on the dog's leash. "Come on, crazy girl. Look, you got me in trouble." He shambled down the sidewalk and around the corner with a cocky gait that reminded Milly of John Travolta in the opening shot of *Saturday Night Fever*, his dog, Sonya, all the while straining her neck back to glower hatefully at the pit-mix puppy.

"Good Lord," Milly finally said, exhaling.

"Why's his dog so mean?" Mateo asked.

"She's just not well trained, Mateo," Elysa said.

The four of them made their way into the park. At the dog run, Elysa took the puppy inside, let him off his leash and into the scrum of wrestling canines, then walked to the gate, where Milly and Mateo waited on the other side. (Milly would not let Mateo into the run, fearing he'd be mauled. It had happened to other children. Horribly, in fact.)

Mateo ran along the fence to follow the dogs at play, leaving the two women alone for a moment.

"He was so high, Milly," Elysa said, disapproval in her voice. "Hector."

"That's what everyone's saying," Milly replied. She didn't have much drug experience except for college-era pot and one episode each with mushrooms and ecstasy, so she wasn't quite sure how to tell if people were high, or what they were high on. "His dog sure was crazy."

"Probably because he's been holed up in his apartment since yesterday doing drugs and hadn't taken her out. The poor thing. That's animal cruelty."

Milly shook her head. "He was such a big deal once in the whole world of AIDS research."

"You told me. He used to work with your mother, right?"

"*For* my mother," Milly corrected. "He started under her, like, twenty years ago. And then he got fed up because nobody was doing anything and he became one of the activists, and then he became a huge deal and was working in the Clinton administration to release all those new medications. He was always in D.C. I think he even lived there for a year or two before he moved into the Christodora."

Elysa slowly shook her head. "He looks worse every time I see him." She paused. "I think I know what drug he's on."

"It's coke, right?"

"No, it's called crystal meth. It's like a hundred times stronger than coke and it makes you stay up and have sex for, like, days."

Milly laughed. "That doesn't sound so bad!" She glanced over Elysa's shoulder to check on Mateo, who seemed to be happily feeding a leaf to a little dachshund through the gate.

"No, no, no, it's really bad," Elysa insisted. "You don't eat or sleep for days and you get all paranoid and then you finally crash and you wake up, like, three days later and you're a total mess. It's horrible. All these gay guys I know in theater are talking about it and saying that guys are having unsafe sex because of it and getting HIV."

Milly processed all this for a moment. "I don't know if my mother ever told me if Hector had HIV or not. He had a boyfriend, or a lover, who died from it. My mother told me that much."

"Well, that's sad," Elysa said, softening a bit. "But if he doesn't already have it, he's probably going to get it with the parade of guys he has coming in and out of the apartment all the time."

Milly paused, last night's wee-hours interlude coming back to her. "I think I saw one of them last night. In the elevator at, like, four A.M."

"What were you doing in the elevator at four A.M.?"

Milly blushed, embarrassed. She didn't like people to think she was peculiar. "I was going to the bodega."

"Are you still having insomnia? I wish you'd go to that hypnotist I told you about."

"I was only up for about an hour. But there was a gay guy coming down in the elevator from a higher floor and he seemed really drugged up."

"How do you know he was gay?"

"He had gelled hair and a tank top and one of those armband tattoos."

"Oh." Elysa nodded.

"I wonder if there's anything we can do—" Milly began. *For him,* meaning Hector, she was about to say. But an eruption from inside the dog run cut her off. Kenji was locked in a vicious, humping, jaws-on-neck brawl with yet another pit mix and a dazed-looking wire fox terrier. Various owners were screaming at the scrum, one of them trying to break it up with a big stick. Elysa ran toward the spectacle, screaming Kenji's name. She pulled him out of the melee by his collar, only to be scolded by an older woman, her frizzy gray hair askew as she cradled the fox terrier.

"I'm sorry," Elysa pleaded. "I'm so sorry."

The frizzy woman: "You can't bring him here, Elysa. We've talked about this. He's not trained."

"He is trained!"

"You call that trained?"

Milly and Mateo watched the showdown from the safety of the far side of the fence. "Kenji's being bad today," Mateo commented.

"Mmm," murmured Milly, her hands on the boy's shoulders. "He has more energy than he knows what to do with."

Shamed, Elysa dragged Kenji out of the dog run back toward them. Kenji's eyes were wild and googly with exhilaration after his brawl. Elysa's social ostracism was lost on him.

"It's a catch-22," said Elysa, looping Kenji's leash on to her shoulder so she could refasten her hair, which had come undone during the scuffle. Her minidress was covered in dust. "He'll never learn to behave at the dog run if I don't take him regularly. But every time I take him, something like this happens and they ban me again."

"Well," said Milly, trying to soothe, "technically they banned Kenji, not you."

Elysa looked perplexed by this. "Why would I want to come to the dog run without Kenji?"

"*Freets!*" Mateo suddenly shouted. "Can we get freets?"

"Can we get what?" asked Elysa.

"He means *frites*, the Belgian fries," said Milly. "They're his newest obsession."

Elysa's eyes widened. "Oh, *frites*! You're so cosmopolitan, Mateo."

Mateo was already crouching again, covering Kenji with kisses. "What does that mean?" he asked, looking up.

"Umm," began Elysa as the trio plus the dog wended their way out of the park. "It means very, um, fancy and knowing about things from different places all over the world. Very sophisticated."

"The *frites* are right on Avenue A," Mateo said.

"Yes, I know, but they come from Belgium."

Milly steered Mateo around an unwashed teenage white girl with dreadlocks who was crouching and rocking on the sidewalk. "You know where Belgium is on the map, Mateo," she said. "It's in Europe. Where we're going next year."

"Oh, yeah, I know that," he said confidently.

They bought their fries, collected their napkins and tiny cups of ketchup and mayonnaise, and crossed back into the park to sit on a bench. A shirtless middle-aged black man rode by on an old bike mounted with a boom box that blared "Try Again," by Aaliyah. He wore a top hat with a sign affixed to it: R.I.P. AALIYAH, 1979–2001.

Elysa followed his trajectory, shaking her head. "That's terrible about that poor girl," she remarked. "Every single person died in that plane crash that weekend."

Milly nodded in that silently clucking way that, when she caught herself doing it, reminded her of her mother. "She was such a beautiful girl."

Her cell phone bleeped. It was Jared, not far away. Five minutes later, there he was, brandishing his own cone of fries. At thirty-one, he betrayed the first flecks of gray on his temples and the trace of a belly underneath an old, grease-smeared Pavement T-shirt. He set down on the bench a clanking messenger bag of tools he'd brought from his studio, then kissed his wife, son, and neighbor hello.

"You're looking very industrial," Elysa noted.

"I'm a macho art guy," he deadpanned. "Big tools, big mess. No pussy watercolors for me."

"I don't use watercolors!" Milly protested.

Jared raised his hands defensively. "Whoa, Nelly! Did I say you? I meant, like, archetypally."

"I don't exactly think early Georgia O'Keeffe watercolors are pussy-ish," Milly said.

"The pussies came later!" exclaimed Elysa.

But Milly didn't seem to hear the joke. "And I don't think the watercolors I've done are pussy-ish either," she said.

"Millipede, come on," Jared protested. "You've barely worked in watercolor."

"But you know that I have," she countered. *Why else would he have said that?* she was asking herself.

Jared just stood there, exasperated. He shrugged.

Elysa put an arm on each of their shoulders. "Come on, you two," she singsonged. "We all know there are two talented artists in the household."

"Three, actually," Milly said, pointing to Mateo. "He just gets better and better."

"I know!" Elysa exclaimed. "I've seen it! Mateo, when did you start using actual paint?"

Mateo was lost in his fries, meticulously pairing different ones with different condiments. "I dunno," he said absently. "A few months ago?"

"This summer," Milly clarified. "In a summer class."

"Yo, bro," Jared said, clamping his hand over Mateo's hair and scratching it. "Are you gonna be the first in the family to start bringing in some money with your art?"

"I dunno," Mateo repeated, still lost in his fries. "I wanna do big metal things like you."

This caused Milly to look up at Jared, her eyes bright with pleasure.

Jared paused a moment. "Nah," he finally said. "I think you're going to be a painter like *mamita*. You two have that whole color thing going on."

Moments later, Milly kissed everyone good-bye and made off to her studio in Chinatown. She shared the space with Bogdan, a Russian guy, a friend of a friend, and she found him there, ignoring his canvas, smoking and reading the *Village Voice*. When she was in her studio—whose windows, wide-open today, gave onto a view of the Manhattan Bridge—she felt macho and badass and free, and she allowed herself only a moment's guilt before she pulled a cigarette from Bogdan's pack and lit up with him. This reminded her of long nights in the studio in college, before the first wiry gray strands had emerged on her own head of hair, when Jared was first falling in love with her, he later told her. That was an interesting thing to think about, because Milly hadn't truly fallen in love with Jared until much later, once they'd had sex.

"Are you productive today?" she asked Bogdan, whose shaved head, she always marveled, was almost rectangular.

He blew out smoke and frowned. "My arm hurts."

"Did you call the physical therapist my mom told me about?"

He shook his head, smiled sheepishly.

"Your arm is your livelihood," she chided.

"I don't have insurance!" he suddenly barked at her.

"My mom says he has a sliding scale. You can't take chances with your arm."

"Okay, I'll call him." He stubbed out his cigarette in the old Café Bustelo coffee can they'd filled with sand to make an ashtray. "Why are you so late today?"

"I lingered in the park with Mateo and a friend. The weather this time of year is so perfect."

He nodded appreciatively. "Labor Day happens too early. Summer goes all the way to October."

She nodded back. They gossiped about other artists and finished their cigarettes. Milly let out a long sigh and pushed her hair back. "Okay, here goes," she said.

"Hit it! Attack it!" Bogdan laughed.

"Attack it!" she echoed. "Plunge in!" She went and squared herself by her canvas, put the crook of her finger to her lips and stared at it for a minute or two. She looked back at Bogdan a few times, casting him an aggrieved look to elicit his sympathy over her creaking start, but he'd already turned his back on her toward his own work. Her canvas wasn't more than a five-by-three rectangle that she'd scraped down to a background field of dusty rose, so pale you could see plenty of canvas through it. She hadn't touched it since the prior Saturday, and all week she'd held it in her head and wondered what to do next. Finally, she went to her table and squeezed some white paint and a little yellow paint into a cup, then stood before the window mixing it, looking out at the bridge, which seemed to pop toward her off a hard enamel-blue sky. A very unpleasant wave overcame her, a mix of sadness and anxiety, which was odd, because mixing paint usually soothed her.

What is it? she asked herself, looking uneasily at Bogdan, as though to check if he'd felt it as well, but his back remained to her. She scrunched her forehead. If she applied herself, she thought, she could pinpoint the source of the wave and address it. She ticked down items in her head. But the truth was life was okay at the moment. She'd been having these tics since she was sixteen. After years of therapy, she'd come to see them as depressive synapses signaling absolutely nothing going on in life. *Nothing is wrong*, she told herself. The sky was absolutely blue and she'd had a perfect morning. The path ahead was clear.

She applied a large blob of the pale yellow paint on the right side of the canvas and watched it leak downward a moment until she picked up a scraper and drew it leftward. Thirty seconds later, she was in a sweet spot, a deep voice applauding her for painting her way away from her bogeyman. Ninety minutes later, the thought of a cigarette blooming in her brain like a flower, she shook herself out of her reverie, and at that moment, Bogdan let out a kind of cathartic groan. They turned to each other and laughed and moved toward the table in the center of the room and Bogdan's cigarettes.

"Are you staying here tonight?" she asked him.

"I have a date," he growled.

Her face lit up. "You have a date? Who is she?"

"She's a teacher. A public-school teacher. Like you."

"Ooh," she said. "Hot for teacher."

He frowned. "Why do you say that?"

"It was a song," she said. She paused. "Oh, wait. I don't think you were in America yet then."

She didn't have much focus left after her cigarette. She applied and scraped for another twenty minutes, then cleaned up and wished Bogdan good night and a good date. Outside, the night was sweet, the sky streaked with wild pinks and golds as the sun set. She stepped into Two Boots pizzeria on Avenue A and ordered two large pizzas, a Saturday ritual. Idling with her cell phone while she waited for them, she noticed Jared had called her but not left a message. Peculiar, she thought, not dwelling much beyond that. They called that her pizzas were ready.

As soon as she walked into the Christodora, Ardit flagged her. "There was a problem," he said, his tremulous blue eyes narrowing.

Her own eyes grew large. "What?"

"You know Hector?"

"In the building? Yes, why?"

"His dog bit Mateo."

"What?" She gripped Ardit's arm. "Is he okay?"

"Jared took him to the hospital. I think he's okay. It just looked like a little cut."

"What hospital? Beth Israel?"

Ardit nodded. Milly put the pizzas down on a handsome, high-backed wooden bench in the lobby, pulled out her cell phone, and called Jared. Her heart was pounding.

"Hi," she said when he answered. "Ardit just told me what happened."

"He's fine," Jared said. "He got, like, two stitches and he's waiting for a rabies shot. We should be home soon."

"Is he doing okay?" Milly asked. "Can I talk to him?"

"Sure, he's right here."

"Hi, Mommy," Mateo said.

"You're okay, sweetheart?"

"I'm okay. I gotta get a shot."

"What happened, Mateo?"

"I was running down the hall and Sonya came out the door and chased me and bit me until Hector grabbed her and took her back inside."

"Oh, sweetheart! I'm just glad you're okay."

"He's okay." It was Jared, back on the line. "We came back in from the park and he wanted to run up the stairs instead of taking the elevator, so I let him. And I guess at some point he decided to run down the hall on Hector's floor and Hector's door was ajar and the dog came out."

"Oh my goodness." Milly kept glancing up at Ardit, who was shaking his head balefully. "Did Hector say anything?"

"I didn't wait. Mateo was crying when he got to the apartment so I took him right to the hospital. But I already took pictures of the bite and called a lawyer. Milly, we have to do something about getting Hector out of the building."

That felt like jumping a step ahead, she thought. The dog, maybe. But Hector himself? "You think so?" she asked weakly.

"He's becoming a menace. The drugs, the sleazy guys in and out of the apartment at all hours, the negligence with that crazy dog. Some folks think he's dealing drugs out of there. He's going to burn down the building one night."

"Maybe I could ask my mother to talk to him," she said. "Reconnect and see what he needs."

Jared harrumphed lightly over the phone, as though he thought it was far too late for that, and slightly as though he was annoyed by Milly's softness. "Anyway, we'll be home soon. Don't worry about Mateo, he's okay."

"I have pizza here," she remembered to add.

After she put away her phone and stood up, a bit dazed from the swift unfolding of events, Ardit said, "That Hector, he's bad news."

"Do you think he's dealing drugs out of the apartment?" she asked.

"Oh, yes," he said. "Guys in and out of here all night."

"He's deteriorating," Milly said. "He once was very prominent."

Ardit shrugged, seemingly unimpressed by this news. "He's got a problem now," he said.

Milly made her *mmm* sound again before thanking Ardit and getting into the elevator. Then she did something strange. Instead of pressing "6," she pressed "9," Hector's floor. Stepping out there, she walked down the hall. Even before coming to his door, she could hear the thump of the dance music emanating from his apartment. She stood before his door and pressed her ear to it, able to hear nothing but the music. Should she knock or ring the bell and try to say something to him? Then she thought about Jared calling the lawyer and how he might not like that because it might interfere in some legal proceeding.

Suddenly, she heard the sound of the dog barking its way toward the door, as if it sensed her presence. Panicked, she ran down the hallway with the pizza and slipped into the stairwell, fast enough that she never knew if Hector came to the door. She caught her breath and collected herself before taking the three flights down to their apartment, where she called her mother, who was still at Judith House, not very many blocks away.

"You're not going to believe what happened," she told her mother. "Hector's dog bit Mateo and Jared had to take him to the hospital for stitches and a rabies shot. And Jared wants to sue Hector and get him out of the building."

"Oh my God," said Ava slowly. "Is Mateo okay?"

"Jared says he's okay. But—should I say something to Hector? Should we? Would you? I feel terrible. Apparently he has a huge drug problem now. And he's not taking care of that dog."

Ava sighed. "Everyone he's ever worked with has tried to do something for him. He doesn't want anyone's help. He stopped returning my calls three, four years ago."

"Really?"

"I think he did actually go to rehab a few years ago, but it didn't stick, apparently."

"People are worried he's going to start a fire or an explosion or something in the building one night."

"You might have to look into some legal recourse," Ava said. In the background, Milly could hear the laughter and conversation of the women who lived in the AIDS residence her mother ran. "That's very sad to think."

"That's what Jared says, too."

"You're still coming for dinner tomorrow night?"

"Of course."

The pizzas had gotten cold. Milly put them in the oven and leafed through the sections of the Sunday *Times* that had already come to the house, in advance of the parts that came Sunday morning. Thirty minutes later, Jared and Mateo were back.

"Look!" said Mateo. He showed off the three stitches in his left calf, where the dog had sunk her teeth in.

Milly held him close. "I'm just glad you're okay. It must have been scary."

"I was really scared."

"We're going to talk to Hector about his dog," Milly said. "She won't hurt you again."

Later, after they'd finished the pizza and Mateo was absorbed in TV cartoons and his drawing, Jared told her, in a low voice, "Me and a few others are going to see a lawyer this week about Hector. I wanna try to get him out of here."

Milly shook her head. "It's so sad," she said. "I told my mother what happened. She said people have tried to help him the past few years, but nothing changes."

"I don't really give a shit about him," Jared said flatly. "I care about the building."

"I know," she said. "I'm just saying he wasn't always like that. It's sad how someone can just go downhill."

Jared shrugged. "Nobody's making him be a tragedy. It's his choice."

"Well, he did lose a lover."

"A lot of people did."

Milly said no more about Hector. There was clearly no point, she realized. "Funny, what a perfect day this was up until this," she said.

Jared took her hand across the table, played with it finger by finger. "Did you get some good work done?"

"A bit." She paused. "It's strange . . . I was in the studio looking out the window and I had a moment where a—like, a dark rush came over me, like something was wrong. It had to be Mateo and the dog."

"You have a sense," Jared said gravely.

"I wonder—" she began. Then she caught the glint in his eyes. "You're mocking me!"

He laughed. "You're always having those dark rushes," he said tenderly.

She flushed. "I know. But this one was so . . . vivid. Staring out at that clear blue sky."

They curled up as a trio in front of the TV and watched their new DVD of *Dinosaur*. Mateo was enthralled. Dinosaurs had been a favorite drawing subject of his since he was four or five, when they'd first met him in the group home in Brooklyn, and the movie had barely begun before he'd run for his pad and crayons and was trying to capture the baby dinosaur, Aladar. Milly absently ran her fingers through his curls while he drew. Their living room was dark, save for the alternating shades of blue flickering on the walls from the TV. Through the open windows, the sounds of Saturday night East Village revels floated up to them from the street, the whoops and shouts and scraps of music from cars and bars. In turn, Milly and Jared napped on each other's shoulders, under the afghan, while Mateo remained rapt before the screen. In the moments that Milly came half to, she had the drowsy, soothing sense of being nested between her husband and her son, grounded, in no fear of flying away.

TWO

A MAD SICK NIGGA

(2009)

He's the coolest; he's got swagger, but he's also sensitive and open. He's a hip-hop hipster; he lives art-school thug life. He's walking down the halls at Art and Design High School in midtown with Lupe Fiasco on his iPod, his massive hair pulled back in one of those comb-type headbands for boys, a long white T-shirt coming down over skintight Levi's, which scrunch into high-top Airs. Sometimes he pulls up the T-shirt to show the tat on the left lower back that he designed, his tag—the grinning tiger with the mob cap slouched down over one eye, with M-DREEM 92 in stitching on the cap. That's him, M-Dreem 92, the star of his high school, graduating three days from now and then going on to Pratt.

He loves this Lupe song, "Superstar"; he's been listening to it for over a year and he mouths along with it. And then Ms. Courtney, one of his design teachers, twenty-eight and from Williamsburg and so sick cool with her retro bangs and her miniskirt and combat boots, flags him in the hall, so he pulls out his earbuds. She and some of the kids from Honors Design are meeting in July, after school's out, to catch the opening of the Emory Douglas retrospective at the New Museum, all that fucking amazing graphic design for the Black Panthers, and does he want to come? Yeah, sure, he says, I'm down. He's working at Utrecht, the art supply store, that summer, but he'll request that afternoon off, so he'll be there, yeah, sure.

"Awesome," she says, with that hint of irony he loves about her, and he moseys on, noting that Ms. Courtney didn't tell him to put the iPod away—which, technically, she should have, because it's against school policy to use them in the facility—but then again, it's the last day of school, there's a loosey-goosey atmosphere along with the humidity, and, also, he suspects Ms. Courtney has a secret crush on him. She can play it cool and appropriate, but by now he knows how to pick it up in inflections. And he knows what he projects, how to turn it on and off, all the dials—the artist, the homeboy, the gifted child and all his drama.

So, his last day of high school. He's alone in the hallway and he feels so good. He shows up late to Advanced Illustration, but it doesn't really matter because half the class is absent for different reasons—all sorts of administrative loose ends to tie up today with transcripts, graduation rehearsals—and everyone's just sitting around doing a crit on one another's final projects, with cool Mr. Adeyemo and his massive locks tilted halfway back in his teacher's seat, presiding over it all sleepily. Dude's even wearing Birkenstocks today and damn those feet are ashy and need a cocoa butter rub.

He sits down next to Zoya, with her half-Egyptian, half-Boricua indie fierceness, her Amy Winehouse eyeliner, and rests his leg against hers. She rolls her eyes but doesn't move her leg. He remembers when she spooked him back in March. They had been dating for all of two weeks, but it was complicated because there was that shortie, Vanessa, from Professional Children's School whom he'd met at a rave in Greenpoint about the same time. He was at Zoya's place in the East River Houses, overlooking the water and the condos going up in Billyburg, smoking herb, listening to Portishead, and feeling retro. A cold March night and they were wrapped in her Care Bears blanket from when she was little, giggling about stupid shit. And then that herb kicked in good and there was this period where the two of them just stared flat into each other's eyes during "Roads," and that line that hit him: *I got nobody on my side. And surely that ain't right. And surely that ain't right.*

"That's me," he told Zoya, and she spooked him because she said, "I know. I can see that about you so obviously."

He tried to giggle off her penetrating stare. "What do you mean?"

"You said it yourself," she answered. Then she burrowed into his concave chest, making this kind of mewing sound that was half cute, half annoying, and she left him to himself and his stoned brooding.

But they stayed friends—hey, it's senior year, everybody's friends by now—and now they're leg-to-leg on the last day of school. And she's like, "You going to Oscar's tonight, right?" And he's like, "I wouldn't miss that shit." And finally the crit comes up on his final project, *After L.B.*, which was this intricate illustration of spiders using forced perspective. He called it *After L.B.* because earlier that year he got really into Louise Bourgeois, especially her big spider sculpture that he saw at the Dia center upstate, and he wanted to pay an homage to that cute old French lady with her sick, scary, genius art.

"So what do we think about Mr. M-Dreem's study?" asks Mr. Adeyemo in his faint Nigerian accent, which M-Dreem loves. He adores Mr. Adeyemo, partly wants to be him. "What's working and what's lacking?" That's a favorite catchphrase of Mr. Adeyemo's.

The class is lethargic today, drunk on dreams of flight. "Good use of values," says Horatio Cordero, sweet faced, bespectacled. "Good lines. Organic."

"There's good movement from top left to bottom right," drawls Zoya. She says it in as bored a way as possible without looking at M-Dreem, then finally glances his way. He grins at her. She rolls her eyes and looks away, but it's nice, he thinks, how their legs have been pressed together still this whole time.

M-Dreem finally speaks up on his own behalf. "I wanted the spiders to, like, make their own web. Not a spiderweb, but a web of actual spiders."

Oooh, goes Zoya and another shortie, Alexa. "You're so deep," says Alexa.

Everybody laughs, including M-Dreem. "You just can't handle all my levels," he flips off.

Mr. Adeyemo leans forward, does that dramatic openmouthed thing where he's going to speak and gets the class to shut up. "Let me tell you something, Mr. M-Dreem." Another quiet round of *ooooh*s goes up—everyone knows that when Mr. Adeyemo gets all enunciative, he's about to get pronunciative, too. "We all know here you got mad skills."

More laughs.

"We've all known that since day one you came in to Art and Design," he continues. "You had good classes before you came." Now this pricks M-Dreem a little bit and he frowns slightly at Mr. Adeyemo, hurt. Why'd he have to throw that in? "But it's clear you had that thing." Is Adeyemo trying to mollify him now? "And you're just going to continue developing your skills and your technique next year at that fine school."

"At Pratt, oooh," goes Alexa.

M-Dreem shoots her a look. "Don't make me," he says.

"Double oooh," she goes.

"But here's my question for you going forward," continues Mr. Adeyemo. "With all your form and skills, what's M-Dreem trying to tell us? What's up with the spiders?"

"What's up with the spiders?" M-Dreem echoes defensively. "Nothing's up with the spiders. I just think they're cool. So did Louise Bourgeois. The work," he says, pointing to his study, "it's a pure expression of form." He loves this term, which Ms. Courtney uses all the time, and he says it now maybe just a little haughtily. He and Mr. Adeyemo stare at each other for more than a natural moment, both of them with half-smiles on their faces, but there's a strange, face-off vibe. There are some nervous titters. Zoya gives his leg a squeeze.

"I got two words for you going forward, my gifted M-Dreem," Adeyemo finally says. "Be open." He's mad enunciating now. "Be open to it all, the form *and* the feeling."

"That's, like, twelve words," Alexa remarks.

"You're right, it is, Ms. Quiano," Adeyemo says. "So let's talk about your study now. *Girls with Good Hair Jumping*. What's working and what's lacking?"

The class starts in on Alexa's study, which is just what it sounds like: little girls with flowy long hair doing double Dutch, which M-Dreem thinks is kind of a mess technically, but he's too distracted by Adeyemo's strange injunction to him to really care. He's glad the spotlight's off him. *Be open. I'm fucking open*, he thinks, and he doesn't even realize he's sitting there slumped back, his leg off Zoya's now, kind of brooding, until Mr. Adeyemo catches his eye amid the chatter and mouths to him, "It's cool."

M-Dreem sort of rolls his eyes and looks away, and he can't really bring himself back to the here and now after that. He wishes he had a blunt. As he often does when he's uncomfortable, he thinks about the snapshot with its date stamp: 04/14/1984. The short, pudgy, goofy-looking Dominicana thinking she's fly with the Sheila E. asymmetrical haircut and the studded leather jacket, the lace leggings under the denim mini and the high heels, big dark eyes darting just to the left of the camera's gaze, one arm up on the shoulder of that gay-looking *moreno* with the boom box on the ground under his left high-top. Damn. M-Dreem can't believe there was ever a time in New York City called the 1980s; how could he have missed that shit, Basquiat and Haring and Fab 5 Freddy and all the rest? But miss it he did. He was born in 1992.

At least his grandma, his *bubbe*, told him about the woman in the picture, the woman who gave birth to him, Ysabel, who died of AIDS before he was old enough to have a memory of her. Bubbe fought for the AIDS people alongside Ysabel, and Bubbe took care of Ysabel at Bubbe's special home for women with AIDS when Ysabel was pregnant with him, then after, right up to her death.

"Issy went from being a scared girl from Queens who didn't want anybody to know she had AIDS," Bubbe told him once, "to an amazing activist and fighter. And she had you! And I told her I'd make sure you were taken care of and loved." Bubbe stroked back his hair. "Do you think I did an okay job?"

He smiled. "I think you did okay," he told her. He loved his Bubbe, the loud, strong, pushy Ava, who got things done fast. Ava wasn't all soft-spoken and mushy like her daugher. That is, his mother.

Bubbe had told him all this when he was twelve, "old enough to fully understand," as his parents put it. He'd felt better knowing that Ysabel had been able to accomplish things before she died and hadn't lived a totally sad life. But he thought a lot about that disco-party boombox side of her, too. The Sheila E. side. The side that looked a bit like a good-time party ho.

"She didn't know who my real father was?" he asked Bubbe.

She sighed, stroking his hair more. "She got really lonely and scared sometimes and she reached out to different places for love," Bubbe said.

He was old enough at that point to read between her lines. Nobody knew who his real father was. He could've been anybody. He was embarrassed to feel tears, hot tears of shame, pool in his eyes.

"Now, hey," Bubbe clucked, holding him by the chin. "That man was handsome, whoever he was. That's obvious."

That made him smile a little bit.

He comes back to earth, back to the final crit with Adeyemo. After that, school's out—forever! He's back downtown in the hood now, the East Village, at Two Boots pizza with Zoya, Alexa, Horatio, and Yusef and Ignacio, these two art-head juniors who want to inherit his mantle—Ignacio with his Mohawk and obsession with *lucha libre* masks. They're all just talking shit, swapping around iPods. Eventually Oscar, who's having the party at his place that night on East Broadway, comes around. Oscar, who graduated from the not-special neighborhood high school, Seward Park, three years ago, and nobody really knows what he does—something tech related in a warehouse in Red Hook. But Oscar has his own place and always has beer and herb, which is key. Oscar, with so many cornrows you can't count them, and his vintage 2 Live Crew T-shirt on today, and his vague coolness without purpose that could be M-Dreem's own fate, he knows, if he hadn't had certain opportunities handed to him by—well, by them. Mr. and Mrs. Parental.

"Look at the children about to graduate," Oscar says, sitting down with the crew. "The future of New York City."

"M-Dreem, show him the future," Horatio says. "Show him your spiders."

He pulls out his big spider illo. "You like this, Oscar?" he asks.

Oscar's eyes pop out; he jerks back from the image. "Fucking spiders, damn! You one mad sick nigga, M-Dreem. But you got skills, I'll say that."

M-Dreem beams; he doesn't know exactly why Oscar's opinion means so much to him, but it does. "Thanks, my nigga," he says. Zoya looks at him and smirks, sensing his self-consciousness with that word; he smirks back at her. *What?* he wants to ask Zoya. *Are you my fucking conscience?* But he knows the Parentals hate that word, too. Maybe partly because when he uses it, he reminds them that, not being white, he can sort of use it, but they can't.

"You niggas coming tonight?" Oscar asks. Hell, yeah, they chorus. "That's good," he says. "I gotta go get this party ready." And then Oscar's gone.

It's hours till the party, but M-Dreem doesn't go home. Home always makes him feel vaguely uncomfortable, even though he doesn't know quite why. Ever since that flare-up with the Parentals last year, that incident with him punching the wall and calling her the B-word, it's never been quite the same with them, even if therapy and time have softened the impact. So today, he and Zoya and Alexa go to Alexa's place a few blocks away and smoke herb and listen to the new Mos Def. They end up in a cuddle puddle, Zoya and Alexa spooning him on either side, him wondering if Zoya can feel his boner as he falls asleep, knocked out from the weed. They all wake up at ten o'clock, Zoya and Alexa taking an hour to dress and fix their hair while he smokes more herb and watches stupid reality TV, and then they head over to Boots again for dinner, two slices between the three of them because they're all mad broke, then over to Oscar's, where his friend Nanyelis, the shy bi girl, is DJ'ing: Ghostface Killah, *Back Like That*. A bunch of kids from school are there plus Oscar's crowd of slightly older, scarier, intriguing who-are-theys. M-Dreem's drinking Negras from the fridge, and Oscar comes over. He always hooks people up. He offers M-Dreem and the girls X, and the girls decline but M-Dreem does a whole one, and in about an hour, and a little more herb, he's dancing, having the best time. Someone's got a rainbow-patch clown wig on, clothes are coming off, he's graduating from high school, he's going to Pratt, he's got mad skills, *Madvillainy* sounds sooo sick coming out of the speakers right now.

At some point the girls are like, "We're leaving, you coming?" and he's like, "No, I'm gonna stay," and Zoya gives him a long hug and she's like, "Be careful, baby," and they're gone. The kids from school thin out; he feels like he's going into a deeper, darker zone, dancing now mostly with this older white girl with a cute tooth gap and short bleached hair like that English model Agyness Whatever's Her Name, reaching out, holding hands, eventually with his hands slipped into the back of her jean shorts, and finally she grabs his hands again and says, "Come on, let's find Oscar." And she winds him back through the apartment.

They find Oscar in a back bedroom, behind a door only cracked open, with some of his friends. They all look half asleep and happy, passing around a plate and inhaling something off of it with a straw. Oscar looks up and smiles when M-Dreem comes in. M-Dreem whispers to the Agyness girl, "What's that?" and she goes, "It's heroin."

"Ah, shit, man," he says. He hasn't tried that one. That one's a no-no.

Agyness girl kind of frowns at him and tugs at his arm. "Snorting a little isn't very strong," she says. "You're done with school, right?"

"Yeah."

"Sooo?"

Artists must have these experiences, M-Dreem thinks. Out of pure experience comes pure expressions of form; he needs to have new visions, see new forms. He sits down on the floor with Agyness, hand in hand, his heart pounding. The plate comes around to Agyness, who passes it to him.

"Here," she says. "You go first. Just do a little bit."

He uses the straw to separate out a bit from the pile of tan powder, which looks like a tiny mesa on the plate.

"Not that little!" Agyness laughs. So he separates out more until Agyness nods her approval, then he nudges it into a jagged line.

"Don't stop snorting until it's all gone," Agyness says.

He doesn't. He's repulsed by the dirty, bitter taste that stings his nasal passage, then the back of his throat. His vision goes cross-eyed and he thinks, *I can't believe I just did heroin. I'm a scumbag. This would kill the Parentals.* But five seconds later, he's exactly where he's wanted to be his whole life but never knew it, back with her, before he was born, inside her; nothing's begun yet, just this warmth and protection, this liquid blanket. There hasn't been any separation or detachment or ache yet.

He snorts another messy line into his other nostril and burrows down deeper into the liquid blanket. Everyone else in the room sort of falls away like a movie camera rushing backward from a set. He locks eyes with Agyness, but it's not Agyness, it's her, 04/14/1984.

"I wanna know you so badly," he says. "I wanna ask you so many things."

"There's so much I wanna tell you," she says. "Most of all, honey, I'm so sorry." Now she's crying.

"Don't cry," he tells her. "You didn't know."

He curls up in her lap, his Airs up by his butt, his arms between his knees. He can hear himself purring; *I'm a little baby kitten,* he thinks. *I just came out of her and I'm getting my sustenance from her.* He loses any sense of the floor underneath him or the sounds around him; he and she are like a balloon they let go of. And she's telling him the whole story of what happened, New York City before 1992 and him.

Four hours later, at 4:30 in the morning, he drifts back from a reverie to look up and see Agyness running her hands through his hair.

"Are you okay?" she asks.

"I'm itchy," he says.

She smiles. "That's just the H, it's normal. It goes away."

"I'm cold, too."

She pulls a blanket from the bed, where Oscar's curled up on his side with Tamara, his sometimes girlfriend the past two years, and arranges it over M-Dreem and herself. All has gone silent and dark in the other rooms; the party has ended.

"I should probably get home," he murmurs, wiping drool from the side of his mouth.

She pulls him tighter. "Don't go."

"No, I have to go." He rises and vomits slightly on the two of them.

"Oh God," Agyness groans, in slow motion.

In the bathroom, where they clean up with mildewed towels, he feels itchy and cold, yet still velvety and delicious inside. For as long as his memory stretches back, to those patchy few recollections of the boys' home in Brooklyn, he can't remember a time—even the happy times with the Parentals and friends and fun and art and success in school, at the beach in the summer or those trips to Europe—where a sense of being lost and wrong didn't hover at his right shoulder, and now, for the first time, it's not there. *I am coming back here*, he thinks, meaning the H, kissing Agyness good-bye.

He walks home up Essex Street as church bells strike five, every streetlight an object of blurry, dancing beauty. He crosses Houston Street, absent the baseball cap he arrived at the party with, looks at all the stoops and gated storefronts with wonder, moves like liquid gold up Avenue B, feels a spasm of nausea and manages to bend over a garbage can just fast enough to avoid vomiting all over his T-shirt again. Long after the vomiting ends, he rests bent over the can, bracing himself above it with both hands, falling into another feel-good fugue, starring the funny-looking Sheila E. shorty, for seventeen more minutes before a vague voice far back in his head propels him home.

In the wee hours at the Christodora, Ardit, the Albanian doorman, tends to doze before the tiny TV in his room in the basement, so M-Dreem enters a sepulchral lobby, falls into a blissful nod once again with his right hand on the button of the elevator, and rouses himself from it a good two minutes after the elevator arrives, just long enough to hit the sixth-floor button. When the doors open on that floor, he feels a strong weight pulling him down toward the hallway carpet just outside the elevator, just another short, um, reverie, but he manages to shamble his way down the hall. Fumbling in his pocket for keys, he slowly registers he's lost them—just when the apartment door swings open to reveal, in a nightgown, Millimom. That is what he most often calls his Female Parental, a smirking hybrid name.

She turns forty next year and betrays the first lines emerging on her forehead and in the corners of her eyes—the beautiful, dark, perpetually anxious, and beleaguered eyes of Millimom. And now those pained eyes are burning with five A.M., been-waiting-up-all-night pain. He sees her *New Yorker* and big ceramic tea mug on the dining-room table in the apartment's dark recesses.

She steps back from the door, scrutinizing him head to toe. "Where have you been?" she asks in a half-whisper, trying not to wake Jared-dad in the room beyond.

Stepping inside, he makes his best effort to open his eyes wide, stand up straight, smile with a sort of no-big-deal, nonchalant air of apology. "Sorry I'm so late, Mom. There was a graduation party."

"I'd think that if you're going to party till dawn, you could at least give me a call." She sounds not so much angry as baffled and hurt.

"I know, I meant to, I just got caught up in the excitement and the flow."

"Couldn't you have just texted?"

Now their eyes are in the mother-son deathlock. He resists the urge to scratch his upper body, which is crawling with itches. Then he caves and lightly scratches his rib cage, where the itching is the worst.

Milly's nose wrinkles. "You smell like vomit," she says. "You've been drinking."

He exhales with relief. "I did drink a little," he says. "It was graduation night."

She crumples back, frowning. "I just wish you had called. Dad and I left you a message this afternoon congratulating you on your last day."

"I know, I—" he begins. Then his stomach seizes and he brushes past her and into the bathroom, where he locks the door just in time to stick his head in the toilet and puke again.

"Mateo," he hears Millimom call from the other side of the door, "are you all right?" But even the puking felt good, and now that it's over, he feels especially good. Another hazy wave comes over him, just as he hears his name again, Mateo, on the other side of the door, but this time in Jared's deeper, sharper tone. He'll get up in a moment, he thinks. But for right now he curls up with his head on the ledge of the toilet, and before he knows it, he's nodding on 04/14/1984 again, purring away.

THREE
DIRECTLY OBSERVED THERAPY
(1981)

What if they could ban smoking in all city restaurants and bars? Surely anyone would say it was a crazy idea—New York thrived on smoking, it was a city of smokers, in and out of the bars, in offices and walk-ups, the sidewalks alive with bobbing Marlboros and Virginia Slims and Newports in the neurotic, fearful hands of people in Armani and tracksuits—but what if, what if?

The thought kept nipping deliciously at the edge of Ava's other thoughts—*gotta make a dentist appointment; gotta stop at Balducci's and buy coffee and brie; oh, shit, gotta make a dentist appointment for Emmy* (her endearment of the abbreviation M.)—as she dressed for work that morning, with Sam off already for his run around the reservoir, and Emmy already being walked to school by Francelle. What if she became the health commissioner who banned smoking in restaurants and bars in the first big city in America? It could happen by '86, '87, she thought. First, nab the top spot, then start a public campaign, get Koch's support—she could make her big mark by the time she was forty-three, forty-four. People would say she was crazy, but if you didn't think big thoughts, how could you make anything happen? Isn't that where big change began, with big, bold thoughts? Women, particularly, needed to have more big thoughts, she believed, recalling all the theory books about women and health she'd read in grad school, suddenly wanting to reread them all, just to reconnect, just to refresh.

She was having so many thoughts! How would she get them all down on paper into proposals, outlines, workable flowcharts? She needed to invent a system to catch all these ideas: the public programs, the public-private partnerships, the synergies, even just ways Renny could run the department better. She needed to enlist the help of that intern from Columbia whom Renny was sending her way, the one he probably plucked because he was Puerto Rican, just like Renny. *Renny isn't so bad!* she found herself thinking, though she usually hated the man—well, no, okay, not hated, *chafed* under the man . . . her boss, for God's sake! But Renny could be funny! And warm! All his *"ay coños!"* when he was fed up with red tape and the bullshit stonewalling and inertia out of Koch's office. She was going to reach out to Renny today somehow, touch his arm, set up a lunch date—once she had some of those ideas down on paper!

In the mirror, she examined her hair, her clothes. She tore off her jacket and the metallic-gray blouse with the bow tie and pulled out the purple silk shell with the deep scoop neck, put on a gold chain over it. Why did she always separate day and night clothes? Why couldn't she bring just a little bit of luster into that drab office? She picked out a slightly higher pair of heels, grabbed her brush and the hairspray, and made her hair a little bigger and looser, bumping up the black feathers on either side. A darker lip gloss. Work was more fun this way! Goal number one for today, Wednesday, May 6: Have fun! Do the work, but have fun!

Sam came in, sweaty, once she was downstairs, nibbling a piece of toast—she wasn't very hungry; so much for the all-natural peanut butter she'd usually smear on it—downing a quick cup of coffee, and going over memos for meetings later that day (the infant mortality rate summit in early July, the herpes thing, the problem with the restaurants in Chinatown). He was her hunky Brooklyn boy, her strong-jawed, dark curly-haired Elliott Gould, her lawyer man with the soul of an artist. She was surprised, and pleased, by the surge of attraction she felt for him at 8:14 A.M.—a time they were usually both so busy getting themselves and Emmy out of the house they barely managed a good-bye peck on the cheek.

"Come here, you big sweaty lug," she said, putting down her papers, slouching back, and parting her legs. Which led her to another thought: She wasn't a girl from Queens anymore; she was an Upper East Side woman! She'd made it! She never really thought about that!

Sam looked at her funny, but intrigued. "I thought you didn't like me sweaty. Especially when you're all pulled together for work."

She stood up, kicking off her shoes. "Things change," she said, aiming to sound smoky.

His eyes narrowed at her—a little dumbfounded? A smidge concerned? Then a smile of gratitude bloomed. "No bullshitting me, Aves?"

She shook her head slowly, reaching for him, pulling off his sweaty old Cardozo Law T-shirt. She wasn't bullshitting. Oh my God, her work clothes were coming off! This was happening—suddenly they were on the kitchen floor. "Holy shit, Aves!" exclaimed Sam. "What the fuck!"

Francelle stepped in with a bag of groceries. "Oh, good Lord," she blurted out. She all but dropped the bag on the floor near the door. She retreated, calling back, "I'm running more errands!"

Ava and Sam burst out laughing, mortified and delighted—this would certainly make things awkward around the house with Francelle—and kept going until they were both done, then lay there on the parquet, clothes down around their ankles, breathing heavily, exhausted.

"Was something in your coffee?" Sam asked her, cradling her on the floor.

She giggled. "You just looked so sexy to me, all sweaty. My Elliott Gould."

With a groan of reluctance, Sam stood up, releasing her gently, picking his sweaty running clothes up off the floor. "All right, Aves," he said. "Hanky-panky time's over. I gotta go make deals for Donald

Trump and you gotta go get everybody healthy. And together we'll conquer New York."

"I'm gonna ask Renny to lunch," she said, pulling a brush from her bag and re-fluffing her hair wings. "I have about a dozen ideas for streamlining DOH, doing more with less."

"Go get 'em, honey," Sam said. He leaned down and kissed her dutifully, then trudged up the stairs. She stood up, put her clothes back together, and was slipping her pumps back on when Francelle gingerly reentered the kitchen.

She smiled impishly at Francelle; she couldn't resist—it was fun to tweak her island sense of propriety. "Good morning, Francelle," she singsonged.

Collecting dishes and cups off the table, Francelle gave her a side-long frown, but Ava caught the frown twisting into an amused, awkward smile as Francelle turned away. "Morning to you, Mrs. H.," Francelle said. "Aren't you running late to be downtown?"

She laughed. "You sound so reproving, Francelle!" She picked up her bulging bag. "No, not too much so. It doesn't hurt to throw off the schedule a little bit here and there. Would you do that sometime today, Francelle? Would you leave a load of laundry till tomorrow and call your sister for twenty minutes instead?" *How bizarre!* she thought. She'd never told Francelle to call Jamaica from the house phone before! She liked how it felt: magnanimous.

Francelle turned, looked at her perplexedly. "I guess I might have time for that," she finally said, loading the dishwasher, "seeing as it's Serendipity day. You didn't forget that, did you?"

She had forgotten—in her head, she'd been planning her workday out through six o'clock—but she wouldn't give Francelle the satisfaction of knowing that, not with all the unspoken tension between them over who spent how much time with Emmy and whom, inevitably, Emmy was more attached to, felt safest with. "Of course I didn't forget that, Francelle," she said. "Wednesday is Serendipity day. I look forward to it as much as Emmy does." Did Emmy look forward to it?

"All right, Mrs. H., have yourself a good day, then. I'll leave something for you to heat up tonight before I leave at two."

"Enjoy your half day, Francelle." She strode over to Francelle and put an arm around her. Francelle went rigid, taken by surprise—perhaps a touch horrified? "Thank you for all you do for us, my dear. You're part of this family." As she walked away, she spied Francelle looking back at her, mouth agape, completely baffled now. Oh, she had ruffled the unrufflable Francelle. What fun!

The glorious spring day, the flowers blooming on the dividers on Park Avenue, the rough thrill of the 6 train downtown . . . the preponderance of good-looking men on the subway and on the street, which she seemed to notice with a special zeal, even though she'd just had sex with Sam. *I could have sex all over again right now!* she thought, amazed and delighted, walking down Worth Street, aware of feeling sexier in her scoop-neck blouse, higher-than-usual heels, fluffier-than-usual hair. She was only thirty-eight, for God's sake! The youngest deputy health commissioner the city had ever had. *And maybe the sexiest?* she thought with an inner giggle.

On the way in, she passed Lauren from TB control. They didn't get along usually. But she surprised herself, exclaiming, "Such a lovely day, isn't it?" as they passed. She seemed to surprise Lauren, too, who nearly winced. "Yes, it is," Lauren replied. "I nearly didn't want to come inside."

"I had no choice," she sang back. "I have a full plate today!" She stopped in the office kitchen for a second cup of coffee, then, carrying it with panache and a certain boom-boom in her step, she thought, swung into her own office. And there was a handsome young Hispanic man in a shirt and tie, square-framed glasses sitting on his face, in the chair in front of her desk with a stack of files on his lap—probably not a day over twenty-five!

"Oh!" she exclaimed. "Well, hello there."

He looked up, startled. "Oh! Hello, Doctor." He rose abruptly, some of the files slipping from his lap to the floor, and they knelt down to collect them together. "I'm Hector. Villanueva. From Columbia."

"Oh, of course." She smiled. "You're my intern for the summer. Dr. Ferrer told me about you. Well, hello, Hector." She extended her hand. "It's nice to meet you. Please just call me Ava."

He looked at her quizzically. "Are you sure?"

"I'm sure I'm sure," she said. He was certainly handsome, she thought, settling behind her desk, but so shy and awkward! She could already tell. And those glasses! He had such large, lovely brown eyes behind them. Hadn't he heard of contact lenses?

"I'm sorry I'm sitting here," he said, even though he wasn't sitting anymore, but was standing, nervously, the stack of folders in his arms. "Mrs.—um, Mrs. Conti said it was okay because she didn't know where else to put me until you came in."

"It's fine," she said, her mind already thrumming with all the different projects she could put him on . . . and wasn't this sweet, she already felt a bit maternal toward him! "I came up at Bellevue. I know how to work around distraction. I'm not one of those lab geeks!"

He laughed—awkwardly, she noted; oops, he probably was one of those lab geeks. "So how's Columbia?" she asked. "Renny—" She caught herself. "I'm sorry," she said, all mock contrite. "*Dr. Ferrer* said you were interested in infectious. I.D."

He nodded soberly. "I am."

"But why? Infectious is over, everything's been figured out. Why not cancer or heart? That's where the big work's gonna be—and the big money."

"Well—" he stammered. He was so nervous! Was she talking too hard, too fast, scaring him? "Well, in the developing world—infectious—"

"Oh, I get it! You want to do I.D. in the *developing* world. Oh, well, that's a different story. Lots of work to do there! You're from—where, the D.R.?"

"The P.R.," he said. They both laughed a bit at the inadvertent wordplay. "We came here when I was thirteen."

"Ah, *sí, muy bien*," she said. "Maybe you can help me with my Spanish, among other things, because it's not very good."

"Sure, I'll help you," he said softly. She smiled. She hadn't even been serious, but he'd taken her seriously. He was sweet. If only he'd lose those dorky glasses—he didn't know how handsome he was!

She needed to bring them back on point—her busy day! Her meetings! The outlines and flowcharts she wanted to work through! "Let's talk about what I've got on my plate and how you can help me out," she began. And just then, speaking of I.D., Blum rapped on her door, came in, and handed her a brief, ignoring Hector.

"You seen this?" Blum asked.

She scanned it, eyes widening. "Another Kaposi's sarcoma report out of St. Vincent's? In a thirty-two-year-old guy?"

Blum nodded. "Another homosexual."

Ava handed Hector the memo. "Here's your first task, Hector," she said. "Xerox this for me." Hector took the memo and left the office.

She turned back to Blum. "This is, what? Case seven in the past few months?"

"Eight."

"What the hell do you think this is? This cancer is, like, a few old Jewish and Italian men, once in a blue moon."

"I wonder if it's hep B–related," Blum said. "It's rampant in the gay community."

"A virus-linked cancer," she mused.

"Either that or too much disco or nitrites or sex or something." This bugged her. "Not funny, Blum. You know my brother's gay."

"Hey, I'm serious about the nitrites! What the hell could it be? And you know L.A.'s reporting a bunch of PCP cases in homosexuals."

"Pneumocystis, yeah," she said. "I read about that." Hector returned with her copy of the memo. "What's your take on this, Hector? If it's community based, it feels epi to me."

Hector looked down. "I haven't been following it," he all but mumbled. *God, this boy is uncomfortable in his own skin!* Ava thought. Then again, hey, he was, like, twenty-five, he was a kid.

She told Blum to call a meeting if and when the next KS case came in; she couldn't spend more time on this today—she had multiple meetings to make, projects to push along, briefs to plow through. And all by three o'clock, then Emmy! She set up Hector in a windowless office—well, frankly, it was a large closet—a few doors down. Then she plunged into her day with gusto. She bore down on her folder, scratching out flowcharts on her pad as she picked through briefs, calling in Rosemary a few times to dictate a memo to her.

"You're going too fast for me!" Rosemary complained at one point.

"I have a lot on my plate today!" she snapped back.

Then she put in several calls around the office and around town to float various questions and ideas. Where was that old late-morning sluggishness? Her mind seemed to move along, click, click, click, ticking off tasks, making amazing connections that had never occurred to her before. She'd felt this sort of mental efficiency all week, but it really seemed to have hit critical mass today. As she read and worked, she sat in her chair in a manner that felt, to her, provocative, legs crossed, bobbing one foot, one hand pulling back one feathered wing of hair, imagining a shiny barrette there. She was the naughty deputy health czar, like in some Times Square blue movie!

At eleven, she had the Wednesday briefer with Renny and the other deputies. En route, she pulled Hector out of his glorified closet. "Come on in and listen to the poobahs and learn how the sausage is made, Hector," she said, taking his arm as they walked toward the conference room. "It's your internship, after all."

"I'm nervous," he whispered. And yes, his skinny arm was shaking! "I get nervous in groups." She felt another maternal surge toward him. She'd thought she'd be annoyed to have to find tasks for this intern, this special pick of Renny's, but she actually already liked having him around. He wanted to go into tropical diseases! How noble! She hoped a summer in the health building wouldn't drain him of his idealism.

"You probably won't have to say anything," she told him, squeezing his arm. "Just look admiringly at me when I say things."

He looked at her, confused. She winked to show she was making a joke of sorts.

"Oh," he said. He laughed a little, relieved.

Lauren led with the latest data on the slow outbreak of drug-resistant TB in the homeless shelters. Lauren fumbled around the truth of the matter, which was that patients weren't completing the course of drugs they were prescribed. Ava simply had to break in, and she did, summarizing a study she'd just read out of Minneapolis on the efficacy of directly observed therapy—where you hold the meds and make the patient show up daily and take them in front of you, to be sure they're taken—in wiping out a similar strain of first-line-resistant TB.

"These are precisely the areas," Ava said, rushing—there was a certain soberer affect she assumed in these meetings, her voice a bit lower and slower, but today she couldn't keep the excitement, the speed, out of her voice—"where we could benefit greatly by having a monthly NYC convocation, flying out some of the investigators of these studies in smaller cities for a few nights in New York. Show them a good time, get a block of Broadway seats out of the mayor's office, let them know they're in good hands and they're not going to be knifed on the street, then basically hole them up here during the day—or in, say, a catered meeting room at the Sheraton—and pick out of them how they implemented these programs. Then we'll figure out how to scale them up for New York–size problems."

Renny was leaning in, engaged, but she noted that Lauren had wheeled her chair back from the table a bit, was regarding her in a civil pose but with murderous eyes behind her glasses.

"The funny thing, Doctor," Lauren began—and, uh-oh, she was calling her "Doctor" and not "Ava," which signaled chilliness and maybe a hint of bite, and not collegial warmth—"is I was just about to brief on the Minneapolis directly observed-therapy study and more or less make the same suggestion that we have the investigators come to New York. Or deign to visit them."

Uh-oh. She caught Hector's terrified eyes—though a touch intrigued, perhaps? Renny cleared his throat. Awkwardness hung in the room. "Either way!" Ava finally chirped. "I'll be happy to throw my beret up to the sky in the middle of downtown Minneapolis." She smiled sweetly, innocently, at Lauren.

Everybody laughed. "You're gonna make it after all, Aves," Blum cracked. The boys liked her far more than Lauren, she knew that much. Lauren had no choice but to smile along like a good sport.

"Lauren, talk to the support staff about getting the Minneapolis people here," Renny said. "And Mary Richards here can decide if we'll take them to *A Chorus Line* or *Sugar Babies*."

Everybody laughed again. This was quite a bit of humor for these dry health types! She ducked her head down, smiled. Renny's crack was a reminder that he liked her, was amused by her. Easily now she could touch his arm after the meeting and set up a lunch date. She managed to be quiet for the rest of the meeting, excepting her own briefings, of course, but her mind was racing. Out of any half-baked idea floated in the room today, she might squeeze a truly great one! And that's why, whereas before she'd occasionally jotted down a word or two on her pad, today she was sketching out a flowchart of the meeting, graphic style, to try to capture who said what and what it led to and how it all looped back and connected. Blum was sitting next to her, and at one point, she caught him looking at her pad quizzically.

"What the hell is that?" he whispered.

"I'm capturing ideas," she said.

"Rosemary's taking notes, though," he whispered back. His eyebrows scrunched down, toward each other. "You okay, Aves?"

Oh God, it was because Blum, her best friend at Health, knew; he knew about that period about a year ago, because she'd confided in him, knew about the crying, the anxiety, the inability to concentrate, the insomnia, Sam's worry over it, Emmy's fearful sensing of it, the Valium, then the having to roll back on the Valium, the new drug that finally seemed to make things better over the course of a few months. That's the thing about sharing this stuff with your work friends—they're always looking out for you and for signs, signs.

"I'm great," she whispered. She was!

He shrugged with his eyes, as if to say, *Well, okay, if you say so.* She caught Hector peering at them. Nosy Hector! She winked at him. He half smiled, looked away, exquisitely young and awkward. The meeting ended and she took him down to Chinatown for lunch since she had to check in on a restaurant-hygiene drive down there anyway. They made the round of a few restaurants on Mott and Canal. At the ancient Wo Hop, she noticed the lack of DOH hygiene-rule signs on the wall. She strode toward the woman absently nibbling on wontons at a back table, a stack of purchase orders by her side. Hector followed her.

"Faye! Why no signs? I brought you signs last time. You're violating health rules."

Faye looked up, grimaced. "Kai—" She made a kind of methodical smoothing gesture, then mimed tacking something up.

"What? Faye, I don't know what you're talking about."

"Kai—" Faye began again.

Ava turned to Hector. "Kai's her husband," she said. "The owner. He speaks good English." Hector nodded.

"So to wipe. To wipe!" Faye continued. "To keep clean."

"What?" She felt a bit more aggressive and impatient today toward Faye, and she wasn't sure why, because she considered Faye almost a friend, and Kai, too.

Faye looked at Hector, shrugged helplessly.

"Oh!" Hector said. "You mean to laminate the signs? To wipe them clean?"

Faye broke into a relieved smile. "Yes! Laminate! To wipe them."

Hector turned to her. "He took the signs down to laminate them," he said.

She frowned at Faye. "They go right back up?"

"Of course." Faye said it as though she were an idiot. "They go back up tonight."

Ava felt strangely disappointed that she had to let the whole thing go. She'd come down here today weirdly looking for some sort of crusade, perhaps so Hector could see her in action. "Well, okay," she said. They made a quick round through the kitchen. It looked okay except for some shrimp tails she saw scattered on the floor and an empty soap dispenser over the utility sink. "Pick those up," she told Faye, who knelt and picked up the shrimp tails with her bare hands. "Fill that." Faye turned and barked in Cantonese at one of the workers, who walked toward the back, returning with a plastic tub of bubble-gum-pink soap. "Looks good otherwise, Faye."

"Thank you, Ava," Faye singsonged back to her.

Hector inadvertently laughed. Faye giggled, too. So the minorities were having a laugh at her, eh? Anger stabbed her, then she laughed herself, just as unbidden. "We need to feed this boy, Faye! Two egg-drop soups."

"Special for you," Faye said, leading them out of the kitchen.

She and Hector sat up front. "Did you see that poor guy in the back?" she asked him. "I wonder how much they're paying him. Did you know they're trying to unionize at the Silver Palace dim sum parlor? Good for them. It's slave labor over there."

"They're scared, though, 'cause they're immigrants," Hector said.

She looked up from her soup at him. "Would you do me a favor?"

His eyes widened, frightened.

"Would you take off your glasses for a minute?"

"Take off my glasses?"

"Yeah. Just for a minute."

He obliged her, removing the squarish plastic frames. Now that was better. "Have you ever thought of getting contact lenses so we can see how handsome you actually are?"

He smiled and blushed, exquisitely embarrassed. "I have them, but they hurt my eyes."

"When did you come here from Puerto Rico?"

"When I was thirteen."

"Oh, so you went to high school here?"

"Bronx Science."

She beamed. "My brother went to Bronx Science! I went to Cardozo. Did you have Mr. Levy with the cauliflower growth on his neck for chemistry?"

"I did!" He smiled broadly. "I loved that guy. How do you know about him?"

"My brother!"

"Oh, right."

They were both quiet for a second. She felt an incredible surge of identification with and affection for him. "So—tropical, huh?"

He nodded soberly. "Tropical."

Tropical was not really her bailiwick. "You've read about the dengue outbreaks in Cuba?" she ventured.

"Yeah, and Castro trying to blame the U.S." He laughed.

But she couldn't really focus on a talk about tropical. She was still wired up from the meeting that morning, and even from the brief volley with Faye. "Health is a shark pit," she said.

His eyes widened, confused. "Health?"

"Health. *Health*. The DOH."

"Oh!"

"Lauren St. Hilaire hates my guts. Did you see the way she was looking at me in that meeting?"

Hector grinned slightly. "Well, you kind of hijacked her presentation."

Her mouth fell open. She was shocked and a touch offended, then suddenly amused. "You really think so?" she asked.

"Well, it's—it's—" He was flustered now. "You had a good idea, but she was getting to the same idea, I think."

"I hate how slow people are with their ideas," she nearly barked at him. He popped back in his seat. "Spit it out! Spit it out! Let's save time. The more time we save, the more we can do."

He laughed uncomfortably. "I know, but—"

But. She suddenly felt affectionate, playful toward him again. "You have a girlfriend?" she asked.

"A what?"

"A girlfriend. A girl. Friend."

"Uh. Not right now."

"You like girls?"

He was squirming, and she liked it! How far could she take him? She had no interest in her food. If anything, she wanted a drink. Also, she had to go back to the office and make sense of that flowchart she'd been diagramming during the meeting and bring it in to Renny. Should she call Renny right now, from the payphone, tell him to set some time aside for her this afternoon? Oh, wait, shit, but Emmy! Serendipity at three o'clock! How much work could she get done between now and three?

"I—" Still squirming. "I'm too busy for that right now," he said. "I wanna publish."

"You wanna publish?" she cried. "You're too young to publish."

"I'm ambitious!"

"I can see that! Okay, fine, you wanna publish, I'll help you publish. Don't worry about it, Bronx Science guy."

Now he finally smiled. "Thank you," he said. She let the fish off the hook. Their food came. He ate with gusto, but she barely picked at hers. She felt like she was losing hold of her thoughts; they were running ahead of her now just a bit too fast, and she didn't like the feeling it gave her. A few times, she felt an urge to cry, but she pushed it back.

Hector looked up at her. "You're not eating."

"I'm not hungry at all," she said. "I'm thinking about my daughter, Emmy. I don't do enough for her."

They left the restaurant. On Canal Street, they passed a vendor selling Hello Kitty dolls. "I'm buying one for Emmy," she said. But she ended up buying five of them, each in a different color, and hauling them away in a black plastic garbage bag, the only bag the vendor had. She slung the bag over her shoulder like Santa Claus.

"You want me to carry those?" Hector asked.

"No, I'm fine," she said, barreling through the sidewalk crowd. Back at the office, she dumped the bag, picked up the flowchart from the meeting, stalked into Renny's office. He was sitting there going over something with Lauren.

She pulled up a seat. "Can you just give me five minutes?"

Renny and Lauren looked at her, stunned. And a little scared. "Ava, we're in the middle of a meeting," Renny said.

"I want five minutes of your time." She stabbed her pad with her pen. "I have a way we can get three times as much out of that meeting in probably half the time. It's just a process issue."

"Okay, Ava," Renny said—why so gently? That was annoying. "But not now."

Lauren glanced at Renny. "Ava," she ventured.

"Ava what? Are you angry at me because I stole your thunder in the meeting? Because if you are, I'm sorry. The idea just came to me and I came out with it."

"No, Ava," Lauren said, her voice firm and loud now. "I'm worried that you're cycling."

She sat straight up in her seat. She made a high, indignant sound. She laughed sharply. "You're worried that I'm cycling? That I'm *cycling*? No, Lauren, you're pissed off about the meeting, so you're going to say instead you're worried that I'm cycling, when you well know that I was diagnosed unipolar, not bipolar."

"Ava," Renny said, "I think that, in retrospect, you've been ramping up for the past two weeks, and now you're cresting."

With a Herculean effort, she sat back in her seat, said not a word. Then, slowly, with excruciating enunciation: "Even if I am, this"—again, she tapped the pen on her pad—"is a better way to do things."

Renny and Lauren looked at each other helplessly—how infuriating! "Fine," Renny said. "We'll go over it. But not now."

"Aw, c'mon, Renny, all I wanted was five minutes!" God, she just sounded like a girl from Queens! She stood up, pad in hand, and walked out. She heard Renny mutter to Lauren: "I have to call Sam."

That stopped her cold. She could not see Sam go through the torment he had gone through a year ago. She stepped back into Renny's office. "Don't you dare call Sam, Ren," she all but shouted. "That is *not* showing concern for us."

She stalked back toward her office, well aware that Mrs. Conti and the rest of the support staff had heard her and were tracking her, peering over their fucking glasses as they typed. She stopped at Hector's closet. "I'm going to my office and closing the door and getting some shit done before I go meet my daughter," she announced.

He looked up. She noticed he was looking through the Kaposi's briefs Blum had brought in earlier. "Okay," he said. "Are you okay?"

She put a hand on her hip. "Do you know what I hate, Hector? I hate when people see good, energetic impatience—when they see a touch of activism in the middle of a fucking ossified bureaucracy—and they want to pathologize it because it scares them. Because it means they might have to get off their own fucking asses and actually get something done. And it sounds like—already! even though you know what I'm about—you see me that way, too. You're scared of me."

He shook his head. "No, I'm not," he said. But she could see the briefs trembling in his hand.

She stared at him good and hard. Her affectionate and aggressive feelings toward him were all mixing in her head confusingly. She wanted to cry. Instead, she thought, *He is literally sitting here in a closet.* That was hilarious to her. "I hope you know you're literally in the closet," she said. Then she was horrified. Had she just said that?

He turned pale. His mouth opened. "I'm not in the closet," he said, but it came out a croak, barely audible.

She held her stare. Voices in her head were telling her to continue to taunt him, but something else broke through. A tender voice told her to spare the boy. "I'll see you tomorrow, Hector," she said.

She got back to her office and closed the door. Her fat folder awaited her. She had exactly eighty minutes until she had to leave to meet Emmy. Certainly she could better use that time if she outlined precisely how to use it, how much time to spend on each thing. She flipped her yellow pad to a fresh page, drew a box at the top. "Chinatown Project," she wrote. "Crunch follow-up data. Call Ben Eng. Spreadsheet format!" And so on like that. Thirty minutes later, she'd completed her outline and was ready to execute it with her remaining fifty minutes. Someone knocked on the door. It was Blum.

She gave him a stern look. "I'm trying to knock off about eight things before I go meet Emmy."

He came in, shut the door, sat down and leaned in a bit toward her. "Aves, everybody's worried about you," he said.

She paused. She gave a helpless, bitterly amused laugh. She laid her palms flat and open on the table before her. "Blum, I can't win this one, can I? Every bit of passion or oomph I ever show from now on will be judged through the lens of last year, won't it? If I'm not tamped down with so much lithium I can barely think straight, I'm just a ticking time bomb around here, right?"

He laughed. Thank God somebody could still laugh at her in the way she wanted! "No, sweetheart," he said. "No one's been doing that. It's the past week or so. You've been different."

"Blum—" Her voice broke. "Blum, I've been feeling good." She started crying; she could do that around Blum. "I've had energy, I've had ideas. Don't take it away from me."

"But, Aves." He leaned forward more. "Look at yourself. You're crying. Do you really feel good right now?"

"I'm *feeling*. I'm feeling. Okay?"

He sighed, shook his head. "Would you just call Vikram and talk about the lithium? You want me to do it with you now?"

"I told you I have a million things to do before I go meet Emmy."

"You're meeting Emmy soon?"

"We meet every Wednesday at three at Serendipity."

"Why don't you take a Valium now, then?"

"I will *consider* taking one," she said. But Blum just sat there. "You are not doing directly observed therapy with me, if that's what you're thinking."

Blum stood up, all six feet two inches of him. He was a boy from Midwood; they understood each other. "I know you hate that you have this thing," he said. "But you have to think about keeping yourself and your family safe."

"Safe!" she snorted.

"We all get crap to deal with, and this is yours, Aves," he said in a suddenly sharper voice. "Be a grown woman."

Blum left, closing the door behind him. She cried. She knew the good times were coming to an end. She should be heading uptown, she thought. But she kept tweaking the damn outline she'd made so she could fully implement it in the morning. There they were, the tears and the anxiety wrestling right alongside the exhilaration about all her plans, that lust for life, that rush. Good-bye to all that. She stuffed her yellow pad into her workbag, slung the black garbage bag of Hello Kittys back over her shoulder.

On the 6 train uptown, she gave withering looks to people whose body touched hers. Finally, to a man who bumped into her, she said, "You could be more careful."

"Fuck you, bitch," he said, before getting off the train.

Her head was racing. She should take a Valium before meeting Emmy. But in the pit of her stomach, she could remember the dead Valium haze from last year, the hell getting off those things, how proud she was she hadn't needed one in three months. Being with Emmy would calm her—it always did. She never took her illness out on her child. They were going to have fun today!

She stepped into Serendipity. There was Emmy, sitting on a white chair, alone at a white table, waiting for her, her dark, curly hair pulled back in barrettes that were woven with pink and blue ribbons. Her Trapper Keeper was in front of her, with the big pink sticker letters on the front spelling out MILLY. (Emmy short for M., M. short for Milly.) She smiled when she saw her mother, showing a mouthful of braces. Then, when she noticed her mother was hauling a black plastic garbage bag, the smile disappeared. Her eyes hazed over with fear.

But Ava didn't see that. She barreled into the restaurant, knocking down a chair with the black plastic bag. "You can't leave a chair out in the middle of the room," she huffed at the waitress who hurried over to pick it up. "Emmy!" Suddenly, she was leaning over, kissing Milly, who cringed—she had schoolfriends just a few tables away; she knew they were already looking over, giggling. "I come from Chinatown bearing gifts!" exclaimed Ava. One by one, she pulled the Hello Kitty dolls from the plastic bag, arranged them in an arc on the tabletop. "Aren't they cute?"

Her mother was cuddling up next to her, asking about her day at school, and, *mmm*, were they sharing a frozen hot chocolate like they usually did?

"Yes," said Milly, "but I have to go to the bathroom first; I'd been waiting for you to get here."

Walking toward the back, Milly could hear how loudly her mother was talking to the waitress, as though she wanted the whole restaurant to hear. In the back, at the payphone, Milly called her dad's office, waited for his secretary to put him on the line. Somewhere deep down, she'd broken in two again, just as she had last year. But for now, she put herself above the shock and the humiliation and the knowledge of what the next few days (weeks? months?) would be like. (Well, actually, she thought about Francelle, and how grateful she was that Francelle was not only loving but the same person every day.)

"You need to come to Serendipity," she said when her father came on the line. "Mom's breaking down again."

FOUR

BOYFRIENDS AND GIRLFRIENDS

(1992)

There it was on the plate, in a pool of syrup, a final fat blueberry that had escaped the finished pancake. Milly speared it with her fork and raised it to Jared's lips.

"You have it," she said.

"No, Millipede, you have it."

Milly held the blueberry between her lips, leaned forward, and shared it with Jared—the two of them laughing as they each bit the berry to pull away their half, kissing all the while. The entire transaction took just seconds; they were certainly not the kind of people to engage in ostentatious and drawn-out public displays of affection. But the whole affair had caught the eye of the mid-fortysomething woman sitting across from them in the restaurant, who turned to her companion, another fortysomething woman.

The first woman said, "I don't think I can do any more Sunday brunches at this place."

Her friend looked moderately alarmed. "Why? We love this place."

"I can't watch another beautiful, bedheaded Gen-X couple come in here with their whole drowsy Sunday vibe of we-just-had-amazing-sex-and-now-we're-going-to-drowsily-walk-around-the-Chelsea-Flea-holding-hands-before-we-go-home-and-have-more-sex."

To which her friend laughed. "Oh, them," she said. "Yes, I'd noticed them."

"You just missed the blueberry make-out trick, unfortunately."

Her friend glanced the way of Milly and Jared. "I don't think they'll make it to marriage," she said.

Friend #1's eyes narrowed. Now they were playing one of their favorite single-friends games: Prognosticate the Fate of the Happy Couple before You. "Why not?"

"Look at him!" Friend #2, the harder-bitten of the duo, exclaimed. "Have you watched him run his hands through his lush head of hair? He's so full of himself. He'll get tired of her. She's too needy. You can tell."

"Oh, nooo," said Friend #1. "You have not been sitting from my vantage point. He's crazy about her. I saw the doggy eyes."

And on and on they went, and how amusing and perhaps disconcerting it might have been for Jared and Milly if they could have heard the prognostications made about them by two lonely strangers in a crowded Sunday brunch spot. But this wasn't the case, and Milly and Jared sailed out of the Chelsea nouveau diner as bedheadedly as they'd arrived, back out into the garbage-scented steam of their first postcollegiate New York summer. They were on this side of town, and not in the East Village, because they were meeting friends from school at a new park along the Hudson for some sort of Frisbee/picnic thing, hastily arranged the day before via a batch of messages left on answering machines. This was their life now, Jared having achieved his goal of Milly and hence free to pursue his myriad other goals, and Milly forever glancing over her shoulder, trying to identify the shape-shifting unease that cast a shadow over their happiness.

At any rate, when they arrived at the picnic, they met someone they'd never seen before, a brunette commanding the crowd on a cluster of blankets under one of the few trees on the pristine grassy expanse. Her name was Drew: tall and skinny, hair the color of dark chocolate brushed back off her face like a boy's, an assertive nose dotted with freckles, big white teeth that were just slightly and adorably chipmunk-like in the front, a skeptical West Coast drawl, and ten toenails painted deep red like Chiclets glinting on perfect, bare feet. She was a fact-checking friend of Colleen's from *Vanity Fair*, but she was really a writer who woke at six each morning to work on her novel before heading to work.

When Milly and Jared arrived, the gang was discussing Václav Havel's resignation as president of Czechoslovakia. The conversation devolved into puns on his name.

"Václav Havel resigns wearing a—" Drew paused. "Sparkly balaclava." Her fey lisp and her timing were flawless. Everyone laughed. Those were the first words spoken by Drew that Milly ever heard.

Colleen introduced them. "Drew, this is Milly and Jared."

"Oh!" Drew pealed with delight. "This is the Jackson Pollock and Lee Krasner of the new millennium you told me about! So nice to meet you."

She sat up on the blanket and crawled forward a few paces to shake their hands, which was when Milly spied the breasts peeking from beneath Drew's shoulder-strapped vintage green floral sundress: two small but wickedly full, darkly nippled orbs that all but whistled from their shadows, *Why, hello, Millicent!* Milly felt that feeling she had felt periodically since she was twelve and acted on only twice, in college, and not very deftly at that: girl desire. Her eyes caught Drew's; the glint was unmistakable. But wait? Was Drew conferring the same glint on Jared?

Milly collected herself. "Umm," she began a reply, aiming to seem game. "How about the Kiki Smith and—um—"

Drew followed her eyes minutely, rapt. "Who is Kiki Smith with, anyway?" she asked. "Is she married, or with—?"

Nobody seemed to know, though Jared's friend Asa said that a friend of his parents' had just bought a Kiki Smith sculpture.

"Well, anyway," Milly continued. But what did she want to say? She kept bouncing her eyes ridiculously between Drew and Jared, who seemed to wait amusedly for her to finish her thought. "I mean, Lee Krasner? Give me some credit."

"Lee Krasner is *awesome*," said Drew.

So that's how it began. Drew began spending a lot of time with Milly and Jared, the three of them out late with their high school and college friends, the fledgling filmmakers and painters and actors and, of course, the endless editorial assistants. And it would always end up that Jared and Milly and Drew would stay out the latest, at some East Village dive like 7A or Blue and Gold, talking drunkenly and intensely about, oh, how could Bret Easton Ellis even put himself in the same category as Donna Tartt just because they went to college together, or who was really more subversive from a gender-deviance point of view, Sinead O'Connor or k.d. lang or even Prince. Or, ironically, they'd put "Man in Motion," the theme from *St. Elmo's Fire*, on the jukebox and then recast the movie with themselves and their friends (and Drew would laugh and be like, "Oh God, no!" when Jared and Milly would cast her in the Demi Moore part). Or they'd make up names for one another's memoirs. Jared's, because he was an installation artist, would be *The Boy with the Blocks: The Jared Traum Story*. Milly's: *BrushStrokes: A Life*, then, beneath, in smaller type, *The Millicent Heyman Story*.

Drew's memoir would be *Prose in the Fast Lane*. Milly came up with that one, which they all had a good laugh over. Milly had never had a friend quite like Drew before. Most of her friends she'd known so long they treated her like a little sister, with affection but also a certain carelessness, whereas Drew was attentive, solicitous, always wanting to know how Milly was—how was her work? Her relationship? And Drew entertained Milly; sometimes Milly sensed, with both confusion and delight, that Drew was almost performing a certain kind of wise-cracking, all-knowing, tough but goodhearted best girlfriend, like in old movies. Drew seemed happy to perform like this for Jared as well, which turned Drew into a subject of enchantment and fascination for both members of the couple.

"I think you're in love with her," Jared would joke to Milly, after Milly had told him in some detail about something Drew had said, a one-liner she'd concocted, or something slightly outrageous Drew had worn the night before, such as a gingham baby-doll dress with scrunchy white ankle socks and Dr. Martens.

"I think *you're* in love with her," Milly would toss right back.

One night in a bar, three in the morning came around and there were just the three of them left, with "Desperado" on the jukebox. They slipped for a moment into drunken quiet. Jared looked at Drew. *"Prose in the Fast Lane,"* he said out of nowhere, and the three of them fell into one another, laughing.

"I love you two," Drew said. "I feel safe when I'm with you."

"You're like our daughter," Jared said.

"Mm-hmm," said Milly. "You're our little girl."

"I finally have two intact parents!" Drew exulted.

But very quickly the relationship between Milly and Drew also became one of those twisted mirror games, a very complicated mix of love, lust, competition, and shared terror over what would happen to them in the areas of vocation and romance. One night, Milly had two paintings in a small group show. Everyone went, including Drew, who later said to Milly, "Your paintings and my writing are alike in that they're both about artifice and posing, except you kind of celebrate it and I lament it."

This dismayed Milly. "What am I supposed to say to that?" she asked.

"I'm not saying it's a bad thing," Drew insisted demurely.

Still, the comment obsessed Milly. "Do you think that's true, what she said?" she asked her gay high-school friend Ryan one day over lunch. Ryan was petite and half Chinese and had a job working part time as Nora Ephron's administrative assistant. Nora bullied him and he loved it.

"I think you're becoming obsessed with Drew," he said. "You talk about her a lot."

"Jared says that, too." Milly twirled a forkful of pasta off Ryan's plate. "I don't know why—I never had a sister, maybe that's why? But even before she made that remark, I'm always thinking, *What would Drew think of this painting? What would Drew think of this dress? Of my hair like this? Of this other friend of mine?"*

Usually, Milly and Jared would put Drew in a cab to the West Village before walking the few blocks home to the Christodora, but one very alcoholic night, Jared said to Drew, "Come over and see Horace"—that was the new cat—so the three of them walked there arm in arm, with Milly in the middle, which gave her the new and wonderful feeling of holding love on both sides of her body.

"Hello, Horace," said Drew, covering the cat all over with kisses. "Are you a great Roman thinker? A great Roman cat of letters?" Jared found a stub of a joint that they all shared and put Matthew Sweet on the stereo.

Milly was relating all this to Ryan a few days later. "And then," she continued, "we had a three-way!"

"Shut the fuck up," Ryan said slowly. "How did it start?"

"I don't really remember because we were all stoned," Milly replied. "Just that it was really like Drew was the little girl who was desperately hungry for love, and we wanted to hold and protect her. It was a total inversion of the usual Drew. She was totally quiet, for one thing. We all fell asleep holding each other with Drew in the middle."

Ryan stared at her blankly for several seconds. "You are fucking with me, right?" he finally asked. "This really happened?"

"Yes! And it was really sweet. She woke up before us and left a note saying, 'Thank you, I wanted to let you sleep. I'll call you later.' But she didn't call later that day, and we didn't call her. And I said to Jared, 'I wonder what it'll be like with Drew now,' and he said, 'Me, too.' So finally yesterday I called Drew and we met for lunch and we hugged and we were both, like, 'Hiiiii!'" The tone of Milly's inflection for Ryan was a sheepish *Oh my God, I cannot believe we did that!* "So we're making chitchat, ordering salads before we take them into the park, and finally she was like, 'So how have you been?' And I said, 'I'm okay. I've just felt weirdly protective of you ever since Friday night—like I'm seeing you differently, making me feel like you can have those kinds of feelings for more than one person at a time.'"

And Drew had said: "Did you tell Jared that?"

And Milly had said: "Not quite like that. I'm afraid it would freak him out."

Then Milly leaned over on the park bench and kissed Drew softly near her ear. "You were so quiet that night!" She giggled. "It was so unusual!"

But Drew didn't giggle back; she just smiled tightly and kind of sadly and looked away. Then she let out a kind of restrained noise that said *Mmmmnggh, I can't stand it anymore!*

"I'm so lonely, Mill," she said. "I cannot be falling in love with a couple. That is not a good plan for me."

A few weeks prior to the three-way, Drew had finally, agonizingly split up with Perry. Perry had been her tall, deep-voiced, WASPily good-looking boyfriend, an editor at *Harper's*, who once, at a party right after Drew said something particularly funny about *Thelma and Louise*, asked her in a good-humored way, "How does it feel to be a swath of glitter wrapped around an echoing void?"

Nobody could silence Drew like Perry could, but she had been crazy about him and his whole Brideshead aura, his swoopy Edwardian haircut. It was Drew who finally broke it off, but only after Milly and a few of her other friends told her bluntly that Perry was sucking away her last dribs of self-esteem. There had been a whole month near the end of the relationship where Drew didn't write at all because she couldn't banish the idea of Perry standing over her shoulder, rolling his eyes at every line.

After Drew spoke, Milly blinked, quiet. "We love you, but we don't want you to do anything you don't want to do," she finally said.

Drew looked up at Milly, then turned away from her. "Anyway," she finally said, "don't you and Jared have some stuff to work out?"

Milly sat up straight. "What do you mean?"

"Well . . ." Drew minutely examined her salad while she talked. "Are either of you making any actual art? A lot of times, when artists date, it's because they want to distract each other from actually working."

"I've been working!" Milly insisted. "I've been applying for grants and residencies all week, putting slides together. I've been running all over town."

"You have to do stuff like that, obviously," said Drew. "But, sweetie, that's not working."

"*You* spend a month applying for eight grants at a time and then tell me it's not working," Milly snapped back.

They walked out of the park together. Milly slipped her hand in Drew's, comforted by that and feeling a bit subversive about it, but Drew gave it a quick squeeze and pulled her own hand gently away.

After that conversation, Milly became obsessed with the idea that Jared was distracting her from producing meaningful work. When she was working in the room she painted in, the small bedroom Jared had helped her convert to a studio, she resented it when he had the TV on too loudly, when he shouted random things to her, even when he brought her tea. She got stuck on the fact that here she was, working from the apartment like a hobbyist, while he had a separate workspace in an old warehouse in desolate far-west Chelsea. (Granted, he worked with concrete and old train-track spikes, materials the apartment could never accommodate, but still.) She fixated on the idea that he'd already had a solo show, albeit one in a makeshift gallery in a garage in Park Slope, but she'd only been in group shows.

She thought of all the times she'd put her brushes down and sunk into his arms when he got home, happy for the break and for the chance to bury her face in his flannel shirts, which smelled like sawdust and diner bacon. Why had she always abandoned her work so readily, to greet him as though it were her duty? And most of all, she grew to resent his routine query: "How're your pictures?" *Pictures.* Before, she'd always thought that sounded sweet and ironic; now it just seemed condescending, diminutizing.

One night she was frustrated, mixing paints to get a particular shade of murky taupe, and he came in with a dishrag over his shoulder and said, "Millipede? You want pasta with asparagus or broccoli rabe or both?"

The words were barely out of his mouth before she turned on him, exasperated. "Why can't you just give me this space? Just pretend that if I'm in here, I don't exist."

Jared winced, as though he'd been slapped. "Jesus Christ," he exclaimed. "I just wanted to make you dinner. But fine. *Have* your fucking space." He grabbed his jacket and left the apartment to go get his own dinner. Milly thought she'd done the right thing, asserted her need for space. But when she heard the door slam, she felt like somehow she hadn't gone about it the right way.

Ryan liked Jared and tried to tell Milly she was crazy. "Who planted this idea in your head that Jared is holding you back?" he asked her. "Drew?"

Milly blushed, as though she'd been caught out. "It's not about who planted the idea," she said. "It's about: is there truth there? I picture Drew getting up at six every morning and making coffee in her French press and sitting down and writing for those two hours in beautiful, utter solitude. No static flying around her head."

Ryan laughed derisively. "Drew's a cokehead! I doubt she's gotten up at six A.M. in a while, unless she was already up all night."

"She's not a cokehead," Milly balked. "She likes to do a little coke at parties once in a while."

At that same moment, however, Milly remembered the last time she'd seen Drew, at a party that Drew and some of her flashy advertising and magazine friends, the ones Milly never liked, had given three weeks ago. The party was loud and obnoxious, and Milly was not having a very good time, so she was relieved when Drew finally came over to her. But Drew looked so gaunt, seemed so jittery, so distracted!

They hugged and kissed. "I'm so happy to see you!" Drew exclaimed. But as they stood there trying to make conversation, Drew couldn't keep her eyes focused. They kept darting around. Milly thought they looked like hollow orbs desperately radiating forced cheer.

Now Ryan asked her, "Do you want Drew's life or yours?"

But Milly ignored the question. "It's not just problems with Jared per se," she continued. "I think I may like women more than men."

Ryan sighed. "I am not going through this whole topic with you again," he said. "You've never had a relationship with a woman that lasted more than two weeks. Meanwhile, you and Jared have been together—what? Three years now? You're telling yourself a story in your head about Jared and your work and now you want everything to fit it. The point is you are doing good work, you are productive; Jared is not getting in the way, and you need to chill out a little."

Milly laughed sharply. "So you're dismissing me out of hand," she said. "Too bad you can't be so blunt with Nora. Maybe she wouldn't make you microwave her salmon four times."

They both laughed.

"I just wish you weren't so suggestible," Ryan finally said.

That quieted Milly a bit. "I just—" She sighed. "I just need to *work*."

Ryan, and everyone who heard this mantra from Milly at the time, thought that she was blowing off steam. But then, to everyone's astonishment, Milly left Jared. She simply left him and got her own apartment in Cobble Hill, out in Brooklyn. Her anger at Jared didn't evaporate—in fact it deepened to the point where it certainly wasn't just about Jared but seemed aimed at something just over his shoulder. She sensed as much herself, but that didn't keep her from hardening into a kind of icy, sealed-off rage that perplexed and dismayed everyone, including herself. The rage put laser pinpricks into her melty brown eyes and began wearing furrows into her forehead. This was shortly after she'd turned twenty-three.

She'd packed her things and left the Christodora one night when Jared was out of town. He returned to find nothing of hers there save a Guatemalan mitten on the living-room floor that must have fallen out of a hastily stuffed bag. He picked it up, bawling and cursing all over it for ninety minutes.

"You're fucking crazy, Milly!" he repeated, wiping his snot on it. "You're fucking lost!" He finally fell asleep there on the floor, exhausted, he and Horace the cat nuzzling the mitten.

As for Milly, the serenity she was looking for after leaving Jared was a long time coming. She kept waking up every day, thinking, *Okay, now, my life begins*. But by eleven A.M. she'd often feel as though she'd already run off her own rails and had no idea how to salvage the afternoon, what to do next.

One evening, she found herself alone in the West Village after dinner with some high-school friends she wasn't very close to. She watched a middle-aged woman with a bushel of scraggly salt-and-pepper hair shuffle out of the Häagen Dazs store, licking her cone with manic precision, and a terrifying wave of loneliness engulfed her. *I don't know how to give or receive love*, she thought. *I'm trapped in this prison.* A cold sweat crept over her and she felt disoriented, as though she'd never seen the corner of Hudson and West Tenth before in her life. She sat down for a second on a stoop, scared to meet eyes with passersby, who'd clearly signaled to her that she looked insane.

Eventually, she stood up. Drew lived three blocks away. In her disoriented haze—tears beginning to well in her eyes and crest over, despite her best efforts to hold them back—she walked to Drew's and hit the buzzer. She waited fifteen seconds and hit it again. Just when a new wave of emptiness was building inside, telling her that she was still completely alone with nowhere to go, Drew came over the intercom, asking who it was.

"It's Milly," she barely choked out. "Will you let me up?"

Her arm reached for the door, waiting for the buzz and the click. But a strange second passed before Drew's voice came back on. "Sweetie, this isn't a good time."

Milly pressed the "talk" button. "Well, can you come down for a second? I really need to talk to someone." Just as she said it, a couple passed, looked at her with glancing concern. She was mortified. Seconds passed. "Can you please come down for a second?" she asked the intercom again.

"Give me a second," Drew replied.

Milly sat down on the stoop, exhausted. In a moment, Drew would come down with cigarettes and they'd sit close, they'd talk, as they had done on this stoop so many times before. But minutes passed and Drew didn't come down. This realization settled slowly into Milly, first puzzling, then humiliating and enraging her. Finally, at the ten-minute mark by her watch, she buzzed again. A minute passed with no answer. Milly pressed her finger to the buzzer for a full twenty seconds, feeling insane. No answer. She walked to a payphone and called Drew, whose answering machine clicked on. "I so long to hear your voice," Drew's recorded voice said. Then the beep. For a moment, Milly said nothing, half expecting that Drew would pick up. But she didn't.

"You are blowing me off right to my face," Milly said flatly into the phone. "I can't believe you!" She hung up. Her shock and outrage had somehow trumped her wild despair, and, too exhausted to walk to the train and take it home, she stuck out her hand automatically and hailed a cab she couldn't really afford, then sat there, spent and dumbfounded, as the taxi took her to her silent new apartment in Cobble Hill.

Not for a month did her fury melt into something more like sober resolve. *You asked for all this empty space around you*, she told herself. *Now you better make good on your word and do something with it.* And she endeavored to. She began painting more productively, with what felt to her like more focus. Her galling obsession with the idea that she had been living in thrall to Jared and his ambitions dissipated, and with that came a modicum of calm for Milly.

As it did, of a sort, for Jared. He went out every night and drank with his high-school buddies. Bombed, he would wordlessly approach friends and give them long, rocking hugs. They'd ask how he was doing and he'd shrug slowly, searching for words.

"I'd say I just went from the period of unbearable, scalding misery to the period of abiding but somehow just barely tolerable misery," he'd finally say. "Like, from waking up in the morning and thinking, first thing, *I'm alone, I want to die*, to thinking, *I'm alone, I want to die, yeah, so fucking get some coffee and the paper and get on with your day and deal with it.*"

"Well, that's a step," his friends would say, and laugh.

And he would snort out a laugh. "Yeah, I guess so."

Then his eyes would glass over. A tiny tear would race down his cheek, which he'd flick away, ashamed. His best buddy, Asa, would notice and rub his back while continuing to extol the brilliance of *Reservoir Dogs* to any interested parties.

As a sidelight to missing Milly, Jared missed Drew, too. He missed her against his better judgment, since he'd been bright enough to put two and two together and realize it'd largely been Drew who'd planted the idea in Milly's head that Jared was holding her back from her personal best. But he still missed her. And, like everyone by this point, he felt badly for her.

Everyone knew that, when it came to Drew, there was some sad shit there, which most people only knew about elliptically, concealed as it was beneath the hardworking sparkle of her party chatter. That honeymoon picture on her dresser: those handsome parents in Italy—the pretty, dark-haired Jewish mom with her Marlo Thomas flip and that fair-haired, smirking dad; how they met at Berkeley; how Drew was raised a double-dissertation baby. And just the dad, the dad. *Don't pull a my-dad on me and tell me you're going to be at my reading and then not show up, or maybe you slip in just when I'm finishing.* Or *One really good tactic in life that's underrated is, when you blow people off, just pick up where you left off the next time you see them and be lovely and pretend it never happened; that always worked for my dad.* Or *When you go on about how you don't know what to do with your life, I feel like I'm talking to my mom when she goes on about my dad. Like, she goes into this trance state of loss and confusion and resentment that's somehow really comforting for her. And finally I have to say, "Enough, I know it feels good, but now you have to go on a date, or go out with your fucking girlfriends, or go to the gym or quit smoking—basically acknowledge that every day you stew in those yummy sad juices, Dad wins."*

The cards from Dad, the checks from Dad, that mysterious visit from Dad, whom nobody got to meet, which rendered Drew invisible and inaccessible for five days. The handsome, suave, cruel older men who came up again and again in the short fiction she'd read at bars, her own Harlequin-pulp Achilles' heel. So much complexity spinning around the dad!

Drew lived so voraciously. It was all very self-conscious, built around references to past eras. How many times had Drew mentioned Lily Bart, Jordan Baker, Dorothy Parker, Holly Golightly, Edie Sedgwick? Throwing out these names took the edge off the random sex and the unhappy mornings after the drugs. How far would she go? She had left her best friend down on the stoop when she was clearly in pain and in need, because she couldn't have her up with the four random maga-zine people in her living room and all the drugs, and she was too high herself to even go down and talk to her.

"You are blowing me off right to my face," they'd all heard Milly say over the answering machine. "I can't believe you!"

They'd looked at one another, cracked out. The guy from *Details* did the totally inappropriate thing and laughed out loud. The girl who'd been so busy with the *Harper's Bazaar* relaunch, the one with Linda Evangelista's arm in front of her face on the cover ("Enter the Era of Elegance"), looked at Drew sympathetically and shrugged.

"You can't always be available," the girl said.

Drew pulled into herself after that, as though the drugs had snapped off—which, increasingly, they did, dashing her into sulky gloom in the middle of the chatter—but remarkably, nobody noticed and everybody stayed till five thirty in the morning.

That was the start of the six-week dark period: Drew having those random magazine and PR people over, usually with a boy staying after; the morning hours of fitful sleep; the dread upon the shallow wake; the afternoons watching crap TV and trying to nap or clean the house; the half hours pretending to work in a café; the evenings pulling it together for somebody's book party or birthday drinks; the bullshit debates about Tina Brown in the dive bars afterward; the inevitable repairing back to her house. She saw Milly through none of it, too mortified to call her.

Then one late night in September, when everybody had left her apartment, including the boy who'd stayed the night before, Drew got into bed and heard the clicking in the walls and at the windows. She snapped on the light, but the clicking continued. It was in her throat. She lay very still and concentrated on her breathing, but the strange clicking continued. She was trying to cry but couldn't, she realized. Her heart was beating so fast. She got up, stood in front of the mirror. She didn't see 1904, 1926, 1963, or 1968. She realized it was 1993, too much upon her to make romance out of it, and for a moment, she saw the Drew whom other people saw—the kind Drew, the compelling Drew, the scary Drew, the sad Drew.

The phone rang at Milly's five times, then came the answering machine. "Tell me who you are and I'll get right back to you," said Milly's voice. Then: "Mill? Are you there? Can you pick up? It's me." A very long pause. "I know I don't deserve this, but . . ."

Milly picked up. "I'm here," she said, her voice hoarse with sleep. Drew still heard the chill in it. "What's wrong?"

"I'm so scared, Mill. I can't cry."

"You can't cry?"

"I try, but I can't."

"Why do you want to cry in the first place?" There was a pause. "Are you high again?"

"I can't stop."

Milly winced, horrified. "Is it in front of you right now?"

"Can you please just come over?"

Milly laughed sharply. "So now you want me to come over. Are you sure you'll buzz me in?"

Drew knew this was coming. "I'm sorry."

"How could you do that to me?" Milly pleaded.

But Drew was silent on the other end of the line, which disconcerted Milly. "If you're that scared," Milly finally said, "you can come over here."

"But I'm scared to leave the house!"

"I'm not coming to you!" Milly fired back, now fully awake. "I'm infuriated at you! You're not a good friend!"

This was the lance that pierced Drew's pent-up tears. "Don't say that," she sobbed. "I want to be. Sweetie, please! Give me another chance."

The low break in Drew's voice, the snuffly snobs, took Milly aback. She sighed deeply, pushed her sleep-tangled hair back from her face. "If you're that scared, get in a cab and come over here," she said. "I'm not leaving Brooklyn at three in the morning."

"I don't even know where you live now," Drew snuffled.

Milly gave her the address—Drew said she'd be there soon—and put the phone down. She was annoyed, and annoyed at herself for acquiescing. Hurricane Drew was about to come sweeping through her safe, well-ordered home. She went to the medicine cabinet in the bathroom, took out the Ativan that she barely ever took anyway, and hid it in a dresser drawer so Drew wouldn't steal it. She turned against the wall a canvas she was working on so she wouldn't have to bear some casual remark Drew would make about it. How else could she protect herself? She went into the kitchen and made a pot of chamomile tea and sat there in her bathrobe, fake-mulling over the crossword puzzle in yesterday's paper.

In the Village, Drew put down the phone. Again, the clicking started and she thought it was coming from the windows and the walls, the neighbors and the authorities trying to get into the apartment in a subtle, quiet way, then arrest or hospitalize her. The thought of pulling herself together, locking the door behind her and venturing down the bright, empty stairwell, braving the sidewalk and hailing a cab, giving the cabbie the impression of normalcy all the way to Brooklyn, terrified her. But she also knew that if she didn't leave, it would just be her and the clicking until dawn, and she'd go insane. So she blocked out the clicking, dressed, got her bag and keys.

Oh, and the coke. There was that baggie in her bureau she hadn't told the others about, because surely they'd have gotten her to bring it out, and she'd wanted them to leave. She took it out and, fully acknowledging how crazy she was, scooped a fair-size mound on the end of her key and snorted it. Then she put it in her bag and lay on her back on her bed with her head hanging off the edge until she felt the familiar, comforting tang in the back of her throat. She got up and swaggered out of the apartment—the heels of her boots criminally loud in the echoing stairwell with the buzzing fluorescent lights—and walked to Seventh Avenue and hailed a cab. She even made small talk with the cabbie, careful not to talk a blue streak like a cokehead on a new jag.

When Milly opened her door, Drew embraced her and sobbed. Milly stood there, dumbstruck, finally embracing Drew in return, gingerly.

"When did you start doing drugs tonight?" she asked Drew.

"I don't want to talk about drugs," Drew said through tears. "I just want you to know that I stayed away because I want your life too badly, and I hate that feeling."

"I don't think I'm awake enough for a big, deep talk right now," Milly said. "You should try to get some sleep. I found an Ativan. Do you want it?"

Drew nodded yes, following Milly into the kitchen. Milly went away, came back, and set the Ativan down before her on the table with a glass of water. Drew took it. She reached into her bag for her cigarettes.

"I don't smoke in the apartment," Milly told her, concealing rapid waves of pity, morbid fascination, horror, and sadness. She'd rarely seen Drew high or so wrecked. In a way, it was a relief to see Drew letting herself fall apart, finally abandoning her bravura performance. "Come on, we can go up on the roof."

Up there under a night sky with a wan sliver of a moon, sitting cross-legged on the roof's gravelly floor, they smoked, Drew's hand shaking. Milly had all but quit smoking and—*Wouldn't it figure*, she thought—was having her first cigarette in weeks with Drew.

"Can I just tell you one thing?" Milly asked. "Believe me, you wouldn't want my life if you fully knew what I went through with my mother growing up. I know you didn't have it easy with your father, but if you could only know what it was like. Because it was really awful. It was like growing up with Patty Duke for a mother."

Milly said this gravely, but Drew laughed, which made Milly laugh, which made Drew feel a bit better suddenly. The first cool edge of the Ativan was creeping in. She would know peace soon; she would sleep with Milly nearby, perhaps close beside her. A thought dimly formed, which seemed too much to ask for: there could maybe be moments of peace when she could put down the exhausting project of Being Drew.

"And," Milly added, "I hope it's obvious to you that you have to go to rehab. Everybody thinks so."

Drew continued to nod, staring at the ground. Then she pulled the baggie of coke out of her bag and handed it to Milly. "Will you get rid of it for me?" she asked.

Milly looked at the small plastic square of white powder in her palm. "What should I do with it? Sell it?"

"Dump it down the toilet, then rinse the bag and throw that out," Drew said. "That way I won't try to find it wherever you're hiding it."

"Oh my God," Milly said. "You are *so* addicted."

This made them both laugh again. They finished their cigarettes and went downstairs. On the stairwell, walking behind Drew, Milly put her hand on Drew's shoulder, and Drew pulled it around to nuzzle it against her face and kiss its back. Drew went into the bedroom to undress and Milly took the baggie of coke into the bathroom. She knelt down by the toilet and tapped its contents into her left palm, moving it around a bit with the index finger of her right hand. She marveled for a moment at the ability of a lump of inert white substance to so completely steal someone away, to the point that she was barely recognizable anymore. Milly had tried coke only once, in high school, and hadn't liked the effect at all.

She dumped the coke into the toilet, brushed her palm, rinsed the baggie in the sink so as not to leave even a powder film of remains in the trash bin that might tempt Drew, and tore the baggie in two. She felt a bit like she'd felt when she'd spied Perry on the street, rushing self-importantly back to the *Harper's* office, unseen by her, a few weeks after he and Drew had finally broken up. Both cocaine and Perry had given Drew a sense of being all right in the world, but then had turned on her. Now they were things that Drew would have to put huge amounts of energy into saying good-bye to rather than enjoying.

It was exactly how Milly felt about Jared. *How can I really judge her when I'm going through that myself?* Milly thought. That allowed her, amid her exhaustion and annoyance, her first tiny wave of forgiveness toward Drew. In the bedroom, with pale strips of light in the slits between the blinds, the Ativan had put Drew to sleep. She lay on her side, in her T-shirt and underpants, her head tucked under both hands. Her face, Milly thought, looked childlike, unguarded, not straining for wit or charm. Milly undressed and lay down the same way, her arm holding Drew below her breasts, her nose in the scent of Drew's hair. It was much the same way Jared had once held her in bed, before she learned she wasn't free.

FIVE

I WANT TO THANK YOU

(1984)

Ysabel was having so much fun. The music sounded amazing and the men around her were beautiful. Whatever she and Tavi had taken—MDMA, she thought Tavi had said—had made her feel euphoric, and she and Tavi were dancing close, bumping, grinding. In the song, the woman sang something like, *Had enough of all the pressure . . . had a life that felt like pouring rain . . . Then I turned around. I was so astounded by your smile. Finally there was light . . . and this is the moment of my life!*

That's just how Issy felt. There could not be more than a few dozen other women in this packed club, going on two A.M., and she knew none of these men was going to fall in love with her, but she didn't care. She was with her best friend, Tavi, and a bunch of Tavi's friends. The music was great, Tavi was holding her close, it was a Saturday night, and she didn't have to be back at work, in fact, until Thursday, the day after The Fourth of July. She and Tavi locked eyes, held that stare, smiled. Then Tavi kissed her—not his usual kiss on the cheek, but on the lips, openmouthed. Not with his tongue, but still . . . it lingered!

She put her hand over her lips. "Oh my God, Tavi!" she said. "You did not just!"

Tavi laughed like a hyena. "Hahaha, yeah, princess, I just did!" That boy was fucking crazy. He was skinny with a big Boricua 'fro and a gap between his two front teeth, wearing Sergio Valente jeans, a tight yellow T-shirt saying WHERE'S THE BEEF?, and three gold chains. Tavi, her best friend from the block in Corona, Queens. Whom she'd pretty much known was gay since they were fourteen. What other boy ran around the neighborhood in tiny orange gym shorts, a rainbow headband, and Mork from Ork suspenders singing at the top of his lungs, *Hey, mister, have you gotta dime? Mister, do you wanna spend some time?* Yep, that was Octavio. Tavi-boy, she called him. They did everything together.

She showed Tavi some of her best moves—kind of like if she were Sheila E. in the new "Glamorous Life" video she was obsessed with, in that shiny tight coat, rocking her shoulders while she thrashed away on those drums. Sheila E. was her new idol. In her mind, she *was* Sheila E. She did have hair nearly as big as Sheila's, styled asymmetrically, and she thought she had Sheila's attitude. Yet Issy was not deluded; she did not think she was as beautiful or sexy as Sheila, even as she tried to make the most of what she had: her large, bright eyes; smooth caramel skin; and fairly good curves. Even though she stood at only five feet four inches, and even if her nose was a little flatter, her forehead a little higher, and her lips a little thinner than she'd have liked, she did her best to distract away from those things with makeup, fashion, and attitude.

In her neighborhood, she was well liked. She was, after all, the younger sister of Freddy Mendes, a big guy with swagger who'd nearly made the farm team for the Mets and who, frankly, had never much paid her the time of day. But lately, having just turned twenty-five, working toward her dental hygienist certificate while watching all her friends get married and have kids, or *not* get married but still have kids, she'd started to wonder, *What'll become of me? Will I be alone my whole life?* She would then catalog in her head the good qualities she possessed: *I'm a caring person*, she thought. *I have a good sense of humor. I can cook. I take excellent care of my teeth. I don't take things too sensitively—I can go with the flow!* Putting this list together in her head helped her, and she would always top it off with a prayer that she meet the right man for her before she turned twenty-eight. (The previous cut-off had been twenty-five, until she'd turned twenty-five.)

Sometimes—often, strangely, in church, when she imagined she was supposed to be feeling her best—she would get deep pinpricks in her stomach that all was not right with the world, and that her usual daily belief that people were good and everything was as it should be was, well, a sham. She would think about how her father and brother held sway over the household, how she'd heard the words *bitch* and *puta* from them and other men, including her uncles and cousins, since she was a little girl, before she even knew what the words meant. She'd think about all the love children in the family and the neighborhood, about men who got off with impunity, and she'd think about the beat-down, sullen workaday indignance of her grandmother and her mother and so many older women she knew, and how those women seemed to take it out on one another in the form of backstabbing and gossip, and she would suddenly not feel so great, or that the real answers were not to be found here, in church, listening to this old, light-skinned Dominican priest drone on about rejecting the glamour of Satan. And she would seriously wonder if there wasn't perhaps some other life out there for her that promised more than a dental-hygienist certificate. Then, to herself, barely perceptibly, she would sigh and dismiss her own thoughts.

But her head wasn't in that melancholy place tonight. She was just having fun—and oh my God, she felt amazing! Plus, these men were *hot*. Here was one coming up to her right now. The DJ had just changed the song. *Baby, you make my love come down*, the whole room shouted along with the singer. *Oh, you make my love come down*. And suddenly this guy, this big-assed, hairy-chested *moreno* with chains dripping over a mesh purple tank top, was bumping up against her.

"Hey, baby," he mouthed over the music. He held up poppers to his nose, inhaled, then held the tube up to her nose. She'd been watching guys inhale them on the dance floor all night and she wondered what they did, so now she allowed herself a demure sniff. Suddenly, she was feeling deliciously woozy and clinging to the guy's neck while he stroked her breasts and buttocks. Her knees buckled in her leggings. She was going to go out of her mind if she didn't have sex soon, she thought. She hadn't had sex since—well, two years ago, that sort of bad incident at that party. That hadn't been what she was looking for. Even the first time, at fifteen, with Ricky Malandrino, it hadn't been what she was expecting, either—it had hurt, and it was over before it even began. It hadn't seemed very romantic. And then Ricky not so much as even talking to her in the street after. That didn't feel too great.

But this moment—wow. They were sort of swaying and grinding, and she was holding on to his neck for dear life, feeling like her whole body below was giving out under his big hands. Then, as she felt the breathless, scary swoon of the poppers fade away, he pulled back. He put a hand under her chin and smiled at her and kissed her gently on the lips. "You're beautiful," he told her.

"Shut up!" She laughed good-naturedly. "You're just high."

He lost his smile, got stern. "No, baby, you are," he said. "You gotta believe that." He kissed her once more, then slipped away, leaving her there, barely moving amid the dancers. Tavi, who'd witnessed the whole thing, sidled back over to her.

"*Puta,*" he said, then cackled. She shoved him, pleased with herself.

They kept on dancing—hours, it seemed. At different times, other men came over to them, danced with them, did the bump-and-grind with Tavi—he came to this Paradise Garage club a lot and he knew a lot of guys here—and even sometimes with her. Ooh, now the DJ was playing "Heartbeat"—ooh, she loved this song, that slow beat, *heartbeat, you make me feel so weak*—that's how she felt! Weak from dancing and elation. She had her head up looking into the lighting system, her arms up over her head. She felt sexy!

"Girl, this song is turning you out," Tavi shouted at her over the beat.

She shoved him. "You're so disgusting!"

Some guys came over and danced with them. Kisses and gropes went all around. One of the guys, Issy noted, was very darkly handsome, a Boricua probably, with a somewhat serious, non-effeminate air about him. He looked a bit nerdy in his large, square-framed glasses, which he repeatedly took off to wipe steam from the lenses. There he was, dancing along with the rest of the guys in his tight T-shirt and designer jeans and Nikes, a bit of gold around his neck, but he seemed a little uptight.

Tavi introduced everyone over the music; she and the handsome nerdy guy—who was how old? not quite thirty yet—met eyes. He gave her a kind smile, not that kind of "Heeeeey, girl!" greeting she got from most of the queens here.

He took a few steps toward her, kissed her cheek. "I'm Hector," he said over the music.

"I'm Ysabel," she shouted back. "Issy."

"How do you know Tavi?" he asked.

"We grew up together in Corona," she shouted. "Since we were little kids."

Hector nodded his understanding. "He's crazy," he said.

Issy laughed. "I know!" she screamed. "He's crazy, it's true! But I love him!"

"I do, too."

"How do you know him?" she asked.

"First from out in the clubs, but now we volunteer together at GMHC, too, on the phones."

She knitted her brow in puzzlement. "What's that?" she asked.

"Gay Men's Health Crisis," Hector said. "It's an AIDS organization."

"Oh." She frowned. Then a horrible thought struck her. She glanced over at Tavi. "Is he okay?" she asked Hector.

"Oh, I think so. As far as I know, I mean. The test for it isn't out yet. We're just trying to provide direct services because the Health Department isn't doing anything. Which I should know, because I work for them."

Issy nodded gravely. She hoped Tavi was okay. Otherwise, she hadn't caught much of what Hector had said. He seemed so serious for a guy on the dance floor! He'd even fully stopped dancing for a moment.

"It's a terrible thing," she offered.

He nodded in turn. "Yep. You gotta be careful, protect yourself."

Tavi came over. "What you bitches talking about?" he shrieked.

Issy shoved him lightly. "Tavs, you didn't tell me you do volunteer work for AIDS!"

Tavi looked briefly freaked out, like he hadn't wanted Hector to tell her, then he cackled and threw his arm around Hector. "Yeah, we're like fucking Florence Nightingale and Mother Teresa up in there! I'm like Lily Tomlin with her receptionist-headset thing going." He did his Ernestine imitation, with an overbite, stretching out his face. He hip-checked Hector. "This one's always recruiting queens for the cause."

Hector shrugged. "If we don't do it, nobody else will," he said. *So serious!* Issy thought again. *Yet very handsome.* Could he loosen up and have fun? She took his hand, made him spin her. "Come on, *papi*, no more heavy talk, you gotta shake it more!"

"Ooh, what a pushy bitch!" Tavi screamed in delight. "You heard her, Hectorina, she needs you to bump her pussy!" Hector smiled goof-ily and shrugged and obliged her and did the bump with her a little bit before politely excusing himself and disappearing into the crowd.

Suddenly alone in the spot where she'd danced with Hector, Issy felt briefly bereft. She momentarily lost her footing, reached out in-stinctively for someone to break her fall. And someone did. But it wasn't Tavi, as she expected. It was the hairy-chested, pillow-lipped *moreno* in the purple mesh tank.

"Oh my God, thank you," she said, regaining her footing. "I almost went down."

"I saw you!" He laughed, showing a mouthful of very white teeth, which Issy noted approvingly. "You were, like, whoa!" He did a funny impression of her tottering on her heels and reaching out wildly for support.

"Oh my God," she said, "I'm so embarrassed."

"Don't be," he said. "You're up in the club."

Then the DJ put on a song she loved from a few years ago, "I Want to Thank You." *I want to thank you, heavenly father,* went the lyrics, *for shining your light on me. You sent me someone who really loves me and not just my body.* The song was a bit of a prayer for Issy. It was a dance song, but a mellow one, and she couldn't help but exclaim to the purple tank guy, "I love this song!"

His eyes popped open in delight. "I do, too!" he said. He took both her hands in his and led her into a bit of an old-fashioned hustle step, sending her twirling through the bridge of their two arms, then reeling her in close again until she could feel his moist chest hair against her cheek and smell his cologne, which reminded her of her older brother's. Here, their dancing stopped. She became more and more aware of the feel of his body against hers—the width of his shoulders, the taper down to his slim waist, the feel of his jeans against her leggings, the warmth of his breath in her ear.

"*Dios mío*," she said, surprising herself.

Purple Tank laughed and took her chin between his thumb and index finger. "You know how beautiful you are?" he asked her.

"You told me that already!" she protested. "You're just high on whatever drugs you're on."

"I'm not on any drugs," he insisted. "Well, okay, I took a Quaalude."

She laughed triumphantly. "See! You're just fucked up."

But he held her chin in place and fixed his eyes on her. "No, baby," he said. "I think you're beautiful. Why is it so hard for you to believe that?"

Issy felt both touched and uncomfortable all at once. *Why* is *it so hard for me to believe that?* she asked herself, still rocking to the song in his arms. Maybe because this was something she'd never heard before—not from family or from girlfriends, and certainly not from boys. She was just—well, she just *was*. She didn't think she was a *fea* and she didn't think she was a beauty queen. She didn't give much thought to herself. She probably spent more time thinking about her *abuela* upstairs and what groceries she should pick up for her on the way home from dental school, or what she should fix her for dinner, than she did about herself. But now, she had to admit to herself, it was damn nice to have a handsome—albeit a somewhat strangely handsome—man looking her deeply in the eyes and telling her she was beautiful.

Then she realized she'd forgotten something. "You're gay!" she said.

"I'm bisexual." He shrugged. "I probably like women more than men, to tell you the truth. I just love the music and the vibe here. I love the crazy mix of people."

"It's a great club," she said. She certainly had to admit that. Tavi had been telling her for a year he'd take her, and tonight they'd finally made it. Speaking of that, where was Tavi? She glanced around, failing to see him nearby. Suddenly, she saw nobody she knew, even vaguely, nearby.

Then Purple Tank's lips were on hers. They felt unbelievably pillowy and insistent. Her throat constricted for a moment. *This isn't right*, she thought. But apparently Purple Tank sensed her unease, because he pressed his hands firmly into her lower back, and she felt herself give out beneath him.

"Just relax and enjoy it, baby," he whispered. "It's okay. It's a holiday."

This was true, she thought. She lost herself in their necking. She clung gratefully to the solidity of his upper body. *It took a long time for it to happen*, went the song. *But I knew those nights I prayed that you would send me someone who's real and not someone for play*. Issy desperately wanted someone like that, she thought. She remembered Freddy, just last week, rubbing his hand over the belly of her pregnant sister-in-law, Vanessa, and how her brother, usually so full of bravado and bluff, had a tender, almost reverent look in his eyes. She wanted a man to look at her like that. Maybe it was this man! she thought. And how funny that for the rest of her life she'd tell people that she met the man of her dreams in a gay club!

She got so caught up in this reverie that she at first didn't notice that Purple Tank was leading her off the dance floor. She opened her eyes, feeling deliciously sleepy and removed from her body, and pulled him back. "Where are we going?" she asked.

"Let's get some air outside, baby," he said. He sheltered her in his arm and guided her toward the exit.

"Just let me tell Tavi," she said, straining to be heard over the music.

"Tavi—" he called back to her. She couldn't quite make out what he was saying. She stood up on tiptoes and scanned the crowd, much of which had divided into couples who were slow-dancing, just as she had been a minute ago. She couldn't see Tavi. Well, she thought, a few minutes of fresh air wouldn't be so bad.

There was a crowd smoking and laughing outside the club, amid a cool and lovely May night boasting a sky where even a few stars, westward toward the Hudson River, were visible. Still feeling sparkly from the MDMA, Issy reveled in the breeze on her neck and arms. Purple Tank put his arm back around her and led her away from the crowd, down the street. "Let's sit in my car," he said. "It's around the corner."

"I don't even know your name!" she said, dragging back a little bit.

He turned. "I didn't tell you? It's Chris. Your friend Tavi and I see each other out all the time." Oh, Issy thought. So he knew Tavi. That gave her some reassurance. "And what's your name?"

"It's Ysabel," she said. "But just Issy."

"That was my *abuela*'s name," he said.

Issy put her hands on her hips. "You are too much!" She laughed.

"I'm not fucking with you," he said, laughing along. "I can show you pictures."

She stood there a moment longer, regarding him. "You are too much," she said again, moving back toward him. He put his arm back around her.

His car, around the corner, was a powder-blue Ford Fairmont with a plastic pendant of San Cristóbal hanging from the rearview mirror. "Oh, now I get the name," Issy said when she saw it. "Cris-tóbal."

"That's right." He laughed. "*El santo de los viajeros.*"

They sat in the backseat with the windows open to let in the breeze. The street, in an industrial part of town deserted at night save for the club, was still and silent. She closed her eyes, tilted back her head. In an instant, she could feel those lips back on her own. She curled in toward him until she'd thrown her legs over his. She felt one of his meaty hands, so hairy, slip between the lower buttons of her untucked, oversize shirt with the pink-and-yellow graffiti print on it. Then she felt two of his fingers slip underneath her bra. At that moment, she surprised herself again with an eruption of tears.

The saint of travelers pulled back a moment. "Why are you crying, baby?"

"I don't know," she said, and she truly didn't. She vaguely remembered Tavi telling her that the MDMA would make her feel all emotional and open, that shrinks used it to get patients to open up about their feelings. "I just feel really happy. It's been a great night."

He laughed. "It is a great night," he said. "Because we met."

Her blouse and bra were coming off; her leggings were coming off. The saint of travelers certainly appeared to be truly bisexual, she noted, impressed. As he penetrated her, as she sank deeper and deeper into the cushions of the backseat, she drew her arms more tightly around San Cristóbal's neck, letting everything fall away but the power of their conjoined bodies. Eventually, as their rhythm intensified, she felt the stirrings of a massive inner thrill. She was going to have her first orgasm with a man! She was so overwhelmed by the sensations racking her. She thought it would never actually happen, it would just build and build, but then when it finally did happen, she thought it would never end. Amid that, San Cristóbal himself came, deep inside her. They held each other, saying nothing, just breathing and shaking, until the sky changed from black to a deep blue.

San Cristóbal finally sat up unceremoniously, disentangled himself, and fished a cigarette from a compartment near the front seat. "You want one?" he asked her.

She was a little disappointed these were his first words after sex. They were hardly very romantic. "That's okay," she said. "I don't smoke. It's bad for your teeth." She began to pull her clothes back on.

"I brush and floss," he said, blowing smoke out the window. He was now sitting a foot or so away from her. He put his free left hand on the back of her neck as a halfhearted concession to intimacy. Issy didn't want the moment to end, though. She lay down again, resting her head on his thigh.

"I can't believe we have to go in there again and I gotta find Tavi," she said.

"Yeah," he said hesitantly. Then, after a pause, "Actually, I think I'm gonna just be getting home, now that I'm out of the club. I made some plans for today. You'll be okay getting back in yourself."

This crushed her, deepening the cheap feeling that the oozy MDMA couldn't quite override. "Of course I will," she managed to say. "Don't worry about it."

"No, I didn't mean it as a question," he said. "I meant, I knew you'd be okay getting back in because the guys at the door are cool. I know them."

Double crushed. He didn't even sound mean about it, Issy thought, just matter-of-fact, as though he genuinely wanted to clarify his intent.

"No," she said. "I mean, I know how you meant it." At this point, she made herself sit up, then check and fix her hair in the rearview window. Everything she saw—the streets and the buildings and the passing cabs—looked sparkly and extra-sharp from the MDMA, all of which made for a strange counterpoint to the core of badness she was suddenly feeling.

"Well"—she turned to him—"good-bye." This, she thought, was the moment of truth. *Please*, she thought, trying not to betray herself with her eyes, *ask me for a phone number or something.*

"Good-bye, baby." He took a final drag off his cigarette, flicked it out the window, and leaned over to kiss her dutifully on the lips. "Get back in there safe, okay."

The final crush. She could feel tears welling in her eyes, so she turned quickly and stepped out of the car. She made a point of not looking back as she walked toward the corner of Hudson and King Streets. She would just go inside and find Tavi and forget that had ever happened.

She was approaching the rather forbidding-looking bouncer, a muscular black man with a yellow Mohawk, to ask politely if she could reenter the club, when Tavi's handsome, nerdy friend walked out of the club.

"Issy!" he called to her. He remembered her name, and she felt bad for having forgotten his. "You waiting for Tavi?"

She wondered if he could tell how disoriented and jangled she felt, between the lingering druggy feeling and the prior moment's encounter. "Huh?" she asked. "Oh. Well, I'm going back in to find Tavi. I needed to get some air."

He peered more closely at her behind his glasses. "You okay?"

"I'm fine," she said. "I just really needed some air."

He studied her a moment longer. "Well, come on," he finally said, putting an arm around her. "I'll go back in and help you find him."

"But you were leaving, right?"

"It'll only take a minute. Besides, there's a guy I met whose number I should try to get. A little blond kid."

"Oh, boy," Issy managed to say. "Well, okay then, thanks."

The bouncer, who'd witnessed this exchange, brushed them back inside. Issy couldn't believe how crowded the club still was, even though it was now early morning. She'd certainly had enough for tonight, though. The DJ was playing something instrumental, heavy on African-sounding drums and a weird sort of flying-saucer sound. The nerdy guy reached back for her hand, which she offered, as they navigated themselves through the dancers.

She pulled him back toward her for a moment. "What's your name again?" she shouted.

"Hector," he shouted back. "Hector Villanueva."

"Thank you, Hector," she said. "You're sweet." This was enough, somehow, to trigger a runaway tear. All she really wanted was a sweet guy, she thought. Why was it so hard to find one?

Hector put his hands on her shoulders. "What's wrong?" he asked.

"It's just been a crazy night."

"Well, don't worry," he said. "We'll get you to Tavi now and then you can get home." He gave her an awkward little hug, as though to reassure her. Issy hugged him back and found it hard to let go.

SIX

LEARNING TO BREATHE: AN EARLY MEMOIR
(1995)

At LaGuardia, waiting to board her flight to L.A., Milly made two calls. First, she called her mother, something she did pretty much every day.

"I'm exhausted," Ava told her. "Two deaths in the house so far this month. Two lovely ladies gone."

"That's horrible," Milly murmured. "I'm so sorry, Ava." Milly mostly kept her distance from her mother's work; it just made her too sad.

"Plus," Ava continued, "the boiler's on the fritz and we had to run out and buy space heaters for the entire house because you can't have a houseful of immune-compromised women sleeping without heat in February."

"You have to be careful, Mom," Milly told her mother. When had she started toggling between calling her mother Mom and Ava? Probably when she was around sixteen; by that point, she'd done so much mothering of her own mother that "Ava" instead of "Mom" had started popping out of her mouth—sometimes with something like barely suppressed indignation, with a sardonic bite that felt good to the tongue, and yet sometimes tenderly, like, well, let's face it, she was the little girl here, not Milly, and you needed to say her name gently so she heard it.

And now, often, Milly had to admit, she said Ava's name with respect. Because for over a decade now, her mother had bitten the bullet, soldiered through the heavy doses of lithium, the weekly psychopharmacological visits, the support groups. She'd said good-bye to her own manic pleasures so she could be there for others. For whom, exactly? For the sick, the poor, the dying. By 1989, what had started as a few strange cases of Kaposi's sarcoma had blown up into one of the worst epidemics the city had ever seen, one that seemed to prey on homosexuals and drug addicts, groups that people already shunned. Yet the city had done so little about it—for many reasons, certainly, but mainly because the city was run, everyone knew, by a closeted mayor terrified of getting his hands dirty with a gay disease.

At the end of the 1980s, Ava had finally had it with the entropy at the Health Department. She would no longer be demonized and vilified as the enemy in the AIDS epidemic; she would not stand there with that uncomfortable, hateful, oh-isn't-this-cute smirk on her face that her colleagues put on while those angry boys—including her own former intern, for that matter—chained themselves to her desk and called her a murderer. Oh, no, Ava had told Hector after she'd finally left, that was the last straw! That's when Ava grit her teeth and summoned all her resources and friends with money and clout and bought that run-down building on Avenue B and started Judith House, a care residence for women with full-blown AIDS. No one would ever look back on this whole thing and say she stood by, a useless bureaucrat. There was only so much more helplessness on her own part that she could tolerate.

But had Ava also bitten the bullet for her own family? For her daughter? Because even now that Ava had clamped down on her manias with heavy drugs, she still felt crappy much of the time and was a scattershot mother at best. Things had gotten a little better, but there were still a million little ways Ava let Milly know that, well, there was simply too much going on—too much sickness, too much death—for Ava to dote over Milly and her homework and her art projects the way other Upper East Side mothers did with their daughters. Sam, Daddy, was there for that. Ava was simply not that sort of mother.

But Milly had had to concede that she still needed her mommy. That was the poignant, humiliating truth of it. And since the breakup with Jared, Ava hadn't been half bad about being there, Milly had to grant that. The Sunday dinners. The calls that had now become daily, even if they were brief, more about her mother's travails than her own. (Because, it had to be understood, her mother's travails were the travails of the city, while Milly's were merely the travails of one twenty-four-year-old, middle-class woman, and they took place mostly inside her head, the venue of much quibbling and second-guessing and angst.)

So, now, the airport call to Ava. "You have to be careful, Ava," she repeated. "You're going to run yourself down like you did last year, then you'll have to take a week off again and work from home and drive Daddy crazy."

Ava laughed dimly. "I'm not staying late at Judith House tonight," she said. "Daddy and I are going to Blue Ribbon for dinner."

"You guys are so trendy," Milly remarked drily.

Ava chuckled. "I suppose." Another pause. "How's Esther?"

Milly loved the way her mother said that: *How's Esther?* In that dutiful, I'm-a-good-mom-for-acknowledging-my-daughter's-lesbian-partner singsong. The I'm-being-such-a-good-sport-about-this-whole-lesbian-thing-and-biding-my-time-till-it-passes kind of tone.

Milly laughed. "She's good. She's away this weekend, too. She's on a panel at Oberlin."

"Oh, that's nice," Ava said. "Is that about women and—and fiction and identity?"

Milly laughed again. "Sort of. It's all about Willa Cather, actually, in some way."

"Oh, that's nice. And how about you, honey? Did you get the NYCHA grant?"

"It's NYFA, Mom. NYFA. New York Foundation for the Arts."

"Oh, that's right. Sorry, NYFA, NYCHA!" NYCHA was the New York City Housing Authority, which Ava had to tussle with regularly.

Milly rolled her eyes. "Right. No, I haven't heard about the NYFA grant yet. Hopefully in the next week."

"Right." Her mother sounded distracted. Milly could hear rowdy gals in the background, the Judith clients and staffers mixing it up, finding daily laughs amid their troubles. Her mother was probably leafing through paperwork right now, as they talked. Well, at least here they were, checking in.

"And what are you and Drew going to do in L.A.?" her mother managed to ask.

"I don't know!" Milly said brightly. "We'll probably see friends. Drew said she'd take me to see this, like, cabaret act I've always wanted to see—it's a husband and wife, I guess, a really bad Steve and Eydie, who do lounge versions of Michael Jackson songs on a synthesizer at this cheesy old lounge where everybody—well, you know, like Generation-X types—goes to see them ironically, but they take themselves seriously. I've always wanted to see them."

"That sounds like fun," her mother said, but so absently that Milly knew she'd lost her mother's tenuous attention. "And—and—" Her mother was trying to pull back into the conversation. "What about Drew? Is her book out?"

"It comes out in a month, I think."

"And what's it called, again? *Breathing Lessons*?"

"No, that book already exists. It's called *Learning to Breathe*."

"Oh, right. It's a novel, right?"

"It's a memoir."

"A memoir? She's twenty-six years old!"

Milly laughed. "I know! Well, she's written a memoir."

"About her whole drug thing."

"I think so."

"Well, I hope she portrays you nicely. You certainly were nice to her that whole time."

"Oh God," Milly moaned. "I don't even want to know if I'm in it."

"I should hope that you are. At least a little bit. In a nice way."

"Well, I'm sorry about your clients who died. Try not to push yourself too hard, Ava."

They gave each other their love and ended the call. Then Milly called Esther at the place she was staying at Oberlin. "I wanted to call you before I got on the plane to L.A.," she said, with that strange, especially girlish and delicate rush of feeling whenever she first spoke to or met up with Esther.

"I can't talk long, Babyturnip, I'm frantically leafing through these Cather books before the panel starts at one." Esther called her Babyturnip. Once, when they were having sex, Esther started calling her every manner of fruit or vegetable—pumpkin, kumquat, parsnip, turnip. My little turnip. And somehow, Babyturnip had stuck. On one hand, it goaded Milly just a little bit. She was sufficiently aware of her own beauty to know that she looked nothing like a turnip, and she wondered if this was Esther's way of debeautifying her, of taking her down a peg. On the other hand, she liked it when lovers, and people in general, had a nickname for her. Jared had called her Millipede, and Drew continued to, and she liked that nickname even though some people said that the thought of a millipede grossed them out. Not Milly, though. When people gave her a nickname, she felt that she must be special to them. So that's why she hadn't objected to Babyturnip.

"It's okay, I won't keep you long," Milly said. She thought of Esther, spread out on the bed in faculty housing at Oberlin, her heavy dark brows knitted together, clamping a chewed-over pen between her teeth. Esther, who was thirty-eight to her twenty-four, who had short, sensible, brushed-back salt-and-pepper hair; wire-rimmed glasses perched low on her nose; generous hips underneath her overalls; a winter parka full of lecture notes, cab receipts, tobacco that she rolled into her own cigarettes—lip balm her only concession to vanity. Esther, the CUNY Grad Center professor, the prolific author of thoughtfully outraged books about women's sexuality in an age of sexual destabilization and disease stigmatization, even a(n admittedly highly conceptual and allegorical) novel, *Cantaloupe Cowgirls*. Esther, who people thought was cutting and acerbic in her comments, but who really, Milly knew, was just blunt and assertive and quickly knew whom she liked and respected and whom she didn't, and couldn't help but show it.

How alone Milly had been only a year ago! First, Drew went off to rehab, then she was back for only four months or so—four months of unrelenting twelve-step babble, Milly recalled wearily, though not without relief that Drew had found some organizing principle to keep her stable. Then suddenly Drew was off to L.A., having determined that reliably good weather was key to her mental health. Apparently more so than certain good friends, Milly thought, not entirely able to quell her feelings of abandonment.

And Jared was certainly not in Milly's life anymore. So Milly was alone a great deal, burrowing into the comfort and safety of her Cobble Hill apartment. Then Esther came and spoke to the women's book group Milly had joined in her neighborhood. Milly—Milly!—had had the gumption to ask Esther to come join the group for coffee after Esther spoke. Milly had looked plain, powerful Esther straight in the eye and leveraged every bit of beautiful-girl power she knew deep down that she had. And Esther, who had a full, complicated schedule and no time for games or the follies of a long, subtextual courtship, looked right back at her and accepted the invitation to coffee.

Pretty soon, they were having the kind of relationship that all the arty media lesbians in New York talked about, including even the kind of sex they had. The girls said that, when Milly showed up at places with Esther, Milly had the oozy glow of a straight girl who was finally getting the kind of daily working-over she'd waited her whole life for without knowing it. But honestly, Esther worked Milly over like that, oh, maybe once a week—in the past few weeks, possibly even less! Once Esther made it clear to Milly that she was capable of working her over like that—effectively putting a kind of sexual lock on Milly and distracting her from melancholy memories of Jared—Esther went back to her life baseline, which was, basically, that she was too busy to put someone else's pleasure before her own important work. And this was actually comfortable and familiar to Milly—on one level just how things seemed like they should be—so she didn't even think about it so much.

"I just wanted to say I'm thinking of you," Milly told her now over the phone.

"Aw, I love you, Babyturnip," Esther said. "I'm thinking of you, too." Funny, that, Milly noted—Esther was talking to her in the same distracted tone her mom had used a moment ago.

"Are you really?" Milly asked coyly.

"Yes, I am," Esther replied in the cadence of a grade-school teacher. "Are you excited about seeing Drew?" (Esther and Drew got along; Esther was clearly attracted to Drew, and Drew respected Esther's literary success, and wanted it as well.) "It's quite the run-up to her book launch, isn't it? There was a half-page ad in the *TBR* today. That's no small change."

"They're putting a lot of money behind the marketing, it's true."

"It's *Prozac Nation* with a way out of the madness!" Esther proclaimed. Milly laughed. One thing a lot of people didn't know about Esther was that she had a rimshot, Borscht Belt sense of humor that reminded Milly of her dad.

"Now go catch your plane, Baby-T, so I can pull these notes together, and don't let me find out you were letting other girls nuzzle your turnip top in L.A."

Milly laughed weakly. When Esther betrayed jealousy, she suggested only that Milly would be attracted to other women, not men. Why? Milly hadn't brought that up, though. It was okay for Esther to bring up Jared, and how there were simply layers of Milly that he never could've understood or reached. But when Milly brought up Jared, Esther would murmur, in that same grade-school tone, "You know I think it's better that you talk about Jared with your friends and not me, if you really have to talk about him."

And Milly would nod and say, "I know, I'm sorry," wishing she hadn't hurt Esther and perhaps even distracted her briefly from her important work.

Milly read Jeanette Winterson's *Written on the Body* on the flight because Esther had wanted her to. Now they could have good conversations about this, holding each other closely, spooning each other yogurt and berries. Then she slept and dreamed, and in the dream, walking down Avenue B with Jared toward the Christodora, Jared took her in his arms and turned up the edge to her wool cap (because it was winter in the dream) and whispered, "I love you, Millipede." And she said clearly, in her sleep, "Jared, I miss you so much," and woke herself up saying it, a thread of drool running out one side of her mouth.

The thirtysomething Persian-looking guy sitting next to her, in a Lakers cap, reading the *Economist*, glanced sidelong at her, startled, but said nothing.

She wiped her mouth, absolutely mortified and disoriented.

"Milli-peeeeeeeede!" There was Drew, sitting inside her cherry-red VW Cabriolet, sunglasses on, waiting for her outside the terminal. Milly felt a little joyous starburst in her chest as she hurried toward Drew, who looked amazing, her chocolaty hair cut in two soft levels, one framing her cheeks, the other curling inward around her shoulders. Thankfully, she wasn't tan, which relieved Milly, who had a horrible idea that everyone in L.A. was roasted a blood orange. But, Milly noticed, Drew wore an ankh pendant around her neck.

"You're wearing an ankh!" Milly exclaimed as they embraced in the car. "So New Age of you."

"Yeah," Drew said airily, "that's my little spiritual lodestone compass type thing. Just a little something to keep me centered on this new journey."

"Wow, you're so West Coast now," said Milly, which made them both laugh. Drew was playing L7 and turned it down a bit. She gestured at a slim paperback on the dashboard.

"Check that out," Drew said.

Milly picked it up. It was a glossy advanced reader's copy of *Learning to Breathe* with a pen in it; Drew had been marking it up, doing final corrections.

"Oh my God, this is amazing!" Milly exclaimed, flipping through the 224 pages. "Look at you, you glamorpuss."

In the cover photo on the back, Drew leaned forward seductively into the frame, a black jersey falling off her shoulders . . . and there was that ankh pendant again! And there was Drew again on the cover, just half her face this time, with *Learning* spelled out in coke lines against a black background and *Breathe* spelled out in Zen-like black stones against a white background. (Then, in quiet, small letters, *An Early Memoir*.) Milly snuck a look at the book's first line, after the copyright page and quote page (from *The Little Prince*, she noted). The first line was: "Before I breathed, I screamed." *Hoo boy*, Milly thought.

"I am so fucking proud of you, Drew-pea," she said.

"You skipped the dedication page," Drew said coyly, her eyes on the road.

Milly turned to it. "For Milly," it read, "who buzzed me in."

Milly looked at Drew, who, eyes on the road, snuck a wary side-long glance at her. Milly thought about that night two years ago—how enraged she had been! How close she had been to telling Drew simply to go to hell and slamming down the phone! But what Jared had always called her basic Milly-ness, what she thought of as her pushover sucker-ness, had prevailed, and now here Drew was, thanking her publicly by name for all the world to see, basically saying that Milly's decision that night had sort of been the pivotal event in her life . . . the event that had brought her from abject drug use to this: looking gorgeous; with a lovely boyfriend Milly had yet to meet but would shortly; exuding a peace of mind that, Milly had to concede, was slightly puzzling and maybe even a bit suspect because it involved an ankh, but, well, there it was, it could not be denied. And Drew really did seem to have her shit together; she'd made the down payment on a tiny little house in Silver Lake with her book advance.

"It's a good thing I buzzed you in that night, or I might not have gotten the dedication page." Milly laughed.

"I know," Drew said. "But you did buzz me in, sweetheart. Because you're Millicent Sophie Heyman, angel of mercy."

Milly blushed and put her hand over Drew's hand on the stick shift. Then they drove in silence for quite a bit, listening to "Andres." Milly felt incredibly happy—happy to be in L.A. underneath all that sun, having a reprieve from New York's brutal winter. She felt happier than she'd felt in quite a while, even during her happiest moments with Esther the past few months. As for Drew's ankh pendant, she thought—whatever! What did it matter? Whatever worked!

At Drew's adorable little new house, Milly met Drew's boyfriend of the past eight months, Christian, a film editor from England who, like Drew's old boyfriend Perry, was slim and pretty and had floppy Edwardian hair, but, unlike Perry, was quiet and sweet and not peremptory. Christian talked self-deprecatingly about being one of about two hundred editors on James Cameron's movie about the *Titanic*, which was probably going to end up being the most expensive movie of all time. Christian also adored Drew; there was a moment when Drew was reading aloud a snippet of her own *Publishers Weekly* review, in a comically theatrical voice—"a bracing tonic after the navel-gazing narcissism of Elizabeth Wurtzel!"—and Christian, Milly noted, beamed with pure delight and devotion at Drew as she read.

This moved Milly, and gave her a pang, too. Jared would sometimes look at her that way, and she had found it rather puppyish and suffocating, whereas now, Esther—well, Esther seldom looked at her. Esther had said, "Let's not feel like we have to be cheerleaders for each other's work; let's let those be parallel universes." But the problem was Milly had already read a great deal of Esther's work, so it came up all the time, and Esther certainly didn't seem averse to discussing it when it did, whereas the first time Esther had seen some of Milly's work hung up at Milly's apartment, and again at the tiny studio space in downtown Brooklyn that Milly shared with three other artists, she had said, "The best gift I can give you on your work is not to comment on it and let that be entirely yours." Which, at the time, had made sense to Milly, except that—well, couldn't Esther say *something* about it? Every time Esther stared at it and said nothing, merely squeezed Milly's butt and said something cryptic like "You have *ideas*," Milly had inner paroxysms of dread. Did Esther hate it?

"How's your mom, Millipede?" Drew asked when Christian had stepped out for a bit.

Milly sighed. "She's okay." She paused, sipping the chai Drew had made her. (If this were the old Drew, she'd thought, they'd certainly have cracked open a bottle of red by now, but there was no alcohol in the house. Drew had met Christian at AA, so he didn't drink, either.)

"She's amazing, actually," Milly continued. "I mean, the poor woman is so tamped down on meds, it really messes with her focus and energy, and yet she manages to run that residence and keep raising money for it and increasing services. I think she might open another branch uptown. It's so funny. You know when she was at the Health Department, the AIDS activists would protest her with, like, her head on a stick with a witch's hat, like in effigy, and now she's, like, the Liz Taylor of downtown Manhattan!"

Drew laughed. "She's amazing." A pause. "I think so much about John Russell." He was a playwright friend of theirs who'd died the prior year of AIDS. "Thirty-one years old. Isn't that the cruelest?"

"I know."

"I read that some new drugs are in development that are really promising."

"I know. My mother talks about them all the time. She has some clients in trials for them. The ones who can stay off drugs, that is."

Drew went *mmm* knowingly.

They fell into a comfortable silence for a few moments. Milly's eyes fell on a photo of a cute little girl in a striped sundress held with a magnet to the refrigerator.

"Oh my God, is that Blanche?" she asked. Blanche was Drew's niece in Menlo Park, a picture of whom Milly hadn't seen in years.

"That's Blanche!" Drew said, beaming. "Isn't she adorable and so pretty?"

"She is," Milly conceded. "But do you know something? I don't think I'll ever have children." As soon as Milly said it, she was surprised at how the thought had simply flown out of her mouth, unbidden.

Drew laughed. "Why? Have you actually been thinking about that?"

"I'm afraid of having what my mother has."

Drew sighed and put her hand over Milly's. "Honey, I know you are. But you've never shown any signs that you do. Usually, you know, there are signs, even in childhood, right? Hyperactivity and childhood depression. You didn't have any of that, did you?"

"I had my share of childhood depression."

"Of course you did! Look what you went through with your mom. But, sweetie"—and Drew laughed softly, maybe with a tinge of her old jealousy—"you are one of the most stable, even-keeled people I know."

Drew had said this to her many times before. Sure, when you compared Milly with people like Drew and her mother, it was true. But what a pain in the ass it was being the stable, even-keeled one! *When do I get to be the mess and have people take care of me?* Milly thought.

But she didn't say that. She just said: "I mean, why take the chance? Why go through the pain of watching someone you brought into this world go through the pain of going through that?"

"Sweetie, look at the pain we've both been through," said Drew. "And we're not even thirty!" Milly laughed a bit in spite of herself. "Would you rather not have been born than go through it?"

"Hmm," Milly said. "Now *that's* a tough one."

Later that night, right after midnight, they were at the extremely burnt-orange-looking Rat Pack–era Dresden Room, in a banquette with Christian and a handsome screenwriter friend of his named Fabrice and Fabrice's girlfriend, Sonya, a handbag designer from St. Louis. Milly, Drew, and Christian drank Pellegrino and Fabrice and Sonya drank martinis. Milly looked around; it was all about trying to look like *Pulp Fiction* these days, she noticed, the guys in their white spread-collar shirts underneath black jackets, the women with their Uma Thurman blunt cuts. The singing duo, Marty and Elayne, were noodling ridiculously over their synthesizer to Michael Jackson's "Beat It."

Milly, bobbing her head, threw an affectionate look at Drew, as though to say, *This is so cheesy, I love it!* But she caught Drew's eyes following the arc of someone's path in the club, a path that led right to the banquette, and suddenly Drew was exclaiming, "Oh my God! Well, hi, guys!"

Milly turned—and felt the blood drain from her face. There was Jared with his New York high school friends Asa and Jeremy. What on earth was he doing here? Was this some kind of a setup? Had Drew said something to the boys? Would Drew do something like that to her?

But Milly made the snap decision to try to deal with the situation like an adult. "Oh my God," she exclaimed to Jared, trying to sound cheerful—or at least not dismayed. "I didn't know you were here this weekend."

"I didn't know you were here," he said. He'd grown his hair out. He looked—older? Just a bit—thicker? Sadder? Milly couldn't quite determine. He was wearing his dad's maroon corduroy Pierre Cardin jacket from the 1970s. Milly felt her whole body prop up in the banquette.

"I—" Jared fumbled. "Jeremy just moved out here."

"I knew that!" Drew said, eyes wide, standing up to kiss hello Jared and the boys. "I'd heard that!"

There was dead silence around the banquette for a moment, then everyone laughed ridiculously to dispel the awkwardness. "Well," Drew continued. "Are—did you guys just get here? Do you want to join us?" Drew started bumping Christian, Fabrice, and Sonya to the left, opening up the right flank of the banquette. Milly had no choice but to bump to the left as well, and soon Jared was sliding in beside her, right up against her—oh God, she could smell that bacon-y smell of his!—with his boys to his right. Jared didn't kiss her, didn't touch her.

"Hi," he told her. "Uh, I had no idea you were going to be here this weekend."

"I had no idea, either," she said. "I mean, I had no idea you'd be here."

Asa and Jeremy were saying hello to her now, asking about her mom and dad—they'd known her since junior high school, as had Jared. They got talking about New York friends and what they were doing now. She was sort of talking over Jared, who, when he wasn't talking over her to ask Drew about L.A., was fairly quiet. Their jawlines were in near proximity at a strange angle. She glanced awkwardly at him; their eyes briefly met and she saw that same flash of sadness again, or was it anger? His thigh, pressed against her own in the too-crowded banquette, flooded her with memories of his body, of the different ways their bodies had fit together. Already, she could see Drew settling back into conversation with Fabrice and Sonya, Asa and Jeremy back into each other.

It was just too loud and too difficult to maintain conversations across the banquette. They would have to talk.

"When are you here till?" she asked him.

"Monday. I'm flying back with Asa Monday morning, then I have to go back and work on MFA apps."

"You're applying to art school? I didn't know." Of course she didn't know that; they hadn't been in touch. "Oh, wow. That's so great. Where?"

"Yale, Columbia, Chicago, NYU. That's it."

"That's *it*? That's a lot!"

"I know. I've been crazy pulling it all together."

"I'm sure!"

Then they instantly fell into a miserable black hole of silence.

"Well," she continued, "I'm really glad to hear you're applying."

"Yeah." Jared shrugged. "How about you? How's your work?"

"It's good, it's good. I like my new place. The light is great."

"That's good." He sounded severe saying it. *He doesn't want to hear about my new place that I ditched him for,* Milly thought. "How's your mom and dad?"

"They're good." She laughed. "They were going to dinner at Blue Ribbon tonight."

He laughed, too. "So trendy."

"That's exactly what I told them! And my mom is—she's very busy, but she's good. She's . . . stable."

"That's good."

Milly could feel herself sinking into a miasma of sadness. How many nights had he sat with her, lay with her, while she bitched and cried and anguished over her mom? How many times had he told her that she had to take care of herself and not get caught up in her mom's madness, while never saying a mean word about Ava? How many times had he chatted amiably with Ava when Ava called and Milly was out, or in the shower?

"How're your folks?" she asked.

He nodded slowly, as though to say good. "They can't wait to get back to Long Island when winter's done." He meant Montauk, where their summerhouse was. All the days and nights at that house, Milly recalled: the sketching on the beach, the sex on the washing machine in the pantry while his folks went to buy fish and corn for dinner. His hand was lingering not three inches from her own. She desperately wanted to take it—the impulse was overwhelming, maddening; she could feel her own hand twitching to jump, her gaze flicking back hopelessly to the curve of his jaw, the hereditary faint dark circles under his brown eyes that falsely gave him the air of fatigue.

"How's your work?" he asked her, as though reading her mind.

"Oh! Oh, it's good," she said. She actually meant it. She'd been very productive in the past few months; she certainly couldn't complain about that.

"How's the big canvas with the—you know, with the impasto—the flowerlike things?"

"Oh, it's beautiful, thank you!" she said. How weirdly formal this was! But she could remember Jared's excitement about that painting when she started it. "I finished it; I think it's going to be in a group show in a few months."

He smiled with the same tints of melancholy and resentment. "That's great."

Under the table, Drew squeezed her knee, a supportive gesture. Marty and Elayne were finishing up "Time after Time." Then, impossibly, they began "The End of a Love Affair," a Billie Holiday song Milly had loved on a mix tape Jared had made her.

She and Jared looked at each other helplessly, then started laughing. What else could they do? Jared rubbed his head in his hands.

Milly turned to Drew, who looked—wait, that first instinct had been right—didn't she look a bit smug and triumphant? Still laughing, but perhaps with some rage seeping in, Milly asked, "Drew, honestly, did you plan this? Did you stage this?"

Drew gasped. "What? Did I stage this? Are you kidding me? Millipede, I have a life, too."

But, strangely, Milly could feel her rage growing. "It's just the kind of thing you would do." Had she really just said that?

"Mill, come on," Jared said, but she ignored him, continuing to stare at Drew, who looked startled, said nothing.

"Milly . . ." Drew began. "Yes, Jeremy told me Asa and Jared were visiting this weekend. I didn't want to tell you."

Milly's eyes narrowed. "But you told them to come here."

"Milly, I most certainly did *not* tell them to come here."

"Milly, she didn't," Asa popped in.

Drew continued: "I told them we'd probably take you to the Dresden Room one night to see Marty and Elayne, because that's what everyone does with their friends who are visiting."

"And, Milly," Jeremy said, "I did *not* tell Jared you were in town."

"He didn't," Jared said flatly.

"I didn't want to twist his head all weekend," Jeremy said. "But, I mean, come on, I had to show these guys Marty and Elayne. They're an L.A. institution."

Milly crumpled back down in resignation, bewilderment.

"It's just so hard, Mills," Drew began, "with friends and . . ." Drew shrugged, gestured helplessly at Jared, who shrugged in turn.

They all just sat there. *Will this song ever end?* Milly thought. This was torture. Finally, she said, "I think I really need to go to the bathroom." Jeremy, Asa, and Jared all had to get out of the banquette for her, a process that was prolonged and awkward.

"You want me to come?" Drew called. Milly shook her head no as she walked away.

She didn't go to the bathroom, though. She walked outside, went and sat on a bench down at the corner of the block. If she still smoked, she'd have smoked now. But she didn't smoke anymore. She just sat there.

First she thought how it was true, nobody walked in L.A., because the streets were all but empty except for people getting in and out of cars.

Why had she just gotten up and walked out? Because she was angry. Paranoid, she felt Drew and the boys had conspired to put her and Jared back together. How hard she had worked to have a life apart from Jared! She thought of her apartment in Cobble Hill, of the pride she'd taken in every piece of furniture or old rug or painting or plant she'd hauled in there from off the street or a thrift shop or her parents' house. She thought about Jake and Frodo, the cats, lolling around, pressing against the calves of her jeans while she painted. And she thought about the light that came in from the back windows that faced the landlord's garden, that dusty amber light that floated in the room over her head while she painted, purring to herself over the absolute depth of the paint colors and Leonard Cohen on her little, unfussy CD player, and the smell of the roasted chicken she had in the oven while she painted, the red wine she'd drink with her girlfriends at her very own table that night while they ate the meal. And also how she'd spared no expense on her bed—the best fluffy-white pillows and comforter, the lovely duvet cover, and the quilt her grandmother had knitted—Jake and Frodo settling in around the crooks of her knees when she went to bed at night, a stack of about six books she was reading simultaneously right beside her. She had wanted this life, Milly's Life Alone, and she had wrapped herself in it completely.

And yet Milly was always half terrified. The silence whispered to her, *Go down this dark, leafy path.* In the middle of the night, when she'd wake to go to the bathroom, she could hear it—she could put on slippers and throw a coat on over her boxer shorts and T-shirt and walk outside, down some imaginary forest path in the snow that wound all the way down to a quiet but vast river. That's why she was terrified, because she could simply keep on walking and never come back. All the trappings of Milly would fall away behind her as she strode deeper into the forest toward the river—the paintings, her mother and father, her friends, the birthday parties, the clothing swaps with her girlfriends, the gallerists, the skirts she'd worn in high school and the fringed suede coats from college, the cats (well, no, she might carry the cats with her into the woods). It would all fall away behind her like well-braised meat falls off the bone, leaving her clean, naked, vulnerable. The silence would whisper for her to do it, and such a deep, terrifying part of herself wanted to, so she would put on Leonard Cohen in the middle of the night and try to ground herself back in the matter of the living, of the very tethered and connected. In the morning, peeking out the window from bed and seeing her landlord in the garden, she was relieved, reminded that it'd all been a four-A.M. half-dream.

But Milly in the middle of the night longed for Jared, who saw through to her terror. By day, his ungroomed, bacon-smelling self—the sheer amount of space he took up, like a farm dog; his hopeless shedding all over her life and her work!—could send her screaming into the forest. In the middle of the night, though, when she'd stumbled back from the bathroom and he'd throw his arm around her and pull her close, she'd melt into that stinky, warm mass and say "I love you" and think *Thank you for Jared* and fall back asleep.

And suddenly there he was, standing over her on the bench on the corner of North Vermont and Melbourne Avenues.

"What's up, Millipede?" He lit a cigarette. She moved over on the bench and he sat down beside her. She folded her arms and stared straight ahead, boiling inside with warring feelings.

"Jeremy really didn't tell me you were here," Jared finally said. "I freaked when I saw you. But we were right up on the table."

Her eyes flashed at him with anger. "They planned it," she said. "Even if they didn't spell it out, they planned it. I bet Drew said we'd be here on Friday. They think they're doing the right thing." She was dismayed to find she was becoming furious again, just as she had inside. "How dare they? How dare they? I have a right to set my own course. I don't just have to take shit." She was surprised to find herself suddenly sobbing. "I have a right to myself."

Jared had been sitting close, but now he slowly backed away. He stood up, stared down on her. The cigarette fell from his hand. "I'll leave you then, Milly," he said.

She stood up and pulled him back down again by his jacket. "No, I don't want you to leave me," she sobbed. She buried her face in his jacket. "I miss you. I love you. I miss you so much. I'm just trying to hold on to myself."

She was racked with sobs, and he held her and rocked her. She felt that rage she'd always felt with him, not at him but something she couldn't quite make out just over his shoulder, and whatever that hideous, massy thing was, she'd just gone to town on it with a baseball bat. And the relief of it was her realization, while she sobbed, that whatever it was, it wasn't Jared! He hated it as much as she did—he hated it for her, alongside her.

She cried until her face was raw, until she felt exhausted in his arms.

"We need to go back inside because neither of us has a car," Jared said.

She rolled her eyes. "I know. So pathetic."

"I don't want to swallow you, Milly. All the room is there for you, as wide as you want it."

She was truly exhausted now. "Let's just get back to New York and figure it out from there," she said. "I can't even think straight in this good weather."

She pulled away from Jared once they were inside; she was certainly not giving Drew and the boys that satisfaction. They had to walk directly in front of Marty and Elayne to get back to the banquette.

"Aww," drawled Elayne into her microphone. "Look at you two! You two kids look like you want to know what love is. Do you want to know what love is? I know I do. Don't you, Marty?"

"I sure do," Marty said into his mic. "I think I already know."

Marty and Elayne then began their inevitable lounge version of the Foreigner song. Milly and Jared got back to the banquette. Drew looked up at Milly's blotchy face.

"Did you request the song, too, just to put a cherry on it?" Milly asked Drew.

Drew gasped. "You're so *paranoid*, Millicent Heyman! You are crazy, you know that, right?"

She and Drew exploded in laughter. "You are crazy, Drew For-man!" Milly cried. "Learning to breathe! I'll show you how to breathe!"

Milly lunged at Drew, wrapped her arms around her. "You're crazy, you're crazy!" Drew shrieked, cackling madly. The boys and everyone else leaned back, like, *Uh, what the fuck just happened?* And Milly didn't quite understand herself, except that it was the first time in a long time she felt full of joy.

SEVEN
PORTRAIT OF THE ARTIST
(2010)

Mateo has grown. He thinks back bemusedly on his high-school persona, M-Dreem, just over a year ago, so fly in his high-tops and massive T-shirts, the little prince of Art and Design High School. Well, he's moved on. At Pratt, there are these slightly older kids—the steampunk kids, they're called—who wear only vintage lace-up boots, tight trousers, vests, old watches on chains, and black hats or slouchy old newsboy hats, and Mateo has become sort of enamored of them, hanging out with them—and they, all being from way upstate or New Jersey, love him because he is "New York" and "real" to them.

He affects some of their look, spending a lot of time when he's not on campus cruising around thrift stores in the East Village, where he still lives with Millimom and Jared-dad, buying anything black or old looking. The big 'fro now goes in pigtails underneath a bowler, for example, and the fat red-and-black Airs perhaps with knee stockings and twill breeches. He likes the look—he's mixing genres, listening to less Outkast and more old Josephine Baker and early Cure. And his art: What the F was he thinking back in high school with that glorified notebook doodling? He laughs at it now. As soon as he started seeing more work, hitting the New Museum and the Chelsea and Lower East

Side galleries, he changed up his game, became much more minimal, abstract. For the final project of his foundation drawing class, he was taking details from these old Josephine Baker photos—one eye, her feet, her breasts—and drawing them into planes of endlessly repeating water drops, food blobs, or strange, jellylike swirls. He inwardly cringes when he remembers that spider thing he did for his final high-school project. What had he been thinking?

Today, mid-April, it's the first warm spring day. Everyone's lying out on campus, shoes off, portfolio cases cast aside, Lady Gaga coming out of the dorm windows. He's hanging out with Keiko, a sculptor from L.A. who dresses like a Tokyo Harajuku girl (schoolgirl kilts, combat boots, shock of purple in her black hair), whom he's made out with at a few parties, and with Fenimore, whose real name is Carl, from Rochester, one of the steampunk guys. Keiko's talking about the Marina Abramović show at MoMA, where Marina just sits there and a visitor sits across from her and they stare at each other for as long as the visitor wants. Keiko went and waited in line for six hours.

"So I finally sit down across from her," Keiko says, "and it's amazing, she is almost like a wax sculpture except that she allows herself to blink, and I can see her chest move up and down breathing."

"But she doesn't talk, right?" asks Fenimore.

"Nooo," says Keiko. "And you're not allowed to make any sort of faces at her or say anything, you just stare and see where your mind goes."

Mateo ponders this for a second. "That is so intense," he says, because, after thinking about it, he feels that it is. He'd like to go. But it also sounds kind of scary to him.

"It is soooo intense," says Keiko. She lies down in the grass, puts her head in Mateo's lap and starts lacing his fingers in her own. Mateo glances at Fenimore, who's looking away behind his sunglasses, as though he's lost in thought. Is he jealous? He'd said the other day he thought Keiko was hot. But then there's his whole obsession with *My Own Private Idaho*, so Mateo thinks he might really be gay, or at least bi.

"Sooo intense," Keiko says again. "So at first it was awkward—I was thinking, *Why am I sitting across from you and staring at you? I don't even know you.* Then your mind starts to wander. You're still staring at her face, but your mind wanders, like I started thinking about my grandmother." Keiko's grandmother, in San Francisco, had died six months ago. "And before you know it, I'm crying! I'm welling up. And then—and this is the part nobody believes—"

"She hands you a tissue?" Mateo asks. Fenimore laughs. Mateo would never want to admit it, but he always thrills a little when Fenimore laughs at his cracks.

"No!" goes Keiko. "I swear, even though she's not supposed to talk or make faces, I swear I see her mouth the word *no.* As in, *Don't cry.* And I stopped short. I was horrified! Had that just happened? Then I was, like, confused, like had I imagined it, like at my grandmother's funeral when I thought my mother said to me, *Stop crying, Keiko, you're embarrassing me.* It was so humiliating. Where was I? But she—um, Marina Abramović—was just like a blank slate. Suddenly I thought I'd imagined it. I'm like the 450th person she's sat across from now for, like, six weeks—she could care less if I cry or what I do. And that kind of killed it for me, so I got up and left."

"How long were you there for?" Mateo asks. He's heard people wait hours in line to sit across from her and then some of them sit there for hours, which they're allowed to. They can stay as long as they want, until the museum closes.

Keiko considers. "Probably twenty, twenty-five minutes in all. I don't know how some people stay for two hours and just ignore all the people waiting in line behind them."

"The people waiting in line," Fenimore says, "are part of the show."

Keiko takes Mateo's hand again, plays with his fingers. "I guess so," she says uncertainly. "I still can't do that, though." When her hand goes into Mateo's, he feels a warm rush, and it reminds him about the baggie in his pocket, which gives him a double warm rush in his stomach, that recall. Ever since that party at Oscar's last year, he's been snorting heroin once or twice a month—not more than that, and never more than snorting it, which is way less hard-core than smoking or shooting it. Nobody knows except a few guys on the Lower East Side whom he buys it from and does it with. The fact that he has been able to control it and to keep his occasional mild dopesickness from Millimom and Jared-dad is a point of pride with him. (That morning after Oscar's party, they thought he was merely drunk.)

He has no one in his life to ask him why he snorts heroin. But if he did, and if he were even able to articulate this, he might say something like: ever since he was twelve, when Millimom and Jared-dad finally sat him down and explained to him that his mother, that woman in the snapshot dated 04/14/1984, had died of AIDS when he was just a baby and left him in the legal guardianship of his *bubbe*, Ava, and that's why Millimom and Jared-dad had taken him in as a foster child and then adopted him—well, ever since then, and more every year through his teens, he had felt increasingly disconnected from the world he was being raised in. It felt like a shadow world, a fraud world, the second-best fake version of the world he'd have grown up in if the woman in the snapshot hadn't disappeared, and if he'd lived with her and with his father. Then he'd have grown up in the world he was supposed to grow up in. As it was, nobody knew who his father was. His real mother, a woman named Ysabel Mendes, had apparently claimed she didn't know who the father was, which, as Mateo aged and wised up, left him only with the angry, bad feeling that his mother, so sassy and fun-looking in that photo, had been a slut who couldn't even keep track of her sexual encounters. Often, Mateo fantasized about seeking out her family somewhere in Queens, showing up on their doorstep in some neighborhood an hour's subway ride from the East Village, with that snapshot in his hand, and saying, *Hey, I'm your nephew, or your grandson, or your cousin,* and *Hey, come on, I want to know my real family.*

But Mateo never did this. The thought of actually doing it terrified him. Instead, all through high school, even as he cultivated his cool factor, he grew angrier inside. He felt duped that he'd grown close to Millimom and Jared-dad in his prepubescent years and now looked upon them with increasing suspicion, wondering why they'd adopted him rather than have their own child. They never broached this topic and he certainly didn't know how to bring it up, so instead, he distanced himself from them, growing chillier even as he realized they were giving him a life he probably wouldn't have had otherwise. Hey, maybe he didn't want this fancy white life! Maybe he wanted to be the ghetto thug, the son of a woman who died of AIDS and an unknown baby daddy. But then, of course, he did want his life. He loved it. He loved his high school, his teachers, his friends, his art projects. But then he'd have to go home to them, to his mystery benefactors. Why had his feelings changed? He'd torment himself with this question. Why couldn't he accept their love and their hugs like he had when he was ten, eleven? Did he *hate* them? Was that the word? It was all very confusing to him; it brought up all sorts of unwelcome feelings, and he seldom knew how to make them go away, except to lose himself in painting and drawing.

And then he'd discovered heroin. How perfectly 04/14/1984 had blended into that moment. The mysterious past and the confusing present felt continuous. Or perhaps he just felt good and didn't give a fuck about reconciling the two. He felt perfect, and even when he wasn't high, he consoled himself with the thought that he soon would be again—on the weekend, say. He felt he had found a way to cope with what he wanted for his future even when the past came knocking too loud.

But now, in this moment with Keiko and Fenimore, he pushes past the warm anticipatory feeling in his stomach. "I have to get home and work," he says. He has a school crit in three days.

"Can I come to your place for dinner?" Keiko asks.

"Why do you wanna come all the way to the East Village for dinner?" he asks. "I'm just gonna have to send you back; I have work tonight."

"I like your parents," Keiko says. "I like being in a real home with people's parents, especially when the parents are artists. It makes me feel good."

"Me, too," Fenimore says. "Can I come, too?"

Mateo sighs, but he's not against it, because it's easier to be around the Parentals when his friends are around. The friends kind of fuzz them out. He pulls out his cell.

"What's up, honey?" Millimom says when she picks up.

"Hey," he says. "Can I bring Keiko and Fenimore over for dinner tonight? They want to come."

"I thought it would be just us tonight!" she answers. He hears cars in the background; she's on the street. "Dad's in his studio—they won't even get to talk to him about building and welding. It'll just be me, a boring, bougie old-lady painter."

"I'll tell them that," Mateo says. He relays the information.

"We still want to come, Millimom!" Keiko shouts into the phone.

"Yeah," Fenimore shouts. "Bougie old-lady painters kick butt."

"Tell Fenimore I'm very flattered," Millimom says. Then: "Why does he call himself Fenimore anyway if his real name is Carl? Is that an art project?"

"Sort of," Mateo says. "He's a work in progress. What do you want me to bring home? Is there wine?"

"None of you should be drinking wine," she says. "You're all under-age. They'll send me to jail for being an unfit parent."

"Dad would let us."

"We'll bring wine, Milly!" Keiko shouts.

Millimom sighs. "Whatever. Also bring a head of romaine lettuce and a baguette. And, um, a good jar of red sauce. We're only having pasta, Mateo."

"We don't care." She starts to say something else but Mateo says, "Bye, see you soon!" and hangs up. In a few minutes, he and Keiko and Fenimore are on the train into the city. After they pick up the grocer-ies, walking into the Christodora, they bump into Ardit, the humorless, square-headed super, and nod hello. Mateo's stomach jumps a bit, as it always does now when he sees Ardit, because once a few months ago, Ardit caught Mateo nodding by the elevator at three A.M. and Mateo had to make up some bad lie about being so tired that he'd fallen asleep standing up. A few occasions since then, when Mateo came home nod-ding, he watched the building until he saw Ardit step out for an errand, or ducked immediately into the stairwell and climbed the six flights to avoid waiting at the elevator. That was murder. He'd slump down in the stairwell for up to an hour after that haul, undiscovered by anyone because it was the middle of the night.

When Mateo and Keiko and Fenimore enter the apartment, Milly is at the kitchen table, in front of her laptop, drinking iced tea. Hellos and hugs go around.

"Look at this work, you guys," Milly says. She's grading final projects at LaGuardia Music and Arts High School, where she's taught painting the past thirteen years, and she shows the trio some gouache on wood abstracts by a girl named Cláudia Torres. "What do you think?" Milly asks.

Milly enlarges the image and the three peer at it awhile. "I don't mind it," Fenimore finally says. "It has some energy."

"I like the pale colors," says Keiko brightly. "She has ideas, I can see them."

"I hope she's taking an accounting class," Mateo says.

"Oh, come on, Mateo!" Keiko protests. "Mean."

"Harsh, bro," Fenimore drawls. "We can't all be as brilliant as you."

Milly turns and looks at Mateo. She opens her mouth to say something, then just closes it and shakes her head, still looking at him. *Yeah, yeah*, he thinks. *I know all your beefs with me, lady.* How full of himself he is. His swagger as an artist. It's very unbecoming to her, he knows. *This isn't an easy life*, she always says, *the artist's path, and we have to support each other, be generous and gentle with our words, pay it forward, and all that.* Fucking Saint Milly, who teaches city kids how to make art even though, with her and Jared's family money, neither of them really needs to teach. But they've both taught all these years, to be "real people," to show Mateo "values," supposedly. He knows his *bubbes* and *zaydes* are paying for his college, but Jared and Milly still make him have those summer- and winter-break jobs so he learns these "values."

"You're impossible," Milly finally tells him softly. Milly had turned forty this year, but the moment after Fenimore left the Christodora the first time meeting Milly, he grabbed Mateo's arm and said, "Dude, your mom is a fucking babe." All Mateo's friends think that, the guys and the girls. The guys are in love with her and the girls either want to be her or are in love with her, too. That warm, kind, but gently droll Julia Roberts thing she exudes. That thing Auntie Drew, who's not really Mateo's aunt but he's always called her that, describes as "*l'air de Milly*."

Mateo tilts his chin at Milly and grins and says, "It's too bad you think I'm impossible since you gotta live with me."

Milly laughs; she's game. "No, my friend, I think that might be the reverse unless you can come up with the money for your own rent while you're in school."

"Don't be a turd to your mother," Fenimore says, grabbing Mateo and Keiko. "You work, Milly, we'll make dinner." Fenimore opens the bottle of red, pouring everyone a glass, and the three of them make a salad and pasta while Milly continues working, chatting here and there. At one point Mateo looks over at her: ebony hair up in that loose knot, cat-eye glasses perched on her nose, legs in skinny jeans crossed, bare foot bobbing, toenails painted glossy black. That permanently worried frown on her face she gets when she looks at art. Mateo allows himself a moment of affection for her. Then Milly glances upward and catches a soft look on his face. Taken aback, he sticks out his tongue at her and looks away—not so soon, though, that he doesn't see her face break into a small, triumphant smile as she turns back to her laptop.

The wine relaxes Mateo. The dinner is good, informal, everyone passing around the baguette and tearing off pieces for themselves to mop up the spaghetti sauce. Keiko retells her Marina Abramović story; Milly plays down the fact that she and Marina have known each other for years, just saying, "It's amazing she's doing this, good for her." Keiko and Fenimore babble and bitch about school and professors. Mateo fuzzes out on his wine, twirls his pasta, clears the table and loads the dishwasher when everyone's done so folks can keep talking.

He comes back to the table with ice cream for everyone. "Thank you, sweetheart," Milly says when he sets hers down in front of her—just one small scoop, all she'll ever have, because it's not like she stays looking the way she looks without putting some thought and discipline into it. Then after the dessert Keiko and Fenimore are getting up to leave.

"I'll walk you guys down," Mateo says.

"You have a crit in three days," Milly says. "You should hit your room."

"I'll be right back!" Mateo whines.

Down on the street, he walks Keiko and Fenimore to the subway. Fenimore thoughtfully walks ahead a few paces while he and Keiko make out for a second on the way. "I love your mother," Keiko says.

"Yeah, she's okay."

Mateo watches them disappear down the subway stairs. Such a warm night! The East Village is vibrating with warmth, everyone's out. He lights a cigarette, takes a roundabout route back to the apartment. He thinks about what's in his wallet and his stomach twists deliciously, his skin flushes.

And then, when Mateo's walking past a row of tenements on Second Street, he sees him: Hector. The crazy gay guy whose dog, Sonya, bit him in the Christodora when he was a little kid, right before 9/11. It had been a horrible situation, with Jared-dad wanting to sue Hector but then Millimom's mom, his *bubbe* Ava, imploring Jared not to, saying that Hector had fallen on hard times after the death of a lover. Instead, Jared had a lawyer send a letter to Hector saying that if Hector got rid of the dog, which was a menace to the entire Christodora, then Jared wouldn't press charges over the bite. Jared had received no reply to the letter and was infuriated a week later to see Hector in the lobby with the dog, who seemed as keyed up as ever.

"Now I'm pressing charges," Jared had said to Milly moments later.

"Well, you might want to wait," Milly said. "Because Ardit just told me that Hector's sold his unit and he's moving out. He's broke apparently; he hasn't worked in two years now, and he can't make the mortgage payments."

Some of the angry color drained from Jared's face. "Are you sure?" he asked Milly.

"Ardit told me today that Hector told him yesterday he'd closed on a sale."

Jared was silent for a moment. "He and that dog can't be out of here soon enough," he finally said.

Everyone in the Christodora had known about Hector, once so famous and important in the AIDS movement but now a total meth addict. To the great relief of everyone in the building, he and the dog finally vacated and moved into a rent-stabilized basement dump a few blocks away. There, it was reported through the Christodora grapevine, he continued to smoke away, on a glass pipe, the money he'd made on the apartment sale. Through the first decade of the 2000s, he unraveled before the neighborhood's eyes, from a handsome, muscular man in his early forties to a mumbling mess in his early to midfifties, screaming in the street at the dog he cooped up in that tiny basement apartment. Everyone on the block knew what went on there, who came and went.

And now Mateo is standing right in front of Hector as Hector yells at a new dog, another shepherd-pit mix, this one tan with black and white markings, straining on her leash to go into the street.

"Get the fuck back, animal," Hector shouts. Mateo stands back and observes; people approaching Hector and the dog on the sidewalk abruptly cross the street, startled. Hector is bald and overtanned, with a three-day growth of black beard flecked with gray; a cigarette in one mouth; a dingy wifebeater over a shaven, sunken chest; cutoff denims too short for even the East Village; flip-flops with a rainbow-stripe thong; and a thick leather band around his wrist. *He looks like a holy gay mess*, thinks Mateo, *some cracked-out Alphabet City version of Big Gay Al from* South Park.

But Mateo can't bring himself to cross the street to avoid him. He just keeps watching the spectacle with the big dog, mesmerized.

"Hector, right?" Mateo finally ventures from a safe dozen feet away.

Hector turns to him. "Brisa, sit the fuck down!" he yells at the dog, who ignores him, straining into the street, howling miserably. "What's up, *negro*?" he asks Mateo.

"I'm Mateo. From the Christodora. You remember us, the Traums on the sixth floor?"

"Oh, shit!" Hector exclaims, breaking into a smile revealing a lost tooth on the far upper right. "Shit, you got big, man! I haven't seen you in a long time."

"I know, it's true," Mateo acknowledges. He wonders if Hector has any recollection of the biting incident nine years ago with the prior dog. Gingerly, Mateo tries to pet this new dog, who strains away from him toward the street, as though she wants to gallop around the block a few times to release pent-up energy. "This is your new dog, right?"

"You got a light, *negro*?" he says, ignoring Mateo's question.

"Huh?"

"You got a light? My cigarette went out."

Oh, Mateo notes, *it has. It's just sitting there dead in his mouth.*

"Yeah," Mateo says, pulling out his lighter. "Sure." He steps toward Hector to relight his cigarette, smelling what he once smelled when he went into a leather bar on Christopher Street for five minutes with friends in high school as a joke—it's like BO, cigarettes, stale beer on the floor. "Fagfunk," they called it upon leaving the bar, knowing they shouldn't say that but cracking themselves up nonetheless.

"*Gracias, negro*," Hector says. Mateo wonders if Hector knows he doesn't speak Spanish—well, not very much. He thinks about his crit—he should get back to the Christodora, he tells himself. But he can't pull himself away for some reason. Hector, though, appears indifferent to the encounter, contentedly puffing on his relit cigarette.

"That's your new dog?" Mateo asks again.

"New?" Hector laughs. "Brisa's not new. She's a fucking middle-aged bitch."

"But I mean—not the one you had in the old apartment, right?"

"In the—" He looks confused. "Oh, you mean the Christodora, right? No, no, yeah, that was Sonya. That poor bitch died a few years ago."

He laughs, and Mateo laughs awkwardly with him. "Yeah, I remember Sonya," Mateo says. "She was crazy."

Hector smiles. "Yeah," he says. "I loved that bitch." He drags on his cigarette again. "Hey, wait a second," Hector says. "You're the little guy she fucking bit, right, and your white daddy wanted to sue me, right?"

Mateo feels himself flush in discomfort. "That was me," he says. "The weekend right before 9/11."

"Shit, *negro!*" Hector exclaims. "And now here you are. All grown up." He cracks another grin.

"Here I am," says Mateo. "I survived the dog bite!"

They both laugh now. Hector flicks his cigarette into the street. Mateo follows it into the gutter with his eyes, acutely aware that he should be getting on home but unable to pull himself away.

He points down toward the basement apartment. "You like your new place here?" he asks, fumbling to prolong the conversation.

"It's a cave," Hector says. "But it's fine except for winter, when I go live in Palm Springs. In another cave." Hector laughs jaggedly. "At least people leave me alone here and mind their own business." Unceremoniously, he turns to go back inside. "Come on, baby," he says to the dog, yanking the leash. *"Está bien, negro,"* he says to Mateo.

"Can I see it?" Mateo asks. *Did I just ask that?* he then asks himself.

Hector turns, looks at Mateo curiously, then shrugs. "Sure, come on in."

Hector was right. It's a fucking cave inside. A wreck. Assorted dog stuff everywhere, dog food scattered here and there on the floor. Piles of newspapers. A torn-up, scratched-up black leather couch with an old blanket thrown over it. A large-screen TV with the local news on, volume off. Construction boots, bomber jackets, baseball caps lying around. A picture on the TV table of Hector, probably twenty years ago, with some gay blond guy—one of those really gay beach pics, both of them in their tiny Speedos and wraparound glasses, arms around each other.

Hector goes to the fridge, pops open a chocolate-flavored Ensure, holds it up to Mateo. "You want one? I live on these things. They're easier than eating."

"No, thanks," says Mateo. The dog's humping his leg now and he's absently massaging her head. Hector goes to the back bedroom, turns up some gay house music, comes back. *Thump, thump, thump, thump-thump, thump, thump, thump.* Some diva screaming, *You got me feeling high,* some bullshit like that. Mateo's heart is pounding, his hands are shaking, and his legs are weak. He feels like he's gone into some kind of fugue state. The crit seems a million miles away.

"Why'd you come in here, *negro*?" Hector asks him. He's standing behind the kitchen counter, drinking his Ensure. "You wanna get high?"

Finally, Mateo thinks, *he asked*. "You wanna snort H with me?"

Hector's eyes brighten. "You got H?" Mateo nods. "I haven't done that in a while," Hector says. "You wanna smoke it?"

Mateo doesn't say anything. Smoking it—he hasn't done that yet. He's always considered that the next step into the beyond, the one that leads to needles, which makes you a full-time junkie and not just a functioning, recreational user. "I never did that," he finally says.

"Hold on," Hector says. He goes back to the bedroom, turns up the music, comes back with a carton of tin foil and a toilet-paper roll, draws the dingy sheet on the front room's one window, which reveals people's feet walking by on the sidewalk above. He sits down on the cracked, ripped-up couch, lights another menthol.

"Come sit," he says. Mateo does, so close he's deeply inhaling the fagfunk. He pulls the baggie out of his wallet, hands it to Hector. The dog, who'd actually been chilling out in a corner, bounds up and comes and sticks her huge head between the two of them like she wants to get high too.

"Sit the fuck down," Hector yells, pushing her down. She goes down with a whimper, looking up at the two of them from the floor miserably, as though she's left out. Hector tears off a piece of tin foil, then folds it and tears it again until it's about five inches square, then taps some of the off-white powder onto its center. Mateo watches him, transfixed, while he does it. *Why are you doing this?* he asks himself. *You are going to fuck up your crit, that much is for certain.* Yet deep within, he is still, still, still just watching Hector, feeling utterly and inexplicably at home. He reaches down, strokes the dog's head, which she rubs desperately against his arm. His foot is tapping nervously to the pounding house music.

Finally, Hector hands him the foil square and the cardboard roll. "Wait to inhale till you see smoke," he says, snapping the lighter to life beneath the foil. As soon as Mateo sees blue smoke curl up off the foil, like a genie appearing from the ether, he sucks it up into the roll. And then, even faster than when he snorts it, his world melts and crumples, beautifully and softly, inside his stomach, the velvety crumple blooming through every vein of his body. He sinks leagues down and the world comes into focus from below, almost like looking up at the sun from under the water, everything quavering, tremulous, so kind and lovely.

He smiles at Hector. "Fuckin' crazy gay guy," he says, and cracks up. Hector laughs with him, his eyes popping open. After Hector sucks up his own plume of smoke, he leans toward Mateo with his mouthful of smoke, then he stops short, turns away, blows it out. They each take a few more hits, then Hector sets down the makeshift paraphernalia. They each lie back on the couch. The dog lumbers up on the couch and settles in between Mateo's legs, grateful not to be turned away this time. The fucking house music pounds on. Somewhere inside his head, Mateo's thinking, *Shut off the fucking gay house music*, but he doesn't really care.

"Feels so good," Mateo manages to say.

At first, Hector says nothing. Finally, that crazy mess is quiet! The H has cut his speed high. "So peaceful," Hector finally says.

Mateo's arm twitches deliciously, along with the exquisite, vaguely nauseous twitching in his belly. Eventually, the music goes off and it's just the three of them, lying there, the now-dark room flickering with the changing shots of the silent TV. Mateo can hear voices, cars, an ice-cream truck out on the street. This is the perfect place, his body tells him. The H baggie is the hole in the air we crawl into to get there, like when Bugs Bunny, being chased, saws a circle out of the air around him and jumps into it, then plugs it back up so that Elmer Fudd slams into it and lands on his ass. It's just blue sky, it's just the air, but there is a hole through it. Go through the hole in the sky.

Mateo turns, curls up on his side, wraps his arm around Hector's leg, tucks his feet up to his butt. He's engulfed in Hector's fagfunk, so comforting. The dog feels good in the crook of his legs, her huge, steady breathing. He feels Hector gently stroke his pigtails.

"I remember this crazy fucking hair," Hector says. "Fucking *negrito* in the building."

Mateo cracks up in slow motion. "*Negrito*," he echoes, laughing in a bath of delectable black ooze.

EIGHT

PARALLEL TRACKING

(1989)

There was weak A/C in Reminiscence on MacDougal in the Village, so it had been hot in there all afternoon, and it was hot and muggy on the street, especially for early June. Milly came out of the shop where she was working the summer after her first year of college, pulled her hand back through her moist curls, rubbed her eyes, sighed. She walked a few feet, felt the heat and her own fatigue and, most of all, the suspension of everything, this odd pocket of six o'clock when the little street was silent, when cars and horns sounded miles away—and she surprised herself by sitting down on a stoop and hiking up her black eyelet gypsy skirt and pulling a cigarette out of her fringed brown suede bag. She lit it, then pulled a bandanna out of her bag to blot her face with, then tied the bandanna around her head to hold her hair back. She was thinking about Jared Traum and should she go back in the store and call him or wait till she got uptown? Or maybe they'd stay downtown so better she just go back in the store, where Alicia was working till it closed, and call him now, and hang out down here in some café . . .

She inhaled gratefully on the cigarette, an American Spirit, which was suddenly what everyone she knew smoked. Jared Traum, she thought. She'd known him since seventh grade, the school circuit uptown. Then they ended up at the same college, taking art classes together, that comfort of seeing someone on campus you knew from before, though, being from New York, that really wasn't a rare thing; she was one of eight girls from her school who'd ended up at that particular college.

In May, Jared had told her he'd be in New York for a few weeks before going to some program at Cranbrook—she wished her parents would send her to some summer painting program! But no, it was work all summer, and then they'd all go to a family friend's house on the North Fork of Long Island for a week in August—that was it for her vacation. Jared had said they should hang out. Yeah, she'd said. Then he'd called her last night, from his dad's office in the East Village where he liked to stay because his dad let him use a whole room as a studio.

Did she want to hang out tomorrow night? he'd asked her. Oh, he was serious, she thought. Well, sure, she'd said. She thought about his head of curly, honey-hued hair, his very straight nose, his honeyed face fuzz. Their shoulders touching in that screening room in the dark for that class back in April, watching "O Superman," having to soon write about all it signified. Her relative boredom with it; Jared's fixation, his love of VHS as a medium. What would they do on such a hot night? They could have sushi, then go hear friends play at the Bitter End. Should she change? Put on makeup? It was so very hot.

Two guys came out of the apartment across the street in sleeveless T-shirts, jean shorts rolled up over the knees, and black boots. The dark-featured one put his arm around the blond one. Gay guys were hot, Milly thought idly. They had no issue showing off their bodies. She thought it was empowering. Then: wait! That was Hector, who'd worked with her mom at the Health Department till he'd left and started giving her hell. It had been awful, but he was breaking her down. He'd turned on her, from shy to right up in her face! That image made Milly laugh, her mother confronted by more confrontational, psycho types than herself, including her own former protégé.

The two men were making their way down the street. "Hector!" Milly was surprised to hear herself call out. The pair turned back, and she dropped her cigarette behind her back and strode across the street. Hector was ridiculously good-looking, so her mother had always said, and indeed her mother was right. He had considerable muscles in all the right places. His boyfriend, the blond guy, was good-looking too in that classic blond, blue-eyed, forever-a-boy way. He was a bit smaller, younger, than Hector.

"I'm Milly Heyman," she said. "I'm Ava's daughter. We met a few years ago—at an awards . . . thing." Her mother had received some dry public-service award for something having to do with food-service hygiene and they'd all dressed up and gone.

Hector peered at her. "Oh, riiiight," he said slowly. He and the blond guy both had canvas bags loaded with flyers and folders. He stepped forward to shake her hand, then stepped in more and gave her a short, slightly awkward kiss hello. He nodded toward the blond guy. "This is Ricky," he said.

She and Ricky shook hands, swapped hellos. Ricky's voice was about two octaves higher than Hector's—he sounded southern or midwestern or something.

They hit that bump of silence. "Well, I saw you," she said, "and recognized you and just wanted to say hi."

Hector nodded, smiling—a little patronizing or judging? Milly wondered.

"You're in college now, right?" he asked.

"Yeah, I just finished my first year. I'm working there this summer." She gestured back at Reminiscence. "I just got out."

"Yeah, we saw you smoking that after-work cigarette, you bad girl," Ricky teased her. They all laughed. Milly blushed and shrugged, a bit delighted to be called a bad girl.

"I know, not a healthy choice," she said.

"We all have our vices," Ricky said. They all laughed again before falling into silence.

"Well, okay," Milly said brightly. "I just wanted to say hi. Hey, you're not at the Health Department anymore, are you?"

Hector shook his head, seemed to frown. "No, no," he said. "I'm doing activism full-time now."

"AIDS activism, right?" Milly had noticed some of the stuff sticking out of their bags, the pink triangle that had become ubiquitous the past few years. "We have a chapter of that in college," she said.

"That's good!" the blond one—what was his name again? Billy?—piped up. "Are you in it?"

She shrugged, blushing with guilt. "Uh, I went to a fund-raiser dance?"

Hector and the blond one laughed. "That's a start," Hector said. "I also have a grant to help design clinical trials—that's what's supporting me right now."

"Baby, I'm the one that's supporting you," the blond guy said, kicking Hector lightly in the thigh. "That grant money is—" He turned to Milly. "I think it pays the phone bill."

"Okay, fine, you're supporting me right now," Hector conceded, putting his arm around the blond guy.

Milly laughed. She was charmed and touched. She knew a handful of gay guys and lesbians in college—she'd had her own inner (and at least one outer) flirtation with that in the past year—but she didn't know any gay couples who actually lived together and schlepped bags around and bickered about the bills like her parents did.

Again, a moment of silence passed until Hector nudged the blond one. "We should go." He pulled out a flyer with the pink triangle on it and waggled it toward Milly. "We're off to a meeting right now."

"Okay," she said. "Oh! I think my mother's going to that meeting."

Hector's eyes widened. He and the blond one looked at each other. "Your mother?" Hector asked. "Are you serious?"

"This morning I remember her saying she wanted to go to a meeting tonight for that." Milly pointed at the triangle. "She was reading the *Times* and pointed to an article about it and a photo with you guys with your signs. Like, at a demonstration I think?"

"Montreal," the blond one said. "We just did big demos at a big conference in Montreal."

"I guess that's what it was," said Milly. "Anyway, yeah, I remember her saying something like, 'That's it, tonight I'm finally going,' or something like that."

Hector broke into a grin. "That should be very interesting to see," he said.

"In-*deed*," said the blond one.

"She—" Milly began. She had to choose her words carefully. "I think she's frustrated with—"

"What she can do at Health?" Hector asked.

Milly sighed. "You said it, not me."

"Maybe she can be an inside-outside," the blond one said to Hector.

Milly wasn't sure what that meant. "I guess you'll have to see if she comes!"

They walked together a few blocks, making bits of small talk. Were they sick? Milly wondered. They certainly didn't look sick. But she knew that years could go by before people got sick. They were arm in arm, and at a certain point, on a crowded sidewalk, they had to sidle ahead of her, leaving her trailing them a bit like an urchin. At a café, she announced she was going in.

"Come to the meeting with us and see if your mom shows up," the blond one said.

Milly laughed. "Me? No, no, I—maybe I would, but I have plans. And I know better than to bother my mom when she's working."

The blond one laughed. "If she shows up, you won't be the only one bothering her, believe me."

Milly had no idea what to say to that. Hector leaned in and gave her a little hug good-bye. He smelled good, she noticed, something like nutmeg. "I'll protect your mom if she shows up," he said. "I know she's on the right side of this."

Then Hector slung his arm around Ricky again and left Ava's clueless Ivy League daughter behind. He thought maybe he should wait until they turned a corner away from her, but he didn't care—something about the conversation had been tiresome and oppressive and, leaving it, he felt a surge of tenderness, lust, and heartbreak toward Ricky, and he dropped his bag and held Ricky intensely by the nape of his neck with his left hand and by Ricky's pert, taut right buttcheek with his right hand and thrust his tongue into Ricky's mouth. When Hector kissed Ricky in public—okay, granted, it was the Village, but still—he felt like he was falling back, back, back, crashing backward through years of self-denial and self-containment, making up for lost time like a starving dog. He was thirty-two! How many years had he wasted?

An overweight middle-aged man, perspiring in a shirt and tie, sidled by them. "Jesus Christ, right out on the street?" he muttered, clearly just loud enough to be heard.

"That's right," Hector called back. "Right out on the street. Sorry to offend you."

"And look at her," said Ricky, his arms still around Hector. Ricky jerked his head leftward and Hector turned. Ava's daughter was watching them, mesmerized, from the doorway of the café she'd stopped at, but when she saw them both turn back to her, she ducked inside, mortified. Hector and Ricky laughed. "How's that for college?" Ricky said.

They walked on. Hector kept his arm close around Ricky's waist. Hector was almost addicted to that gesture, squeezing Ricky around the waist until he felt his head growing like it was going to explode. Then Hector's ravenous, mad hunger kicked in and Ricky would say, "Oh God, no, here we go again, *el voraz*!" And it was true: when it came to Ricky, Hector was voracious. He marveled at how it never got old; just put that butt between his hands for a few seconds and he would be groaning and marveling, "Holy shit, holy shit!" Ricky laughing with delight at his powers of assitude, a colorist who'd become a potentate. Sometimes Hector would nearly cry; it was too much for him to bear: a full, complex effusion of feelings that encompassed past, present, and future all at once. Past: How had he gone so long without this? All those nights in the office, boxed away. Present: Was this really happening? Could he possibly be so happy? He was exploding! Future: What if he lost this? He would surely die. Get more now! He plunged himself back into the assitude with a renewed burst of psychotic joy, a mix of gratitude and terror, making Ricky cry, "You're crazy, you terrify me!"

Walking down Bleecker now, Hector crept his hand down lower, lower.

"Stop it!" Ricky hissed, yanking up Hector's arm. "Have some decency."

Hector glanced at him and smiled a silent, wicked smile. Then, the wires of lust and fear crossing in his head, he asked, "You went this week, right?"

Ricky dropped his self-satisfied grin. "Went where?" he asked.

Hector knew Ricky was thinking: *Oh God, here we go again.* "Come on, you know what I mean," he said. "Went for a test."

Ricky straightened, almost imperceptibly picked up his pace, jerked his bag up more securely on his shoulder. "I'll go next week," he said. "This week was crazy. Work and all this shit." He jerked his head at the bag full of flyers and folders.

"Wednesday I said I'd meet you there and I called you at the salon and you didn't call me back."

"We got crazy. Ivana came in."

Hector snorted a laugh. "Oh, Ivana comes first."

"Well, she kind of does," Ricky said in his *duh* voice. "She's brought in, like, a hundred friends."

There was no point, Hector knew, in doing the whole spiel: everything they were working out at these meetings to get drugs faster; this whole miracle of parallel tracking they were working on, where you could get the new, experimental drugs even if you didn't qualify for the actual clinical trial because this or that picky lab test of yours wasn't quite right and you weren't their perfect trial specimen. They were going to get thousands of people access to a drug in the baby phase, the drug ddI, and when you took it along with AZT it was very likely going to do what AZT alone couldn't do. Well, Hector amended himself, maybe not *very* likely, but likely. But Hector knew that Ricky knew all that. So instead, he just said: "Can we go this coming week, please?"

"Oh!" Ricky exclaimed, infuriated. He stopped dead on the sidewalk, making Hector stop, too. "I've told you a hundred times, Hector. I don't want to know. *I don't want to know.*" He was saying it in a nasty singsong. "I don't see the point. *La-la-la, la-la!*" He walked on a few more paces, then stopped again. "And if you're so concerned, then use a fucking condom when you fuck me. Okay?" He kept walking.

"You're fucking pissing me off," Hector called to him. "You know it's you I'm concerned about, not me."

They stood there, about twelve feet apart, an awkward standoff. Finally Hector caught up to Ricky. "Let's just go to the meeting," he said. They walked on but they didn't touch. A car went by blasting "Cherish," Madonna's new song. In the video, Madonna played in the waves with the hot merman and the cute, curly-haired little black girl.

Half a block from the meeting, they ran into Chris Condello, one of Hector's fellow science wonks in the movement, with his unkempt shock of jet-black hair, tote bag, Bronski Beat T-shirt sweaty and worn down to crepe over his modest spare tire. They exchanged hello kisses. Hector noticed Ricky hang back ever so slightly, the way Ricky always did, a bit insecure about his non-braininess when Hector encountered another data geek.

"You ready to present with me tonight?" Chris asked Hector. "You do background and I'll do prospectus?"

"Sure," Hector said. *Why don't you do background and I do prospectus?* he thought flickeringly. But for the most part, he avoided those stupid ego wars in the group. He brought the same clinical, businesslike calm to the group that he'd provided in his closeted days at Health, and he knew people respected him for it and respected that he had a real clinical background. The difference between working with multiple-degree Health bureaucrats and working with people desperate for their lives, and their friends' and lovers' lives, stunned him. When he wanted to go off on people at the meetings for being stupid, impetuous, angry, or uninformed, he reminded himself that he was taking what he'd been expensively educated to do and was using it to help save the lives of his own people—and he got to have fun and flirt and plan major disruptions and then go dancing along the way—instead of shuffling papers in a closet in a city agency.

They arrived at the meeting. "Holy shit, it's packed tonight," Ricky said. And it was, noted Hector, slightly in awe, as he always was when he showed up to a full house. These meetings: such a mix of righteous anger and complicated lust, social energy, bitterness, and hurt that preceded AIDS and went back into childhoods, adolescences. Such a sea of white boys in sleeveless T-shirts, jean shorts, and combat boots! Then his other fellow members of what they all called Brown Town, maybe about thirty of them in all. There was Ithke Larcy, the social worker with his massive head of locks, and Ithke's white boyfriend, Karl Cheling, the wild-eyed left-wing evangelical minister. The two of them were trying to force the city to let homeless people with AIDS live in real apartments and not the chaotic cesspools of the shelter system. Then there were all the lesbians. That novelist Esther Hurwitz, the kingpin of the downtown arty dyke rat pack, was here, Hector noticed; she'd been coming around and getting all vocal, but some people suspected she was just collecting material for a novel she'd write about them all someday. You couldn't hear yourself think in here, it was so loud.

Hector and Ricky found some boys Ricky called friends, boys in their twenties who worked in fashion or at salons and came here because they knew on some level it was the right thing to do—but also because, the past few years, there was no cooler place to be. Here you could be angry but sexy at the same time, all riled up about a plague, which made for great carnal energy that you could take out of the meeting, then dance or fuck it off at Boy Bar or Meat, Dusty Springfield singing, *Since you went away, I've been hanging around, I've been wondering why I'm feeling down*, over a hand-clap backbeat. The boys were there with Micki, a five-foot-four magenta-haired dyke who said she'd come to the meeting when she heard that the federal definition of AIDS, which drove benefits and funding and research, didn't include symptoms that showed up only in women, like the early lesions of cervical cancer. "That fucking pissed me off," Micki had said. "Dykes get AIDS!" In fact, this is exactly what Micki had screamed at Barbara Bush at an event in D.C. Micki had managed to infiltrate, posing as a young congressional page, looking hilariously straight in pumps and a skirt and a blond bob wig with a headband.

Hector felt a hand at his elbow. It was Chris. "Let's get this party started," Chris said.

They wove their way through the crowd. Halfway through, Korie Wright, just three years ago a skyrocketing thirty-one-year-old graphic designer, stopped them. Oh God, he looked frail, his chest virtually concave underneath his tank top.

"I have to ask you guys something," Korie said.

"You'll probably hear your answer in the presentation," Chris said, pushing forward.

"Chris, Jesus!" Hector said. Sometimes Chris's callousness stunned him. He and Chris exchanged a quick, nasty look. Was Chris even HIV-positive? Hector wondered. Was that the source of the callousness? Or was it that he wasn't? It was strange to him that, even here, people could be coy about their own HIV status. Of course, there were plenty of people like Ricky who were simply too scared to get tested or didn't see the point of knowing. Some of them saw not knowing as a political choice; if nobody knew their status, then they were all on a level playing field, everyone compelled to have safe sex with one another, nobody branded a pariah.

Hector, with Korie's arm on his, took Korie's other arm. "What is it, Korie?"

"Marty Delaney in San Francisco called me back about Compound Q. He's doing an illegal trial."

Hector nodded. "I know."

"You think I should fly out and do it?"

Hector caught Chris rolling his eyes. Hector knew Chris thought Compound Q, the Chinese cancer drug, was a dead-end path for AIDS— Hector pretty much thought so, too—but he couldn't believe Chris's insensitivity. "We should talk about it later," he told Korie. "It's a complicated decision."

Korie's eyes flickered with fear. "You think so?"

"There are major toxicities to consider," Chris all but barked at him.

Korie frowned. "What?"

"He means that it could have side effects," Hector said. "It could mess with your head. But let's have coffee after the meeting and talk about it. I still have to talk to Marty but I think it's worth considering."

To Hector's surprise, Korie hugged him. "Thanks, sweetie. Nice to know that some of you data guys can stay human." Korie shot a hateful look at Chris, who looked suddenly stricken, then Korie turned on his heel.

Chris and Hector pressed forward. "What the fuck did that mean?" Chris asked him. "I just told him there was a toxicity risk."

Hector stopped, leveled a stare at Chris. "He didn't know what toxicity meant. And neither did you two years ago, probably. Stop throwing your knowledge around. People are really sick."

Chris just looked at him, openmouthed, but said nothing. Hector stared him down for a second, then, with a quiet new sense of authority, continued to push forward, glancing back once to see if Chris was following him. Which he was.

The meeting was called to order. Various committee leaders gave reports, questions were taken, motions to vote were made, votes were cast, actions and new committees were elected into being. Esther Hurwitz went on a long tangent about identity and marginalization until someone in the crowd, breaking the rules of order, shouted, "Wrap it up!" Hector and Chris stepped up to the mic to present.

"This is the data committee's report on the experimental drug ddI," Hector began. These public presentations had helped him get over his shyness; the sense of usefulness he felt taking these arcane lab-bench and FDA-backroom goings-on and putting them into simple, blunt language for the people who needed the information most took him out of his self-consciousness and had brought him a new poise, a maturity, he felt. "This drug—"

"*Hector Villanueva, you're fucking hot!*" It was some queen way in the back of the crowded room. Hector felt his face go crimson, smiled. The room broke into hysterics and wild screams. "*It's true!*" and "*I second that!*" came from other points in the room. Hector caught Ricky in the crowd, smiling and shaking his head with mock resignation.

Hector took a breath and continued: "This drug looks like it will probably be the first drug approved by the FDA to fight HIV since AZT in 1987." Boos and hisses. "I know, I know," he said. "AZT is a fucking fortune and it hasn't panned out the way we hoped. But there's a lot of hope that when ddI is combined with AZT, that'll be the punch the virus needs to—"

There was a stir in the back of the room. "Ava Heyman, Health Department, AIDS killer!" someone shouted. People in the crowd pulled back. There was Ava, his old boss, her graying hair pulled back in a ponytail, her work glasses low on her nose, her groaning black leather workbag slung over her shoulder. She stood alone. Hector watched her from the dais, mesmerized.

"I'm not an AIDS killer," she said in her loud Queens honk, a touch of her trademark disgust in her voice. "I'm here to listen. And help."

"You guys at Health have done bullshit for eight years," someone shouted. It was Ithke Larcy, the housing activist.

"Ithke, you know that's not true," Ava shot back. "I'm not going to let you grandstand in front of a crowd. You and Karl were in last week and we mapped out a plan for subsidized housing units for HIV/AIDS-affecteds, and you know it's under way."

"AIDS-affecteds!" spat Ithke, the locks on his head shaking with righteous rage. "Listen to how you talk. We're people."

Ava flung her hands in the air. "Oh, come on, Ithke, gimme a chance here!"

Chaos was erupting in the back, and Hector noticed a few folks advance toward Ava. "People, hold up!" he found himself booming into the mic. "Hold up!" The crowd quieted, turned back toward him, curious. Some knew, some didn't, that he'd worked for Ava. Many relied on him to be a conduit to her, to Health. And here she was.

"I know Dr. Heyman," he told the crowd. "I worked with her at the Health Department for seven years." Everyone stared up at him, eyebrows raised, as though to ask, *And?*

"I knew she'd be here tonight," he continued. "And believe me, if someone leaves work at the bureaucracy of the DOH and comes to one of these meetings, it's because they want to help. So let's build allies where we can use them and give Dr. Heyman a chance to listen in tonight and see what we do, and see what she can do for us." He paused. "And please step back from Dr. Heyman."

Those aggressive combatants who'd stepped toward her backed away. The room was unusually silent. Across it, Hector and Ava locked eyes. Then an enormous, satirical smile broke across Ava's face.

"Thank you, Hector," she called out. "You always were chivalrous."

Most of the room laughed. Ava felt her jaw and shoulders slacken. *There*, she thought. The worst was over. Her psych meds made her sweat, and she hoped the sweat under her blouse wasn't spotting through the back. She put her heavy bag on the floor. Ithke and Karl came over to her, hugged and kissed her. It was amazing how these guys could turn on a dime on you like that! she thought. They were like hurt, impulsive little boys. What were they like to their mothers? What were their mothers like to them?

She focused on what Hector had resumed saying: "So, yes, ddI . . ." How the clinical trials for ddI were so rigid, so exclusionary—God, Hector explained this heavy stuff to a lay audience so well, so clearly, no bullshit!—that nobody who really needed the drug could get in the trial. So, as activists, they'd forced the FDA and the drugmaker into meetings with them where they'd come up with a novel concept called parallel tracking: the drug company would fill its classic trial as best it could with patients who met the strict criteria, but it would also give the drug in a parallel-track trial to whoever needed it and met only minimal basic criteria. The whole thing would start in a few weeks.

Ava nudged Ithke. "It's amazing they pulled that off," she said. "That kind of model at FDA is unheard of."

Ithke smirked. "Little by little, you're all learning not to shut us out," he said.

So cocky! These boys . . . really! She could only smile back at him in the half-charmed, half-reproving way a mother might to her bratty son. Was Ithke HIV-positive? she wondered. Who around her was? A few looked sick, but most looked great—sexy, young, lithe. She felt like she was at a gay disco but with slogan T-shirts and sign-up boards instead of throbbing music. She thought about pills. All the fucking pills she'd had to take the past several years—the exhausting, rotating mix of pills and their weird, sweaty, enervating, weight-gaining, narcolepsy-inducing, strange-tics-and-sparks-in-the-brain-provoking side effects—the constant titrating up and down, the mind-numbing trips to her autocratic psychopharmacologist, all the tinkering and tweaking, constantly trying to get to that point where you felt balanced and minimally stable but not like a walled-off zombie. The mood swings and the pills had made her not only a public-health official, but a patient, conferring on her an empathy for sick people she hadn't particularly asked for and still half resented.

So many pills for her to choose from, and so hard to know how to use them. Whereas these guys—hardly any pills at all. The only real pill, AZT, so nasty and toxic. She'd probably never die of her disease as long as she stayed on her funky pharmaceutical soup. But who here would live? What if she knew that Milly might decline and die in the next five years? The thought gave her a wave of stomach sickness. What did the mothers of these boys think, feel? Did they even know their kids were gay? And Hector. Did he have it? She could never bring herself to ask him, not even in his final year at DOH when, for the first time, the edges of his anger and disgust started showing, more and more, in meetings and random conversations for the first time since he showed up as her shy intern in 1981.

Ithke and Karl left her side now to present on housing issues. Hector stepped down from the dais, was working his way through the crowd to her. Before he reached her, a woman with wire-framed glasses, in a pair of overalls and massive black boots, approached her.

"I'm Esther Hurwitz," the woman announced. "I'm an activist and a writer. I chronicle the death toll. And I'd like to ask you: With how little you've done in this plague, can you live with yourself as a woman and a Jew?"

Ava's eyes grew wide. Then she laughed, incredulous. "I can live with myself as a woman and a Jew just fine," she said. "How about you?

And another thing: Is that really how you think you make allies with the health establishment in an epidemic?" she asked.

"You've hardly been an ally," Esther shot back. "You've been useless."

Hector joined them. Ava turned to him. "Who is this woman? She just accosted me."

Hector, baffled, said nothing. Ava glanced at him again. She missed him so much! She was . . . she found the word: she was *proud* of him.

"Esther, she's on our side," Hector finally said to Esther. "Honestly."

Esther eyed Ava for several seconds behind her glasses. "None of you guys," she finally said, "have done much to make us believe that."

Something in her tone softened Ava up. She was moved to see how many women—lesbians mostly, it seemed—were here tonight, when the women easily could've said this was the boys' problem, not gotten involved. "That's why I'm here tonight, honey," she said.

Esther folded her arms over her chest and frowned. "We'll see, then," she said. "*Honey.*" She turned and walked away.

Ava turned to Hector. "Tough fucking crowd," she said.

"You don't even know the half," he said. He led Ava out of the main room toward the foyer, which was quiet. They sat down on a bench. "I saw your daughter tonight."

"Milly?"

"She's working across the street from our apartment."

Ava cocked her head quizzically. "Oh my goodness, that's right. At a café, right?"

Hector couldn't help a smile. Poor Milly. Ava'd never exactly been the most attentive mother—she'd had the city's health to think about. "At a boutique," he said. "Reminiscence."

"Oh, of course, I knew that. Isn't she a beautiful girl?"

"She is," Hector agreed.

"I'm proud of her," Ava murmured absently.

They fell into silence. They could hear shouts and scattered applause in the great hall, but they were alone for the moment in the foyer. Their eyes met; they both smiled awkwardly. Ava took Hector's large hand in hers for a moment, moved it to her lap, set it back on his own. "You're a grant recipient!" she joked.

He shrugged. "That's me."

More silence. "Are you all right, Hector?" she finally mustered the nerve to ask him.

He looked at her, shrugged again. "I am," he said. "At least I was as of February, the last test. And I haven't been with anyone but Ricky since."

"What about Ricky?"

Hector pursed his lips. "This is between us, right?"

"Of course."

"I think he might be. Swollen lymphs and a long cold this winter. I want him to get tested but he won't. He's afraid."

Ava said nothing for a while. Finally, she turned on the bench and said to him, in a deadly serious whisper, as though she was afraid someone might hear, because she was: "I care about you and I want to apologize to you. I didn't do enough when this emerged. None of us did. Because of who it affected, and we didn't want to get our hands dirty with it. We kept putting it off. Everyone has."

Hector laughed a bitter, soft laugh. "You think I don't know that? You think that any of us don't know that? Ava, why do you think we're here, showing up at your offices with the *New York Times* on our tail, trying to embarrass you? This is what you pushed us to." His hands were clenching as he spoke—oh, he hated showing his anger! "I would much rather be fighting this fight from inside Health, with my fucking colleagues."

"You know I spoke up for this, Hector," she said. "With Steve. With Ed!"

"Ava, you know that fucking closeted queen of a mayor hasn't done enough. And neither have you."

Had he just said that square into the face of his boss of seven years? Apparently. A moment later, guilt stabbed him. For seven years he'd watched her drag herself to work, sometimes sweaty, sometime bloated, walking through the haze of new meds, new med combos. She had virtually bolted her mind down with meds to show up for work, for her daughter's high-school years, so she'd never humiliate her husband and daughter again. Through it all, she'd missed only two weeks of work, for a hospitalization upstate in '87, a kind of support camp to come to grips with her illness and, together with others in the same situation, learn to live with it. The deep lines in her forehead and around her eyes and jaw, at not even fifty, traced every sweaty, depressed, off-the-beam year of her past decade. Her hair was salt-and-pepper now, frizzy, pulled back in a plastic clip; she didn't care much about being stylish and sexy anymore. She'd lost something and she had that dark nimbus, embodied by her ridiculously heavy old black workbag, to prove it.

She met his level gaze. "You know a massive corps of new case-workers are coming on in a few weeks at DAS." She meant the city's Department of AIDS Services, which, the past three years, had done an anemic job at best of coordinating services in the city. "I'll tell you this confidentially right now. In a few days, Steve's announcing me as DAS point person for Health. And I am going to ride that agency like you've never seen."

Hector smiled and laughed. "I'd like to see that!"

She laughed in turn. "Ride them into the ground! And if, in three months, I'm not getting what I want—what we want"—and she gestured back at the great room—"I am cutting loose and going maverick like you. So, in other words, I have nothing to lose at this point. I stopped wanting to be the first female chief at Health about two years ago, so—so fuck it."

Hector studied her. "You know that all the information you just gave me, I now hold over your head."

She shrugged slightly, as though to say, *So?*

"And you know that, as much as I like you, if I need to, I won't fail to put it out there."

"Why the fuck do you think I told you?" she rasped. "You're going to hold me to account. You and I are going to be in close, close touch in the coming months, my friend."

If I give you my trust and you let me down, I'll kill you, he wanted to tell her. But he thought better of that. *It's good to be working with you again,*

Ava, he was going to say. But the corner of his eye caught a woman—a short Latina with her hair pulled back in a scrunchie had wandered into the foyer in acid-washed shorts and a baggy T-shirt, looking terrified. Ava, noting Hector's attention break, caught the woman, too.

"You need something?" Hector called.

The woman turned, seeming scared to have been spotted. She said something and choked on it.

"What did you say?" Hector asked. He felt his face and his voice softening, trying to calm the woman. That seemed to work. The woman walked straight over to him and Ava. "Is this the AIDS meeting?" she asked in a half whisper, as though invisible passersby might hear her.

"It is. *Las activistas*," he said with a laugh and a little bit of a gay flourish, something he had modestly refined in the past few years, though not very convincingly. He just never would be one of those flourish-y gays, like Ricky. "You wanna join? We need Latinas."

The woman bowed her head. It seemed like her face was twisting into some kind of embarrassed smile. But—no! She started crying. "I'm gonna die," she sobbed. "I'm think I'm gonna die soon."

Hector and Ava looked at each other, parted on the bench to make room for the woman, who didn't look much older than thirty. The woman put her head in her hands and continued crying and saying, uncontrollably, *"I'm gonna die."*

"Shh, it's okay," said Ava, putting her arm around the woman. "Why are you saying that? Because you're HIV-positive?"

The woman nodded. Still crying, she said, "I have a hundred and thirty T cells. I don't ever feel good any more. I have problems with my periods. They're not normal anymore."

Hector and Ava exchanged another look. *"Chica,"* Hector told the girl, "a hundred and thirty T cells is a lot. Why do you think you're gonna die any time soon? There's meds and treatment for you."

"They didn't help my friend," she said, coming up from her tears for air, with what seemed like a bit of fighting spirit breaking through. "He took AZT and it just made him sick and he died anyway, in February."

"Oh, honey, I'm sorry," Ava said.

But Hector was connecting dots in his head. Of course. Tavi Peña. That crazy, cackling queen he'd worked with at GMHC. But Tavi, once he found out he was positive, as he got sick, didn't want to come here, didn't want to fight. He retreated back to Queens, to his family, which, thank God, loved him and took him in and nursed him. Hector had been to the funeral, to the memorial service in Jackson Heights, with its Spanish drag performances. But he hadn't seen this sweet *chica* there. And then he remembered, now, that night at Paradise Garage so long ago, when this woman—a girl then!—and Tavi were so messed up. It was the night he met Ricky!

"You mean Tavi, right?" Hector said to the girl.

She snorted back tears. "Oh my God," she said. "You knew Tavi?"

"Yeah. And don't you remember that night I met you with Tavi at the Paradise Garage? Like, five, six years ago?"

The girl looked blank for a minute. Then, locking on to a new depth in his eyes, her face colored. Her hand flew to her mouth. "Oh my God," she said. "Oh my God. That night."

"Yes." He laughed. "That night!" He put his hand in hers. She just hid her face behind her hand and laughed quietly, mortified.

"I guess I had to be there," Ava said.

"Oh, no, you didn't!" the girl said. "No, no, no."

"Well, okay, whatever," Ava murmured. "No, no, no. Well, anyway, stick with this one"—she nodded at Hector—"and you'll be okay."

"I've known for a year now," the girl said, "and I can't tell my family. My father and brother will kill me."

"Why don't you just come back into the meeting with me?" Hector said. "You don't have to figure everything out at once. What's your name again? I'm Hector."

"It's Issy. From Ysabel. But just Issy is fine. I need advice. This doctor wants me to take AZT but I'm scared to take it after what happened to Tavi. He was so sick from it and it barely even helped him."

Hector stood up, lifted Issy up gently under her arm. "Come into the meeting."

Ava rose. "I'm gonna get home." She kissed Hector on the cheek. "Let's talk tomorrow. I'll have more intel for you on the caseworkers."

"Thank you for coming," Hector told her.

"Don't thank me, that's insulting." Ava turned to Issy. "Stick with him," she said again, nodding to Hector. Ava put her hand on the girl's arm. *You'll be okay*, she was about to say. But how could she really say that?

She walked out of the building into the sweet June night. Absently, her thoughts still at the meeting, she wandered into a bodega and bought a pack of gum. Gum had become a kind of soothing cud for her through all these years of medication-related misery. She stepped back outside, pulled out a stick of gum, and walked. After a few blocks, she came upon a black woman wearing flip-flops, jean shorts, and a filthy-looking old Rick James concert T-shirt, sitting on a cardboard box. The woman's face was emaciated—she looked like Munch's *The Scream*.

"You got a cigarette?" the woman asked her in a hoarse voice.

Ava's jaw dropped. *You're sick, you shouldn't be smoking*, she was about to say. "I don't smoke" was all she said, though.

"Well, can I have a piece of gum then?"

Ava handed a stick to the woman who, rather than unwrapping it and putting it in her mouth, tucked it away jealously in her pocket.

"Do you have any place to live?" Ava finally asked the woman, swallowing a fear she was being rude. She was always torn between her everyday New Yorker's instinct to ignore street people and her health worker's instinct to get real information about how city systems were working.

But the woman didn't seem perturbed. "I don't wanna live in no shelter," she said. "I won't move somewhere unless I have my own room."

Ava took twenty dollars out of her bag and gave it to the woman. "Can you buy some food with that?"

"Ain't you scared I'm gonna spend it on crack?" the woman asked gleefully. "Because I might!"

Ava couldn't help but laugh with the woman. "It's your choice, but I really hope you buy some food with it."

The woman shrugged noncommittally. "Well, thank you," she finally said. "That's mighty kind of you."

Ava smiled wanly and moved on. She knew that by going to the meeting tonight, by giving Hector that information, she'd made herself vulnerable, and that made her feel . . . free. Her own illness had enraged her. To her psychopharmacologist, to her doctors, she was a puzzle to be resolved. They had no idea of the terror she experienced taking the subway. Would she lash out at someone against her will? Or of the hell of the crash from mania, or the fear of the crash, which was almost as bad. The inner landscape of sickness was wild, roiling, and her doctors were so dry, so cold! She didn't want to be that way.

Finally, at Union Square, she got in a cab going uptown. Idly, she watched pedestrians—and, good Lord, there was Milly, her own daughter, walking side by side with a tall, honey-haired boy. What was she doing in those saggy, fringy hippie clothes? Ava twisted around in her seat to watch them until they were out of sight. The sensation was peculiar—Milly had been home for the summer for a few weeks, but this was as though Ava was really seeing her for the first time in years. That's because, though Ava could not articulate this, guilt had forced her to think of Milly, and even look at Milly, as little as possible. Ava knew too well that her own illness had eclipsed Milly's growing up.

But—Milly had turned out okay, right? Graduated with all sorts of honors from high school and brought home a fine transcript from her first year of college. She was going to be an artist! Certainly the Heymans, having scratched their way from Russian peasant stock up into the New York professional classes, had never had an artist among their ranks before. That was cause for pride. And Ava was proud of Milly. But Milly also had two qualities Ava was jealous of. One was beauty. Ava had been sexy, but her looks had been muddled, a bit Streisand cross-eyed, whereas Ava's best features had harmonized with Sam's in Milly, who had almost Disneyish brown eyes, a delicate nose, and loose dark curls.

The other quality, part of which probably came out of the beauty, was quietude. Milly was quiet. Ava was not. Ava was loud and showboaty and got what she needed, or sometimes didn't get what she needed, because of it. But Milly was so delicate, amused, wry! Milly had always been this way, Ava thought. It had to be the gentle, loose-curled influence of Sam, who was also quiet, forbearing. Milly's beauty and quietude made her almost unbearable to her mother, a thought so awful that Ava wasn't even fully aware of it.

The cab drove on, dropped her in front of her brownstone. Inside, she found Sam in front of the TV, watching the videotaped *MacNeil/Lehrer NewsHour*, his tie cast aside and his black-stockinged feet up on the coffee table. She dropped her bag on the floor, kicked off her low heels, and collapsed alongside him on the couch.

"Can I beg you for a foot rub, handsome man?" she asked.

Sam lifted her left foot in his hands and kissed it before setting to work on it. "You're back later than usual tonight," he noted. He'd had to stop running because of a knee problem and he'd gained fifteen pounds in the ensuing two years, but Ava found his new thickness comforting, if not exactly arousing, to the limited extent she cared about being aroused anymore.

"I went and met with the AIDS activists," she said, then groaned in pleasure from the massage, her head falling back on a pillow.

"And how was that?"

"They reamed me. But I had it coming."

Sam laughed gently. "You can take it. You're a tough lady."

She lifted her head, looked at him. "Too tough?" she asked. "Not a good person? Not a good mother?"

Sam blinked, taken aback. "Where's this coming from?"

"I was coming uptown in the cab tonight and I saw Emmy on the street, walking with a boy. It was such a strange feeling. She looked so—" Ava paused, grasping for the word. "Foreign. To me. Like I hadn't seen her in years. And suddenly I wondered—" Ava began to cry, feeling as though the entire evening was catching up to her. She swiveled on the couch and crawled into Sam's chest. "I don't know, Sam, I just got a really bad feeling and I wondered, have I—"

Sam shushed her, stroking her hair. "No, you have not," he said firmly. "No, you have not." *She had*, he thought, but he would never tell her so. What would be the point of that?

"You okay?" Jared asked Milly.

She looked up at him, put her hand in his large hand, flecked on the back with red hair. "I'm okay, just hot. Do you want to have a drink?"

They walked to the Blue and Gold on East Seventh Street. Friends of Jared's from high school, Asa and Jeremy, were inside, and they fed the jukebox and drank pitchers for the next several hours, listening to Fleetwood Mac and Steve Miller. Milly got drunk and felt happy and carefree for the first time in over a week. There was a long, messy conversation about George Bush and what a dickwad he was, and about how sad it was that Barbara Bush couldn't just come out and say she was pro-choice. Around three o'clock, Milly and Jared parted in front of the bar from Asa and Jeremy, and Jared asked Milly to come to his place at the Christodora, which his dad had bought just the year before—at the bargain-basement price of $90,000, Jared noted proudly.

Milly said yes, and as they approached the entrance of the very plain, handsome, and boxy brick building that towered over Tompkins Square Park, Milly looked up at the bizarre bit of frieze work over the door, which featured eerie winged creatures, and asked, "What does Christodora mean?"

"I dunno," Jared says. "It reminds me of Stella D'oro cookies. This building used to be, like, a settlement house in the Depression. Can you believe the city bought the whole building in the seventies for, like, fifty thousand dollars? That's what a shithole it was."

"The name reminds me of a Rossetti poem or a pre-Raphaelite painting," Milly said.

Upstairs, in a dark, high-ceilinged apartment littered with dirty clothes, secondhand furniture, and art supplies, Jared pulled out pot and a pipe, then put Sinead O'Connor on his CD player.

He drew on the pipe, then held it out to Milly. "You wanna?" he asked.

Milly frowned. "I probably shouldn't," she said. She'd had some bad, paranoid experiences with pot the past few years. But then again, that was in groups of six, seven.

"Just have a hit."

"Will you light it for me?" she asked.

He did, the two of them standing face to face in the middle of the dark living room. Milly felt the rush of stonedness overcome her, the confusion, the heightened sense of Jared's body against her own. What was she doing? Jared took another hit off the pipe and put it down. The room suddenly seemed enormous, and scary, to Milly. She suffered that unfortunate effect of pot, of suddenly doubting whether she really knew whom she was with, even though she'd known Jared since she was eleven.

"Can we light candles?" Milly asked.

Jared darted away, rummaged in the kitchen, came back with about half a dozen candles and holders, lit them all. Now the room danced with shadows—theirs and that of the boxy, tweed-covered sofas and chairs. Jared came back to her and took her in his arms, pulled her hair back, tied it loosely behind her head, drew her by her nape toward his lips.

"Do you have any idea how beautiful I think you are since we were in ninth grade?"

She laughed. "That sentence came out pretty ungrammatical," she said. She was overcome with lust, pulled Jared's T-shirt over his head, pressed her face into the amber-colored fur on his flat chest.

"You're so beautiful," she said, as Jared pulled the bandanna out of her hair, which he ran his hands through, then slowly lifted her batik sleeveless jersey off her chest, her arms rising in the air. He unlatched her bra in the back, then, as she stood there with her arms out, crouched down and kissed her nipples all over until they rose.

He looked up at her, his hair wild where she'd run her hands through it. He smiled.

"I love your little crooked tooth," she said.

"I was going to get it fixed, but now I won't," he said. Gently, he put her at arm's length. "Get naked in front of me."

She smiled. In her stonedness, Jared was both Jared and not-Jared; he was also some hot frat creep she didn't know who scared her a little bit, and she liked this duality. She stepped out of her huaraches, out of her skirt. They both lost their smiles and stared at each other flatly. She pulled off her panties in front of him until she was naked.

Now he smiled again. "Fuck," he said.

"Now you go," she said.

He pulled off each dirty Chuck Taylor low-top with the toes of his other foot. He was sockless and Milly could smell the faint, sour smell of his large, sweaty feet, his toes flecked with light brown hair. He unbuttoned his Levi's and stepped out of them, his erection tent-poling his light, paisley-patterned boxer shorts.

She laughed a little bit, raising her eyebrows. "Wowza," she said. "Are you gonna show me the goods?"

He cocked an eyebrow. "It's big, right?" he asked, without a hint of humor.

Milly laughed. "It looks that way. I'm a little afraid. Can I see it?"

Jared blushed, but he was clearly so proud. He pulled it out of his boxers. It was sizable and stood there, bobbing, pointed at her like a greedy weapon. Her mouth fell open; she was amazed, but also a bit scared.

"I'm sorry," he said. "I know it's huge."

She laughed. "Don't be too self-deprecating or anything!"

Jared just shrugged. The chorus of the song came up. *Nothing compares to you*, she sang to him, then cracked up.

His face lit up. "Millicent Heyman," he said slowly. He stepped in toward her, sang, *All the flowers that you planted, Mama, in the backyard.* He knelt down, put his arms around her waist, brought her down to the shag rug with him. He reached up, pulled a rough shantung roll pillow off the couch, put it behind her head. He sank below her again, his hands up over her breasts, lying on his stomach.

"Oh my God," gasped Milly when she felt his tongue inside her. "I'm new to this rodeo."

He looked up at her, his mouth glistening. "Really? A cunnilingus virgin?"

She giggled and nodded.

"I've been jerking off to this thought for about a year," he said.

"Oh my God!" she gasped again. She was horrified and delighted. "You really had to share that with me?"

He looked up again. "After all those art classes. Looking at your picture in the freshman directory."

"No, please tell me you haven't," she said. She arched her head back on the roll pillow and put her hands up to her face, but he pulled them down and held them. She lay there. Oh God. She was terrified, mesmerized. *Every arrow in the world is pointing right at me*, she thought. *It's like a white-hot spotlight. I don't deserve this much attention.* She writhed and moaned. It was almost as if Jared had disappeared in the dark and there was just a lapping demon on her. She felt almost unbearably uncomfortable having the world focused on her so completely like this.

She gripped his hands, choked out, "No, it's too much."

He gripped her hands back. "No, it's not."

She started crying.

He stopped and pulled up to her, head to head, brushing back her hair. "What?" he asked. "You don't like it?"

"It's too much." She couldn't believe she was crying. What a—what a wuss she was! "I don't deserve it." Now she was mortified. Had she really just said that? She wanted to die.

Jared laughed. "That's the issue? Did you like it?"

"I can't take that much pleasure. I'll go nuts on you."

His face lit up again. "I want you to. Such a good girl."

"You don't really know me," she told him. She was fully stoned now and had no idea what she was saying. "I can't lose control."

He sighed a bit. "I might know you more than you think," he said.

"No, you don't."

He ran a finger around her lips, over her nose. "People show themselves," he said.

This possibility truly dismayed her. Jared put one arm around Milly and moved the other one back down between her legs, which she'd absently left open.

"What do you want, Milly?" he asked her.

Why did he have to ask her that? But—she locked into the deepest center of his eyes, and in that random moment, she had the blessing of having her self-consciousness taken away, replaced by the full gratitude of feeling him naked against her in the big room with jumping shadows on the walls.

"Okay," she managed to say. "If you really want to know. I want us to fuck and to feel you inside of me and feel incredibly close to you." A fire truck blared by several stories below and threw crazy lights against the ceiling for a second.

Jared smiled, quite self-satisfied. "I can give you that," he said.

After that, it got better for Milly. She had lost her virginity that past year to a guy from Atlanta she'd dated for exactly seven weeks in the fall and she'd had her share of sex, but she'd never felt both so satisfyingly base and so safe as she did in this moment with Jared. The allure of his honey-fuzz-covered pale skin, that little bit of white softness right around the waist, the claylike flatness at the end of his nose. He was very close to entering her with his prize trophy when he reached over for his pants, pulled out his wallet, and took out a condom.

"Here," she said, sitting up and rolling it over him. In the time between his first entering her, with the gasps and fits and starts, and the thirty, thirty-five minutes when they simply didn't stop, her world spun over her. There was her senior year, that bizarre road trip with her dad when they'd visited Vassar and then visited her mom on the way back, that image of her mom—Milly and her dad entering a living room of zombielike people sitting in front of *Sally Jesse Raphael*, no Ava in sight, until a tight ball on the couch covered in a hospital-issue thermal sheet turned out to be her, out cold. Then the spittle around her mouth as she tried to talk once they'd woken her up. These were the images going through her head as Jared slowly moved in, their eyes locked, their lips grazing. It really didn't pay for her to get stoned before sex, she noted, feeling like her brain would burst as Jared's widest point approached.

"What is it?" He stopped, looked at her. "Where are you?"

"I'm here," she said. She pressed his hips down harder into her. The two guys that night, Hector and the blond, the kiss she'd caught on the street and how they'd caught her looking, how she'd darted away. What had she wanted to say to them? Jared was so deep inside her now, sweating in the air-conditionless, ceiling-fanned apartment.

"You're so fucking beautiful, Milly," he told her, just resting there, before the wildness really began, as she took huge breaths and adjusted. "I'm in love with you."

The words shook her from her roving images. "You don't know that yet," she said.

"I know it so well."

Thunder shook the apartment. In a second, rain was pounding on the window screens. She could hear it instantly pooling on the sills. "We have to close the windows," she said.

But Jared's smile was so wide! "No, we don't," he said. Then—and how did he do this?—staying deep inside, he twisted them both until he held her from behind, his lips on her shoulder blades. Milly stared deeply into the complicated rattan weave on the front of the stereo console, and, as Jared began to move, for the next several minutes she forgot about him and about all the moving images and she let the world focus on her, and she was finally comfortable with it.

The rain—and obviously it was a very warm rain—had already pooled so deeply off the curb that Issy was about to step into it in her sandal up to her ankle when Ricky, his bag of flyers already wet, went, "Whoa, girl!" and sort of lifted her from the waist so she missed the big puddle. They were leaving a diner where they'd gone to eat after the big meeting— her, Hector, this guy Ricky who was obviously his boyfriend, and a guy named Korie who really didn't look good.

She had stood alongside Hector throughout the rambunctious meeting, a bit overwhelmed and dazed but also strangely relieved and safe, and then when it adjourned, Hector—and she could tell that Hector was a big shot here—had introduced her to a bunch of women, some of them Latinas but most of them looking like *lesbianas*, and before she knew it she was on a committee to try to get the federal definition of AIDS expanded to include more symptoms that only women had. Like not getting your periods regularly! That had been happening to her! And after, Hector had said, "Come on, we're getting something to eat at Joe Jr. Come with us." So she had, sitting there with a bowl of tomato soup and a grilled cheese (Hector picked up the tab) while the guys talked mainly about a Chinese drug and whether you could take it for AIDS or not, because Korie wanted to know. Overall, Hector didn't think it was a good idea.

"I think you should wait and get into parallel tracking with ddI," he told Korie, who took a deep breath, as though he was digesting this new idea. Everyone had been talking about this new drug ddI at the meeting, Issy had noticed. Could this be the drug that was going to change everything? What if she lived? She sipped her soup and listened quietly to Hector and Korie go back and forth. There was a lot of new terminology she was learning tonight. Some folks had told her they didn't know jack shit about AIDS or science or the body or anything before they started coming to the meetings, and now, only a few months in, they could hold their own, read medical papers, follow a conversation. Maybe that would happen to her, too! She already had dental knowledge. (And, at her dental hygienist job, she suffered intense guilt that she had told no colleagues she was infected, as well as terror that someone might somehow find out and she'd be fired, or—worse—that she might somehow bleed into a patient's mouth and infect them.)

Ricky put his arm around her. She knew he was in his twenties, but he looked like he could be twelve with that little-boy face! "How's your soup 'n' sandwich, girl?" he asked her.

She laughed. "It's fine. I didn't eat much today before. I was nervous about coming to the meeting."

"Well, you came and you made a splash!" he said. She liked Ricky. He reminded her of when you were flipping TV channels and came across an old musical set on a farm or something, that kind of guy. All-American and smiley and wholesome, even though he had a punk haircut.

The boys were getting up now and talking about going to dance at a bar called Boy Bar. She didn't think she'd ever been there with Tavi—maybe it was new.

"What are you going to do now?" Ricky asked her.

She shrugged. "I guess I'm gonna take the subway back to Queens." God, it was so stressful living with her family, hiding this from them. What if she started looking like Korie? How would she hide it then?

"Come dance with us!" Ricky said.

She laughed. "Me? No, you guys go ahead."

Korie put his arm around her. "Oh, honey, please, if I can go for a while, so can you."

She looked up at Hector. "Come out with us for a while, *chica*," he said.

The place was basically a dark pit with loud music, like Paradise Garage had been. *Tavi*, she thought when she walked in, the music's throb hitting her. They were walking forward in a crowd of guys and she felt herself shuffling, her hand rising to her neck. Oh, she had pushed down these feelings about Tavi! Oh God, he had been like her brother, far more than her *real* brother. Well, maybe he was more like her sister. And she couldn't bring herself to tell him, in his final months when he was so sick, that she had the same thing. He'd died without knowing. She'd pushed down all this Tavi stuff for months now. She hadn't set foot in a club, heard this *thump-thump* music, since Tavi.

Hector spied her, put a hand on her neck. "You okay?" he shouted in her ear.

"I haven't been to a club since Tavi," she shouted back into his ear, on her tippy-toes.

He put his arm around her. "It's too much for you? I can walk you out."

She didn't share that she'd barely stepped into a club since that night five years ago, the night she was fairly certain she'd gotten the virus from that *moreno* in the back of the car. Four years later, she'd started having the private-area problems, catching colds that seemed never to go away, noticing her glands were always hard and swollen. The doctor she'd visited asked her if she had any reason to believe she might have HIV.

She didn't have to think back too hard. Literally from the week after the encounter with the *moreno*, she wondered if she'd done a stupid thing, especially as she read more and more about the disease. She'd insisted on a condom the two times she'd had sex with someone since.

"I had sex once with a bisexual guy," she told the doctor. "Without a condom."

The two weeks she waited for the test results, she stopped in a church every day to light a candle and pray she didn't have it. When the doctor called her back in and told her she did in fact have it, she felt an immediate disgust with herself for being so naive and trusting as to think God would have cut her a break. What a fool she was! She wasn't getting a thing she wanted out of life, the deck was stacked against her, and this was fate's last laugh at the sad, not-much life of Ysabel Mendes. That sense she'd long buried, that perhaps the world really wasn't a fair and good place, as dictated by the church, came rushing up in a hot, humiliating blaze in her throat.

"So I'm gonna get more sick and die?" she asked the doctor, tears welling in her eyes. And meanwhile, she calculated to herself, she'd be fired from her job and would have to endure the scorn and rejection of her family, the neighborhood. That would be fun. "How soon do I have?"

"Don't look at it that way," the doctor had said. "You're in decent health now. Your T cells are high. We'll monitor you and if they ever get really low, we can talk about AZT."

"What?"

"It's a drug for HIV."

"Does it cure it?"

"No, but it can keep it in check for a while. And other drugs will be coming down the pike. So meanwhile, eat well, don't drink or smoke, exercise, don't get too stressed. You'll be okay."

Taking out her anger at a cheap gym after work was Issy's concession to the doctor's advice. Otherwise, she suppressed the diagnosis, pushed it down inside her. If the doctor said she didn't have to worry about it, she wouldn't. And she wouldn't tell anyone, either. But life became very stressful and she found herself constantly short-tempered, or breaking out privately into tears. She felt as though she may as well be walking around wearing a sign that said I HAVE AIDS. She feared that if her brother ever found out that she knew all along she had the virus after she'd held and played with her little niece, he'd turn on her in a rage, hit her.

Then, a few months before, she started noticing in the papers and on the news that there was this group, mostly gay guys, who were out there blocking traffic and getting arrested, demanding that the city and the country do more to stop the disease. She followed them with a secret thrill. They weren't afraid if anyone thought they had the disease or not—they were all over the papers. It had all led to her creeping to the meeting tonight, and to a feeling of colossal relief.

So now, the music stealing up into her feet, she let herself collapse in Hector's arm a bit. "No, I'm okay," she told Hector. "I wanna dance a little!"

"Yeah, I know, girl, we haven't danced together in a while."

"Oh my God, shut up!" She slapped his arm, mortified but smiling. He tossed back his head and let out a deep, satisfied laugh. Suddenly she realized he'd lost those nerdy, chunky glasses he'd had the night he met her. That's why he seemed sexier and looser. That, she figured, and his new muscles. And maybe because he was so popular in this activist crowd.

"Come on, *chica*," he said.

They got beers and went downstairs, which was packed and sweaty. A huge drag queen with oversize false eyelashes and a blond cotton-candy wig sailed through the crowd like a cruise ship, kissing hello left and right. "That's the Lady Bunny," Ricky shouted into her ear. "She's a southern girl."

Issy nodded *Ohhh*. The music got her excited and she jacked her body along with the boys. Except for her periods, she wasn't sick yet—she felt fine! She started to let herself think that maybe everything would turn out okay.

Then she noticed frail Korie standing by the bar, alone, with his beer, sort of staring into space. But Hector and Ricky were with her. They watched her jack her body, went, "Work, girl!" They were bumping and grinding on either side of her, pressing her in the middle. "Wooooh!" she went. She felt better, and she didn't see, nor could she hear them over the music, when Ricky pressed a little pastel smiley-faced pill into Hector's hand.

Hector glanced down at it. "Where'd you get that?" he shouted in Ricky's ear.

"Korie gave them to me," Ricky said.

"Korie? He shouldn't be doing this shit."

"That's why he gave them to me."

Hector frowned. "I have a lot of work and meetings tomorrow."

"One pill's only gonna last you a few hours," Ricky said. "You'll be fine. It's only ten thirty."

"I suppose you already took yours."

Ricky grinned a Cheshire cat grin. But Hector felt a rage rising. "You don't fucking care about yourself, Ricky! You make me so fucking mad."

Ricky grabbed his arm. "Don't go there tonight. Let's have fun with this poor girl."

"Don't you dare fucking give her an X."

Ricky looked offended. "Do you think I would?"

They just stared at each other for a second, mechanically dancing in place. Finally Hector shook his head and popped the pill in his mouth, washing it down with a swig of beer. "Ooh, bad boy," Ricky gibed him.

"You just don't care," Hector said again.

Ricky shrugged. "You care too much," he said, but said it smiling, then thrust his tongue in Hector's mouth before Hector could respond. *We always hang in a buffalo stance, we do the dive every time we dance*, went the song now. Hector could feel Ricky's powers of assitude begin to exert themselves over him now, and when he finally pulled away from the kiss, he saw the new girl, Issy, slipping away through the crowd, which now included about three dozen people from the meeting. Where was she going? He resigned himself to wait for the X to kick in, danced—something he'd "taught" himself to do in the intervening years, how to move his body. They should feel good about themselves, about parallel tracking, he told himself, watching Ricky bump it with Micki, the magenta-haired dyke. Ricky was in really good spirits now, Hector knew, because Ricky loved X'ing and dancing all night, even if it was a Monday night with Ivana's roots to do in the morning.

Data suggested that AZT plus ddI would squelch the pathogen, Hector reminded himself. Things were probably going to change in the rest of 1989: symptoms and mortalities were going to plunge. Then bang! That moment when the X kicked in and the world popped to life in Day-Glo colors. That feverish wave of horniness and joy.

"Can you feel it?" Ricky asked, in his arms. And now, oh God, the Shep Pettibone remix of the song of the summer: *When you call my name, it's like a little prayer. I'm down on my knees, I wanna take you there.* The room screamed and collapsed into the pounding beats. Hector followed suit with some of his more extroverted buddies from the meeting and pulled off his T-shirt, stuck it in the band of his jean shorts. Ricky's ass was in his hands, Ricky's tongue in his mouth—Ricky was here, Ricky was here, it was summertime, Madonna was on their side, parallel tracking was coming. Everything was going to be okay.

PART II

THE LEFT COAST
1992–2012

NINE

SILVER LAKE

(2012)

Should she walk to the AA meeting or jump in the Prius? After nearly twenty years in L.A., Drew still believed in the goodness of walking places. Like all New Yorkers who move to L.A., even those like her who'd lived in New York but briefly, she clung to her New York identity. It didn't matter if life in L.A., frankly, was sweeter, milder, easier, prettier. Being a New Yorker was cooler, partly because it was such a pain in the ass to live there. So walking Lewy—her drooling English bulldog—around Silver Lake while she did errands and such was one of the ways Drew held on to that New York period of her life, when she was a messy, lost party girl booty-grinding to Mary J. Blige on a coffee table at somebody's after-hours party.

Of course, nearly twenty years after the fact, Drew felt she could finally afford to set aside the tragedy of her life back then just a bit and allow herself some nostalgia for the sassy New York girl she'd been, despite her messiness. And when she allowed this, she pictured herself walking: her hair, with not a strand of midforties gray, pulled back from her forehead with one cute barrette; wearing some kind of black eyelet minidress and chunky platform boots, a duffel coat if it was cold; walking at a breakneck clip in the morning, her breath exploding before her eyes as she exhaled her Camel, which had deep red marks on it from her Mac lipstick.

So she walked to the AA meeting. She was supposed to meet Mateo there. A few hours before, when she was writing in her study, after Christian had left for the studio for a long day and night of editing, Mateo had called through the door.

"I'm going to Intelligentsia to do some sketching, okay? I'll meet you at the meeting later."

Intelligentsia was a coffeehouse down on Sunset where Mateo had a part-time job. When he'd said he was going to see if he could get work there, Drew's first instinct had been to tell Mateo to wait, that she could call a friend who owned another coffeehouse that might be easier. But then she checked herself. Mateo was taking responsibility for himself, trying to make his own decisions. That was good.

"Okay, hon," she called. "I'll see you at three."

She'd heard the door close. Then she made more coffee and wrote for two hours. She was writing a fairly simple piece, actually. She was preparing for the release of her fourth book, *Couples*, her account of having lived for a week each with six different couples around the United States, including two blue-collar black lesbians in Inglewood, white teen parents of two toddlers in a trailer in West Virginia, and an affluent Christian husband and wife in an open relationship in Overland Park, Kansas. Each one of these weeklong trips had been a very intense, bizarre experience, plunging her headlong into the intimate terrain of another couple's existence, and every time she returned to L.A., when Christian would pick her up at the airport, she would take his face in her hands and smother him with kisses and say, "Just talk to me, talk to me."

"What do you want me to say?" he would reply, and laugh.

"Anything, I just want to hear your accent. I missed it so much."

Christian would take a theatrical breath. "Whether I shall turn out to be the hero of my own life," he began in an especially stupid, plummy version of his own English accent, "or whether that station will be held by anybody else, these pages must show. How about that?"

"I love you, I love you, I love you," Drew would say, tearing her hands through the floppy hair she adored, and then they'd go home and have sex in the living room and lie on the floor with the dog listening to Arcade Fire, and Drew would sigh on Christian's pale chest and say, "I am so grateful to be back in my own life."

"It's very odd how you go and live in somebody else's life for a week," Christian would remark. And Drew would nod and say, slowly, *"Mm-hmm."* But this was how Drew had ended up making a living. After *Learning to Breathe*, about her drug addiction and getting sober, became a reasonable success in 1994, she realized that she didn't have enough life experience beyond the timeline of the book to really write another memoir, but also that she had no idea what to write a novel about. And at the time she was watching Hillary Clinton tank because of how she'd handled the health-care thing—even after all those men in Congress had stood up and applauded her because she seemed so smart!

The whole thing gave her an idea. It was called *When You Have the Ball: How Women Handle Power*. And Drew had politely reached out to a half-dozen powerful women around the world and asked if she could come spend time with them, and thus followed her second fairly successful book. Drew proved she was not only a talented memoirist but a journalist, too. Then came *Soft Power: How Men Are Changing*, sort of the same book, but with men. (Secretly, Drew didn't feel that men had really changed—the crunchy environmentalist leader she had spent time with was the biggest blowhard of all, she thought—but she hadn't come up with the title anyway—her editor's assistant had.) Books two and three had even been optioned by an emerging network for a sitcom that never happened, but at least Drew had made a nice extra chunk of change from the deal.

So all this had brought her to the latest book, and today she was banging out a sort of promo piece for it to run in *Cosmopolitan*. "The Secrets to Successful Couples: What I Learned." This is what Drew worked on for two hours, which, because she was an extremely efficient writer, she felt was far too long for such a puff piece. The gist of the piece was that successful couples communicated ruthlessly and constantly allowed each other, and the contours of the relationship, to change and grow.

Trying to live by her research, she'd even suggested to Christian that they devote Tuesday nights to having a "ruthlessly honest" conversation about their relationship. He'd sighingly agreed to that, and they'd even dutifully done as much for a few weeks—but Drew had to admit privately that she was relieved upon realizing later that an entire month had passed and they'd both forgotten about the rather tiresome pact.

So that was that for the afternoon. She could finally leave the house and get some fresh air. She put Lewy on a leash—you could bring your dog to this meeting as long as the dog didn't bark, pee, or poop inside, and Lewy had done the last only once, when Drew was almost certain he had had a stomach bug, but, smartly, Drew had some plastic bags in her purse so the cleanup wasn't so bad.

She got to the meeting, in the back room of an old café on the corner of Sunset, a few minutes early and chatted with the regular crowd. There was Boaz, a former daily pothead and children's TV producer whose wife was going through breast-cancer treatment; each time it seemed he was about to cry, he would sort of pull himself together, something Drew thought was very sexy and reassuring in a very traditionally male way, even though she never would have said that, because you were certainly allowed, even encouraged, to come here and cry, rail, swear, curse out the room, whatever it took to keep you from taking your out-of-control feelings out into your life and, God forbid, picking up alcohol or drugs. There was Justin—the broad-chested, ginger-bearded gay TV-commercial actor who was trying to get a stage musical about Susan B. Anthony off the ground with his husband, Doar, with whom he was raising two foster kids from Compton. Justin had no problem crying in the meetings and did so frequently. Drew loved Justin—they'd often go out for tacos together after meetings—but she always cringed just a little bit when he would raise his hand and say, in a sort of high, inquiring voice, "Justin, addict, alcoholic?" and then simply gulp for words and not say anything.

They all knew what was coming. Justin would softly, mournfully cry for up to sixty excruciating seconds—inevitably, whoever was sitting next to him would put an arm around him and stroke his back—before talking, and sometimes he wouldn't say more than, "It's just so hard, that's all. It's really hard today. But I'm grateful to be here. Thanks."

Drew sometimes wished he'd say more than that and give everyone something to work with. But then again, having gone to meetings for nearly twenty years now, she'd mostly learned to accept people on their own terms.

Well, probably except for Susannah. Beautiful, raven-haired Susannah reminded Drew of Milly if Milly, rather than being too awkward to make a self-sealed temple of her beauty, had simply run with it and lived in a bubble of navel-gazing self-regard. Susannah would say things like, "I mean, honestly, I don't think I'm *built* for this industry, I'm too *raw*, unfortunately I *feel* too much." But that rawness hadn't kept Susannah from being a super-successful writer of about every other original movie on Lifetime—she was writing the scripted TV-dreck equivalent of the real-life women's stories that Drew actually went and lived in a trailer park for a week to find. At least, Drew's sponsor pointed out to her, a fearless moral self-inventory had given Drew the self-awareness to realize that some of her dislike for Susannah was competitive, and, in knowing that she was driven by selfish fear, she could pray to a (nongendered, faceless, non-anthropomorphized) G-d of her understanding to remove that shortcoming from within her. And Drew had several years ago stopped wearing the ankh pendant that had so disconcerted Milly upon spying it, but Drew was still quite spiritual and spent her first twenty minutes upon waking in meditation, even though usually her focused inner mantra would stray off into to-do lists and various petty, nagging resentments, such as irritation at her gardener for leaving the sprinkler on in the middle of a summer drought.

Once at the meeting, Drew made herself a cup of tea in a Styrofoam cup and chatted with Boaz, who'd spent the morning in bed watching DVR'd episodes of *The View* and *Ellen* with his wife after they got back from chemo at City of Hope.

"I mean"—he shrugged—"it was a blessing that I just wrapped a show and I have that kind of time to spend with her when she's going through this."

Drew lightly put a hand on his arm. "Boaz," she said, "you know you'd find a way to be with her even if you were in production."

She'd mastered this gesture, the light touch on the arm, along with the remark that reminded people they were better than they thought they were. About three years into meetings, she'd realized what she had slowly, inadvertently become: the cool, good-looking, smartly self-knowing successful woman with a very good haircut who served as an example to smart, pretty young women who were coming into the meetings, with all their self-conscious hair-flicking, face-picking tics, because they'd messed up their lives just like Drew had, probably because of some terrible father relationship or a mother who subtly had always told them that they had to be pretty and speak in a high, questioning voice and put their own needs behind those of others and never, never show anger. Drew had sponsored dozens of girls like this. She even called them "my girls," and, because she had a formidable Jewish-mother streak (something she'd come to realize and embrace about herself in sobriety, which had led her to explore the more intellectual, dialectical side of Judaism), these girls were almost a salve as she realized that she and Christian probably would not have kids. They were—they could admit, laughingly—"just too selfish and devoted to Lewy," their bulldog, to take that on.

So Boaz kind of shrugged in that slightly inchoate, menschy way of his that she rather loved. "Yeah, I know," he said. "So where's the foster son?"

Drew laughed. "He's coming. He's down at Intelligentsia sketching a little, I think."

"He's gonna have ninety days clean soon, right?"

"On Tuesday!" Drew said brightly. "Forty-five days at Gooden and the rest with us."

"That's amazing you guys took that on," Boaz said.

Drew lowered her eyes. "It's my amends to his mother. I mean, I made my amends to her many years ago. It's my living amends."

"Where are his parents? New York?"

Drew nodded. "They're old New York friends of mine. They're artists. They are *such* New Yorkers. Both born and raised."

Boaz nodded slowly. "Maybe it was tough for him growing up with two artist parents, being one himself."

"They're working artists but they're not wildly successful." She paused. Was that mean to say? No, she decided, it was just true. "Actually, they fostered him when they were just—they were really young. Like twenty-six, twenty-seven. Just a few years after I left New York, actually."

"Seriously?"

Drew nodded. How stunned she'd been back in 1998 when Milly told her over the phone that, only three years after she and Jared had gotten back together, they were taking in this kid! "It's kind of a crazy story," she told Boaz. "He'd been in, basically, a boys' orphanage for a few years after his mother died. Of AIDS. And my friend's mother had standby guardianship of him and was keeping an eye on him, trying to find him a home."

"Holy shit." Boaz rubbed his jaw. "Holy shit."

"I know," Drew said. "And they formally adopted him a year later."

The meeting was being called to order and they took metal folding chairs alongside each other in one of the back rows near the door. Drew coaxed Lewy to lie under the empty chair to her right, putting a paper bib around his neck to catch his drool, and placed her bag on the chair to save it for Mateo.

"The shit people go through, right?" Boaz muttered.

She nodded and gave his hand a squeeze. The meeting started. The speaker was Julia, an insecure trust-fund kid from Seattle who fumblingly dabbled in filmmaking. Drew had heard her story twice in the past few months, and it irritated her when she realized she'd have to sit through it again, but she said a quick prayer that her Higher Power would help her hear something new and valuable this time, at least so the next twenty minutes weren't a total bust.

"I'm really, really nervous and unfocused right now," Julia began. *Really?* Drew thought. *After speaking twice already in two months?* Then she admonished herself. She was not being openhearted. And she realized, as she twisted her head back every time a latecomer came in behind her, it was because she was irritable and distracted that Mateo was not there yet. Seven minutes into the meeting. Thirteen minutes. The end of Julia's qualification, the round of applause, the passing of the basket for dollar donations to pay rent on the meeting room, the beginning of the individual hand-raising and identifying with Julia's story before going into one's own spiritual and practical challenges of the day.

"What's up with Mateo?" Boaz finally leaned over and asked her.

She looked sidelong at him darkly, folded her arms over her chest. "I dunno," she muttered.

Toward the end of the meeting, when he still hadn't arrived, Drew raised her hand and was called on. "I'm Drew, a grateful recovering alcoholic and cocaine addict," she said for what felt like the fifteen thousandth time.

"Hi, Drew," came the affectionate chorus.

"Thank you for your qualification, Julia. I've heard you a few times the past few months and every time I hear something new and feel like I know you a little bit better."

Julia smiled a genuine shy smile of gratitude, which made Drew happy she'd said what she just said.

"But I have to admit," Drew continued, "I was distracted all through this meeting because a newcomer, which a lot of you know—Mateo, who is sort of my godson from New York—was supposed to meet me here at this meeting and he never showed up, and I know damn well at this stage of his recovery, just a few weeks out of rehab, he has nowhere else he's supposed to be other than this meeting."

A round of knowing "mmphs" went through the room.

"So I'm nervous," Drew went on. "I'm thinking the worst, and maybe I'll be embarrassed when he walks in the door right now and hears me talking about him, and he was late because he ran into some AA-ers there and got caught up in a conversation and he doesn't know the right way yet of saying he has somewhere to be in twenty minutes. But as far as I'm concerned, when I was in early sobriety, the meeting always came first."

Another round of "mmphs."

"It still comes first," Drew pitched higher, buoyed by the support, "because you know what? If I don't put it first, I'll lose everything else. I'll lose my amazing husband, I'll lose the writing career I love, I'll lose my house in the hills, I'll lose my dog." Often she enumerated in meetings these things she'd lose; it was a comfort to her because it was her way of vocalizing vigilance, but also of subtly signaling to the newcomers how good they could have it if they stayed sober for nearly twenty years like she had.

"So, I'm sorry, I'm nervous," she continued. "But I have to tell myself that if, God forbid, he's relapsed, it's not my fault. I have to tell myself that even when, God forbid, I call his mother in New York and tell her I don't know where he is. Because I'd taken him in for a few weeks after rehab and given him this shot, thinking it might help him to live for a while with two sober people while he figures out how to live his first year in sobriety—because it's going to take time for him, because this kid blew up his chances at a great art school"—she glanced warily back toward the door to make sure Mateo didn't walk in amid her exegesis—"and drove his parents to the brink and lashed out at them hard. That's where this disease can take you. A brilliant kid with brilliant parents and all the shots in the world. I've seen this kid's work, and it is fucking brilliant. I mean, I wanted to introduce this kid to Deitch if he kept sober."

People were shaking their heads in accordance and dismay. "If he's disappeared, it's not my fault," she said, now actually a bit alarmed at the bite in her voice. "Because nobody can get you sober. You have to want it." God, she sounded like the hard-ass old program cranks that she always complained about! Boaz put his arm around her.

"Anyway, thanks for letting me pipe up, and I'm grateful to be here and grateful to be sober today, because it doesn't matter that I have almost twenty years sober. This is what I have. This is what matters. Today."

"Thanks, Drew," the room chorused. She sighed and sank back down in her seat. Others were called on, but she couldn't hear what they were saying; she found that she was stewing in fury. Surreptitiously she pulled out her iPhone and texted her sponsor: "Mateo didn't show up to meeting, I'm freaking out." Three minutes later, her sponsor texted back: "Relax, don't jump to conclusions." That's what she needed to hear.

After the meeting, Boaz asked if she wanted a ride home and she accepted.

"Can we swing by Intelligentsia?" she asked.

He glanced at her sidelong. "Sure," he said.

Mateo wasn't sitting outside the huge hipster café and he wasn't sitting inside. She told herself not to, then she did: she asked the manager if Mateo had been in, but the manager, a pretty blond girl with a tiny diamond stud in her nose, had seen no sign of him. She felt a sick, cold pang in her stomach and walked out to Boaz's Prius.

"He never was here, the girl said," she announced, getting in.

"Oh, shit," Boaz said. He drove her home.

"Will you wait here one second?" she asked him when he pulled into the driveway. "I want to check something."

"Sure," he said. Drew hurried into the house and found exactly what she'd feared she'd find. Her wallet, which stupidly she'd left in her purse on the kitchen table, since she was just walking to a meeting, was shorn of cash and credit cards. And in the room where Mateo had been staying, all his stuff was gone. She charged back out of the house toward Boaz.

"Well, that's just as I feared," she said. "My cash and credit cards are gone and so is his stuff."

"You're kidding," Boaz said.

"I'm not." She started crying. "We were fools! He could've stayed in the halfway house and we could've just met at meetings. But no, I wanted to help my friend." She pushed back her hair. "Well, the joke's on us, I guess."

"You want me to come inside?"

"No, sweetie, get back to Becca. I'll go inside and cancel my cards and call Christian. And, oh God, then I have to call his mother."

She and Boaz hugged good-bye. Then she went inside. Her eyes were throbbing and she wanted a glass of white wine. It amazed her that she could still have that instinct in times of freaking out, even after nearly twenty years. She poured herself a glass of water instead and called the bank, gazing around the house while she waited for the service rep to come on to see if Mateo had left a note. He hadn't.

The rep finally came on. Yes, said the rep, a withdrawal at a Silver Lake ATM had been made at 1:37 P.M. for $400, the maximum, and another at a nearby ATM at 1:47 P.M., also for the $400 max. That was it so far. Drew froze the bank card and did the same to her credit cards, which, somewhat miraculously, hadn't run up any charges yet. It occurred to her that, somewhere along the line, somehow, Mateo had gotten her ATM PIN number. How on earth? she wondered. No cokehead, no crackhead, she thought, was ever as conniving, as utterly zombielike and self-serving, as a fucking junkie.

Then she caught herself and took a deep breath. When she and Christian took Mateo in, she reminded herself, they'd acknowledged to each other that this could happen. It had already happened to Milly and Jared in New York. So it had happened again, and it was pointless, she told herself, to be infuriated about it; it was simply beyond her control. But the most curious feeling, which she couldn't shake, was that she was letting down Milly all over again, nearly twenty years later.

She called Christian and relayed the news.

"This is making me incredibly fucking sad to hear," Christian said.

"You said he should spend the year in a halfway house after rehab and I was the one who pushed and said we should make him the offer," she said. "And I have to come clean: after all these years, I did it out of guilt. I couldn't believe Milly was going through a drug thing with somebody again—first her mom, then me, then her own son—and I did it out of guilt."

"You didn't do it out of guilt. You did it out of love," Christian said. "You know that."

Drew slumped in the kitchen chair and felt more tears coming. "I wanted to pay her back."

Christian laughed lightly, startling her. "Because you're in love with her, darling," he said agreeably. "I've always known there's one other love in your life besides me, and it's Milly. Saint Milly."

"That's a mean thing to say to me right now," she complained through her tears.

"Well—" he protested. Then he had a long pause. "I'm sorry. It was. But I still think you did it out of love, not guilt. We don't have anything to feel badly about—"

"Except he probably already has a needle in his arm."

"Eight hundred dollars is not so much. Why don't you wait until I'm home in an hour or two to call Milly?"

"Because you think he might come back?" she asked.

"He can't live with us again," Christian said swiftly. "The most we'll do is make calls to try to put him in a halfway house, or in detox if he needs it."

Drew let out a very deep sigh. "This is the day it all went south," she announced.

"Call your sponsor, darling. I love you and I'll see you soon."

She sat there for another fifteen minutes, crying weakly. She walked around the house, looking for signs of Mateo. He'd denuded the guest room of his belongings, except for the black knit skater-boy-type cap he'd been wearing day in and day out, as a kind of security blanket, pulled down low so that the fold touched his massive opaque-black sunglasses. Now he was out there with a needle in his arm without his security hat, which prompted Drew's first raw, excruciating pang of true maternal misery over the situation.

Because she'd been growing to love Mateo. "What's the biggest moment you've ever felt in your work?" he'd asked her just last week when they were walking Lewy—he'd asked her very, very casually because he was a very, very cool customer who never gushed or effused or let on that he derived any satisfaction or thrill from making art. And they'd ended up talking for a very long time about their creative processes, and Drew had wished Milly could've been a fly on the wall and overheard her son's amazing, articulate thoughts about making art, which obviously Milly and Jared had infused him with. He had loved cooking at night with her and Christian, and after dinner the three of them would watch that stupid but addictive art-competition reality show on Bravo together, then maybe a movie like *Opening Night*, because she and Christian had gotten Mateo hooked on Cassavetes. And she'd also loved going to meetings with him, presenting him with his sixty-day chip, and she was going to present him his ninety-day chip. She was bringing the story with Milly full circle.

We just don't control how things go. That's the gist of what her sponsor told her over a forty-two-minute conversation. Then she put down the phone and cried a little more and picked the phone back up and called Milly, got her voice mail. "Hi, it's Milly, leave a message and I'll get right back." *I'll get right back.* So brisk and confident. Milly'd had that message on her voice mail since before this whole drug thing with Mateo had started, three years ago, and she still sounded on it like everything was okay.

The beep went off. "Millipede," Drew said slowly, warily. "Mateo's gone. He took off. Call me. I'm so sorry. Just call me."

TEN

RIGHT BACK THERE AGAIN

(2012)

In a one-room efficiency on West Second Street in a nondescript part of downtown Los Angeles—all low-rise beige apartments and a paucity of palm trees along the sun-baked streets—DJ Khaled's "All I Do Is Win" coming out of the cheap speakers attached to the laptop, Mateo sits back against the futon and plunges into vacant bliss while Carrie shoots the syringe into his arm.

"Thank you, thank you, thank you, I've been waiting so long for this," he manages to say, before his eyes all but close and he's with her again, her million little fingers scratching through his belly insides so nicely. God, it's been so long since the last time in New York—eighty-six days exactly—and now it feels so pure, so pristine. It was worth the wait.

Carrie pulls out the needle. "Can you shoot me now?" she asks.

Mateo met her at a meeting in downtown L.A. when she had been only a few weeks clean. The minute he saw her—the cropped, bleached hair; the huge, beautiful, wary brown eyes; the pale skin and the perfect Cupid's bow of a mouth twisted into a scowl; the large birthmark by her right eye; the nipples murmuring underneath her tank top and the skinny, tattooed arms folded across them—her whole surly, I-don't-wanna-be-here energy—he knew he should stay away from her, knew exactly how she'd make him feel. He was at that meeting alone, no Drew or Christian, and later, he didn't tell them he'd met Carrie and taken her cell number on the cheap phone Drew and Christian had bought him so he could stay in touch with them and other twelve-step people. This transaction took place while chatting after the meeting.

It was a very gritty meeting. It wasn't the posh, arty, sober people of Silver Lake, the mostly yuppie former alcoholics and potheads with a sprinkling of fairly successful gay guys with meth problems and a couple long-ago glamour cokeheads like Drew. It was the derelicts and the quasi-homeless dirty, crusty kids of downtown, mostly junkies who'd either fallen from creative grace or, like Carrie, who said she was a singer, only ever fumbled on the fringes of L.A. creative life before sliding totally off the radar. Mateo felt at home there, relieved, with nothing to prove; there were even some blacks and Mexicans there. He sat there with his black knit cap pulled down low and his black shades pushed back up on it, his arms crossed over the threadbare green-striped T-shirt he found in the royal-blue duffel bag of clothes Millimom had thrown together for him when she came to see him at the airport before he schlepped out to rehab in L.A. and then, after leaving rehab, to Drew and Christian's. His life had more or less been reduced to this bag, even if Drew and Christian had given him his own room to set it down in for a while.

So he sat there in the downtown meeting with his legs spread in the black skinny jeans he'd bought somewhere back in 2010, 2011—that whole foggy period when he was still managing to show up at Pratt but his life was becoming more and more of a nodding dream. That was when needles—spikes, with their horror and then their vise-grip allure, their absolute necessity—floated into the picture. That first time he'd let someone shoot him up, his gut told him there'd be no going back, and his gut had been right.

And in this meeting, he was horrified to learn it was one of those round-robin formats where everyone who has under a year's sobriety has to speak when it comes to them. And he'd been exchanging glances, and then even a half-smile and a shrug, with Carrie, when the round-robin came to him.

"I'm Mateo and I'm a addick," he said. Every time he said it like this, he thought of the Parentals and how horrified they'd be to hear him talking this put-upon slang—*I'm a addick*—but he loved it, because he felt it put him squarely with the subterraneans in the whole class structure of Twelve-Step World. At Silver Lake, once, he'd allowed himself to say it like that.

Drew, sitting beside him, smiled at him sidelong, amused, and asked, sotto voce, "You a *addick*?" Minutely, he nodded and smiled, and she scratched his knee for a quick second.

That was back when he had about seventy-two days. He liked Drew, he had to admit. She'd been a flickering presence in his life growing up, her trips to New York where she would down endless cups of tea in their kitchen with Millimom, and one vacation he and los Parentales had taken to the West Coast the summer he was thirteen. Drew was more or less Millimom's best friend, and he'd always kind of liked her because she had a saucy, direct pushiness and deadpan bite that Millimom, with her perpetual air of just-barcly-contained mourning for the planet lacked.

"You a gangsta," Drew would say drily upon first spotting him on her New York visits, as he stood in front of her, just home from school, in jeans falling off his butt, his high-tops splayed out in every direction around the scrunched bottoms of his pants legs, his hair pulled back in a rubber band popping out the slot of his flat-brimmed Yankees cap, his backpack hanging precariously off his shoulders.

"He talks like a gangsta now," Millimom would observe drolly, falling into her slow, signature nod.

He would tip his chin toward Drew, sitting there sipping her tea with her big, expensive leather bag at her feet, and pop back, trying not to smile. "Maybe I am a gangsta."

"So come here, gangsta," she would say, laughing, and he'd slouch toward her. Then she'd stand and give him a big hug and kiss while he stood there and maybe just barely put one arm up loosely around her back. "Your art is amazing," she would say. "I am blown away."

"How do you know about my art?"

Drew tipped her chin toward Millimom. "Who do you think e-mails me pictures of your art all the time with every tiny update about your awards?"

Millimom was staring down into her mug of tea, trying to look neutral, inscrutable, but with that bleeding-heart, just-about-to-cry look around the eyes that both touched him and drove him fucking crazy.

"You didn't tell me you were doing that," he finally said to Millimom.

Milly looked up at him, gestured innocently. "I thought your new work from school was good and I wanted to show it to her," she said. "Are you mad at me about that, too?" She turned to Drew. "He's always mad at me these days."

"I'm not mad at you," he said. "I just—I just didn't know that."

"And I send her my chapters," Drew added. Drew wrote some kind of weird books, like she was a journalist who traveled around interviewing people and then wrote books instead of articles, he was fairly certain. He didn't know what to say. He was sensing some peek into their back-world, which he didn't really understand; he could just sense that it had been weird and maybe slightly lesbionic in that sensitive, touchy-feely white-girl way, and he didn't want to really know more than that. So instead he just looked at Drew and shrugged and said, "Well, thanks. Welcome to New York." He headed toward his room.

"Thanks for having me," Drew called back drily.

"Mateo," Millimom said to him.

He stopped short. "Yeah?"

"I just wanted to know if you remembered about six o'clock tonight."

Inwardly, he crumpled in humiliation. She meant the shrink. There'd been some incidents—okay, there'd been a lashing-out incident with Jared-dad that had involved a halfhearted fist to his face, and a verbal lashing-out incident involving her and the word *bitch*—and, after a few horrible, frozen days when he considered just running away in the night, they'd come into his bedroom very gently and asked if he'd be open to seeing a man in the neighborhood they'd found, a guy a few blocks away named Richard Gallegos, MSW. He wanted to say no but he felt, after the fist and the curse word, maybe there was no way out of it. And this night, he wished he'd forgotten, but unfortunately he'd been thinking of it all day; it was supposed to be his first night seeing him.

"Yeah, I remembered," he mumbled back, before going in his room and shutting the door and playing Young Jeezy off the speakers in his laptop and doing homework until five thirty, when Millimom knocked, stuck her head in the door, asked if he was readying himself to leave.

"It's only five thirty," he said, not looking away from the laptop.

"I just think you should be a little early for the first one," she said.

He sat up, sighed deeply, saved what he was working on. "Okay," he said, "I'll get ready."

"You want me to walk over with you?"

Finally, he looked at her. "It's, like, eight blocks away, right? Why, are you afraid I'm not going to go?"

Now she sighed, ran a hand through her hair. "No, Mateo. I just thought—" She stopped. "Forget it, of course you can walk over yourself."

"Okay," he said rather pointlessly. He caught her eyes; she caught his. He could clearly read hers. They were saying, *Why? Why? Why do you hate me?* And he felt his were saying, *Please, woman, leave me alone!* And then he and she cut their eyes away from each other and she closed the door.

A few minutes later, he pulled his ponytail back through the gap in his cap, grabbed his keys and cell phone, and walked back out into the kitchen, which smelled like something Asian-y that Millmom was cooking—something ginger-y. Millimom and Jared-dad were at the kitchen table, Jared-dad drinking a glass of red wine, Millimom and Drew drinking Pellegrino. He barely nodded to them all as he stalked toward the door, hands shoved in his pockets.

"We'll eat when you're back, okay?" Millmom called to him.

He grunted, but he knew it wasn't loud enough for them to hear. He didn't mean to slam the door that loudly behind him, but he still kind of did. Downstairs, he lit a cigarette and pulled out his cell to check the text that Millimom had sent him with the guy's address. He walked there, rang the buzzer, and was buzzed in to a waiting room with smart-people-type magazines and a few comfortable club chairs and a weird white machine in the corner that made a whirring noise that, he would later learn, was meant to muffle the conversation in the other room.

He was alone in the waiting room and he just sat there and his anger rose. There they were, the three of them, probably sitting there with their drinks talking about him and what a problem he was, and he . . . why was he the one who had to come here? Why weren't they here with him? Had he asked them to adopt him? No. And why had they, anyway? Why didn't they have kids of their own? Oh, he knew the whole story by now. They'd told him when he was twelve. She'd died of AIDS. And Bubbe had known her, blah, blah, blah. Often, he felt that he hated her, his real mother, whoever she was, or had been. What a dumb spic slut to go and get AIDS! He hated everyone, pretty much, except Zoya from school, who he decided right there, on the spot, was actually his girlfriend after all, just like she'd wanted, and he pulled out his cell and started texting her: "Im at the fuckin shrinks office my parents sent me 2."

And he had barely sent it when the door opened and a middle-aged white woman, very East Village with her chunky black square glasses, walked out and slipped away. A middle-aged, kind of chubby, sullen-faced Latin-looking guy with very neatly coiffed, short hair and a leather cell-phone holder on his waistband held out his hand and said, with a faint Puerto Rican accent, his name was Richard Gallegos.

"Mateo."

"Come on in."

The guy's office was warm and small and all beigy-type inoffensive colors and smelled nice, like aromatherapy candles, and had two leather club-type chairs facing each other in the middle. There was some ethnic-type banana-lady art on the walls. The guy sat down and talked about some boring insurance stuff and about how Mateo would have to pay anyway if he missed an appointment or canceled later than twenty-four hours in advance. Then he said, "Okay. Okay, Mateo. So, not your idea to come here, right? Mom and Dad's?"

I don't call them that, he was about to say to him. But then he was gripped with such a ferocious anger—even hearing someone say "Mom and Dad" was more than he could take—that he did something very strange. He just looked at this Gallegos guy with more hatred and contempt than he thought he could possibly muster, then pulled his cap down over his face and curled up sideways in the chair, his own face smashed against the back. He knew this was kind of ridiculous and childish, but he just couldn't deal, and he didn't know what else to do.

Mateo waited for Gallegos to say something. For a long time, he didn't. Then Gallegos said: "You know, whatever's going on, you might find it a big relief to come here once a week and talk about it. I'm not your parents and you can tell me anything. I won't judge you and you don't have to even like me."

Mateo stayed in his crouch facing away from him. He allowed himself to consider this idea. Maybe if he just didn't look at him? He pulled his face away from the leather a bit.

"It's just that I don't really want to be here," he started.

"That's okay."

"I wanna just go away. They're not my real parents anyway. They probably told you that, right?"

"They're your adoptive parents, right?"

"They're not even really my parents. And it's kind of fucked up that they even adopted me. Why didn't they have their own kids?"

"Have you ever asked them?"

Mateo hadn't. They had never touched on that, the three of them. "No," he said.

"Why don't you?"

This gave him pause. Would it be so wrong to ask them that? Maybe it would. Then he thought again of the three of them sitting there in the kitchen, talking about him, and his anger redoubled. "I don't really fucking care why they didn't," he said, "I'm just kind of over it."

"Well, we don't have to talk about them now," Gallegos said. "We can talk about anything."

Mateo finally allowed himself to turn, still curled up, his high-tops hanging over the chair's arm. He glanced at Gallegos, whose face was big, chubby cheeked, soft, feminine with its wire-framed glasses. At least it was brown, Mateo thought. That was kind of a relief amid his parents' world of white people who thought they were so fucking liberal and multicultural. Gallegos kind of cocked his head and smiled at him a bit.

Mateo ended up going to him for almost two years, learning to make amiable chat about school and art and future plans, but, really, he never opened his heart to him. He would often look into Gallegos's broad, caramel-colored face, with its soft, kind brown eyes, and feel strange and uncomfortable stirrings of grief and yearning. Once he'd found this so disconcerting that, right in the middle of Gallegos saying something to him, he had cut his eyes away, his face coloring.

Gallegos stopped, peered at him. "What just happened?" he asked.

I wondered for a second if you were my father, Mateo almost told him. That's the thought that, unbidden, had floated into his head. But he didn't tell Gallegos that. "I lost track of my thoughts," he said instead.

For eighteen months, Gallegos helped Mateo focus on the future, so that by the time he graduated from high school, he was a bit of a star. He'd been able to quiet that bubbling resentment he'd felt toward Millimom and Jared-dad and live peaceably with them. That was the summer of '09, after high-school graduation, when he knew he was bound for Pratt, when he parted ways amiably with Gallegos.

And that's when that slow free fall into the drug H had begun—at Oscar's party after the last day of school, then intermittently throughout that summer before college. Just when his life was more or less his for the making. He really didn't understand it, how inevitable it felt that he'd go into that free fall. But he also didn't want to understand it. It felt like a gift, a solution, beyond the need for understanding. It made him feel like he was finally where he'd wanted to be his whole life—very far away.

True, Hector had gotten him smoking the stuff—those long, infinitely serene sessions with Hector, the becalmed dog, the shadows of feet passing by the curtained window in the filthy basement apartment. And it was after the second or third smoking session with Hector that he started to feel truly dopesick for the first time, the onset of what felt like the flu from hell, a shaking, sweating fetal-position misery tinged with a panicked need to get more H to cut the sick. In one of those sick spells, not at Hector's, who'd left town to spend the winter at some friend's empty apartment in Palm Springs, but at a using friend of a using friend's place in Jersey City, he'd let someone shoot him up for the first time—a fucking pimply New Jersey high-school kid named Eddie!—and in that moment, he relinquished that bit of mental dignity of the user who tells himself that he can control things, that there is a line he hasn't crossed. *I'm a slave to this*, he thought, not with horror but relief. Now he could simply go there. When he closed his eyes now, needles, syringes, ties, and fat, willing veins danced in his head.

At noon on a Tuesday, returning dopesick to the Christodora, relieved to know that the Parentals were at work, he waited for the elevator in the empty lobby—Ardit had stepped away from the desk, where a game show murmured on his tiny portable TV. Before the elevator arrived, he heard a clambering down the stairs around the corner—footsteps, but also dog steps, the rattle of a dog leash.

"Shit!" It was the voice of Elysa, Millimom's actress friend. In a moment, he heard her footsteps recede back up the stairwell. He peered around the corner to find Katsu, her new pit mix—Kenji, his childhood love, had died years before—double-tied to the stair railing, panting just aside Elysa's wide-open pocketbook. Apparently she'd forgotten something and run back upstairs. He peered inside her bag, absently stroking the panting Katsu's head for a moment, then plucked out Elysa's wallet, extracted the wad of bills in the fold, dropped the wallet back in the bag, and ducked out of the Christodora just as the elevator doors were parting for him. Not until he was halfway across the park did he dare to thumb through the cash, which totaled $187. He'd intended to rummage around inside the apartment to pull together the bills and change for his next fix, but now he didn't need to. In less than an hour, he was back in Jersey City, nodding—as was the pimply high-school kid and a few other randoms, all of it compliments of Mateo. He'd safely averted the worst of the dopesickness.

When he looked at his phone seven hours later, he saw a voice mail from Jared-dad: "Do you know you were caught on camera?" went the message, in an impossibly flat tone of disgust. "You need to get home right away and tell us what exactly is going on. We are assuming you have a drug problem and now basically the whole building knows, too. You are in deep shit, Mateo."

There was also a text from Millimom: "Please please please come home."

He didn't come home until the next day, protected from dopesickness with the rest of the stash he'd bought, tucked between his shoe and his sock, terrified they'd find it and take it away from him. Ardit glanced up at him as he shuffled in and looked away, disgusted, shaking his head.

"You better get upstairs now," Ardit said.

Upstairs, he found them sitting at the kitchen table—they'd stayed home from work waiting for him to come back. His jig was up. At least he didn't have to sneak around them anymore. He stood there, staring at them, fighting the urge to scratch himself or hug himself against the oncoming achiness, and they stared at him with a hollow, resigned look. They were sad, he could see, because their best-laid plans were blowing up in their faces.

"Is it heroin, Mateo?" Jared-dad asked.

He nodded. Millimom started to cry.

"You," Jared continued slowly, "have to go upstairs with us and apologize to Elysa, so she understands you have a drug addiction. Then you're packing a bag and we're getting on Metro-North with you and taking you to a rehab in Connecticut. We've already called. This is all part of the deal, and if you don't like it, you can get your things right now and turn around and never set foot in this house again. We didn't sign up for this."

"Why'd you sign up at all?" Mateo was surprised to hear himself shoot back through his achy malaise.

Milly stood. "Mateo, sweetheart, *please*, just go along with us on this. You need help before it gets worse."

He capitulated to her—not him, but her. He went to the rehab. But a few months after that, it got worse anyway, culminating with the infamous Sculpture Incident of October 2011, which had gotten him kicked out of the apartment for real. That's when Drew stepped in and got him into that rehab in California, then to her place—and to the AA meeting that day with Carrie, track marks fading under his long-sleeved jersey. And the round-robin coming around to him. "I'm Mateo and I'm a addick."

"Hi, Mateo," everybody said, singsongy.

"I have seventy-nine days today," he said. Everybody clapped and said things like "All right!"

"Uh—" What should he say? "I guess I'm grateful for my sobriety." Then—he didn't know why—he kind of laughed a little. Like he was laughing at what he just said. It did sound mighty clichéd. "Uh, I have a lot of cravings. A lot of fantasizing."

Heads bobbed in accord around the room.

"And a lot of—like, about the future. I wanna go back to New York. I'm an artist. I wanna finish school. L.A. freaks me out."

People laughed.

"It's too fuckin' warm, man, this is fuckin' January!" he said, egged on a bit by the laughter. "But I guess—some nice people are putting me up. And my parental figures in New York really can't deal with me now anyways. So I guess I'm just trying to stay focused on today and not freak out over the future." *Always best to fall back on a twelve-step cliché if you're stuck for your next line*, he thought. *So, voilà*. "Thanks."

"Thanks, Mateo," everyone chorused.

Carrie was sitting across the room from him, three rows back in the concentric circles of chairs, so the round-robin never got to her. But when he finished speaking and was twisting his torso in his seat to stretch, he caught her eye and she smiled sweetly, as though to say, *Nice job*, and he smiled back.

At the end of the meeting, when he was helping put away chairs, she came over and asked if he was going out to coffee with the others. At the IHOP, they sat together at the end of a long booth full of their fellow struggling derelicts, some crankily silent, some too boisterous, no one at ease in their skin.

"I want a cigarette but I'm gonna wait till we leave instead of going outside now," announced Carrie, apropos of nothing. She had something like twenty-two days clean—unless you counted chain-smoking, the last acceptable fix of the recovering junkie—and she was a mess, a ball of bad, shaky, nervous energy, constantly pulling at her lip and looking away. But fuck, she was cute.

"You look a little like Jean Seberg," Mateo told her.

"Who's that?"

"Are you serious?" he asked. "You never saw *Breathless*?"

"No. What's that?"

"It's a Godard movie."

She shrugged at him. "I don't know what that is, either."

"He was a filmmaker." Okay, he thought, so a cutie, but not so well versed. Where had she said she was from originally? Arizona? That probably explained that.

"Maybe you can show me the movie someday," she said. She was glancing at him sideways while she pretended to look at the vast breakfast options on the laminated menu.

"That could be arranged," he said in a coy kind of maybe-maybe voice.

It's not like H ever came up. It was more like, when they swapped numbers before everyone parted ways outside of IHOP, he just knew it wasn't a good idea. He didn't tell his sponsor about it, just like he hadn't told his sponsor he'd been thinking more and more about Hector, missing their dream sessions, wondering if Hector was in Palm Springs, not two hours away. He didn't tell Drew and Christian. No wonder he felt so crappy that afternoon throwing all his shit in his bag, plucking those credit cards out of Drew's wallet, out of her bag, on the kitchen table, and slipping out of the house while he knew she was deep in her writing time. He took the cards almost as a kind of self-guarantee; from here on out, it'd be easier to go ahead and use than to turn back around, hand over the cards to Drew, fess up to his aborted plans.

His heart was pounding as he clomped his way down the winding streets out of the hills toward Sunset. On some level, he knew he was going back to square one, undoing absolutely anything he had achieved in the past eighty-six days—that whole expensive time he'd spent at that second, fancy rehab with the yoga and the organic food, the goodwill he'd built up with Drew and Christian since he'd been out. And he knew the text he was about to send was wrong, that he was pulling someone else down with him. But he had no choice. The time had come. In his heart, he never really believed he'd go more than, say, ninety days without the stuff. That just wasn't a viable way to live, and part of him pitied the AA people who truly believed it was. In fact, he liked the hard, pragmatic focus it took to sideline every other intervening thought and wend his way, deftly and efficiently, toward the prize. It was a bit like making art at its best—a clean, totalizing focus.

"U feel like hanging out?" he texted Carrie while waiting for a bus on Sunset, where every stray glance from the folks around him—the elderly ladies in faded housedresses and the Honduran cleaning women in T-shirts and jeans—seemed to signal: *We know what you're about to do.* But whoa, he was free! L.A. had never felt like this before, a wide-open playground. He could probably hook this up with Carrie, but even if he couldn't, he knew he'd do it by some other means, probably within hours. There was the joy of that wild, blank canvas in front of him. Which reminded him . . . ATM? He knew he had only so much time to get resources before Drew and Christian discovered the cards were absent and canceled them. He hit an ATM outside a convenience store, withdrew the maximum allowed sum of $400, then, still enjoying the hard, lean focus of liberation, trucked it with his bag a few more blocks until he came to another ATM and took out another max of $400.

Right after that, he got Carrie's text: her address, then "u coming now?"

"u bet," he texted back.

"u r not far. take the bus south on Alvarado."

She gave him more detailed directions after that and he started walking. Eventually he got to Westlake, her nondescript neighborhood, found her pale yellow apartment complex with the scraggly palms outside, buzzed her unit until she let him in, then walked down a dim hallway with faded industrial carpeting and water stains on the ceiling.

Carrie answered the door in a tank top and cutoff jean shorts, barefoot. "Heeey," she said, her eyes widening at the sight of his huge duffel bag. "What's up with the bag?"

"Well," he began, taking in her place: an ill-lit studio with a futon, a thirty-two-inch TV, a laptop and speakers, piles of clothes everywhere, and a poster of Debbie Harry circa 1979 on the wall over the futon. "I'm over it. I'm just over it. I've had enough."

She took a few paces back from him. "You're going back to New York?"

He hadn't even thought that far ahead. "First I really just wanna get high," he said. There, he'd said it. He shrugged and laughed sheepishly.

Carrie put a hand to her mouth. "Oh, shit. Really?"

"Couldn't you kind of get that's what I was talking about when I asked if you wanna hang out?"

She put her arms around herself. "Well, I mean, I wasn't really sure." She continued hugging herself nervously. He knew she had about thirty days clean at that point, her most time ever. But here was where he had to have discipline, focus! Human feeling must be pierced through with laser precision if he was going to pull this off.

"I would like to do this with you just once," he said. He knew he had to work fast. He stepped toward her and took her face in his hands, massaging toward the back of her neck, down her bare shoulders. "We can both go back and start counting again after that."

"Oh God," she said. She had her hands on his arms now but she wasn't exactly pushing him away. "It's been so hard getting to this point."

"I need a break from the effort," he said.

She made a tortured sound, digging her nails into his arms. "Mateo, you have to go," she finally said.

They stared at each other. He knew he was giving her the blank, lost, little-boy sheepdog look. How to play this? he wondered. Perhaps best to walk it back for a moment.

So he did, literally. "It's okay," he said. "I'll find my own. Sorry I came over. I shouldn't have done that."

"I wish you'd just go to a meeting," she said. "Do you want to go right now?" Carrie had a car, a crappy little 1994 Civic.

He couldn't tell her he felt it was too late for that—his bag was packed, the credit cards were stolen. "I'm just gonna go do my own thing," he said, reopening the door to leave. He turned back, kissed her quickly on the forehead. "Take care of yourself."

He felt the loneliness he was leaving behind: her single, sad room; the total lack of connection to L.A. except for those early, tenuous friendships in meetings; the TV with a talk show on low volume. He was counting on it.

And it worked. Carrie sighed. "Put your bag down, Mateo. We can drive over to a guy I know."

Ding, ding, ding. Now was the time to play it carefully. He turned. "You can just call him for me and I can go myself," he said. "You don't have to be part of this."

She'd turned to put on her flip-flops, grab her car keys and sunglasses. "Just shut up," she said flatly, averting her eyes as she walked past him toward the door. And there he felt the moral split! *Look what you've just done*, he thought, *you are the devil, basically*. But he also thought: *Mission accomplished*. Now he just had to be steely and keep all ambivalence and feeling tamped down until the spike went in.

Neither of them talked as she drove. On Sunset, he noticed a girl, semi-obscured in a doorway, nodding in short-shorts and a tank top, and he hoped that Carrie hadn't seen her. Carrie drove west on Third Street into a pretty neighborhood on Windsor Square, pulled up in front of a peach-colored apartment building on a corner.

"You didn't call him first?" he asked her.

"He's always here," she said.

Carrie buzzed.

"Yeah?" came a guy's voice.

"Hey, it's Carrie!" she called breezily.

The buzzer sounded, the door clicked open. The halls of the apartment smelled like some sick orangey cleanser. Mateo heard MGMT blaring on the other side of the door, which opened. The guy was a fucking hipster with graying temples; he looked like he could be a screenwriter. The place was midcentury-thrift trendy, a big photo of topless Bardot over the teak-frame couch.

"Hey!" the guy said. He kissed Carrie and then, strangely, turned up the music so that everyone had to strain to talk over it. Oh, Mateo realized, he was afraid of clients wearing a wire. Carrie didn't seem nervous. She just seemed sort of glazed and sad. Well, Mateo thought, too bad. The guy wanted them to hang out. Carrie looked at Mateo questioningly. Had they fucked before?

"Nah," Mateo said, "let's just go back and chill out." He handed the guy $200 and asked for spikes, too.

The guy looked at him anew, impressed. "You're serious, aren't you?"

Then the guy shrugged, going off into the bedroom. Mateo sat down on the couch next to Carrie, saying nothing. He put a hand on her neck, massaged it. She looked at him and shook her head. Oh, shit. Her eyes were welling. Time to take action. He leaned over, kissed her gently on the lips.

"We are going to have a very nice time," he said softly, smiling.

"I know," she said, sounding more resigned than excited.

The guy came back with a paper bag, which Mateo put in his jeans pocket. He thanked the hipster douchebag in his completely non-suspect, pretty neighborhood.

"Don't be a stranger, Carrie," the hipster said as they were leaving. Carrie looked back at him and smiled weakly. They drove back to her place in silence. The TV was still on—she'd forgotten to turn it off.

"I want to take a shower first," Carrie said.

"No, no, no, come here," Mateo said, pulling her back, taking her in his arms. He couldn't wait. His heart was throbbing right out of his chest and he was sweating all over, so he had to make this sexy if he wanted it to happen right away. "I like you like this," he said. "I wanna smell you."

"Gross!" She laughed, squirming in his arms. He eased her down to the floor.

"Hold on," she said.

She went to the kitchen and came back with stuff they needed: the spoon, the lighter, paper towels, and alcohol. They sat down on the floor together. Mateo already felt high. He'd done it; he was sitting here with everything he needed right in front of him. His heart was in his throat, a swarm of butterflies were dancing in his stomach, his arms and legs were already delicately twitching with what he'd learned in rehab was called "euphoric recall." He pulled off his belt and took off his shirt and looked at the left inner elbow where the dim quarter-inch track mark he'd had was fading, then tied his belt loosely around his arm. Carrie was setting things up for him resignedly. He dared to look at her. She was slowly shaking her head.

"What is it?" he asked.

"I'm right back there again," she said.

Mateo couldn't avoid a moment of shame. He said nothing, but there was a beat when their eyes met, when she had to have seen his shame, and perhaps that helped him in the end, because it reminded her that he was human and not a heartless using machine.

But he didn't nurse the moment. In fact, he said, rather coldly, "You know how good you're going to feel in a second. Block everything else out. That's what I do. In a second, it won't matter."

"Why'd you even come to L.A.?" she asked.

He looked at her and laughed, taking the loaded spike from her. "Why are you asking me that now?"

He was ready with his needle. He looked at her one more time. She was just looking at him blankly, openly, with DJ Khaled boasting and braying out of the speakers wired to the laptop. Just a fucking anonymous, hot, sunny, blank L.A. afternoon, in an anonymous apartment, in an anonymous part of town, with a next-to-anonymous girl. He was once again off the map; he could be anywhere in the world right now—and he was about to fly away, erase himself, and that was the best feeling in the world. The moment before was almost better than the actual doing. But then in went the spike. And then: Oh, the shudders!

Oh, the violence inside him! Then: the fall, the fall, the fall. She was always there during the fall, 04/14/1984, the big 1980s hair pouf, the denim miniskirt, the leggings, the studded leather jacket. Why was this the only time she came to him?

Now he was deep in the fall. He didn't know Carrie had watched him in horror and brutish, lustful jealousy. Or that, up to this minute, she'd reserved a tiny piece of her mind to walk away—to just run to the car and drive to her sponsor's—a drive that might have led to disaster because her heart was racing, her whole body racked with chills and shakes. But now that she'd seen him like this, getting fucked by the H god, she wasn't going anywhere, she needed it too badly herself.

A million miles away, he could feel her taking away his spike, undoing his belt. "Can you shoot me now?" he heard her say dimly, across a stratosphere. A hundred layers inside himself, he laughed. *Can I shoot you now? Do I look like I can shoot you now? Fucking shoot yourself up. You're straight and you've got everything you need.* He felt tremendous gratitude, though—not to Carrie, who, again, was now many miles away, but to the simple state of being high again. He was relieved that that long period of eightysomething days of pretending that he didn't want this . . . well, that was only half true. He didn't want this up until he ran out of energy to do what he needed to do to keep from doing this when he wanted this, which was, admittedly, a good deal of the time. He was just tired from the mental back-and-forth. On the floor, leaning against the bottom of her futon, he sank orgasmically forward into the Crouch. The Crouch! God, it felt so good to be back into the Crouch! And soon . . . the Rocking!

"Mateo, can you please do me?" Carrie asked again. He reached for the belt and crouched toward her. He wasn't computing time but his arm held the belt out, frozen, for thirty seconds before she finally took it from him and began tying herself off. Thank God! He crawled toward her and buried his head between her legs, her smell there mingling with his high and plunging him deeper into bliss, in slo-mo, the same way he'd watched his blood cloud back in the spike. God, how fucking gorgeous that was!

He mustered the energy to push open her legs and rest his open mouth over the crotch of her shorts while she readied her works—it was his way of telling her what she had to look forward to if she could just, could just, get over the moral hump and get herself high. He kept falling—it was the coming-true fantasy of falling down the endless rabbit hole without fear of the thud, the impact—while she did herself up, focused on the work. Then her shudders and tickles went through him, plunging into his own. Holy shit! Again with the delectable slo-mo, he felt his dick bloom to life, as it often did after he'd shot, not that he could ever have an orgasm in that state.

Mateo knew to wait until her shudders and shocks subsided and she was falling, crumpling forward. It felt like a million hours but, lying atop her, he took off her clothes, then his own, then, with the two of them like near-corpses on her sisal rug, he worked open her pussy with his fingers, then gentled in his blood-hard dick, taking the long, slow, mind-shatteringly excellent plunge inside.

She stretched her arms up and back on the rug, her crotch rising to push him inside as deep as he could go. "Mateo." She said his name like a four-year-old. "Thank you, Mateo. You were right."

He reached forward, held her hands bound over her head. He'd won. He felt powerfully evil, somewhere fathoms beneath his slo-mo bliss. He was still M-Dreem!

"I was right, baby," he said, smashing her mouth down into the rug with his own, rising and falling on her like a weapon of destruction. *Oh fuck*, he thought, *I shouldn't have been born, but since I was, this is what I was put here to do. Spiking and fucking.* He was delirious. For maybe twenty seconds, which felt like two hours, he felt that his body had melded with Carrie's body, but now, even as he fucked her, more and more slowly, he felt himself soaring away from her in black space. It was all about him and that woman, their unholy alliance, him carrying on her whorish work of nothingness, until, when finally his head came up and he looked at Carrie, he saw instead her face from that snapshot and his own face, merged into one.

"Fucking God!" he gasped, shattering the slowness, leaping out of Carrie and off her body, flopping with a spasm on his back next to her, grabbing his dick for dear life.

"What is it?" Carrie said, but it was a drooling slur; she could barely fix her eyes on Mateo.

I think this H is cut with something, acid or X, he wanted to say, but he couldn't—he just stared up at Carrie with the pleading, terrified eyes of a child, holding his dick.

"I feel something different, too," she said. She climbed onto him, lowered herself, arched back and out of his view. She was having her revenge on him now. It went on and on. He flopped his head to the side so that the two of them, though joined at the center, could have been leagues away from each other, and he gave himself over to crying quietly. It felt cathartic and vivid amid the more numb bliss of the H high. He cried and cried, letting himself be a little baby, while she rode him, and the next thing he knew, she was nodding on top of him, with him still inside her.

Slowly, slowly, hearing the suck of the sweat around their groins, he pulled her off him. "Mateo!" she protested once, popping awake for about six seconds, before he gently shoved her onto the rug. He crawled toward his pants to retrieve his cell phone; he was feeling an incredible need for Hector, whose beat-up couch in that shithole apartment back in New York had become Mateo's favorite place to nod before he went to rehab; Hector, too manic to be a true heroin fan, would watch over Mateo while tweaking on meth and ushering various visitors in and out of his back bedroom.

Mateo had gotten used to the tremendous feeling of safety of knowing that Hector was watching him as he nodded, and he missed it now and wanted to reach out to Hector, to see if he was in Palm Springs. He pulled out his cell phone, whose battery was nearly run down. There was a text from Drew: "Please come home or go to a hospital. At least text me back and tell me where you are. I love you." There was a text from his sponsor: "What's going on? You don't have to do this, you know. You think you do, but you don't. It's as easy as calling me." Mateo deleted them both. There were voice mails from them as well, but he deleted those without even listening.

Hector's cell number was burned into Mateo's memory, a huge trigger to use just like the sight of a needle. He texted Hector: "Im in LA where r u u fuking freakshow? r u in palm spring?"

The cell in his hand, he crawled on his naked belly across the rug—oh God, all that scratchiness felt good, alongside the scratchiness inside him—and pulled up against Carrie—but wait, was she breathing? Yes, she was breathing. Slowly, but breathing. He held her close, kissing her neck, until his dick was fully erect again. Then he pushed her legs open and eased his way back inside her from behind.

"Mateo," she mumbled, bucking back toward him. Deep inside her, he nodded again, not reviving until the cell vibrated in his half-open hand. He checked it. "Fuck yeah this is crazy Im in ps," read the text from Hector. "Address? Ill cum 2 u."

Mateo smiled. Hector would "cum" and make it all right, take care of him and Carrie. Hector was always going on about how much he loved Palm Springs, the dry air and the sprawling desert-scrub landscapes and the big gay parties. How did fucking destitute Hector even get the money for a flight to Palm Springs anymore, Mateo wondered, or for a rental car? How'd he make it across the country with his drugs without getting busted? Where'd he put the fucking dog? Well, who cared, thought Mateo. He was coming.

"What's the address here?" he asked Carrie, the cell poised.

"Why?" she mumbled.

"A friend of mine wants to come over."

She squirmed unhappily. "Why?"

"It's good," Mateo said. "He doesn't really do H so he can watch us while we nod."

She told him the address and he texted it to Hector, an act that felt like it took an hour. Then, still inside Carrie, Mateo nodded back out.

The door buzzer buzzed. Mateo looked at his cell. It was 3:42 A.M.— more than two hours had passed. It buzzed again. Gingerly, Mateo pulled out of Carrie. He managed to stand and pull on jeans. He shuffled his way to the door, hit the buzzer, looked through the peephole and smiled. There was Fagfunk, dark glasses on in the middle of the fucking night. Mateo opened the door. Hector was with some beanpole, fake-blond, meth-skinned little gay rat, barely dressed in a drooping Lady Gaga tank top and fucking purple leggings under short-shorts. What the fuck? Mateo stepped aside and they hurried in, anxious to get out of the hallway.

"This is fucking crazy, *negrito*, we're both on the Left Coast," Freakshow said, his glasses still on, his fagfunk emanating off his too-tight white jeans and tank top. "Why didn't you tell me you were gonna be out here? You haven't come by in a while. Remember I told you I come out here every year for a big party? I got lots of friends out here."

Hector talked a blue streak while Mateo stared at him, slack-jawed. Hector's torso was more concave on top, flabbed out on the bottom, than the last time Mateo had seen him. His head was shaved and someone had given him a bad tattoo on his neck—some scary-ass kind of cartoon cat. As for his twitching tweaker sidekick—God, thought Mateo, the kid looked like he was twenty-three going on forty-six. His skin and teeth were a wreck.

"What the fuck are you doing out here?" Hector asked again. But Mateo didn't answer. He was nodding, his eyes heavy-lidded, swaying on his feet in front of them.

"Oh, shit," the beanpole tweaker piped up. "They are *out* of it."

But Mateo didn't care. Freakshow was here. Mateo managed to put an affectionate hand on Hector's shoulder. "Freakshow," he mumbled. "New York City freak."

"You've gotten worse since the last time I saw you," Hector observed, guiding Mateo into the room, where the TV, which had been on low for hours and hours, was now broadcasting what looked like a cable-access talk show out of someone's basement. He dropped Mateo on the futon before he noticed Carrie, naked, legs splayed, barely breathing on the rug.

"Holy fucking shit," Hector said. "Is she OD'ing?"

Beanpole just stood in the doorway, looking around frantically, while Hector knelt down by Carrie and pulled up her head. Amid his nod, Mateo felt contentment. Freakshow would fix up him and Carrie. Mateo knew Hector was opening up his backpack with his sex toys and his porn and his lube and his cherished little black box with the glass meth pipe inside; he knew Hector was propping up Carrie and putting the pipe to her lips; he knew she was suddenly sitting up in that dazed, buzzing, time-stands-still nexus between nodding and tweaking Mateo had dwelt in a few times with Hector. Mateo knew she wouldn't OD now. Hector came around to Mateo next, put the pipe to Mateo's lips.

In a second, Mateo felt alert to the scene in the room. There was beanpole tweaker reaching hungrily for the pipe and pulling off his shorts and leggings, shotgunning smoke with Freakshow, mouth to mouth, back and forth; Carrie, naked, legs spread, looking at Mateo in a stunned, fried daze on the rug. Freakshow doffed his clothes, right down to a black jockstrap, and stroked his nipples, licking his lips and sitting back wide on the futon couch. Beanpole shoved a DVD into the player, then the thirty-two-inch screen exploded with the orange-tan flesh and pounding techno music of gay porn. Mateo's eyes felt, after hours of heavy-liddedness, like they were widening so fast, they were about to pop out of his head. He was freaked out and horny at the same time; he pulled off his jeans and started stroking his now-limp dick, then running his hands through his hair.

"Holy shit, oh holy shit," he kept saying. "What the fuck, what the fuck!"

Carrie was reaching for him from the floor, her eyes wide, too. "Mateo, come here," she said. "Hold me."

"I can't yet," he answered idiotically. He looked desperately at Freakshow.

"We need to balance you out," Hector said. He went into his little black box and pulled out some tiny baggies, pulled out a key. He gave first Carrie, then Mateo, then the beanpole, and finally himself a giant bump of something—then of something else from another bag. He put them away.

Whatever Hector had given them, Mateo could instantly feel it working; the wild overstimulation was subsiding and he was descending into a semiparalyzed pool of ecstasy. Hector was guiding Carrie and Beanpole toward the futon, doing that tender hush-hush thing he could do so well.

"Let's all get close," he said. They were all naked now; the room was spinning slowly into a horny, mellow, gooshy lull. In a second, Carrie was straddling Mateo, holding him so tight, working her way down onto him; right alongside the two of them, Beanpole was doing the same on top of Hector.

Holy shit, Mateo managed to register, *they're gonna fuck right alongside us.* His heart was pounding, but pleasurably; his eyes were closed, but when he opened them he realized he no longer had any idea where he was. Freakshow had given them all acid or mushrooms or ketamine or MDMA or some combination; when he looked searchingly into everyone's faces, he saw only his own and hers. Hers, the snapshot. Ah yes, he thought, he was back in the sweet spot! Carrie had gotten him inside her now. She had her head bowed down around his neck.

"Oh, don't do that, oh, don't do that," Beanpole was chanting as he went up and down on Freakshow, clearly meaning just the opposite, as they were echoed by the men on the TV screen. Mateo had a flickering realization that the night would probably not end well.

"Ysabel," he said very clearly, right to her face, as she looked down over him. "Ysabel Mendes."

Usually, he hated to think her name, let alone say it out loud. God, where had it just come from? Well, she was right there in the room, looking into his face! He kept fucking Carrie, his eyes closed. When he opened them, maybe minutes later, he saw that Beanpole was alone on the futon, looking startled, tossed aside. Mateo scanned the room wildly. Freakshow, naked, was standing across the room, just staring at him, horrified, his hands to his face.

Mateo's eyes bugged out. He couldn't help laughing. "What the fuck, Freakshow? Get back here, you're freaking me out." Carrie rode Mateo wordlessly, her head dead on his shoulder, a damp spot growing on the futon where they were joined.

But Hector didn't move for several more seconds. Then, wordlessly, Hector was putting on his clothes, grabbing his wallet and the keys to his rental car.

"You're fucking leaving?" Mateo asked. Alarmed, he pulled Carrie off him and stood up, so fast he fell to his knees. The room was spinning and stretching; it felt like a funhouse one minute and a horror show the next. The techno music from the porn filled his entire head and wrapped around his brain in strange ways. Freakshow was walking out the fucking door! *Where the fuck are you going?* Mateo tried to call to him, but he couldn't—instead, Mateo found himself crawling toward Hector, terrified he was leaving.

You can't leave me now, Mateo tried to say, but could not. He watched the last of Hector's construction boot as he closed the door behind him. Mateo reached for the door, opened it, crawled and stumbled down the hallway of the apartment, but Hector could still somehow run, and he did.

Mateo watched Hector from the window in the stairwell as he drove away. Sunlight was emerging. Mateo was naked, stinking and sweating, in the stairwell where anybody could find him. Carrie and the beanpole were back in the apartment, with all the drugs, doing God knows what. *You should go back inside*, he thought from somewhere far away. A huge part of his body and mind were screaming to resume the animal coitus. But he was paralyzed, standing and staring out at the street. He couldn't muster a fully formed thought. Eventually he started masturbating. He watched a stray morning jogger pass. How much time had slipped away? Minutes? Hours?

Then he heard distant sirens. Were they really sirens? Yes, they were. And they were getting closer. But Mateo still couldn't move. With fascinated detachment, he watched the ambulance pull up in front of the apartment, disgorge itself with paramedics charging up the front walk with all their gear. He could hear the commotion on the floor below as they buzzed every buzzer. He finally determined to turn around and go back inside the apartment, and when he did, shuffling naked down the carpeted hallway, he was met with the team of five EMTs.

ELEVEN

MONSTERS AREN'T FRIENDLY

(1997)

There he was, alone. That was the first thing Milly thought when she saw him, in the playroom of the Catholic boys' home in Fort Greene where she'd agreed to meet her mother before lunch. There were other boys about twelve feet away, all of them black or brown, all of them four or five years old and involved in an elaborate game of toy-car smashup, but this boy whom Ava had standby guardianship over until he someday found a real home, whom Ava had said she wanted to check in on, lay alone on his stomach, on the bright orange carpet in the cheerful room full of sunlight and bright-colored pictures on the walls and primary-color beanbag chairs, and drew scary, hairy creatures with dark Crayolas on white craft paper. The first thing Milly noticed about him was his riot of glossy black curls.

Milly and Ava knelt down beside him. "Emmy, this is Mateo," Ava said. "Mateo, this is my daughter, Millicent."

"Hi, Mateo," Milly said. "What are you drawing?"

For several seconds, Mateo didn't stop his work. Then he glanced up at them both quickly. "Monsters," he said.

"Oh, wow, monsters!" Ava exclaimed. Her nasal Queens accent pierced the room, Milly noticed. "What kind of monsters are those, Mateo? Are they friendly ones?"

Mateo looked up at Ava and rolled his eyes, which made Milly giggle a bit inwardly. "No," he said flatly. "Monsters aren't friendly."

"Some monsters are!" Ava insisted. "What about the Cookie Monster?" God, Milly thought, her mother was being so loud. "You know who the Cookie Monster is, right?"

Again—studiously, it seemed—Mateo let a few beats pass, colored a few more strokes, before looking up with his exquisitely bored brown eyes. "No," he said.

"We don't have a TV in the house."

Milly and Ava looked up. It was Sister Ellen, who ran the house, a stocky, short-haired woman in jeans, a sweatshirt, and a Yankees cap. "It's a good thing," the nun added.

"Not even for *Sesame Street*?" Ava asked. "You can't deprive kids of *Sesame Street*!" She was half joking, Milly thought, but she also wasn't— she was bossing. "Emmy, can you imagine if you hadn't had *Sesame Street*? It's the best babysitter!"

"You can't miss something you don't know that you don't have," Sister Ellen said lightly. "When these guys get placed in foster homes, the TV thing is out of our hands, but as long as they're here—" She broke off. "That's a policy I set. I'd rather they read. Or play, like they're doing now."

Amused, Milly watched her mother pretend to consider and respect this point of view. "Of course," Ava said. "I just thought you might make an exception for *Sesame Street*."

"No exceptions," Sister Ellen said.

Chastened, Ava stood up and continued chatting with Sister Ellen. Milly turned back to Mateo. "Can I draw with you?" she asked him.

"If you want," he said, not looking up. He was, what, four? Five? Milly considered him for a second from her perch a foot or two above him. She couldn't really see his face, just that mop of curly black hair. He wore an oversize Yankees T-shirt (in fact, Milly noticed, several of the boys did; Sister Ellen, in her staunch Yankees fandom, had worked out some charitable thing where the boys got visits from the players and free shirts and hats) and painters shorts and sneakers that looked like they were from Old Navy. She noticed his little chubby hand and how it held the crayon (raw sienna) masterfully, loosely. She reached for a blank piece of paper and the box of Crayolas.

"Do you mind if I use burnt umber?" she asked him.

"Nope."

She set to her drawing, plucking other colors from the box. She was delighted when she noticed he'd begun peeping over from his own drawing, with longer and longer glances.

"There," she said, holding up her work. "What do you think?"

"What is it?" he said, not looking up.

"It's you holding hands with a friendly monster." And that's what she'd drawn: her best rendering of Mateo, dressed as he was in this moment, holding hands with and smiling alongside a big, smiling, fluffy, blue-and-yellow-colored creature, a New York streetscape sketched in behind them.

He rolled his eyes at her piteously, as though she'd failed to comprehend him the first time. "Monsters *aren't* friendly," he said, then went back to his own drawing.

"I figured I'd make up one that was. The world's first friendly monster! That's okay, right?"

He didn't bother to answer this. Milly sat there and looked at the top of his head. Then she looked at his picture. She could see his skill. She knew he had looked at pictures in books and instinctively knew how to recreate lines. She gave up trying to engage him and just watched him draw. Coolly, he didn't acknowledge her once, though he certainly had to know she was still there.

Her mother and Sister Ellen came back in the room. Milly stood.

"So you're an artist, your mother tells me," Sister Ellen said. Milly was starting to see why her mother and Sister Ellen had ended up working so closely together the past few years. They were both bossy, blunt women who probably got things done very quickly.

"I am," Milly said.

"She just started teaching at LaGuardia High School," Ava said. It annoyed Milly slightly that her mother had seemed more impressed by Milly's getting this job than any piece of art Milly had ever created. "That's one of the best arts high schools in the city. And her boyfriend teaches at Art and Design High School."

Sister Ellen seemed wholly unimpressed by this and cut to the chase. "The two of you could come out here Saturday afternoons and do art with the boys," she said. "You could bring your artist friends. You could rotate."

Milly glanced at Ava, who stood slightly behind Sister Ellen, smiling amusedly, wondering how Milly would handle the nun's bossiness.

"It's our day off," Milly protested feebly. "But, I mean—"

"Well, you could come Sundays, then, after you've had a day off," Sister Ellen pressed on agreeably. "Just for a few hours." She gestured around at the boys. "They're always here."

Milly glanced at Ava, who shrugged slightly, as though to say, *Don't ask me, it's up to you.* Then Milly looked down at Mateo, at the top of his head and the chubby fingers holding the crayon.

"Of course we'll come," Milly said. She pulled her little black notebook and a pen from her bag, handed them to Sister Ellen. "Write your number here and I'll call and we'll arrange it."

The nun took the little book and pen, looking quietly pleased with herself. "You won't consider it work," she said as she jotted in it.

Milly knelt down again and, in a flash, scratched the curly black head. "I'll come back and we'll draw more monsters together?"

He looked up at her, as though he was indulging her. "Sure, okay," he said. "But I hate to tell you, there aren't any friendly monsters."

"Are you absolutely sure about that?" Milly asked.

He took a big breath, as though he was about to answer but then stopped to consider the question. "I'm pretty sure," he said, nodding his head for emphasis.

Milly and Ava went to a Jamaican restaurant, got out of the stifling Labor Day–weekend heat into the A/C and ordered mint lemonade and jerk-chicken sandwiches. "You wanted to go there today just to see, um, Mateo?" Milly asked her mother.

Ava, her mouth full, shook her head. "We're talking about replacement of a few of the boys back with their moms," she finally said, dabbing at the corners of her mouth in a ladylike way with her napkin—an affectation Milly found funny and strangely touching.

"Are you serious?" Milly said. "Because of the new HIV drugs?"

Ava nodded. "Yep. That's what everyone's calling Lazarus syndrome. People are starting to live again. It's a total mindfuck. And now they gotta figure out their lives. But it means, for a few of the moms, they want to try to raise their kids again. They're not afraid they're gonna die on their kids any time soon. So for some of them, we're working on finding a group home where they can raise their kids together."

"That is amazing," Milly said. "Whoever would have thought . . ." Words failed her.

"That people would finally stop dying?" Ava asked. "Not me! Fifteen years of death, death, death, then the people lucky enough to make it this far start getting better, stop looking like cadavers. Now they have to figure out how to pay their credit-card bills."

Milly looked at Ava's face: lined. Dark circles under the eyes. Hair gone gray and a middle gone thicker, as had her dad's, even though Ava still called Sam her Elliott Gould and he dutifully still called her his Marisa Berenson. Seventeen years of drugs for Ava as well—drugs of a different kind: "My head meds," Ava called them. And about a dozen awards since she'd started Judith House in 1990, including from the White House. The write-ups in the *Times*, *New York* magazine, *Essence*; the *20/20* segment; the *Vogue* thing where they'd styled her and put her in a Donna Karan gown alongside a half-dozen other "contemporary warrior women."

"Ava, don't you get burned out?"

Ava considered a moment. "I wouldn't know what to do with myself if I weren't doing this," she said. "The one thing I'm proud of in life is I left that fucking bureaucracy and actually managed to help people."

Milly looked down at her sandwich, stung by the words. She could feel tears welling, though she wanted to be more adult than that.

"Oh, honey," Ava clucked. Milly wanted to feel her mother's hand on her own, but Ava didn't put it there. "You know what I mean. I meant in my career. Of course I'm proud of you."

That couldn't have felt more cursory, as far as Milly was concerned. Milly dropped her voice. "You know, I turned out okay, Ava. I hold my life together. I have a steady job. I have a good relationship."

"I love Jared!" Ava interjected.

"I know you do," Milly said. Ava certainly loved Jared. Partly, Milly knew, because Jared came from the kind of old-money German Jew family Ava had always wanted to be from. WASPy Jews, instead of Ava's shtetl stock.

"And you *know* I'm proud of you," Ava said. But, Milly thought, she sounded irritated at even having to say it aloud. Milly knew it was time to get off this subject—it would just take her down a wormhole of bad feelings.

"I'm proud of you, too," she told Ava.

"That's sweet," Ava said.

They fell into several seconds of awkward silence. Milly thought about her own pills, the antidepressant she'd been taking. Wellbutrin. After several months, Jared had said to her, "Something's wrong, Millipede, you have to face it. And going on a mild-to-moderate med for your mild-to-moderate depression—*mild to moderate*, like the doctor said—does not mean you're going to go down the same road as your mother. But you can't stop ignoring that you have depression. You feel it every day, and so do I."

So Milly had gone on Wellbutrin. And—it had helped? She was fairly certain she felt somewhat less . . . what? Sad? That sense that it would all never be quite right, that that shadow of dread would always be there, flickering, sometimes rising up forcefully and forcing her down into the bed, into a book for hours as though it were something she could physically crawl into and close around herself, or out of the stifling sadness of the apartment and into the East Village for those long, long walks, just trying to figure it out, to think her way out of that vapor-like sadness. And sometimes the tears that would come out of nowhere on those briskly paced walks, Milly not even really caring who saw her crying quietly.

She wanted so badly to tell her mother about it. But she wouldn't let herself. It was just too awful, the implicit accusatory nature of it—*Look what you've given to me!* That she and her mother might share this awful monster, this mindbeast that plagued women and made them crazy, made them major hassles for the people in their lives—neurotic Jewish women!—was far more than Milly could deal with. So, as they sat there in awkward silence, Milly did what she'd learned to do her whole life: look outward to other people and what was plaguing them.

"So this cutie, Mateo," she asked, "does he know about his mother?"

Ava's own eyes lit up; she, too, was clearly relieved that they were moving on, talking about other people and their problems.

"I don't think he really knows yet," Ava said. "Ysabel had him for only about a year before she went into St. Vincent's for the last time, when Mateo went to Ellen's house. My God." Ava sighed. "That she went through with that pregnancy and that he came out normal and alive. That's a miracle."

"Did she consider"—Milly paused a moment—"having an abortion?"

"She couldn't," Ava said—then, portentously, "Catholicism. Even though her family mostly cut her off when they found out she had AIDS and didn't want to see her. She couldn't bear asking them to raise him, so she asked me to sign papers to be his legal standby guardian until he found the right home."

"Who was the dad?"

Ava laughed bitterly. "She didn't know. She disappeared and went sexually cuckoo for a while. She was gussying herself up and going to clubs and not even telling guys she was positive. A few months after that, she got sick enough to qualify to come live in the house when a bed opened. And a few weeks after *that*, she finds out she's pregnant. So that's when we got her on AZT and—well, voilà," Ava said, gesturing back in the direction of the group home and meaning Mateo. "That's why the kid was born HIV-negative."

"Mmm," Milly said, still thinking about the little boy they'd just left behind with his crayons. "Why don't you just adopt him? You have room."

"Me?" Ava hooted. "With my schedule? Why don't you?"

After lunch, Ava went back to the East Village and Milly got on the LIRR in Brooklyn and took the train out to Jared's family's house in Montauk. This was a yearly Labor Day–weekend ritual.

"Are you okay from your day with Ava?" Jared asked her, kissing her, when he picked her up at the train station. Jared looked handsome, she thought, with his fresh flush of tan. He'd come out here the previous day.

"It was fine," Milly said. She didn't want to bore Jared with a recitation of all the usual feelings she had after seeing her mother. "She took me to a foster home in Fort Greene. Oh my God, Jared!" She put a hand on his arm as he drove. "I wish you could see this little boy who was there, Mateo. He's four and he's such a talented drawer. He was drawing these really scary, mean-looking monsters, so I got down on the floor with him and drew him a friendly monster, and when I told him that, he just gave me this heartbreaking, deadpan look and said, 'Monsters aren't friendly.'"

Jared chuckled distractedly, negotiating a curve. "The kid's right. Monsters aren't friendly. They wouldn't be monsters if they were, and we're just doing kids a disservice telling them that there are friendly monsters, like the Cookie Monster."

"That's exactly what Ava told him! She was indignant that the nun who runs the house—who, by the way, is a total butch lesbian—that she wouldn't let the kids watch TV, even *Sesame Street*."

"Well, you know something?" Jared said, slightly cutting her off. "Monsters are monsters. AIDS and mental illness are AIDS and mental illness. They're not cuddly."

This took Milly aback. "Mental illness? What's that supposed to mean?"

He glanced at her. Milly sensed he was dismayed by what he'd just said.

"I'm just saying," he said, "any disease—AIDS, mental illness, cancer, Parkinson's, Lyme like my sister has—we're better off just calling them what they are and dealing with them and not putting a cuddly name on them."

Milly was silent. She really didn't know what to make of that. Instead, she wondered what Mateo was doing at that moment. Did he ever play with the other boys?

"Well, I have something to tell you," she at last said to Jared. "Sister Ellen—that's the butch nun who runs the boys' home—she kind of strong-armed me into saying that you and I would come out weekend afternoons and make art with the boys."

"Oh, she did?" Jared laughed. "To Brooklyn?"

"It's not that far out in Brooklyn. Just the Q to Atlantic/Pacific."

"We go to the studio on weekends and make our own art."

"I only go Sundays anyway."

Jared glanced at her sidelong but said no more.

Twenty minutes later, they were on the big porch overlooking the beach with Jared's family, drinking rosé, while Jared's dad put burgers on the grill for them. They put on sweatshirts and jeans for the annual beach bonfire with the same group of neighbors Jared had spent Labor Day with since he was eleven, then came back up to the house around midnight and had sex for the first time in two weeks in the twin bed Jared had spent childhood summers in. The room smelled and sounded like the ocean, and Milly was blessed to feel safe and protected in Jared's honey-fur arms as he fell asleep and, moreover, to acknowledge she felt that way for once.

In the morning, when she woke alone in the bed, she pulled herself together and went downstairs for coffee, to find Jared and his family watching CNN.

"Princess Di died," Jared's mother, a good-looking woman with a silver-blond bob who'd run the same hunger nonprofit the last twelve years, said as Milly came in. "Last night in a horrible car crash in a tunnel in Paris."

"Oh, that's horrible!" Milly exclaimed. "Her poor sons!"

They ate breakfast in a disjointed way in front of the TV, each of them retreating to the kitchen to get coffee or a bowl of cereal, then coming back to the drama on CNN. Eventually they pulled towels and umbrellas together and went down to the beach. But the death, and the allegations swirling around it that it might have been murder, followed them down there like a strange pall. It was strange in that Diana may as well have been a fictional character to them; no one among them could think of anyone who knew anyone who knew anyone who'd known her, or even once met her. Milly kept thinking of the two sweet boys being left with their horrible, cold father and their grandmother, the Queen. And this merged back into thoughts of Mateo and what he might be doing at any given hour of the many long hours in the boys' home.

In the late afternoon, when the sunlight spilled a fantastic golden liquid light into every corner of Montauk, Milly and Jared did what they'd done the past several years and grabbed their sketchbooks and a blanket and retreated into some remote dunes and sketched each other. Then they had sex again on the blanket and, after, lay there naked and talked for a long time.

"The year we broke up was the worst year of my life," Jared told her. "I ached through every day of that year. Never a year apart again, okay? Never, never, never."

"Never," Milly murmured. But her own recollections of that year were different. Certainly she remembered the loneliness of those solitary nights in her new apartment without Jared. But she also remembered the clean, open clarity of those days and nights, the feeling that her life, for the first time, was a wide, blank canvas before her. For the first time she had been able to focus intensely on her painting—her own painting, versus her students' work or even Jared's. Since then, she had traded chronic, low-level loneliness and pure artistic concentration for companionship and intimacy and a nagging feeling of artistic superficiality and self-postponement. Someday, she'd tell herself, she would be alone in a studio in the woods with perhaps a few other artists to eat and have a glass of wine with at the end of the day, before they repaired for more painting through the night.

This was her artist-colony fantasy, yet she never got around to actually pinpointing a month on a calendar and finding a colony to apply to. Now she was a woman with a partner, with her own family, his family, her students; a woman engaged in the world.

Back in the city, after the Montauk weekend, she and Jared plunged into their first week of work at new schools. Diana was everywhere: on the covers of papers and magazines, on every channel 24/7. Milly found herself thinking about her in that idle way you think about a public figure and make private judgments about them just because they're thrust in your face all the time. Milly felt that Diana had become rather silly in recent years, saying she wanted to be the queen of people's hearts and that kind of nonsense; it also looked like, in her postmarital thirties, she'd been having the sexy, glamorous fun she'd been deprived of, having been made to put on that ridiculous massive wedding dress and marry into royal suffocation at the age of twenty.

But there was another feeling Milly couldn't escape, which only seemed reinforced by the insane outburst of sadness the death was provoking in England, the people crying out in front of the castle and begging the Queen to show sadness, mercy, a soul. It was that Diana was a martyr to goodness and warmth in a world long governed by arbitrary, cold rules. Why couldn't warmth and generosity prevail? Milly was appalled to find herself wondering this as she went around thinking idly of Diana that whole week—a week of new classrooms, faces, paperwork to wend through. Why were any boys left in group homes? This desperate thought left Milly on the brink of tears. Listening on the radio to the new version of "Candle in the Wind" Elton John had written to sing at Diana's funeral, Milly told herself that she was crazy and probably needed a higher dose of Wellbutrin.

The following Saturday, Jared told her he couldn't go to the boys' home with her. The art faculty at Art and Design had agreed to meet to reconfigure and reorganize the studio space. Milly set out on her own with about twenty dollars' worth of paper and crayons. Sister Ellen greeted her as matter-of-factly as though she were showing up for the hundredth time, not the second, and took her into the sunny rec room where about twelve boys, all between four and nine, were playing. Mateo sat alone in a chair wearing his Yankees shirt again, reading *The Stinky Cheese Man*, idly paddling his feet back and forth in their cheap kid-size Nike knockoffs as he read.

Milly knelt down. "Do you remember me from last week? Drawing the monsters together?"

He looked up. Did she catch just a flash of happiness on his face, of excitement to see her again, before he composed himself? "I remember you," he said dutifully.

"Do you feel like drawing again? I brought new paper and crayons."

"I draw every day anyway."

This deflated Milly, leaving her at a loss for words.

"You can draw if you want to," he added.

She had to rally. "I'm going to lay this all out on the floor here," she said, "and if you want to, you come join."

She moved to the open play area and engaged the other little boys. They broke out the supplies and started drawing. Milly calmly started drawing from last week's memory a certain home in Montauk she liked, all the while encouraging the three or four boys who joined her, giving them gentle tips she thought were appropriate for an art class for four-year-olds. She willed herself not to glance Mateo's way, which was why she was delighted when, twenty minutes later, she looked up and he was standing over her.

"Okay, I'm ready to draw now," he said.

"That's great," Milly said, trying not to sound as triumphant as she felt. She reached for her bag. "Do you want to try some colored pencils? They're more—" Should she use the word *sophisticated* with a four-year-old? "They're for bigger-kid artists, so you might like them."

He lay on his belly with his ankles crossed in the air and started in. Milly was careful to leave him alone, to mind her own drawing and focus on the other boys. Milly felt a tremendous calm overtake her; she didn't feel any sense of having forgotten some urgent other matter, something that often nagged at her. At a certain point, she glanced at Mateo and he glanced up and bugged his eyes out at her, as if to say, *What, lady?* which made her laugh, which made him smile faintly as he went back to his work.

"Here," he said finally, pushing his paper toward her.

A bloblike creature, all shades of blue and green, floated over a streetscape of pitched-roof houses and passersby—sophisticated figures for a four-year-old—walking down the street. The aquamarine creature, which hovered amid some clouds, with a sun nearby, had blank, unyielding eyes and a straight stick of a mouth.

"I like it," Milly said. "I like all the different shades of blue and green you use. What is it?"

He took a breath, about to declare something serious. "It's a monster that's not mean but not friendly, either. It's an in-between monster."

"An in-between monster," Milly echoed, fighting back her delight, trying to keep a straight face.

"An in-between monster that doesn't do bad or good, he just watches everything."

That's what God is, she thought instantly. *God just watches us and doesn't lift a finger.* "Ah, I get it," she said. "An in-between monster. That's very good."

"What are you drawing?" He stood over her now, hands on his hips. He'd picked up a bit of Sister Ellen's bossy affect.

She held the paper up to him. "It's a house that I saw last week that I like a lot."

Mateo examined it blankly. "Whose house?"

"I don't know. I just saw it and I liked it."

"You're a good drawer," he said.

Milly beamed. "Thank you!"

She went back to the boys' home the next several Saturdays. One Saturday, she finally got Jared to go with her. He enjoyed himself immensely, especially with a boy named Tranell who only wanted to draw Mariano Rivera over and over again.

Leaving Ellen's house one Saturday, he put his arm around her and asked, "Can we have a baby? I wanna be a dad and draw with my son. Or my daughter."

She tightened inside. She'd always known that if they stayed together, this would come up. But now? They were both twenty-seven! Jared knew she was on the Pill. She laughed, trying not to sound nervous. "Um, can we table that discussion for another five years?"

"Five years?" he protested.

"Okay, fine, five months," she said.

But she was actually dealing with that very matter in eight days, when she hadn't had her period. She'd forgotten to take her pills to Montauk with her Labor Day weekend, the weekend Diana died. So now, without saying a word to Jared, she bought a test at the drugstore and tested herself positive. Without a word to Jared, she visited the doctor, who confirmed it. She walked out of the doctor's office dazed. Back at work, she went in her tiny little office she'd barely settled into yet—it was only early October—and called Drew in L.A.

"Well, hello, Millipede, what a lovely surprise!"

"Do you have a second?"

Drew paused. "Why, what is it?"

"I just found out I'm pregnant. I just found out, like, twenty minutes ago, at the doctor's. I haven't told a soul yet."

Drew gasped. "Oh my goodness. Well?" She paused. "What should I say? 'Congratulations,' or 'Oh, dear,' or 'What are you going to do?'"

"'What are you going to do?'" Milly said. "And I'm absolutely certain I'm not going to have it. I'm just not going to have it. I'm not even going to tell Jared, I'm just going to take care of it and pretend it didn't happen and I never missed that weekend of the Pill and just move on like it didn't happen."

"Millicent," Drew said sternly, "slow down. You have plenty of time to decide if it only happened a month ago. And why on earth aren't you going to tell Jared?"

"Because he'll want to have it, that's why!" Milly said bluntly, as though Drew were an idiot.

"Well, doesn't some part of you want to have it, too? People are having babies now, Millipede. I'd probably have a baby with Christian now if I accidentally got pregnant."

Accidentally! thought Milly. *What an idiot I am!* "Accidentally!" she shot back at Drew. "There you go. You have no plans of getting pregnant. You have a life."

"Yes, but I'm saying *were* I to get pregnant. You don't want to even consider it?"

Milly paused and composed herself a little bit, lowered her voice. "I am not bringing a child into this world with my genes. I am not going to watch that and perpetuate the cycle."

"Oh my God," Drew said. "You are not even bipolar. And your mother has been on meds and more or less fine for years now."

"No, you're wrong, I'm on antidepressants now. I think the whole bipolar cycle thing is starting in me and it's starting with depression, not the manias, just like it did with my mother."

Drew was silent for several moments. Milly pictured her in front of her computer with the dog on her lap, cold coffee at her elbow. Milly could hear Radiohead in the background.

"Oh, hon," Drew finally said. "Can I ask you one thing? Can I ask you to just sit with this for a few days? You have time. Just sit with it."

"Just sit with it while it gets bigger in there and more human and this becomes harder and harder to do?"

"Listen to me: you have *plenty* of time. And I seriously think you should tell Jared. You live together."

"Can I sit with it just until tomorrow and we'll talk then?"

"Yes, sweetheart. I'm here working all week so call me any time you like. But . . . this could be a wonderful thing, you know."

Milly sighed, crestfallen. "Thank you, Drew-pea," she said, and hung up.

Later that night, she went home. But she did not tell Jared. In fact, she consciously put on a sort of mask before she went into the apartment so he wouldn't even suspect something was wrong. She just blocked it out. And the next day, and the next day, and the next day, she called Drew, telling not another soul. Drew put her in touch with a big psych researcher at Columbia, who told her, in effect, there were no diagnostic tools extant to predict if her child would be mentally ill, or what the chances were. The researcher said instead that by the time the child came of age, treatment would have been fine-tuned to the point where it really wasn't a problem. But Milly kept picturing years of watching a child in fear of the first terrifying signs of morbidity or mania, or both.

Finally, she called Drew and said, in a steely voice, "If I flew you out here, would you go with me to the abortion?"

Milly waited quite a few moments before Drew spoke. "Let me ask you one thing," Drew finally said. "If you were to set aside this fear you have, would you want to have this child?"

Milly tried to consider the question honestly. She liked her new job. She liked teaching art to the boys on Saturday. She liked working on her own stuff in the studio on Sunday. She liked having just a bit of money for her and Jared to travel with. "At this point?" she asked Drew. "Not now. No."

Another long pause from Drew. "Okay then, I will fly out, and you don't have to pay my way. I'll schedule some meetings and write off the trip. But one thing: I can't stay with you unless you tell Jared. That is just too weird for me to be spending a few days with the two of you so we can go off and secretly have an abortion and try to keep that from him and be all, like, la-di-da."

"It won't be so hard if we're doing it together," Milly reasoned.

"I don't think it's right that you're not telling your boyfriend of, what, five years now?"

"Six years, technically."

"Six years, then," Drew said. "You are putting up a wall between the two of you and I think you are going to regret it."

Milly respected Drew's opinion, so this gave her pause. But in her head, she didn't see any reason why she needed to tell Jared. So she went ahead and scheduled the procedure, informing Drew. In doing so, she put up a wall that even she was a bit stunned by. She didn't tell Jared, and in not telling him, she started to resent him in his ignorance of the situation—couldn't he intuit she was pregnant and in distress? She didn't tell her mother—that would go to the heart of the whole painful matter. But what surprised her the most was that she didn't tell her shrink. She couldn't stand one more person after Drew telling her this was something she might regret. She had to stay strong and keep her resolve and just get this over with. Deep down, she had no intention of ever having her own baby—ever. She would not watch her own genetic curse unfold before her eyes in the form of her own child.

Drew came and stayed in the West Village apartment of an editor friend who was out of town. Milly told Jared that much, and that she and Drew were going to meet after work for dinner and have a girls' sleepover. But actually Drew met Milly in the morning at a SoHo doctor's office with a lovely, massive ceramic vase of freesia in the center of the room, real art on the walls, and comfortable nubby earth-toned sofas in the waiting room. Finally, seeing Drew, Milly allowed herself to cry, and Drew held her.

"Honestly?" Drew looked Milly in the eye and asked. "The thing is, Millipede, you think you know what the future holds, and you don't."

"No," Milly protested quietly, scribbling her way through the paperwork, "it's that I don't know. That's what I can't stand. It'd be like wondering if you're raising a time bomb."

Drew sighed. "Oh, Milly," she said, leading Milly to the sofa. A nurse finally came out and summoned Milly.

"I'll be right here," Drew said as the nurse led Milly away.

Milly steeled herself and went into the doctor's office and willed her mind out of her body through the procedure. The Valium helped, which was good because, now that it was actually happening, she was distressed over the fact she was aborting Jared's baby (that he'd wanted!) without telling him. What if she could never get pregnant again? Well, wasn't that what she wanted?

I really need to remove my mind from this situation, she told herself. So she thought about art supplies, which always gave her a good feeling; she thought about the decent budget she had for that this year in her new job and how she'd bring in a nice supply, and how she could discreetly siphon a bit of that away from school and bring it to the boys' home on Saturdays. She'd introduce Mateo to watercolors and a paintbrush—she'd put his fingers around a paintbrush for the first time!—if Sister Ellen would let her. That would be a joyous afternoon.

See, she thought, she was able to remove herself from this situation. And this certainly didn't mean she didn't love children. It certainly didn't mean she couldn't be a good mother. She could be a loving mother, an attentive one, a mother who nurtures her child, not one who merely treats her like an afterthought. This was all still possible. She couldn't even let herself think about what was going on down there, on the other side of her johnny, and she did her best to tune out the gentle, supportive murmurings of the nurse whose hand she gripped through the procedure. It was best just not to be there.

When it was over, they drew a comfy old-style quilt over her and told her to rest for a while. She turned on her side, tucked her hands under the pillow, and lay there. She certainly was relieved that was over with. And she certainly would not be forgetting her Pills again any time soon. She felt vaguely crampy but otherwise fine, a bit floaty from the Valium. Drew came in and sat down beside her and stroked her hair back behind her ear and smiled at her. She loved Drew, that much was certain. She was feeling bizarre alternating pangs of remorse and resentment toward Jared, but she sure loved Drew.

"How are you, sweetie?" Drew asked.

"I'm fine, it's over," she said. "Thank you so much for coming."

"We'll get in a cab and go back to the West Village and rent a bunch of movies and watch them all day and night," Drew said.

"No movies with children," Milly said.

"No movies with children."

She called Jared from Drew's friend's apartment that night. He was making himself pasta and then going to Green Day with Asa and some of his other friends.

"We're going out somewhere ourselves," she told him. "We haven't decided yet." She was lying; she felt basically fine except for a little crampiness, but she was in no mood to sit in a crowded restaurant and maybe run into people. Drew flashed her the tiniest look of reproach.

"You'll be home tomorrow after work, right?" he asked her.

"Of course I will," she said. "We'll cook together."

She and Drew watched silly movies till midnight, then slept together in Drew's friend's comfortable queen-size bed, spooning just as they'd done that night at Milly's Brooklyn apartment before Drew went to rehab. Milly hadn't slept with anyone but Jared in three years, since that window of 1993–1995 when she and Jared weren't together and she'd dated a little, and now Drew's soft, slim body and the cinnamon smell of her hair were comforting, and she slept long and well for the first time in weeks. They went to Tartine in the morning for breakfast before Drew hailed a cab on Seventh Avenue to go to JFK.

They embraced. "Thank you for being such a good friend," Milly told Drew.

Drew cupped Milly's face between her cool palms. "I love you, Millipede. I'll call you when I'm home."

Milly went in and did her half day of work, as had been planned, her heart strangely bursting at the opportunity to see her new students again and assign easels. She still felt that sense of good fortune and happiness as she shopped for dinner after work, and when she came in the apartment and saw Jared in front of his laptop at the kitchen table, some hummus and pita bread beside him, she felt not guilt and remorse but love and contentment, dropping the bags to go sit in his lap, put her arms around him, and kiss him a long, long time.

"You and Drew had sex and she obviously rebooted your libido," he said, face flushed. "I'm lucky she's in your life!"

She laughed. "We did not have sex! We snuggled but we did not have sex."

Fall turned into winter and she continued going to Sister Ellen's home on Saturdays, sometimes with Jared, sometimes without. There were the Thanksgiving art projects, the Hanukkah art projects, the Christmas art projects. She woke up on Saturday mornings happy, dying to fill her bag with art supplies and hop on the train. She loved walking in the sunny room now because the boys cheered and went wild when she came in. All except Mateo, who, immediately upon seeing her, would smile quietly and go sit off by himself at a little table he had designated as his personal art area, out of which he would carefully pull the projects he had been working on that week to show Milly. He waited patiently, professionally, for Milly's attention, his arms folded, watching her every move as she set up the other boys. Milly knew that he knew that they were mere prologue to him, Milly's star student, and he was right. Milly adored him, but she never let herself show it too much because Mateo made it very clear with her that he wanted them both to keep a cool tone.

On December 20, the Saturday before Christmas, Mateo turned five.

"We'll have his cake at dinner tonight," Sister Ellen said. Then Sister Ellen looked at the wrapped gift that Milly had brought for Mateo with Sister Ellen's approval. It was his own paint set.

"Do you want to foster him?" Sister Ellen asked her.

Milly felt like her eyes popped out of her head. "What? Be foster parents?"

"It's not adoption," Ellen said calmly. "It's a trial-basis thing. Your mother would retain legal guardianship for the time being. If it doesn't work out, he comes back here." She paused. "How can I give that boy the opportunities that his talent deserves as he gets older with a whole house to run?"

Sister Ellen scared Milly a little. It seemed like she could read minds, or hearts, because it was as if she knew that Milly had been running this scenario over and over in her head nearly every day for the past month. She found herself taking her cue from Ellen and being strangely, bluntly honest: "I do want to," Milly said. "But I don't know if Jared does. He wants us to have our own baby."

"Who's to say you couldn't?"

Milly said nothing.

"I will tell you this," Ellen continued shrewdly. "I know parents who've fostered, then adopted. They thought they couldn't do it because they didn't have enough money or time, or they wanted their own kids someday. They thought it was going to close up their lives. And what happened was their lives exploded open. Before their eyes."

Milly nodded, taking this in. She glanced over at Mateo, who sat with his arms folded, project in front of him, kicking his legs off the chair into the air, watching her with an air of patient expectation.

She giggled at Ellen. "Just look at him. He knows he's my star student."

Ellen smiled. "Plus," she added, "it's his birthday."

"Well, you've planted the seed," Milly told Ellen.

Ellen gave her a two-second massage on one shoulder. "I know the seed was already there," she said, walking back into the kitchen.

Milly went over to Mateo. "Hello, my friend," she said. "I hear it's someone's birthday."

"It's *my* birthday," he corrected her, no patience with her coyness. "Will you look at this?"

"Will I look at this *what*?"

"Will you look at this *please*, Milly?"

"Thank you, that's better."

That night at dinner with Jared, after telling him about Mateo and his latest work and how he'd reacted to his gift (concern that all his favorite colors were included, followed finally by a cautious thank you), Milly dropped the bomb oh-so-lightly.

"Sister Ellen asked me if we'd ever consider fostering Mateo," she said.

"Are you serious?" He tossed off the question so lightly, Milly knew that he had not ever even remotely considered the idea. Mateo existed to him in a little cozy pocket of an occasional Saturday, something way out in the sporadically visited right field of his life. He wasn't in there taking up space all the days in between. "It must be a whole second job for her trying to find actual homes for those little guys."

She said nothing, scrambling for what to say next, which, in a few moments, alarmed him.

"Did you tell her we'd consider it?" he asked, already incredulous.

She shrugged. "I told her I'd mention it to you." She was trying to sound light, ingenuous.

"Would you really want that? I want to have our own kids, Milly."

She panicked. How long could she go on obfuscating like this with him? "I'm scared of having our own kids," she blurted out. "I'm scared of having a depressed, bipolar kid. I can't watch that all over again, in my own kid. And what if the whole experience makes me worse, in some hormonal chemical way, and I go down the tubes while we have a child to raise? Here is a child who already exists who could use this home."

Jared's jaw dropped lower and lower, ever more deeply stunned. He made a staccato sound to talk, then stopped. "You really think that kid isn't going to be trouble?" he finally asked. "His mother died of AIDS, Milly. We don't even know who the father is or God knows what was wrong with him. At least we know ourselves and our families."

"It's just fostering; it's not a lifelong commitment."

"You see him every Saturday, Milly. I barely see you Saturdays now."

Milly felt herself getting worked up, approaching tears, for reasons she couldn't fully understand. "We have a room that could be his," she pressed on. "He could have his own room. His own easel in his own room. Now that I know him—" She crumpled a bit. "I think about him all the time, Jared."

Jared looked back at her, eyes narrowing. "You do?" he asked quietly. "A lot."

He was recoiling, she could tell. "I thought you wanted our own family."

"It's not that I don't," she said, sort of lying. "It's that—this just came up. He just came up."

Jared looked a bit dazed, slowly shook his head. They dropped the topic.

The next three Saturdays, she went out to see the boys alone, but the fourth Saturday, Jared said, "You mind if I come with you?"

As they were approaching the home, he asked, "How's the prodigy been?" It was probably the first time he'd mentioned Mateo since their dinner conversation.

"He'll have something waiting to show me," she said.

Mateo did. The piece was of about eight kinds of different-colored birds, all with big smiles, flying around in the sky over the tops of palm trees. Sand and water were below, with smiling crabs on the sand, smiling fish below the water.

"Everybody's smiling in your piece this week!" Milly exclaimed. "That's not like you."

"This piece is called *Paradise*," Mateo explained. "It's different from here, so everybody smiles."

"Even the crabs," Jared pointed out.

"You don't come all the time," Mateo noted to Jared.

Milly and Jared laughed. "Sometimes I sleep late on Saturdays," Jared confessed sheepishly.

They worked with the boys for ninety minutes, and when they were getting ready to leave, Jared lightly took Milly's arm and asked quietly, in the foyer, "Do you still want to foster Mateo?"

"Are you serious?" she asked. "Do you?"

"It's not going to kill us. We can try it."

"Let's go talk about it," she said. They went and had brunch in the neighborhood. "Why did you change your mind?" she asked him.

"I didn't change my mind. I just needed time to sit with the idea. And I think it would be cool to do, if you still want to do it. And if it doesn't work—"

"It's not so easy just to dump a child back in a boys' home," Milly said.

Jared seemed to consider this for a long while. "I can take his brooding," he finally said. "He doesn't have to be crazy about us and affectionate. We'll put him in kindergarten in the neighborhood and introduce him to the kids in the park, and if he misses Ellen and the boys at the home in six months to a year, he can go back. I can take anything from him—as long as he doesn't bite us or attack us with a knife."

Milly laughed. "He's not the biting or attacking type. He's too cool for that. He'll just freeze you out with a look."

They started walking back to the home, passing by a discarded pile of Christmas trees. Milly looked up at Jared. "I love you," she said.

He tightened his grip around her shoulders. "I love you, too."

They went back inside and told Sister Ellen they wanted to foster Mateo.

She smiled a slow, triumphant smile. "I'd hoped you guys would come around," she said. She walked them into her office.

They went through the application process with the city fairly quickly. They had the resources, the credentials. They had the dedicated bedroom. They would receive some government money they could put toward child care when they were at work. They could hire Elysa, their actress friend in the building, to babysit him. One Saturday, after they were done working with the boys, Ellen brought them and Mateo into her office and closed the door.

"Milly and Jared want to be your foster parents, Mateo, my dear," she said. Her voice rasped. Milly couldn't believe it—the tough gal was tearing up!

"Would you like to go live with them in the East Village, in Manhattan," Sister Ellen continued, "and have your own room, and you can come back here with them on Saturdays and see me and the boys and do art with us still?"

Mateo opened his mouth slowly but said nothing. Milly, smiling at him, was terrified. Was he going to reject them? Maybe he'd be happier here, even if he wasn't the most extroverted boy in the house. He continued to say nothing.

"We have a really nice room for you," Milly said. "You can paint the walls and . . . it can be like your own studio."

He actually seemed to *tsk* and roll his eyes in annoyance! Milly was devastated.

"That's not what I want," he finally said, sounding plenty annoyed. "I want my real parents."

Milly and Jared looked at each other. How had they not had this conversation with Sister Ellen? They looked at Sister Ellen.

"Mateo," Sister Ellen said, "we had this talk, remember? We don't know who your dad was. And your mom died when you were a little baby. She was very sick."

"I think probably she just got lost in the city and she's better by now and you just need to look for her," he said with startling confidence.

Milly took Jared's hand and squeezed it. She hadn't considered how hard this was going to be. Sister Ellen got up and went and knelt by Mateo and took his hand.

"Sweetie," she said, "your mom is really gone. She died. She can't come back."

"Nuh-uh, I don't think that—" he began in an eminently reasonable voice. Then Milly felt a knife twist in her stomach as she watched his face suddenly contort and he erupted into sobs. "That doesn't make sense," he bawled. "That doesn't make sense. She's just lost."

"Oh, baby," Sister Ellen said. She took him in his arms, where he continued sobbing in her neck—a wild, bewildered sobbing. Milly wept and Jared put his arm around her. The four of them stayed like this for at least a full minute before Ellen mouthed to them, "I'll call you," and they slipped away.

Milly cried two blocks on, Jared's arm around her. Finally she wiped away her tears and laughed. "So much for that!"

"Give it time," Jared said.

Sister Ellen called them later and said to forget the conversation and to keep coming as usual on Saturdays. Mateo knew it was an option and he would either come around or not, and she didn't want him to ever feel she was pushing him out of the house. When they went back the next three Saturdays, Mateo wasn't there—he didn't want to participate. For the first time, he had chosen to go off with the group that went to the playground Saturday mornings and played basketball and such. This killed Milly, weighing heavily on her all the intervening weekdays.

"He doesn't want us," she told Drew over the phone.

"He's mourning his mother," Drew told her. "It's not about you."

By late February, Mateo had come back to the art group—"He's an artist, not a basketball player, and it finally caught up to him," Sister Ellen said, chuckling—but made it clear to Ellen he really just wanted to do his own thing and not be bothered by Milly and Jared. Milly went alone, Jared busy with other commitments, and those weeks when she did not allow herself more than an unreturned smile, hello, and good-bye to Mateo and otherwise pretended he wasn't there were excruciating. How strange that she had ended up staking her happiness on a five-year-old boy's acceptance! With no other choice, and feeling slightly traitorous, she opened herself up more to the straightforward enthusiasm and affection of Tranell, the Mariano Rivera freak, whose warmth was, frankly, a balm to her. Tranell was sweet but he was no Mateo, especially when he insisted on drawing the same bad drawings of Rivera over and over again, with only minor variations in athletic stance or facial expression.

"He asked about you this week," Sister Ellen told her when she came the following Saturday. "He asked if you'd be coming."

"I don't believe you," Milly said dourly.

"My advice would be to go about your business with the other boys and let him come to you."

Milly did just that, happily lapping up Tranell's affection. It was Mariano Rivera time again—this time Mariano Rivera holding hands with the Easter Bunny. When she looked up, Mateo was standing over her, looking impatient, paper in hand.

"I can't do this," he said.

"Do what?" Milly tried to sound casual, as though he hadn't just frozen her out for a month.

"This." He showed her a picture in a comic book of what looked like a *Tyrannosaurus rex* and a giant beetle with menacing antennae, locked in a complicated death grip. He was trying to copy it; she could see his paper with its tentative first lines, scribbled out in frustration.

"Give me a second to finish with Tranell and I'll come over," Milly said. She certainly couldn't just drop everything because Mateo finally acknowledged her. That would send him the wrong message.

Mateo frowned and walked back to his self-appointed art table. Five minutes later, Milly came over.

"With a picture like this," she told him, "you have to look at the primary lines, the major thick lines in the picture. See them?" She lightly traced over them with her finger. "Take a clean sheet and try to recreate those primary lines and I'll do it alongside you, okay?"

They both began. Milly set to her sheet. At one point, she looked up and found him staring at her with what she thought actually looked like tenderness and some amusement. "What is it?" she asked.

"You still want me to come live with you?" he asked.

Inwardly, Milly took a deep breath, careful to modulate her joy. "The offer is still wide open if you want to come," she said. She tried to sound not too desperate. But then she couldn't help adding: "I think you'd like the East Village a lot. There's a lot of artists and a lot of fun things to do."

"Would you mind if I leave if my mother comes back?"

This caught Milly short. Had she assumed that in the intervening weeks he'd accepted the truth? She put her hand over his hand. "Of course you can leave if your mother comes back, sweetheart."

He looked at her hand, then her face, then her hand. Slowly, he put his other hand on top of hers. He smiled at her, as though he had finally come to terms with a difficult decision. "Can I bring my paints with me?"

"You can bring your paints with you," she said, her voice breaking. "You can have your own room and your own easel."

"Why are you crying?" he asked her, a note of frowny disapproval in his voice.

Milly brushed away tears with the back of her hand, embarrassed. "Because I'm happy," she said, all her defenses down.

He took back her hand and put it on his again and rubbed it in a curious, reassuring way. "You're a nice lady," he said.

She laughed, which, amid her tears, became a bit of a snort. "Thank you," she said. "You're a nice boy."

For a few seconds, neither of them said anything.

"So," Milly finally said, pulling herself together. "We'll talk about it after with Sister Ellen, okay?" But he'd already gone back to his drawing.

In just one month, after an afternoon of good-byes at Sister Ellen's where everyone was crying for one reason or another—the boys because Mateo was leaving them behind, Ellen because Mateo was leaving them behind, Milly a bit because the heartbreak of the scene was just too much for her, everyone, really, except for strong, dad-like Jared and curiously matter-of-fact Mateo, who exuded the cool, quiet entitlement of someone who was about to have his own room—they took him home on the subway, all his worldly possessions of his five years, including many, many drawings and paintings and a bit of clay sculpture, fitting in a duffel bag and a box.

He said absolutely nothing on the subway—he could have been riding alone, giving just perfunctory nods when Milly or Jared said something to him, such as how much they thought he was going to like the art supply store around the corner from them, or the great art teacher at the kindergarten he'd be going to. He said nothing to Ardit, the super, or the other building staffers at the Christodora, all of whom had been expecting his arrival for a month now. He said nothing in the elevator, nothing in the apartment, nothing even upon entering the former study/guest room they'd furnished into a boy's bedroom, careful not to decorate or paint save for a few superhero posters, so Mateo could make all the decisions himself and create a room entirely his own.

"You can figure out how you want to make your room, my friend," Jared said. "What colors, what pictures."

Mateo sat down tentatively on the bed. Milly caught his hands trembling. "Can I take a nap?" he asked.

"Right now?" Milly asked. "Do you want to go see the neighborhood? It's really nice outside."

"I'm tired. I wanna take a nap first."

"Take a nap," said Jared. "Get comfortable in your new room." Jared gently drew Milly out of the room.

"Can you please close the door?" Mateo asked.

"Sure," Jared said. He closed it behind them, leaving it slightly ajar.

"All the way?" Mateo called back.

Milly and Jared looked at each other. Then Jared shrugged and fully closed the door. Milly put her arms around herself and walked, in a daze, to the kitchen, Jared following her. She sat down at the kitchen table and looked down six flights at the boys playing basketball in Tompkins Square Park. Jared brought them each a glass of water.

"He's in shock," Jared said quietly. "Give it time."

"*I'm* in shock," Milly said.

They sat there, holding hands across the table. "We can't leave our own house on a Saturday afternoon," Jared said in a low voice full of amazed amusement. He started laughing quietly, gripped her hand. "What the fuck have we done?"

Milly smiled a little, shook her head. "I hope you don't hate me for this."

They heard a high, hiccup-y sound. Milly kicked off her shoes and, in stocking feet, padded to Mateo's door, then padded back. She took Jared's hand again. "He's crying," she whispered. "Really softly, like he doesn't want us to hear him."

Jared came around the table and raised her up, held her. "This is going to take time, Milly."

All through 1998, with the whole soap opera of Monica Lewinsky in the news every day, Milly watched while Mateo glacially adjusted to his new life. Mateo made friends in kindergarten, at the playground. Mateo had playdates. Mateo had white friends, Mateo went with Milly and Jared to galleries and performances, Mateo went to Montauk and saw the beach for the first time and fell in love with the waves—and with crabs, just like the ones he'd drawn. (Real crabs didn't smile, though.)

Milly and Jared would take Mateo back with them to Ellen's home at first, and then after about six months, he said, with no fanfare, he didn't want to go back anymore. Milly and Jared looked at each other, thought it best to leave it at that. Milly went back herself to do art with the boys a few more times, then finally had to tell Ellen she didn't have the time anymore. She was now a mother, or some approximation of a mother, in a nuclear family, and she was feeling the closing in of priorities that all parents feel: that sense of letting go a bit of engagement with the broader, bigger issues of the world; that sense—which seems so solipsistic from the outside, but so utterly inevitable from the inside—that the world of the home was a crowded and challenging enough universe in and of itself.

One Sunday night, in the summer, they took a train back from Montauk. Milly and Jared carried Mateo upstairs in the elevator and put him to bed with sand in his hair, because he'd fallen asleep in the cab home from Penn Station. The next morning, Milly went to change the sheets in his little bed and she found, jammed between the mattress and the wall, a beat-up snapshot of a game-looking Latina with moussed hair and a leather jacket and a denim miniskirt, posing with some guy and a boom box.

She turned it over and read the date stamp: 04/14/1984. She turned it back around and stared at it intently. Neither Sister Ellen nor Mateo had ever mentioned this picture to her. But she didn't have to think too hard to realize that it was likely Mateo's mother, Ysabel Mendes, of whom her own mother had often spoken.

Milly scrutinized the woman's face—not especially pretty but not ugly, either; eyes large and alive—looking for signs of Mateo. Mateo was lighter than his mother. He'd certainly received her wild curls, though. Milly felt tenderness for the woman, and gratitude, and also burning curiosity about exactly whom she'd gotten with to make Mateo. *I hope you know he's okay*, she thought, talking to the picture. *My mom took care of him for you. You can relax.*

Later that afternoon, Milly was in the drugstore and bought a frame for the picture. She got home and took the frame into Mateo's room and intended to put the picture in the frame and place it on Mateo's dresser. But as she began to, she thought better of it. She found some photos she had just had developed of all of them at the beach and put one in the frame and set that on Mateo's dresser instead. She left the photo of his mother tucked between his mattress and the wall, just where she'd found it, and never said a word about it to Mateo.

Occasionally in the coming years, when Mateo wasn't home—and amid an overall new happiness and sense of purpose Milly felt upon being a mother, which settled deeply and comfortably into her bones and went a long way toward dulling the quiver of dread she'd lived with most of her life—she'd slip into his room and examine the photo and ponder the final years of Ysabel Mendes.

TWELVE

BORN THIS WAY

(2012)

On the street in front of the apartment in Westlake, Hector got in his long-term rental car, shaking. *You are so fucking high*, he told himself. The deep, deep-down survival voice told him that if he didn't take a Klonopin right now, he was going to do something very, very bad, like drive the car over the first cliff he saw. He found the pill in the front pocket of his jeans, chewed it carefully and thoroughly, washed it down with the rest of a sticky bottle of Gatorade lying on the floor of the car. The pill wouldn't kick in for thirty minutes, he knew, but he still had to act fast. He pulled out his cell, started to dial 911, then noticed that the young, skinny twink he'd been with had left his own cell phone on the seat of the car. All the better, then. Hector picked it up, punched in 911. The woman on the other end was immediately barking for his name, address, phone number, location.

"There's three people fucked up on drugs in an apartment on the corner of West Second Street and South Union and I think one of them is overdosing. You have to send EMTs."

"Sir, what is the address and number of the apartment?"

He didn't know. "It's right at the corner of West Second Street and South Union. It's off-white with a flat roof."

"Sir, what is your name? Are you at the scene, sir?"

"I told you where it is, you just better get there," he said.

He tried to hang up but the call, an emergency call, wouldn't let him. He backed up the car to the building, where he noted the address and spoke it into the phone. He couldn't remember what buzzer they'd buzzed only—when was that? How much time had passed? Fifteen minutes or three hours? The sun was rising in the east, pushing dazzling grades of red and gold into the sky, the neighborhood still silent. He threw the phone onto the small plot of lawn in front of the building.

The pill wouldn't kick in for a while, but he had to drive—he had to get out of here. No, no, wait! He couldn't go until he knew EMTs were coming. He started the car. The volume of the radio startled him. Had they really been blasting it that loud on the way here? He turned it down. It was that Lady Gaga song from the year before, "Born This Way," the one that sounded like the old Madonna song. Paranoid from the drugs and making too many connections, he freaked out: it was a sign from Ricky, who'd been obsessed with Madonna!

He steadied himself to drive around the corner, where he parked. He blasted the A/C; he was soaked in sweat. He thrust his right hand into his pants and slowly masturbated to give himself something to focus on, to keep himself from going crazy. He dreaded that at any minute someone might walk or jog by with a dog, spot him behind his black sunglasses, but nobody did; he finally glanced at the car clock and realized it was 6:30 A.M. On Wednesday? Thursday? As soon as he'd flown in to Palm Springs over a week ago, as soon as he'd settled into the tiny studio apartment he rented each winter for nearly nothing from an old New York friend who'd long ago moved west but spent the winter in Puerto Rico, as soon as he'd made a meth connection and the glass pipe and torch had come out, he'd lost track of time. After that, it was just the laptop, the porn, the random visitors with their intermittent glances through the blinds at the sun-baked pool in the courtyard, from which they thought they heard laughter but which appeared deserted. Were people playing tricks on them? Hector and his visitors wondered, as the light and dark rotated rapidly outside like in a time-lapse video.

Now, in the car, he thought he was hearing sirens. No, wait, he *was* hearing sirens. He was relieved and terrified, because he often thought he was hearing sirens, getting closer, always waiting for the sirens to crest outside his apartment, stop, the silence, then the inevitable raid he'd been waiting for for years now that never happened, remarkably. (Why not? He had half wanted it to happen, to be delivered finally from his paranoia.) Unmistakably, now, these sirens were approaching. He heard them surge and stop around the corner. Gripping the wheel, he U-turned in the street, saw the ambulances pulling up in front of the building, and drove on. He felt his first wave of something approaching a notch less than psychosis. They might get in trouble with the law—how many drugs had he left in the apartment?—but at least nobody would die.

He drove aimlessly, so anxiously he was driving at a ridiculous crawl. His eyes felt like they were prying their way out of their sockets behind his sunglasses and he kept thinking he was seeing things—children, animals—in his periphery. He was in some truly nondescript part of L.A., all ugly, boxy, sand-hued 1960s apartment buildings, tired old palm trees in front of them, as the sun climbed higher and the same wearying California azure suffused the sky. What to do? Could he possibly get back to Palm Springs?

Then the thought sprang up on him again, hard, for the first time since that moment the boy had said the name aloud—Ysabel Mendes!—and he said aloud, "Oh my God," and had to pull over again. He just sat there. Why had the boy said it? He started making horrible connections: the boy was living in the Christodora because Ava's daughter had adopted him. Ava and Issy. Had he ever heard—had he heard, back in 1994, 1995, that Issy had had a baby before she died? Heard that from Ava or somebody in the world of AIDS? He couldn't remember. By that point, he'd almost completely broken away from the original street activists and was usually either in D.C., in meetings with his elite colleagues and pharma and the feds, or off at big circuit parties, expensive raves for gay jet-setters, fucking everyone he could to forget about Ricky. He was ashamed to admit that when Ava had given him the date for Issy's memorial service, he found the thought of attending too painful, so he'd not canceled his meetings in D.C. He'd sent flowers instead.

The boy looked like Issy, he could see it now. The nose—not as flat as Issy's, but flat. And the fucking wild hair! But the boy's skin was lighter. The boy's eyes and his build. Oh, no. No, no, no, no, no, no. Hector began to cry. No, no, no, please God, no. He found and swallowed half of another Klonopin, started the car, drove onto a wider, multilane road. He drove past a massive, modern yellow-brick building. Then he saw there was a big crucifix on it and, at the ungodly hour of 6:52 A.M., some women were walking into it. He parked his car across the street and walked toward the church. CATHEDRAL OF OUR LADY OF THE ANGELS, said the sign. Hector felt he had nothing to lose at this point. He went inside the church, which was the size of a stadium. He passed a woman on the way in and expected her to grimace, because he knew he stank, but she smiled. In a second, he could see why. A mass was getting under way, with some engaged attendees, but they were clustered what seemed a quarter mile beyond, in the first ten rows.

The rest of the endless sea of pews was dotted with homeless people, some of them with mountains of baggage at their side. Hector sat in one of the last rows. In his youth, in the many churches he'd been inside in San Juan and New York with his mother, grandmother, aunts, and cousins, the only church that approached this one's size was St. Pat's in New York, which he and the other activists had stormed on a Sunday years before to protest the archdiocese's AIDS policies, its opposition to condoms, and its hatred of gays.

"I hope it's fucking okay that I'm here today," he said aloud, as though waiting for approval. Nobody so much as turned toward him, which irritated him slightly. Were they deliberately ignoring him? He could feel the Klonopin kicking in—his eyes didn't feel quite so much like they were straining to crawl out of their sockets. He laughed softly. "Fuck you, Ricky," he said—he thought he said it aloud, at any rate; he wasn't sure, just as he wasn't sure if the legions of characters on the tapestries hanging overhead were moving, watching him, talking about him.

"The thing with you, Ricky," he continued to himself, mumbling parts aloud, "you just didn't want to live. That's why I say fuck you, as harsh as that sounds. Because you didn't even care that there were two people involved, not just you. You put me through that for, unh, what would that have been, from about 1989 when I first knew until '92. You wouldn't get tested, you wouldn't go on meds until they forced you on meds in the hospital and it was too late, and you fucking—what about all my other work? I had to give up all that fucking work, going to Washington, because you wouldn't take care of yourself, and then I had to watch you die, like I didn't have better things to do that year."

He must have really been talking out loud, at least at some point, because a guy with a leathery tanned face and a matted beard four pews ahead finally turned around and said, "Shut the fuck up, man."

So he did, closing his eyes for a minute, one hand thrust in his pants. But at some point, the monologue began again: "You just weren't very educated. And that your father, cutting you off. Well, that's no reason to make me watch you die, you dumb fuck. You never had any interest in the data. Not at all. You were a dumb twink, basically." Hector laughed. "A fucking hairstylist. I ended up with a fucking hairstylist."

He started crying, tears engulfed with lust. "But I miss your beautiful face, Ricky. I miss it so much. Every day. And I miss your ass."

"What the fuck, man?" The matted-beard guy four pews up had turned around again. "This is a fucking church."

Hector didn't even know why the guy was talking to him. He tried to look squarely at the guy through his tears. The guy looked like a filthy, sun-baked version of Charlton Heston. "I'm sorry," he told the guy.

Now the guy's face lit up, laughing. He made an exaggerated sign-of-the-cross benediction in his direction. "Well, my child, I forgive you. Get your hand out of your pants, though, man. You look like a fucking pervert."

Hector took his hand out of his pants. The Klonopin was pushing down on him now like a giant, velvety hand. Probably it would be okay for him to lie down for a little bit, to get twenty minutes of sleep before he got back in the car. So he did that, feeling hugely warm and calm and protected, unable to stop babbling to himself as he fell asleep.

When he woke up, a fat, gentle-faced Latina, probably Honduran or Salvadoran, was standing over him, gently shaking his shoulder.

"Sir, you have to leave the church now, it's almost six o'clock, we're closing."

"It's seven in the morning," he said.

"No, sir, it's six o'clock in the evening. You're the last person in the cathedral. You have to leave now."

Six in the evening! Holy shit. Hector stumbled his way out of the cathedral and onto the street. His car was gone. "Oh fuck me, no," he said. He'd parked it illegally and it had been towed? He had no idea. He'd left his wallet in the car—or at the girl's apartment? He couldn't remember. He hadn't a credit card or a dollar on his person and he really didn't much give a shit. He looked back at the benches outside the cathedral, walked across the street, lay down on one, fell asleep. How much time passed before the same fat Latina was shaking his shoulder?

"Sir, you really can't be sleeping in front of the cathedral."

"Why not, it's not a public space?"

"Do you want me to call our homeless outreach for you, sir?" She was taking her cell phone out of her bag.

Hector laughed. "No, I'm not homeless. I live in New York." He didn't see the need to elaborate, so he lay down again and passed out. How much time passed before the same goddamn fat lady was shaking his shoulder? This time when he looked up, she was standing there with two guys, two more Honduran-looking guys with crew cuts.

"Sir, you want to come to the cathedral's shelter for the night and have a meal and a shower and a cot?" one of the guys said.

Hector gathered lucidity for all of four seconds. He was currently in no position to figure out this mess with the vanished car, how to get back to Palm Springs.

"Sure, why not?" he told the guy, who helped him up. He got inside a minivan that drove for a few minutes on the freeway until it pulled off into a side street, next to a cinder-block building. There was a big room inside with another big old cross on the wall looking down on about fifty men, all of them black and Latino, crashed out on cots, some massed in a corner on old couches watching TV or playing cards. The place stank. As soon as he walked in, in his soiled, too-tight white jeans and tank top, they started jeering at him. "Faggot" this and "*maricón*" that. Hector was still so wasted, he didn't much care.

"Come on, man, leave me alone," he said wearily to one of the guys closest to him who tossed off a *maricón*. One of the worker guys walked him back to the showers, where he stripped off his grimy clothes and stood under the stream, lathering himself, relieved to be getting clean despite the starkness of the cinder-block stall. He realized he had left the rest of the Klonopin in the car and had his first frisson of worry over how he was going to start feeling when everything started wearing off. Couldn't he already feel, standing here under the lukewarm stream of water, the first stabs of depression and anxiety that always came with the crash?

The staffer guy came back with a towel and a clean, used T-shirt and pair of jeans, so big for him he had to hold them up while he walked. A horrible, sinking sense of abjectness—one he could usually fuzz over and modulate after every drug run with a mix of Klonopin and sleep—started seeping in. The worker brought him to a cot with a thin, beat-up pillow, and he lay down on it fetally, wondering if it had bedbugs. Five minutes later, the worker brought him a bologna-and-cheese sandwich on Wonder Bread on a paper plate. He took one bite and realized he was ravenous, that the last thing he remembered consuming was a protein drink twenty-four hours ago. He finished the sandwich in about four bites and lay down and said his usual prayer for when he finally went to sleep during a crash: "*Por favor, Dios, ayúdame a dormir esta noche.*"

When he woke up—eleven hours later, according to the institutional black-and-white clock on the cinder-block wall—the dude on the cot next to him said, "Fuck, man, all you been doing is crying and screaming and tossing around in your sleep like a crazy motherfucker."

Where was he? What was that smell? Bit by bit, his mind pieced the past few days back together. The lost car. The abandoned apartment in Palm Springs. He was in a fucking homeless shelter in Los Angeles?

What was he wearing? He wanted to cry, but not in front of the dude on the next cot. He thought that he could kill himself, that the whole thing had just gone too far this time to try to piece things back together. But how would he do it? He didn't have any drugs or pills to do it with. Should he just walk out in front of traffic?

Then the whole "Ysabel Mendes!" moment came back to him. Oh God, not that again. No, no, no. Please God, no. The fucking kid.

He lay there on his side, crushed by the depression of the crash. His mind kept sorting out that he could do three things. One, he could kill himself, but that would take some doing with no drugs or pills around— he'd have to leave the shelter and go out into the streets and figure it out. Two, he could just stay here. They had no ID for him; nobody would ever come looking for him. He had effectively cut himself off not just from New York City and everything that had ever happened there, but Palm Springs, the half-dozen or so guys he'd had to his friend's apartment before he got the text from the kid. He could just stay here and be a bum and be taken care of at the lowest level—cot, shower, bologna sandwich—make peace with these fellow bums, maybe be brought into their card circle or TV clique.

But there was a third choice, motivated by a dim grain of recognition that, just maybe, because of all the people he had actually helped years before, he'd earned a crumb of credit to be helped in return. He lay there and mulled over that extremely alien thought for several minutes. It motivated him enough, finally, to sit—and oh, that was a miserable effort—then to stand, holding up the too-big jeans, and walk over to one of the staffer guys, who was watching a wrestling match with some of the dudes.

"Can you make a call for me?" he asked the staffer.

The staffer—not the same staffer as the night before, correct? He wasn't sure—looked up at him disinterestedly. "You got somebody to come pick you up?"

Hector nodded yes; it seemed like the easiest answer. Slowly, apparently reluctantly, the staffer pulled a cell out of his pocket. "What's the number?" he asked.

Hector didn't know it, he realized. "I need you to call 411 for the number," he said. "I know it's listed."

"Are you serious?" the staffer asked. Hector was sure now the guy wasn't the fairly nice guy who'd brought him in here the night before. This guy seemed like a dick. "It's like a dollar-fucking-ninety-nine a minute to call 411."

Hector suddenly had a long view of just how much subjugating himself he was going to have to do to take this third choice rather than kill himself or simply say nothing and stay here and rot. Was it really worth it at this point?

"I know, sir, I'm sorry," he made himself say. "But I really need this person and I forgot her number."

The staffer rolled his eyes and dialed 411. He looked up at Hector. "What's the name?"

"The last name is Heyman." He spelled it out. "First name is Ava." He also spelled it out. "New York, New York."

"You gotta call New York?" the staffer asked, more pissed off every minute.

"That's where I'm from," Hector said. He started to cry. "That's where I'm from."

All the guys in the TV clique looked up at him. "What the fuck?" they said. "Why you crying, *marica*? It's gonna be okay, don't worry."

"Okay, okay, relax," the staffer said. He waited for several seconds. "Here, I got somebody here who needs to talk to you," he finally said into the cell, handing it to Hector.

"Ava?" Hector said into the cell, walking away from the blare of the TV.

"Who is this?" she asked. Oh God, Hector thought, he hadn't heard that rasp of a voice in a long time. He came extremely close to snapping the phone shut. He couldn't do this, he told himself. He said nothing.

"Who is this?" Ava said again. "Emmy?"

"Ava, it's Hector."

Silence. Then: "Hector? Villanueva?"

"Yeah."

Another beat. "I haven't heard from you in a long time."

"I need your help, Ava." That was all he needed to hear himself say before the tears flowed again. He sat down on a chair and sobbed choking sobs into the phone.

"Hector, what's wrong? Where are you?"

"In Los Angeles," he said through his tears.

"In Los Angeles? Are you high?"

"I was."

"Who was the other guy on the phone?"

"The guy working at the homeless shelter."

"The homeless shelter? Hector, what is going on?"

"Will you help me get home?" He was still sobbing.

There was silence on the other end of the line. Ava finally sighed again. "Of course I'll help you get home."

"Thank you, Ava. Thank you so much."

"Let me get a pen and—put me back on with that other guy, okay?"

The staffer was already standing over Hector. He put a hand on Hector's shoulder. "Gimme the phone, buddy, I'll work it out," he said.

Hector handed over the cell and put his face in both hands and wept into them. Parallel tracking hadn't worked, he thought. Well, it hadn't worked until 1994, 1995—saquinavir, indinavir, ritonavir—the names of the drugs that had meant everything to them, the ones that changed everything. And Ricky? Until he couldn't talk anymore, he was obsessed with fucking Madonna! It was all mashing together in Hector's head now. He'd had to bring Ricky the September issue of *Vogue* with Claudia Schiffer on the cover—an outsize tome that further weighed down Hector's already overladen work bag, on perhaps the steamiest day of the late summer—because another stylist with whom Ricky had imagined himself in a bitter, unspoken rivalry had gotten to do Claudia's hair color, and Ricky just had to see how it had come out.

"Ooh, thank you, thank you," Ricky had cried from his hospital bed, grabbing for the magazine. "Let me see." He'd appraised the cover shrewdly for a few seconds, then sighed and rolled his eyes. "This is horrible," he'd finally pronounced. "*Horrible.* That color is so flat. No depth."

Hector had laughed. "Are you relieved?"

Ricky had looked up and smiled coyly. "I most certainly am," he'd drawled.

"I'm glad it makes you happy," Hector had said. He really meant it, too. It wasn't the spitefulness, Hector had believed, that had delighted Ricky, but the prospect of curling up with hundreds and hundreds of pages of hair, makeup, and clothes. Ricky could peruse and analyze fashion spreads with a minuteness that amazed Hector, pointing out the tiniest imperfection or oversight in an eyebrow, spotting the faintest telltale wig line that would be invisible to the layperson's eye. Ricky had prided himself on his meticulous work, which he'd not properly been able to take part in for several months.

Then Hector, overcome with longing, had gently drawn the magazine from his hands.

"Hey!" protested Ricky. "What are you doing?"

"I need to lie down with you," Hector said, pulling the curtain around the bed, taking off his boots, lowering the top of the bed with the control switch.

"This is *my* bed," Ricky fake-protested. "It's a very, very expensive bed."

"Good thing you're broke-ass enough that Medicaid's paying for it, then," Hector said. He shimmied in the bed under the sheet, put his arm around Ricky. He buried his mouth in Ricky's neck; deep in his rib cage, he could feel his tears shuddering and he took a breath to quell them. "I don't understand you, Ricky," he whispered.

"Don't squeeze too hard, it hurts."

"I'm sorry."

"I'm cooperating with the regimens now," Ricky said.

"I know," Hector said. He knew the data too well, though. Ricky had lost about eighteen months of good preventive treatment with Bactrim, living in his crazy denial. That had put him so far along. The data wonk's boyfriend who shunned treatment! They were talked about like a tragedy in the movement. Hector slid his hand down into the back of Ricky's underpants, gently ran it over Ricky's right butt cheek.

"Does that hurt?" he asked.

Ricky squirmed happily. "Noooo. *Au contraire*. Are you going to massage my butt?"

"Yes, I'm doing it right now."

"Oooh, hot. Right here in the hospital. Scandalous."

"It's a therapeutic massage!"

"It certainly is."

"I love you so much, Ricky," Hector said.

"I love you, too, *papi*."

"I hate when you call me that."

Ricky laughed. "Well, I've called you that for eight years, I'm not going to stop now."

"It's racially offensive."

Ricky laughed harder. "Oh shut up, you love to be the *papi*."

Hector laughed. "You're fucking crazy."

They'd had exactly eight weeks left after that night. Hector calculated that with clarity, sitting in the cinder-block shelter. The staffer who'd been on the phone with Ava walked over to him.

"A woman named Drew is going to come pick you up," he said. "It's a friend of your friend."

Hector nodded. He had no idea who the woman was. He continued to sit there, beading together the months in a way he hadn't in years. Twenty years ago! How 1992 bled into 1993. Awful fucking 1993. That was around the time he'd started the splinter group with Chris Condello and a few others and they'd taken shit for that from the main group, being called traitors. Then all those trips to D.C. They spent half that year, and 1994, too, in D.C., in meetings with FDA and HHS. That work saved him for a little while. The protease inhibitors—watching the protease inhibitors develop, 1994, 1995. He was already letting go of the work by 1996, 1997. He was celebrating—the work was done! The friends he'd barely seen the past few years were hitting the streets again, looking like something approaching normal. All their fucking credit-card debt, all the black humor about the credit-card sprees, and now they'd live to face the bills! The creepy viatical companies who'd bought all his friends' life-insurance plans and now were making their sinister phone calls, asking, essentially, in the most roundabout, delicate way, "Why aren't you dead yet?" The new drugs had foiled their ghoulish scheme! But still they kept calling. Hector chased the faces, the voices, the attitude, even the asses that reminded him of Ricky. So many new party drugs and a thumping sound system everywhere he went.

A woman walked into the shelter—attractive, white, slim, rich-looking, skinny black jeans, ballet flats, a white eyelet gypsy blouse, dark hair pulled back in a messy ponytail, a leather bag, big sunglasses, iPhone in hand. The catcalls instantly started. She seemed hesitant to venture farther into the room.

"That's the woman for you," the staffer said to Hector.

Hunh? Hector thought. Who was she? He ignored the jeers from the other guys in the room and walked toward her, mortified.

She took off her sunglasses. "You're Hector, right?" She sounded nice enough, but unsure, wary. He nodded. "I'm Drew." She extended her hand, which he took. "I'm a friend of Ava's and her daughter, Milly. You know, from the Christodora? I live here in L.A."

It all kept coming back to that kid! he thought. A friend of the kid's adopted mother. He nodded. "Thank you for coming to get me," he managed to say.

The woman glanced around the room. "Are you ready to leave?" she asked.

Hector turned to the guy at the front desk.

"Nobody's keeping you here," he said.

"Thanks for everything," Hector said.

"Good luck, buddy," the staffer said, reaching under the desk to hand Hector a plastic bag. It contained the dirty clothes he'd peeled off before his cinder-block shower the day before. "Try to pull your shit together."

Outside, the sun hit him like an angry blast. He put his hand over his eyes.

"I think I have another pair of sunglasses if you want them," the woman said. She fumbled in her bag and pulled out another big, dark pair—ladies', obviously. Hector took them, put them on gratefully. The woman giggled a little. "Very glamorous," she said.

He barely smiled. They got in her Prius and she put on the air-conditioning. "I would never do this usually, except Ava told me all about you," she said.

Oh God, Hector thought. He could only imagine what that meant. "Thank you," he said.

"Can I ask you something?"

He nodded.

"You're a meth addict, right?"

God, it stung to hear himself called that by a total stranger, to know that was how old colleagues described him now, too. But he nodded.

"I'll help you sort out your situation here and get back to New York, either way. But do you want to stop?"

"I wanna die," he told her.

She sighed. "Well, so did I. I had a drug problem, too. Can I ask you one thing? Would you be willing to go to an AA meeting with me now?"

"I don't have a drinking problem," he said.

"There's a lot of drug addicts there, too. There are meth heads."

Meth heads! That was all she thought he was—how casually she said it! But, well, she was right. Hector felt a frisson of shame, like maybe he wasn't supposed to have become a meth head. Maybe he was supposed to have dealt with loss the way other folks he knew had, with a certain amount of bitterness, defeat, and fatigue, but with dignity, staying in his post, remaining a responsible citizen, a helper of his community. The idea exhausted him and even bored him a little bit. But he also felt that perhaps he had exhausted the role of a meth head. Hector Villanueva, who had worked alongside Bill Clinton and David Kessler at FDA—a meth head! This woman had met him only minutes ago and it was clear she thought of him, first and foremost, as just that.

"Sure, I don't mind going to the meeting," Hector told her. His life was in shambles, he thought. Where else did he need to be?

"There's one in West Hollywood in an hour. You want to get something to eat first?"

"Sure."

She drove to a Koo Koo Roo, a fast-food rotisserie-chicken place, on Santa Monica Boulevard. There were lots of young gay guys inside, all in tight tank tops and shorts, toting gym bags. Hector knew he looked like a homeless person in his oversize old T-shirt and jeans, his motorcycle boots, but he didn't much care. At least he told himself as much. The woman ordered an unsweetened iced tea and a salad.

"I'll get you something," she told him. "You must be hungry."

He was ravenous. He hadn't had a real meal in what seemed like five days. "I'll pay you back for all of this," he told her.

She put a hand on his arm. "Don't worry about it, just order what you want."

He ordered a half-chicken and two sides. They sat down together. He was still crashing; it was hard for him to keep his eyes open. He felt gutted from the inside and far away from the bright, loud, pop-music-playing world around him. The woman gave him a kind, fatigued smile.

"Did you know Milly's son in the Christodora?" she asked him. "Mateo?"

Oh, no, he thought. What was coming? He nodded. "The little Latin kid."

"Right," the woman said. "They adopted him. Well, pardon my weariness, but he actually—he developed a heroin problem a few years ago. And he'd come out here a few months ago for a rehab I recommended. And he was doing really well and staying with me and my partner, my boyfriend, out here, but he disappeared a few days ago and stole our bank cards, stole our money from ATMs, and we haven't heard from him in two days. So—like I said—pardon my weariness, it's been a very trying past few days."

As the woman recounted this, a fresh wave of self-loathing crept through Hector's gut. He'd abetted the kid's downfall.

"I'm sorry," he managed to say. "Really, thank you for coming to get me."

"I don't mind. I've been there. I'm nearly twenty years sober now, but I was there."

"What was your drug?"

"I was just a drunk and a cokehead. Nothing very hard core. But, well, I mean, I was very young at the time—like twenty-five. And I just couldn't cope with life. I was freaked out and scared and didn't know how to live my life." She looked at him keenly. "Ava told me about all the amazing work you did. Thank you, because I have many friends who are alive today because of the drugs that you helped create."

Her words pierced him with discomfort; they felt too admiring. "I didn't do that much," he said.

"I know that you did. Ava told me."

Hector stared down into his food, which he'd been attacking, his stomach sucking it into his system faster than he could fork it into his mouth.

"Do you have a Valium or anything like that?" he asked her.

She shook her head. "I don't."

"I'm crashing," he said.

"Can you come sit in the meeting with me for an hour and if you're freaking out or feeling suicidal after, I'll take you to the ER?"

He nodded his head.

The meeting was actually around a bunch of picnic tables in a park—Plummer Park. Hector sat there alongside the woman, Drew, looking at the thirty or so people collected: a mix of women and men, some of the men obviously big queens, one or two trannies in the group—but put-together, employed-looking trannies, dressed more or less like Drew. About half the people seemed to have brought their little dogs along with them. Everyone was kissing, hugging, seeming so chipper. Drew introduced him to a few folks, including a sixty-year-old bearded leather bear named Vinny whose cheekbones had the sunken quality of men who had been on a particular, early generation of AIDS medications a decade ago.

It was hard for Hector to absorb it all, feeling like shit. How the fuck had he ended up here? Whenever he happened to make eye contact with someone, they gave him the same sweet, understanding, crinkle-eyed smile that made him cringe and look away. He picked up stray bits of what people were saying. When it got to the bear, Vinny, he went on mostly about how he was praying and meditating to help him take care of his eighty-five-year-old mother with Alzheimer's in Pasadena.

But Hector couldn't really concentrate. Out of the haze of the past few days, jigsaw pieces of anxiety were floating back into his consciousness: he had left Brisa, the dog, his prize bitch and only constant companion, with a tweaker friend in New York whom he thought would be trustworthy because he claimed he wasn't doing meth anymore, just some ketamine. Hector took pride in that he never let his partying keep him from feeding, walking, or showering love on Brisa—he'd take her to the vet when he was crashing if he had to, numbed out on Klonopin—but he hadn't much thought of the wisdom of leaving her with fucking Scooter Rosen, who had twice nearly died from GHB overdoses. Then there was the rental car. He hadn't even thought to tell this lady—um, this Dreena or Deana? what was her name again?—about the car he'd left parked outside the Cathedral of Our Lady of the Angels.

And the kid. This thought pierced the glue of his brain. Walking out on the kid and the girl and the twink from Palm Springs in that apartment, everybody boinked out of their mind on what had to be about four different drugs. The scene started to take up space there again, as he listened to the AA people babble, growing like a vision in a nightmare that was peaking. He knew that the EMTs came. But still . . .

He'd been staring off, absently watching the dogs in the dog run, when he blinked back and realized everyone was giving him that horrible kind, expectant look. He'd apparently not heard someone say something.

The rich woman who'd brought him here put a hand lightly on his arm. "Do you have a burning desire to say something?" she asked him softly.

He felt his face burn scarlet. They were all fucking waiting for him to say something? He shook his head. Everyone held him in their kind, concerned stare for a moment longer, as though they really didn't believe him, before someone else raised their hand and the focus was blessedly taken off him.

Then—oh God—the meeting was ending, everyone was clapping, and they were standing and holding hands and saying that fucking prayer. The rich lady slipped her hand into his. Of course he'd come across this prayer in his past rehab stints. *God, grant me the serenity to accept the things I cannot change, the courage to change the things I can, and the wisdom to know the difference.* What the fuck did that mean? He'd acknowledged the last time he was in rehab that he couldn't change the fact that Ricky and nearly everyone else had died and he hadn't. Did he have the courage to change the fact that he'd become a meth head? He didn't see it that way. He personally didn't have an interest in changing it. He had the benefits that covered his rent, the food stamps, Brisa, and the buddies to party or crash with day and night. He still managed to get to Fire Island or take a plane somewhere now and then. And the way he saw it, the medications had been invented, he'd done his job. Nobody really died of AIDS anymore. He'd done enough.

As soon as the meeting was over, the rich lady and the AIDS bear Vinny walked over to him. "So what's your story?" Vinny asked him. "Where do you live?"

He stared at Vinny blankly. "New York," he said finally.

"Hector sort of found himself in L.A.," the rich lady said.

Vinny had beautiful watery blue eyes that bore into Hector intensely, a look of empathy and connection that made Hector want to crawl in a hole. "You want to come with us for coffee?" Vinny asked.

"How are you feeling?" the rich lady asked him.

He struggled for words, openmouthed. He could walk away again. He could—what? Rudely walk away and go off and try to find the rental car. But he knew he wouldn't do it. He knew he would kill himself before he got that far—the courage to kill himself, at the moment, was far greater than his courage to clean up the mess he'd made.

"I need to talk to you for a second," he said to the rich lady.

She and Vinny looked at each other. "Just me?" she asked him.

"Just for a second," he said. He managed to put a hand on Vinny's upper arm. "Sorry, just a sec," he said.

Vinny and the rich lady glanced at each other again. "No worries," Vinny said. "We're hanging out here for a second. Let us know if you want to tag along." Vinny walked back over to the group at large—the group that was all smiles and chatter and hugs.

"What is it?" the rich lady asked. "You want me to take you to the ER?"

Did he? "I dunno," he said. "I dunno where to go."

Her brows knitted close together, appraising him. "I think we better go to the ER," she said. "I'm worried about leaving you alone."

"I need to tell you something."

"What?"

"You know the kid? Your friend's kid you mentioned who ran off?"

"You mean Mateo?"

"Yeah." Oh God, he thought, this was the point of no return.

The rich lady's face darkened. "What about him?" she asked.

"I was with him out here. We were, um, partying—getting high—together."

She stared at him, baffled. "What? You—you guys are friends?"

"Uh—" He was stammering, shaking. "We would get high together in New York. At my place."

"Oh my God," the rich lady said. She stepped back slowly, her hand over her mouth. "You got him into heroin? In your neighborhood?"

"No!" he said, startled.

"You came out here and found him?"

"No! I didn't even know he was out here. He texted me and told me to come over."

"What? Come over where?"

"To a—to a girl's house."

"When?"

"Like, two days ago."

"That's when he disappeared. Well, where, where? Where is the house?" She was panicking now.

"I don't know, I don't know! It was near the church."

"What church?" Her voice was rising now, attracting the attention of the others. At the edges of his vision, Hector saw the bear Vinny walking back toward them.

"The big modern church."

She threw up her hands, as if to say, *That's a big help.* "Was he okay?" she asked. Vinny stepped up to her side, put an arm around her.

"We were all high. I called the ambulance."

"Did they come? What happened?"

He felt like she was going to hit him. He stepped back a pace or two. "I saw the ambulance pull up and I drove away."

Her hands flew to her mouth again. "Oh my God!" she cried, walking away from him, aghast.

"Sh-sh-sh, it's gonna be okay," Vinny said, taking her in closer. Hector shrank before him—a shame he'd tamped down for years rose up from his chest and seared him in the face.

"Just explain to me what's going on," Vinny said, looked from the rich lady to Hector and back again.

The rich lady gasped in a long breath, took Vinny by the elbows. "A friend's son who was staying with me," she managed to say. "I have to make calls to see what happened to him." She was already rifling through her big expensive leather bag, pulling out her iPhone, a little notebook, a pen. She turned abruptly to Hector. "How could you not have said something when I first told you about Mateo?" she pleaded.

She walked away toward the picnic tables where the meeting had been. Hector felt like his head was on fire with shame. He began weeping.

Vinny put a hand on his shoulder. "I think you better let me take you to the ER," he said. "What's your name again?"

Hector managed to say his first name.

Vinny stared at him a bit funny. "Are you Hector Villanueva?"

Hector looked at him, startled.

"I was an activist, too," Vinny said. "In San Fran. I remember we met at a conference, like, twenty-two years ago. In New York."

Hector looked at him blankly. "We did?" he asked. This was the last thing he needed right now. Ghosts, ghosts, ghosts!

"Look," Vinny continued. "It happened to me, too. It's just trauma, that's all. Don't hate yourself—it's not worth it. We went through enough already."

Hector looked at Vinny dead level in the face. "Sweetie, I have had enough of this life. I'm ready to wrap it up."

Vinny gripped his arm around Hector's shoulders and steered him about, walking him toward the rich lady. "You need to go to rehab and get sober," Vinny said. "Everything else works itself out."

"I'm not going over to her," Hector said.

"You don't have to," Vinny said. "Wait here and I'll talk to her."

Hector turned away while they talked. Should he run? He didn't have the energy to run. Anyway, they'd just call the police, reporting a man who'd said he was suicidal. In a moment, Vinny returned and introduced him to some Asian dude from the meeting, a middle-aged guy named Foster wearing a Black Flag T-shirt. Foster at least spared Hector the treacly smile and merely whopped him lightly on the back by means of hello.

"Come on," Vinny said. "We'll take you to the ER at Cedars."

He walked with them toward the parking lot. And what—what the fuck was this? Two LAPD cops were charging straight toward them across the lawn. *They're coming for me*, Hector immediately thought, then he thought, *No, they're not*, then he thought, *Yes, they are*. And they were. One of them asked him if he was indeed Hector Villanueva. He nodded his head.

"You're under arrest for possession of drugs," one said, cuffing him. "We also need to talk to you about the death of Carrie Janacek." They started walking him toward their cop car, Vinny and Foster following behind.

"I don't know that name," he said, but he felt his stomach plunge.

"It's the girl you fed with drugs two nights ago in Westlake," one of the cops said. "After you left, she OD'd."

The ground seemed to slant forty-five degrees as they were walking. In years of partying, nobody had ever died at a scene with him. He could barely even remember that girl except for those final moments when the four of them had been fucking on a couch.

"Is the kid okay?" Hector asked.

"Which one?" asked one of the cops, the woman.

Oh, that's right, he remembered. That twink from Palm Springs had been there, too. "The, uh—the Latino one."

"He's where you're going, along with the other kid," said the cop. "MCJ."

"What's that?"

"The jail."

They arrived at the cop car, and he was pushed gently down in the backseat. He looked back up at Vinny and Foster.

"I'll tell Drew," Vinny said. "We'll work on getting you out. Try to get some rest, okay, Hector?"

The cop car drove off. Hector closed his eyes, went to lie down in the backseat.

"Sit up, sir," the woman cop said from the front seat. "We need to see you."

He sat back up. He couldn't even care about what would happen to him. The only thing he wanted was to curl up into a fetal position as soon as possible and go to sleep and hopefully never wake up.

THIRTEEN

DARKEST HOURS

(1992)

Hector walked back into the apartment, fully a widower. He took off his suit and tie in the living room, then stumbled into the bedroom, pulled a flannel shirt of Ricky's from the dresser and wrapped it around his neck to deeply inhale its scent, got under the duvet, curled up in a ball, and wept. The worst part of the day had been all that time right alongside Ricky's parents. To have never even met them until earlier that year, when they came to visit Ricky in New York City for the first time because they knew that the end was nearing, to have only really known them as these Catholic Republicans from Reading, Pennsylvania, who, Ricky told him, were responsible for certain intractable elements of Ricky's own personality—Jim and Cathy, Jim and Cathy—to not particularly like them because of what he knew was the stone silence on the other end of the line whenever Ricky, so bravely and brazenly and effortfully nonchalant, ever mentioned to them his being gay, having a boyfriend, fighting the epidemic.

Then to suddenly have to be right beside them for hours, days at a time. Then the moment during the service when Cathy finally broke down—when she began to quietly weep and turned, imperceptibly, timidly, to her husband, who either truly didn't notice or frigidly pretended not to notice. Hector couldn't take it. He put an arm around this small, inconsequential woman, this narrow, Hummel-collecting woman who'd never been anywhere or known anything but who nonetheless had produced Ricky for him—how could he not be grateful, owe her something? He put his muscular arm around her and she crumpled into it, turned in to his chest like it was the soft, understanding place she'd been searching for for the past several months and soaked his suit front with tears, while he brought her into his other arm and freely indulged, crying with her, full of a white-hot rage at Jim, who stood there stoically and pretended not to notice.

After the service, the three of them and the siblings and Ricky's closest friends had lunch at a midtown restaurant. Hector was so grateful whenever one of the siblings or the friends would make a lame joke about how Ricky, with his white-trash sweet tooth, would insist they all get the chocolate-marshmallow-goo-covered dessert. After, Hector had walked Cathy and Jim and the siblings to their hotel, then taken the subway back to the Bleecker Street apartment. He had lived there virtually alone on and off for most of the past year, with Ricky at St. Vincent's.

Eventually, he determined that he couldn't weep anymore or continue on in such a state of acute grief and agitation. He took a Valium, chasing it with a glass of white wine from a bottle that had been in the fridge, half empty, for several months. It tasted sour, but he sat with it at the kitchen table, smoking a cigarette, waiting for the Valium to kick in. When he felt blurry, he took the bottle back to the bedroom with him and walked around the room, gathering up more stuff of Ricky's—a pilly sleeveless T-shirt from an old Whitney Houston concert, a pair of white gym socks, a photo from Fire Island, a red jockstrap, Ricky's astrology book, Ricky's ironic Strawberry Shortcake snuggle doll—and brought them all into bed with him and held them in his arms until he passed out.

Seven hours later, the phone beside the bed half woke him. An hour later, it woke him fully and he reached over and answered it with a cobwebby hello.

"Hector?" It was a woman's voice. He grunted an affirmation. "It's Issy."

Ysabel. He hadn't seen her in—what?—four, five months. A veil of shame descended over his semiconsciousness. "What's up?" he grunted.

"Are you okay?" She sounded timid, small.

"I just woke up."

"I just wanted to call and say I'm sorry I didn't come today. I'm not feeling well."

"I know, Ava told me. Don't feel bad."

"Did everything go okay?"

"Yeah, it went fine, thanks. You can ask Ava about it. I took a Valium when I got home and I'm just waking up from it."

"Oh," she said, sounding mildly chastised. "I'm sorry, I didn't mean to wake you."

"It's okay." Hector sat up in bed, realizing that, half stoned, he'd surrounded himself with Ricky's stuff before passing out. The framed photo of Ricky clattered off the bed and he reached down to pick it up. "How are you doing, Issy? You're not in the hospital still, are you?"

"No," she said. "I stabilized. I'm with Ava. At Judith House."

"I'll come see you this week, okay?"

"No," she said quickly. "I'm not really up to it just now. I'll let you know, okay?"

"Okay," Hector said. "Thanks for calling, Issy."

He hung up. Even in his haze, he felt that bad feeling he'd felt with Issy the past six months. It would never be the same again after what had happened. This, he thought on some murky, inchoate level, was what happened as people—a network of people—faced the end, as they realized their collective dreams weren't coming true, that they were running faster but falling behind, that they were losing coherence and morale. They connected in rash, inappropriate ways, because, most of the time, they were unable to connect at all. The survival instinct was to isolate.

He managed to climb over all his Ricky memorabilia on the bed and stumble to the bathroom, piss, then crawl back to bed. He fell back asleep, but the phone rang again. What time was it? Midnight, one? He didn't care. Was he hungry? Vaguely.

"Hector, it's Chris." Chris Condello, the movement's bedheaded wonder boy, Hector's partner in data wonkery. Hector had barely been to a movement meeting in six months, but he had to say Chris, despite his baseline brattiness, had been a good friend during Ricky's sickness, visiting him at St. V's and calling Hector regularly. He'd been at the memorial service earlier that day.

"You doing okay, Hec?"

"I was sleeping."

"I'm in your neighborhood. You mind if I drop by?"

"What time is it?"

"It's a quarter to one. I was at Uncle Charlie's."

"Are you drunk?"

"Drunk and on coke. You mind if I stop by? I wanna talk to you about something."

"Sure, stop by," Hector said. What did he care?

In five minutes, he buzzed Chris into the building and stood at his open door, scratching at his briefs, while he listened to Chris clatter up the three flights of stairs in his Dr. Martens. Chris came at him, drunk, high, and leering, his jet-black hair sticking up in about three different directions.

"Hot, greeting me in your Calvins like that," Chris said.

"I'm glad you think it's hot."

Chris put his arms around Hector, burying his vodka-reeking face into his neck. "You doing okay after today, Hector?"

"I knocked myself out with Valium. You got a bump for me?"

Chris pulled out his wallet and extracted a little baggie of white powder, popped it open, dipped his house key into it, and held a fat bump to Hector's left nostril, then another one to his right. Hector sucked up both greedily and reveled in the chemical shock to his senses. Chris did two bumps of his own, then put the baggie down on the table. They looked at each other, bug-eyed, swallowing back the coke in their throats, then started making out.

Chris pulled away. "You know how badly I've always wanted you to fuck me raw?" he asked.

"Oh, so you *are* positive," Hector said. "That's what you're finally telling me?" He pulled his dick out of his briefs and pushed Chris down to his knees by his shoulder.

"Of course I am. Aren't you?"

"No."

Chris looked up at him. "Seriously, you're not? I thought—"

"I'm not. You know it's tough for tops to get."

Chris considered this for about as long as his coked-out state would allow. "Great, so you can still fuck me raw then." He put his mouth over Hector's dick, but Hector pushed it away.

"Let me ask you something," Hector said. "Is this why you're always such a dick at meetings? You feel like you can be a cunt to people there who show up for help because you're in the same boat?"

Chris laughed, taken aback. "I'm just there to get things done. I'm not you, okay? They know I'm in the same boat."

"I don't think they all do. How come you never told me?"

"Hector! Of course I told you. I told you when you told me about Ricky."

"No, you didn't. You never told me."

Chris looked up at him and rolled his eyes, impatient. "I think I probably told you, Hector, but if I didn't, I'm sorry. I just assumed you knew."

How comically abject Chris looked right now, on his knees, saliva around his mouth, looking up at him, pleading and flustered. Hardly the Chris Condello that people venerated, that the *New York Times* profiled so breathlessly. "Just suck my dick, you jerk," Hector said, treating Chris how he wanted to be treated. He shoved his dick back in Chris's mouth.

Chris pulled it out for a second. "Then you'll fuck me raw?"

Hector shoved it back in. "We'll see."

Over the next forty minutes, they did a lot of coke. Eventually, Chris was naked on Hector's bed, on his stomach with his head mashed in a pillow and his legs spread wide, moaning away. Hector smeared lube on

Chris's butt and his own dick, but he couldn't stay hard enough to put it in. In fact, the sight of Chris's butt, fatter and less pretty than Ricky's had been, and covered all over with a dark-brown fuzz, just depressed Hector, even through the coke high.

"I can't do this," he said, crawling off Chris and squeezing himself into a fetal position, a pillow smashed to his face.

"Just take your time," Chris said.

"No, you don't get it, I'm freaking out." He lunged off the bed and returned with the bottle of Valium, chewing one to hasten its effects.

Chris looked at him, bug-eyed. "What, you're gonna bring down your high?"

"If you wanna go get high with somebody else and have them fuck you raw, then go!"

Chris looked him, jaw wide open, and laughed. "Okay, fine," he said. "Give me a Valium, too."

"Just fucking go! I don't feel like fucking you, okay?"

"Hey," Chris said slowly. He put up both hands gently, placatingly. "Give me a Valium, too. I'll come down with you." Chris reached for the bottle.

Hector yanked it away. "I'm not wasting my Valium on you."

Chris rolled his eyes. "I'll get you more." He reached for the bottle. Instead, Hector pulled out one pill and handed it to him. Chris put it in his mouth, walked naked into the bathroom, where Hector could see him wiping the lube off his butt with toilet paper, then walked to the kitchen, then back into the bedroom with two glasses of water.

"Drink," he commanded. Hector drank the water.

"Now, come here." Chris pulled him back onto the bed, lay him down, pulled the sheet over them, and put his arms around him. "No fucking, okay? Just snuggling. Two friends snuggling."

Hector put his hand over Chris's arm running across his chest. He was trembling, his heart cannonballing out of his chest from the coke. He lay there, looking straight ahead, terrorized, until the slow, blissful Valium ooze started to leak in. Once it did, he realized that, no longer panicked, he was still coke-horny, an erection growing. He turned around in bed on his side, did the same thing to Chris and fucked him silently, his mouth mashed into the back of Chris's neck the whole time. He came inside Chris, just what pushy little Chris had wanted, then he stayed inside him and started crying again.

When he finally had settled down, when he was wondering absently how to get rid of Chris but falling asleep at the same time, Chris said, "So now that you've made your deposit, can I propose something?"

Hector mumbled his assent.

"Rich and Maira and I want you to leave the movement with us and start a new treatment group. So we can do really close work with the feds and not be held back by all the crazies and the rules of order and the side issues."

Amid his semi-stupor, Hector was irked. He'd barely been to a meeting the past six months, watching Ricky die. He'd told himself he'd checked out, that he'd done his part, that maybe when this whole thing was over he was going to move back to Puerto Rico and do some kind of public-health work there. He couldn't take any more of the movement's bitterness and the bitchiness and the immovable slab of grief and sadness that lay beneath it all, the profound disappointment over the breakthroughs that hadn't happen and the finger-pointing that the disappointments provoked.

"I think I'm done with treatment work," he mumbled to Chris.

Chris turned around, propped himself up on his elbow, and faced Hector, who remained with his eyes closed, his head smashed in a pillow. Chris smelled funny, Hector noted—some mix of putty and dirt. Not necessarily a bad smell, but a weird one.

"I think having this to focus on over the next year or two will be really good for you," Chris said. "We already have a lot of funding promised up front from different private groups. But we also need someone to communicate back to the big movement, and you know you're the only non-asshole of the four of us to do it. The only one people really like."

"That's true," Hector mumbled.

"Clinton's probably coming in in January. We need to be on the protease trials all day, every day for the next few years if they're going to be structured right."

"Protease," Hector sneered out the term. "Fucking protease. I hate that word."

"Oh, Hec," Chris clucked. He brushed Hector's hair off his forehead. "I'm so sorry, honey."

Finally, Hector looked up at Chris. "If only you fucking knew how to say that a little bit more to people," he said.

Chris smiled coyly. "That's why we need you, Hector. We're all major cunts but you."

"I'll give you an answer in a few days."

Chris brushed Hector's bangs again. "I'll let you sleep now."

Chris took a shower, pulled on his clothes, did a bump of coke, and then clattered down the stairwell and stepped out into the cool October quiet of a Greenwich Village side street at 5:30 A.M. He barreled down the street, his fists thrust in the pockets of his denim jacket. He realized he was still high, so instead of going home, he speed-walked toward the East Village, to an unmarked dive between Avenues C and D, where he knew he could find more drugs and probably somebody to fuck him again. Times like this, he could feel himself, almost on a cellular level, masochistically putting more stress on his stressed-out immune system, perversely, pleasurably, pushing it to its limits. How much strain, how much toxicity and decay, could it withstand before his body really turned against him? The guys who got all into the macrobiotic natural juices and the yoga and the Marianne Williamson lectures and the positive visualization—well, how much sadder were they when they finally got sick anyway? At least this way he had some say in the matter. He pulled out a cigarette and sucked on it furiously as he walked.

And yet he only had to think of a term like *pathogenesis* or *prophylaxis* or *cytokine*—or, now most beautiful to him, *protease inhibitor*, because it contained the same shiny promise of future redemption that the term *ddI* had contained a few years ago—and some channel would switch in his brain and self-obliteration was the last thing he desired. The complex words, which put him in a circle of conversation populated only by doctors and a few other lay elites, girded him, gave him the comforting feeling that he could find his way out of the microscopic labyrinth of his own disease. And of course that special knowledge came with prestige, earning him respect from the people with medical degrees and a certain amount of awe from everyone else. All this buoyed Chris and made him hungry to see the future. Then he'd vaguely wonder why he wanted to live so badly on one hand yet behaved as though he wanted to die, bingeing on alcohol, cigarettes, and cocaine. He chalked it up to "taking breaks," rewarding himself by letting off steam between long periods of work—preparing for and then attending a conference, for example—but he had a harder time understanding the visceral and gritty satisfaction he took in his drug runs, how it felt cathartic to tax his body to the point where he could barely get out of bed for three days. When he was finally able to get up, shower, eat, and continue with his important work, he'd feel strangely as though he'd earned back his purpose.

As he walked, he passed a brownstone on East Seventh Street between First Avenue and Avenue A—a building with a discreet plaque near the door reading JUDITH HOUSE. A woman who had not slept well was sitting in the front window on the third floor in a little room she shared with another woman. She looked down and saw him and thought, with an inner giggle because she knew exactly the kind of place he was going to at this hour, sucking on his cigarette, hands thrust into the pockets of his denim jacket, *Oh, that's Chris!* She thought about all the boys and how she had barely seen them in months, not going to meetings or rallies, which was how she wanted it, but it didn't mean that she didn't miss them.

A few girls from the movement—the dykes and the handful of straight ones—she'd let come see her. Esther Hurwitz, whose frowning bluntness had terrified her initially, but who then became one of her best friends, came by faithfully nearly every day, usually with some wheatgrass or wheat-germ or lemongrass—what was it?—drink she'd make for her at her own apartment a few blocks away. Esther sat with her in the sitting room downstairs, or, when the other ladies got too loud and crazy in there, they'd walk around the neighborhood, and Esther would unload on Issy every single story of stress and contention from the movement, from the last meeting or affinity group. The through line was always that people—the boys, mostly, but some women, too—were trying to "undermine" and "marginalize" Esther because they were annoyed by her message of radical change and social justice, one that went far beyond the epidemic.

"Oh, Esther" was all Issy could think to say. Actually, Issy appreciated the updates. They cheered her up and let her know that work was still going on. Prior to Issy's disappearance, the big issue for the women had been getting the government to change the official definition of AIDS to include things that only women got, like pelvic inflammatory disorder or menstrual irregularities, which Issy had endured, and Issy had played quite a role in that effort, surprising herself with how much information she was able to both take in and explain back to other, newer people.

Then, about six months ago, she'd gotten sicker than she'd ever been—and then she was barely over that harsh episode when she got that *other* news. Then her heart just sort of went out of the whole activist thing, and it was too weird to see a *certain someone* at the meetings, and her new level of sickness qualified her for a place at Judith House. Here, she helped out Ava quite a bit with grant writing and any number of administrative things.

"When are you coming back to meetings, Issy?" Esther asked her. "You're well enough now to come back, and we need you."

Issy shrugged, kicked some orange leaves on the pathway in the park. "I feel weird going back right now."

"Nobody's going to judge you because you're having a baby. You're on meds—you're not passing it to the baby. Everybody in the meetings knows that."

Issy felt super-squirmy. "I just wanna break, Esther!" She felt pinned down. "I showed up one day three years ago because I thought I was gonna die and I didn't know where else to go. I didn't show up looking for an activist career." All these were excuses, Issy knew; she'd stopped going to meetings because she didn't want the boys, especially *him*, knowing she was pregnant; Esther and some of the other women had promised her they'd keep it to themselves.

Esther smiled slyly. "But you became an activist there. And you're pretty damn good at it. You showed those boys."

Esther put her arm through Issy's, and Issy smiled in spite of herself. Esther was right. The past three years had been unexpectedly exhilarating. Had Issy ever thought she would stand up at a microphone in Washington Square Park and say to a crowd of a thousand people, "I am a New York City Latina living with HIV/AIDS and I am a citizen, and I want my rights!" And that everyone would cheer wildly for her and that she'd be in the papers and on the local news? Had she thought that, when her father saw her on the news and called her, furious, demanding that she stop shaming him, she'd find the courage amid her hurt to tell him to go to hell? Did she think she'd be part of committees going down to Washington, D.C., to tell her story to government officials and ask that funding be created specifically for women with AIDS?

Is this really happening? she'd thought while sitting in an office in the National Institutes of Health across from a dough-faced, middle-aged white Republican deputy from the South who oversaw a committee that continually refused to earmark more money for AIDS research and treatment. She'd made this visit with two policy people from GMHC, which the movement scorned as too accommodationist, but GMHC had told her she was one of the few HIV-positive Latinas in New York City who could talk about these issues fluently with congressional staffers and they desperately needed her to come along, so how could she say no? And now here she was sitting across from this man, who seemed to be listening to her, his doughy hands folded in his lap and his eyes narrowed in concentration and trained relentlessly on her, but his knee bobbing, bobbing, while she looked him in the eye and explained cervical dysplasia to him.

When she finished, he raised his hands, sighed, and said, "I'm in awe of the work you're doing. I know I could get in trouble for saying this in some quarters, but I think you're doing the Lord's work." He winked at her mischievously.

This made Issy blush uncomfortably. "Thank you," she said.

"But you do realize we're just coming out of a war *and* we're in a recession *and* we already passed the Ryan White CARE Act to help American AIDS victims."

Issy felt her heart rate spike, but she took a breath and thought of her movement friends back in New York. "Excuse me, we're not victims," she said bluntly. "We're people living with HIV/AIDS and we need more research and funding—the women, especially."

The deputy nodded vigorously. "I hear that," he said. "I hear that. I see so many different constituencies and I don't always get my terminology right. I apologize. I'm just saying we're looking at a very tight fiscal picture right now, we're in an election year, and we can't necessarily accommodate every special-interest group in the country, because there are many. Your group's actually received a lot of funding in the past decade."

Now Issy's heart was racing. "My *group*! We're not a *group*. We're people, we're Americans. And we haven't received good funding. Your president didn't even say the word *AIDS* until 1987." By now she'd repeated this angry mantra—that more than twenty thousand people had died before he uttered the word—several times, but it still shocked and enraged her as much as when she'd first learned it, making her realize just how disposable she was to her own country.

The deputy gently raised a palm to stop her. "Now, that was Reagan. Things have been very different under President Bush. He signed Ryan White. Please be fair."

"Sir," said the crew-cutted, young gay male staffer from GMHC who'd accompanied her on the trip, "I think Ms. Mendes would like to talk to you specifically about increasing funding for research on *women* with HIV/AIDS."

"That's right," Issy said, embarrassed that the GMHC staffer had to refocus her. "You guys need a special program to make sure that the drugs are being tested on women."

The deputy turned back to her and smiled in a way that felt, to Issy, both kind and fatigued. "We need a *lot* of special programs, Ms. Mendes. And we're in a recession."

Issy shook her head, enraged. "You know," she said, slowing into a deliberate tone, steeling herself. "I wish you could have my vagina for one day so you knew what pelvic inflammatory disorder was like. I wish you could have the pain, and the nasty discharge, and the *smell*. *The smell!* And then you'd know that that's a *symptom* of AIDS and that you couldn't even get disability benefits from it because it's a woman's symptom and the government doesn't consider it a *real* symptom. And then I think you'd think different about how important this is."

.Issy held his stare, which was a mask of studied concern. "Ms. Mendes, I'm truly sorry to hear about your health troubles. And"—here he turned to his young blond female staffer, so impassive in her headband, beige suit, and sensible heels—"we will bring your concerns into committee. Isn't that right, Shonna?"

"It's in the log!" the young woman said with Teflon brightness, the same drawl and the same faint edge of impatience as her boss.

Everyone was quiet for a moment. Issy had encountered this pause already today in prior visits—that unbearable moment when she'd spilled her heart out, when desperation and need had been expressed, when its expression had been politely acknowledged and documented and now there was no more to say. Other supplicants, with their own dread issues, were queued up in the reception area behind her. It was all so—Issy struggled for the words in her head—it was like lining up for confession, waiting for the priest to tell you something mind-blowing that would make your whole life right, except he never did. He just told you to go off and say some old prayers.

"I didn't mean to gross you out," she blurted out. "I just want you to understand."

The deputy nodded indulgently. "You have been heard," he said. "Very much heard."

Outside, in the hallway, the GMHC staffer grabbed her arm. "Issy, you were amazing! That's exactly what he needed to hear."

"But he's right," she was surprised to hear herself saying, with a realization that was both a strange relief and also cause for a deeper despair. "We think this is everything, but to the government it's just one out of a million things. It's a grain of sand."

"It's *more* than just a grain of sand," insisted the young man from GMHC.

Remarkably, though, they'd won. Later that year, 1991, the government had earmarked money to start a very large national study of women with HIV, tracking problems and issues that were specific to women. Even though the study would not formally start for another two years, the mere fact that the feds had funded it was a triumph. Wonderfully for Issy, many people in the movement pointed to her as someone who'd been brave enough to put her own story out there in D.C. to make this happen, and she'd received a shrieking ovation at the weekly meeting, everyone chanting "Issy! Issy!" Hector and Esther, standing on either side of her, held her arms aloft as though she were Rocky Balboa. She'd beamed with elation and felt a sense of belonging and acceptance she'd never known. There was more work to do—the government still didn't include women's problems in its official definition of AIDS—but they'd scored a victory. *She'd* scored a victory.

And then, of course, there was the fun she'd had the past few years, the friends she'd made. Had she ever thought she'd go to big summertime drag-queen festivals in this very park, Tompkins Square, where she'd wildly cheer on boys from the movement when they got up on stage in wigs and dresses and crazy makeup and did high kicks while lip-synching "Rip Her to Shreds"? Had she ever thought, after Tavi died, that she'd have such great, funny, gay guy friends again? She'd done the right thing showing up at that meeting one night three years ago. She'd had a pretty good three years.

On the other hand, though, there was the sickness. The missed periods and the fatigue and the winter colds that never seemed to go away and the chronic yeast infections and the antibiotics and the supplements—and, worst of all, the waiting for it just to get worse. And the rejection from her family. And the loneliness. Being surrounded by handsome boys who were having sex with each other like rabbits and her getting none of it. Even the other women were having sex all the time. She'd decided she wished she were a lesbian. If she were, a woman might love her and make a home with her and not care that she was no bombshell or that she had AIDS—women were just more like that, she'd realized, especially lesbians.

There had even been this dyke, a *morena* named Tiffany who looked like a tough little fourteen-year-old boy in a twisted baseball cap, who'd asked her on a date. She'd come right up to her after a meeting and said, "Let's go to Nanny's and get a beer and talk about this situation."

"We got a situation?" Issy had replied, smiling.

"If you want one," Tiffany had said, chucking her chin. "You look like you need one, sexy."

Issy had exploded laughing, uncomfortable. "Tiffany, I'm not into women, right? But I think you're really sweet."

Tiffany had just sort of made a sad face and shrugged and twisted her cap around and swaggered away. Maybe she should have given Tiffany a chance. Maybe *that* wouldn't have happened, because she wouldn't have been so lonely.

In the bed across from hers at Judith House, Shirley, her roommate, was waking up.

"How long you been up, girl?" Shirley asked her through a yawn.

"Like an hour," Issy said. "I couldn't sleep. My back hurts."

"You feel him kickin' this morning?"

Issy ran a hand over what she felt was her horrifyingly huge belly. "A little bit."

"Two more months, girl," Shirley said. Issy nodded slowly. Shirley had an air of sullen indifference about everything, but, Issy had noted, she was obviously following her pregnancy keenly because she was always counting down to Issy's due date. "There gonna be three babies up in this house."

"I know, right around Christmas," Issy added. She looked down on the street and watched a junkie crouching and rocking in a phone booth. Did she know him? Living here going on six months now, she was starting to recognize the neighborhood's junkie network by face, or by where each one liked to nod. She was pretty sure the one down in the phone booth was Ronny, who once told her, in one of his more sentient moments, that he used to work in a quarry upstate.

Shirley sat up with a start. "I gotta make breakfast today. Damn! I gotta peel potatoes."

"I'll help you."

"No, you can rest, baby."

"No, no, it'll be good for me to walk. I can't sleep any more anyway. Go use the bathroom, I'll go after you."

"Aw, thanks, baby." Shirley creaked and groaned her way out of bed, wearing a Yankees T-shirt that came down to her knees and sweatpants. Shirley was a tall girl, but damn, was she a reed. You could put your thumb and index finger all the way around her biceps. But Shirley insisted she had always been skinny, that it wasn't just the virus. She'd run track in high school in the Bronx, sometime back in the early 1960s. Shirley wasn't political about the epidemic. She spent most of her day going to Narcotics Anonymous meetings and the rest of it playing cards in the park with a bunch of old guys. She also liked to cook for the house and was proud of her hash browns.

"I'll meet you down in the kitchen, babe," Shirley said. She grabbed her towel and her bag of toiletries and padded down the hall. Issy folded her hands over her belly. Another day at Judith House, she thought. It was Sunday—the one day that Ava didn't come in. The girls would have a quiet day. Maybe they'd go for a walk, buy some magazines and cosmetics for themselves at a ninety-nine-cent store.

Issy would have to take her AZT soon. She'd have to take it right in the middle of breakfast to "bury" it as best she could, then after breakfast she would feel disgusting, nauseated, and strange in the head and have to lie down for an hour. She sat there and thought about the funny permutations and implications of things: if she had never gone to that first meeting of the movement, hadn't met Ava and Hector and Chris and the rest, she would never have learned what inside researchers suspected—what, in fact, had just become a major scientific trial in order to confirm the suspicion—that a pregnant woman taking AZT could all but eliminate the chances of passing HIV to her baby. This had been documented the past two years, anecdotally, in hospitals in New York and elsewhere. She probably wouldn't even be taking AZT otherwise, it was so disgusting, and by this point most doctors and activists believed that, in the long run, it didn't stop HIV anyway.

But then again, she thought, if she hadn't gone to that first meeting, she wouldn't be pregnant now. Well, maybe she would be, but she wouldn't be pregnant with—oh God, she thought. Was she crazy to have this child?

Ava was supporting her. It was tough for Ava, but at least she stood by her conviction that a woman could do what she wanted with her pregnancy, even if she was HIV-positive.

"But whose baby is it, Issy?" Ava would ask her.

"I don't know," Issy had lied. "I've—I haven't been careful with a lot of guys lately." If only that had been the case! she thought, laughing to herself. That might have been fun!

"Can we get in touch with them?" Ava asked.

"I didn't get their last names or their phone numbers. They were just stupid guys I met in a club in Queens."

Ava's eyes widened. "Did you tell them you were HIV-positive?"

Issy nodded, continuing to spin her tall tales. "They didn't care. They were all macho about it."

Ava shook her head and rubbed her eyes, which looked perennially tired from the various psych meds she had to take. "Good grief," she said.

Issy had stopped going to the movement meetings as soon as she started to show her bump in a way that made it clear she wasn't just putting on a little weight. Ava promised her she wouldn't say anything about it at the meetings. Issy didn't want to go to meetings and deal even with the hint that people disapproved of her for carrying this baby. Every time somebody looked at her and her bump, she knew what they'd be thinking—or so she thought. *I can't believe she's going to have that baby.* So Issy withdrew partly to a scared place inside herself that she'd been in before she ever showed up for the first meeting. But not entirely. She did have Judith House, after all.

That, of course, was not the only reason she stopped going to the meetings. And it was well enough that Hector thought she wasn't going because she was ill, which was unfortunately true. She was declining. And she knew Ricky was sick too, and that Hector was preoccupied with him, so better not to bother him with this anyway. She allowed visits from Esther, who lived a block away, and she'd told Esther exactly what she'd told Ava: she'd been lonely and yearning and, when she was still living with her family in Queens, went out a few nights and connected with random men, three or four.

She would have this baby. She would never miss a dose of AZT and she would have this baby and the baby would be HIV-negative. She still thought there was a chance she might live, that she might make it to the new, better drugs that were in the works—that all their work in the movement would kick into high gear in the research trials. It was only going to go faster once Clinton came into office! Then they'd have allies in Washington instead of enemies. But she wasn't taking any chances. Yes, everyone in the movement said they were leaving a legacy, even if they died soon—they were deriving some meaning from all this, that they would leave something better behind. That was how the sick ones in the movement who knew they might not be long for this world kept their sanity. And she was among them. But she was leaving more than that. She was not going out of this world at thirty-three, thirty-four, thirty-five having left nothing behind. She knew her child would thrive. Ava would make sure of that; Ava had promised.

She wouldn't tell Hector. He'd never know. It wasn't fair to put that on him when he was taking care of Ricky. And curiously, Issy thought, that's how it had happened—taking care of Ricky! Hector had told her on a Thursday that he was bringing Ricky home from the hospital that night, and Issy had said she'd drop by with a box of Ensure and some old blankets she'd cadged from her parents' house in Queens. She wanted to make sure Ricky was comfortable and had everything he needed now that he was back in the apartment.

But when she arrived, she found Hector alone—no Ricky. Hector had been drinking tequila on the couch, watching *Beverly Hills, 90210*.

"What's going on?" she'd asked. "Where's Ricky?"

"Turns out he had a staph infection in his thigh so they had to keep him in longer, on an antibiotic drip," Hector said. He spoke louder than usual, thickly, eyes cast down. Issy noticed he'd spilled tequila on the rug.

"Oh my God," she said, setting down the box on the kitchen table. "Poor Ricky. He must be so sick of the hospital."

"Naw," Hector drawled. "He has some gay nurse now he talks astrology and bullshit with all day. About signs and moons and what's rising and what's falling. He feels fine. PCP's cleared up."

Hector was drunk. That much was clear to Issy. "Oh, Hector," she said, laughing a little. She moved toward him and gave him a hug. "I'm sorry you guys are going through this."

He put his arms around her. "We've been through it before. How you feeling?"

"Okay," she said, smelling the tequila on his breath and feeling his large hands on the small of her back. She wanted to stay there. She had not been held close for a long time. But she gently stepped away. "Pretty good today, just a little tired."

"How's your family?" He motioned for her to sit across from him on the couch, and she plopped down, grateful to rest for a moment. He'd asked her in Spanish, which they slipped into occasionally when it was just the two of them.

"It's stressful living there," she answered in Spanish. "They don't mind me going to meetings, but they don't want me out in public. I told you my dad said I was bringing shame on the family."

"*Bochinche!*" Hector exclaimed. Shameful gossip.

"Yes." She laughed. "*Bochinche.* The nice girl brings down *bochinche* on her family."

"You should move to Ava's," he said.

Issy paused. "I probably will soon," she said. She wouldn't mind the support she'd find there. At the same time, moving to Judith House also meant she was sick enough to qualify for a place there. It felt like a death knell. She didn't want to feel that way—she knew it wasn't fair to the other girls who already lived there—but she couldn't escape the feeling.

She and Hector caught each other's eyes for a moment too long, and she looked away. In the sudden silence, she'd felt the specter—*el espectro*. This was what, in her head, she called the dark pit before her when she was alone, when she wasn't ensconced in the comforting shouts and cries of the meetings or rallies, or some of the high jinks they'd have from time to time in clubs. *El espectro* was simply when, in the silence, you realized you'd probably die soon, or that everyone around you was dying. No action against a government office or clever new poster or even hundreds of friends chanting the same words at the same time could really make the specter go away for good.

Still looking down, she shook her head. "It all sucks," she said. She traced patterns on her jeans with her finger, not wanting to look at Hector.

He got up and went into the kitchen, came back with a glass for her. "Drink with me," he said, pouring her tequila.

Issy laughed. "That shit'll fuck me up!"

"Not so much this far along." Hector handed her the glass.

"Don't we get limes and salt?"

He laughed. "You wanna go downstairs and buy limes?"

"No!"

"Then just drink."

Issy knocked back her first gulp. The tequila burned and bloomed in her stomach, filling her with a liquid sunny warmth. She seldom drank; it wasn't good for her liver. "My God, that feels so good," she commented.

Hector smiled bitterly. "I know."

As they drank, on opposite ends of the couch, they idly watched the TV program—an inane plot in which the girl played by Shannen Doherty witnesses a robbery at her favorite diner and then has flashbacks about it.

"Haha, she's having night sweats!" Hector laughed. *"Pobre blanca!"*

"Yeah, she saw a robbery in Beverly Hills!" Issy cried. "How's she ever gonna recover?"

The more Issy drank, the more she felt convinced she was throwing off earthly chains. She and Hector could've been kids growing up on the island together, running on beaches. It all could've worked out so differently! Maybe what they were living through wasn't really happening; maybe they were waking up from a bad dream. The more she drank, the more she admitted to herself that she'd been in love with Hector for three years, that he played the starring role in fantasies she barely allowed herself. Then suddenly she was saying, "Oh, Hector, oh, Hector," over and over again. Then she was in his arms on the couch, tasting his tequila lips.

Hector broke out laughing. "You're crazy, Issy!"

"I know." She laughed, her hands gobbling up every part of his body. "You've been so good to me, Hector. I really love you."

"I love you, too, Issy. But I don't—"

"I know. I don't care. Can you just hold me? I haven't had that in so long."

"Of course, Issy." She felt his hands in her hair.

Then it started happening. *He's humoring me, it's a pity fuck*, a little voice in Issy's head told her. But she couldn't be bothered with that. She felt the all-consuming gratitude of someone who sets misgivings aside and gives over completely to a fantasy coming true. She looked at him. He stared up at her, lying on his back, frightened and awed.

"Just let me show you," she said. And indeed she had to show him. But when she undid his pants and saw that he was semihard, she felt a quiet wave of triumph that allayed some of her feelings of being pathetic. She slid down, fellated him, took pride in his moans, in his hands on her head. When she felt he was not far from coming, she pushed down her own jeans, her wet panties.

"We need a condom," she said.

But Hector pulled her closer. "You're not going to give it to me," he said.

She felt a new rush of gratitude and tenderness toward him. Four years now, she'd lived with the feeling of wearing a sandwich board that said DAMAGED GOODS. TOXIC VAGINA. She often felt certain people on the street could read this information in her eyes, and she could see repulsion or pity in return. She knew it was difficult for a woman to infect a man. Usually, though, that didn't quell her feelings of self-quarantine. It wasn't an easy thing to explain to a man, and the few occasions she'd had sex since her diagnosis—occasions of which she wasn't proud, coming as they did after a desperate, lonely bar visit—she'd felt ashamed that she hadn't told the men, even though she'd insisted on a condom. It was a holy relief to be with someone who understood the disease, who knew about her and didn't reject her.

Issy lowered herself onto Hector. "Oh my God," she exclaimed. She'd barely remembered what *that* felt like. It brought back the feelings of that night in the back of the car outside the club. How strange that she'd met Hector that night, and now—

She looked at him. He was staring at her, his eyes large with bewilderment.

"Are you okay?" she asked. "Does it feel good?"

"It feels good," he said. "It's just—" His eyes welled and his voice broke. "It's just I don't understand anything. I feel like it's all happening around me and there's really nothing I can do about it."

Issy drew in her breath. Her desire simmered for a moment and she clearly saw Hector's confusion. "Let's stop then," she said, bracing herself on the couch to rise.

"No, no." He pulled her back down. "Stay there." He pulled her head down toward his, held their foreheads together, his hands behind her neck. "Stay like that."

Issy moved up and down on Hector, her feelings a queasy jumble. She was using him, for one thing. She'd been pushy about it. Yet it felt so good, like scratching an itch, deeper and deeper. She felt like, as she moved, she was trying to work something out—something that, as she got closer and closer to it, felt like anger. Rage. She'd been so fearful and ashamed and shut down for three years. What she was feeling now was rage at her family, at her neighborhood, at the whole entire city. She'd been royally fucked over! She didn't deserve this! And there was Hector. How dare he not love her the way he loved Ricky! And yet, also, there was Hector, his mouth wide open, breathing hard, his eyes squinched shut, with Ricky back at the hospital. She wanted to blot him out to the point where he was merely an object, a dildo, in this moment, but she couldn't remove herself from his grief. It was all making for a very complicated fuck for Issy, and to mute her own intensity, she refocused on Hector.

"Does that feel good?" she asked him. "Like that?"

"Yeah," he answered. "Yeah, definitely."

Issy worked it like that, focusing on Hector's face, until she felt the contractions and jerks that told her he was moving toward coming. Hector tried to pull away but Issy insisted he stay. He came inside her, noisily and hotly—he looked like a deranged eight-year-old, she thought amusedly as she watched his face—then she put the focus back on herself and made herself come, gouging her fingers into Hector's neck. She felt hugely relieved when she was finished, like she'd thrown off years of misery and frustration. She slid off him and collapsed alongside him on the couch. The full force of her drunkenness hit her now, and the room began spinning. She focused on the feeling of his hairy stomach against her back, his hairy legs on hers, his breath on the back of her neck. He threw an arm around her, and she drew him closer. The room spun and spun, making her close her eyes to it. She spun uneasily into blackness and passed out.

When she woke, she found herself alone on the couch. Sunlight streamed in through a window and she heard traffic outside. She'd barely lifted her head before the wild spinning began again. She was still very drunk—she could feel it. She managed to stand up, spying the empty tequila bottle. The last thirty minutes before she passed out came rushing back to her. She gasped, covered her mouth with her hand. She pulled up her panties and jeans, buttoned her shirt, and walked toward the bedroom. Hector had moved there at some point and fallen asleep in a fetal position in his T-shirt and jeans. His body heaved up and down. Issy knew she should take a shower and leave, but she could barely stand up straight, the room was spinning so fast. She climbed up onto the bed and lay down on her side next to Hector, who sensed her body and rocked away from it.

FOURTEEN

VANCOUVER

(1996)

Champagne glass in hand, Hector turned away from his conversation—he'd been talking with a local activist about where in Davie Village to have dinner later that night—when a nervous treble voice behind his back broke the cocktail din in the small reception room. He was shoulder to shoulder with Chris, whose trembling hand held a coupe of sparkling water, a thin ring of sweat staining his collar, his face a chalky color with another sweat film over his upper lip.

"You okay?" Hector murmured to him.

"I'm scared I need a toilet," Chris murmured back. "Fucking, fucking, fucking meds, they are *so vile*."

Hector briefly massaged Chris's neck. "You gotta hold it, honey, you know she's coming in soon. You can't shit all over the queen."

Chris allowed a grin. "That's how we'll remember this crowning moment." Then he switched into a cheesy British accent. "When I shat myself before the queen!"

"Please, she'd probably help clean you up. You think you'd be the first soiled queen Liz Taylor's seen in the past ten years?"

The treble voice belonged to an amfAR functionary, a handsome PR reptile with a long Italian last name Hector could never remember.

"She is about five minutes away with Kessler's deputy JoAnn Barbour accompanying her," he announced to the room.

"Kessler's not coming in with her?" The question had been asked by Maira Goode, to Chris's left, the sole woman in their breakaway group. A five-foot-four pear whose high-school-lacrosse thighs anchored her into the floor when she spoke before a group, and whose dark curly hair was always disciplined back into a knot, Maira had never in her life uttered anything more charged than a mere incontestable fact, which was how she'd managed to disengage herself from the movement without leaving bitterness and recrimination in her wake. Even Hector, so much more loved than Chris, hadn't fully escaped that fate, perhaps because people hadn't expected such treason from him. When their group reported back to the movement, Maira led, Hector followed, and Chris stayed home.

"Kessler's in front of another group," said the amfAR functionary.

"Pharma?" Chris muttered under his breath to Hector.

Barbour, a fiftysomething ash blonde in a taupe rayon pantsuit, the conference lanyard around her neck, entered just in time to hear the conversation. "Believe me, Liz wasn't happy about it, either," she deadpanned.

That cracked up the room. Even Maira snorted out a laugh. To Hector, the moment felt good, a nanosecond bit of irreverence amid all the pomp, the relentless schedule of the conference, the fact that everyone was slowly realizing that, after more than a decade of meeting like this every other summer since Atlanta in 1985, this was likely the one everyone would look back on as the turning point. Hector couldn't get past a shadow that fell between himself and the data; surely someone had to have missed something—surely it wouldn't pan out. And yet he'd told himself a hundred times that, well, there was the data and there were the results, happening to his friends these past six months before his very eyes. There was Chris, ready to shit himself, but still with computer printouts showing numbers that meant he probably was going to live to see the twenty-first century. There it was, all around Hector. He'd thought that 1992, Ricky's death, had been the most surreal year of his life, but maybe he was wrong. It looked like that title now belonged to 1996.

"So I would say just go on and talk among yourselves for the moment," the functionary said.

The small, crowded room settled back into murmuring chatter. Hector crossed glances with JoAnn; she smiled and came over.

"So you get to be the queen's plus one," he joked.

She gestured at her pantsuit. "I'm sure I'm not up to her standards of glamour."

"Like Kessler is? Come on, neither of you are exactly Rock Hudson circa 1960."

"True, that," JoAnn demurred, glancing down at the floor. Briefly, Hector considered the inner life of a single, childless FDA deputy commissioner. He pictured her reading briefs while microwaving a frozen dinner and pouring a too-large glass of wine at the kitchen counter of a Bethesda condo after getting home from work at ten P.M.

She looked back up, eyed him. "You guys should feel really proud," she said, sotto voce. "Really, *really* proud."

Hector shrugged; now it was his turn to feel awkward.

"You called us out when you needed to," she added. "Every step of the way. On AZT plus ddC. On the d4T data."

He raised an eyebrow at her. "Don't talk about it like it's the past tense, you know." He tried to keep humor in his voice. "It's not over."

"I'm not saying that." Her voice was still low, careful. "I'm just saying—" She paused. "You guys know this one is special."

She briefly put him at a loss for words. "Yes, it's special," he finally averred.

But she caught something in his eyes. "What?" she asked him. "Hector." And here she surprised him by reaching for his hand. "You *have* to acknowledge this. I know it's been really, *really* ugly at times. But this is definitive."

"I *know*." He jumped on her words, startled by the speed in his own voice. "I'm just saying now's not the time to relax."

"*No*," JoAnn insisted. "Now *is* the time to relax a minute. We can un-relax when we get back to New York and D.C. But you should relax a little now and enjoy this." She craned her neck, hearing the clack of heels in the hallway outside. She peered out the door and ducked back in, grabbed Hector's arm. "Oh my God, oh my God, oh my God, it's her," she muttered, gesturing for the whole room to push back along the far wall, near the table with the champagne.

"Are you relaxed right now?" Hector asked her, grinning.

"I'm freaking out a little!" She clutched his arm, pulling them back in baby steps toward the wall.

The amfAR functionary turned to the entire room and panto-mimed a giant *Shush!* as though he were quieting an orchestra. Then he ducked out of the room, returning seconds later with two other officials and *her*. The queen. Who'd just stood before three thousand people and the international press and denounced Canada's prime minister for abandoning a national AIDS program. She struck Hector as a giant ebony nimbus of hair and eyebrows set atop a Lilliputian frame. He was fixated on her eyes. He couldn't believe he was in the same small, crowded room with *those eyes*. He applauded with the rest of the room, exchanging giddy glances with Chris and Maira.

"Well, *hello!*" she trilled over the applause. "Hello and thank you and congratu*la*tions." The functionary shouldered his way from the back through the crowd with a flute of sparkling water for her, which she reached out and accepted without acknowledging him. She scanned the back reaches of the crowd. "Where is my new FDA friend?"

Hector nudged JoAnn. "Go!" he whispered. "She's summoning you."

JoAnn made her way to the front of the room and, her face the color of a pomegranate seed, stood shifting alongside the queen, who looked her up and down with cinematic precision, then, after a perfect beat, said, "You look very fetching in a pantsuit, Dr. Kessler."

The room erupted in laughter. It was a perfect diss to Kessler, who for one reason or other hadn't been able to accompany the queen on the plaudits she wished to bestow upon a small, select group of activists and researchers.

"Now, I don't mean to make this long day even longer for you," continued the queen, whose diction—luxuriously articulated, almost slurry, full of delicious, refined cadences and hints of various medications—rolled over Hector's ears like a thick nectar. "But I asked for the chance to meet some of the individuals I've not yet met through amfAR who've been so instrumental"—indeed, she played that word like an instrument, cresting elegantly toward the syllable *ment* before tumbling back down—"in . . ."

She trailed off, as though at a loss for how to finish. "In . . ." She looked at the faces before her, raised a heavily jeweled hand as though to say, *Help me.*

Panic flashed across JoAnn's face. "Well," she said, "in helping bring about the amazing data that we're seeing here in Vancouver. And celebrating."

The queen's hand fell, relieved. "Exactly. I couldn't have said that better myself." Pause. "And I didn't." Again, she made the room explode in laughter.

"Ahh," she continued, smiling, her head bobbing slightly as she grasped for new thoughts. "What I know is that many of you here in this room today—and I mean not just the federal people and the drug companies, but the young people from New York, from the Drug—" She paused, then sounded frustrated with herself. "Well, you know, the Drug group—"

"From the Drug Movement Coalition," JoAnn supplied.

"That's who I meant," the queen said. "The Drug Movement Coalition. I mean"—her voice rose emotionally—"I mean these five or six people—where are you, anyway? Step out."

Hector, Chris, and Maira weakly raised their hands, accepted applause from the room. Chris, Hector noticed, had gone a shade whiter.

"These people kept the rest of you on your toes the entire way, and they were not even in Washington!" Her eyes were wide with wonder, admiration. "These people were not even doctors yet *they* were the ones telling us, '*No, no, stop! Stop* testing the drugs one by one; you're killing their power. You *have* to put the drugs *together* for them to work. It's as *simple* as *that*.'"

The room was uncomfortably silent. This was the problem with the queen, many said, as beloved as she was. Sometimes the queen spoke beyond the limits of her knowledge and got the science a little bit off. Certainly, here, she was overreaching, Hector knew—everyone knew. Their group hadn't been the first to know or to insist that new drugs had to be tested in combination rather than one at a time; they'd just played a huge role promoting that information to other activists and to patients, then proposing to the feds a trial that allowed for different combinations without being too burdened with qualifying criteria, so that as many patients as possible could participate. And they'd also demanded more safety data on certain drugs before they were released. (In that regard, they were only half successful.)

But the queen was right about one thing: patients' virus levels hadn't plunged and T cells hadn't skyrocketed until the new drugs—including the protease drugs, those slightly villainous-sounding names that had dominated the past half year, like ritonavir, saquinavir, nevirapine—were administered together. Hector felt his heart rate rise and the blood pound in his temples when he thought how, for eight years—*eight whole years, how* stupid *they all had been!*—they'd been giving people one perfectly good drug at a time, letting the virus develop resistance to it, killing a perfectly good drug option for the future. *So* many people now were already failing in their new regimens because they were taking drugs they'd already spoiled for themselves. Who'd still be alive by the end of the year? It was all the more bitter for those who were failing, having to watch others flourish. He thought about the years—1987, '88, '89, '90, '91, '92—when he watched so many friends make themselves sick on AZT and ddI, and all they were doing was spoiling their chances for the future! In retrospect, he grudgingly tipped his hat to Ricky, who—granted, like many—knew in his gut that AZT was toxic and not worth taking alone. Those who'd waited were benefiting now. The ones who'd made it this far, that is. Ricky not among them.

He'd gone off on a tangent in his head. He trained his attention back on the queen.

"—much more work to be done," she was saying. "We have winners and losers right now. We must, *must*"—she pounded a jeweled fist into the palm of her other hand—"work to make sure that everyone around the world who needs these drugs gets them. Because we know the cost of these drugs is exorbitant. But in the meantime"—she raised her glass—"I want you all to toast yourselves, you wonderful people. This is a good year."

Chris turned to Hector, his glass raised. "Did you know it's a good year?" he asked.

Hector smirked. "I've heard that."

The amfAR functionary led the queen around the room, introducing her. When he brought her before Hector, Chris, and Maira, her amazing eyebrows flew upward.

"Good for *you*," she said with a conspiratorial satisfaction. "Good for you for disrupting their little *game*!" She cackled, full of mirth. Then her eyes fixed on Hector. She brought a jeweled hand to his cheek.

"This one looks like Fernando Lamas," she decreed, looking him tenderly in the eyes. "Thank you for your work."

She sailed on. Hector, Chris, and Maira suppressed flabbergasted titters.

"Was that the guy on *Falcon Crest*?" Chris whispered.

"I think it was his dad," Maira said.

"Oh, yes, he was *hot*," Hector conceded, putting the name and face together in his head. "You think they fucked?"

Chris tipped his head in the queen's direction. "I think that was your invitation to visit her hotel suite tonight." But even as he said it, his face flushed and new beads of sweat broke out over his upper lip. "And now I'm hitting the toilet," he said, slipping away.

"You want me to follow just in case?" Maira asked. Hector knew why she was asking. She was thinking about the incident last week in their tiny office in SoHo, when Chris had not made it all the way to the bathroom and she'd found him in the hallway, crying, before running back inside for a roll of paper towels. The new medications had power far beyond their intended purpose, alas.

Chris shook his head curtly and stepped away.

"Wait a minute," Maira said to Hector, tracing Chris's steps and peering out the door a few seconds. Shortly, she returned. "He made it," she reported. "I just wanted to make sure."

Hector nodded. "So, dinner?"

"Where?"

They found the local activist and made a plan to meet up at eight for Thai food in Davie Village. Chris and Maira stayed behind at the reception but Hector was beat; he wanted a nap before dinner. More to the point, he wanted to cocoon himself in solitude in his hotel room for an hour or two; he couldn't understand the dull itch of rage he was feeling just underneath every conversation he'd had that day, as though a deeply immersed part of himself wanted to suddenly sigh aloud and say, *Oh please, shut the fuck up.* He'd managed to quell that inner bitch all day, but he felt that if he didn't get an hour or two alone, she'd surface and he'd regret it.

He wended his way through the vast conference center toward the exit, ducking his head down to avoid encounters with anyone he knew.

"Hector!" he heard a voice behind him. He turned to find David, a fellow Boricua, from the Chicago chapter of the movement, hustling toward him, his lanyard swinging from his neck. David caught up with him and threw an arm around his shoulders.

"Fucking crazy day, huh?" he asked. "Can you believe Liz?"

"We were just at a little reception with her," Hector said. "She's fucking amazing." But he felt suddenly hollow saying it, by rote, as though he were following the standard worshipful script about the queen.

David beamed. "She fucking slammed Chrétien!"

"She did."

"You got dinner plans?"

"Thai in Davie Village. You guys wanna come?"

David nodded. The two walked along in silence for a moment. Hector felt burdened to make conversation but couldn't bring himself to it.

"You think you'll be in Chicago for our conference next month?" David asked him. "We'd love to have you guys."

"I think I'm getting out of the AIDS biz," Hector said, surprising himself. Had he just said that? And then he added: "Before this whole circus falls apart."

David stopped. "What do you mean?"

Hector released a contemptuous snort. "This whole circus! There's no cure coming. Look at the resistance data so far. Look at the failure rates. All these meds are gonna fall apart in about four months and then we'll be looking back on today embarrassed at ourselves for partying."

David stared at him, then laughed awkwardly. "Are you doing a Larry Kramer to entertain me?"

"No."

"But that's not what the data is showing. We get the fundamental concept now. We have other agents coming down the pike. Merck's got a compound. Yeah, sure, cure, maybe not. But suppression."

Hector felt himself soften. What had just happened to him? He put an arm around David's shoulders, continued walking. "Now you know why I gotta get out."

"You're burned out!" David offered. He seemed relieved at Hector's turnabout. Here was something he could understand. "Everyone's burned out. It's been, like, eight fucking years of this. Take some time off, go somewhere warm. Go see your family. But you know you can't leave."

Hector laughed. "Is that, like, you reading my mind or some kind of a threat?"

"It's a threat!" David smiled. "You know I need you."

Hector glanced sideways at him. "How are you doing? Are you pooping all the time?"

"Not as bad as I thought it'd be."

"Chris is having a fucking hard time."

"I know."

They parted ways outside with plans to reunite at dinner. Hector went back to his hotel room, closed the drapes, took a melatonin, stripped down to his underwear, tried to sleep and could not. He thought of what a naysaying bitch he'd been the entire conference, thought of his own anhedonia amid the hope and joy, and, deep down inside, finally admitted it was because of Ricky. He was watching lovers who'd lived in agony the past few years, waiting for one or both of them to die, realize they were getting a second shot, waking up to the reality-of-life shit that wasn't going to go away—bills, mortgages, disability payments, employment prospects. They were cursed with the divine gift of having a messy life to go on living. They would suffer through that debt, that paperwork, that uncertainty, and at the end of a day with all its trials, they would meet in the same bed, they would grasp reassuredly at each other's bodies, however thick around the waist or wasted around the limbs or butt; they might even find their way back inside each other again. They would go on, they would have *more*; they might not even appreciate, amid the stress and fear of putting a life back together and managing dozens of nauseating medications and insurance calls, how lucky they were that they'd won the AIDS lottery, made it to the finish line, run out the clock.

"You should be here, Ricky," he said aloud, his mouth mashed into his pillow. He wanted Ricky's stupid things clustered around him in bed. That's how he'd slept the year after Ricky died, on pills and crying surrounded by Ricky's shit. Then there'd been the excitement of the Clintons. He supposed he owed Chris for dragging him into the Drug Movement Coalition; suddenly they, the scrappy, leather-jacket-wearing bad-boy faggots from New York, were surrounded by feds who wanted their input and expertise, flying or Amtrak-ing them down to D.C. twice a month, putting them up in good hotels, conference-calling them.

If the feds had absorbed their tormentors in order to neutralize them, it had worked. He and Chris had gladly sucked up the bureaucratic royal treatment even if they'd paid for it by earning the rejection of (most of) their former comrades. That wasn't so bad when you were taking meetings with Clinton's honchos, when David Mixner introduced you to Hillary at a cocktail party—Hillary, who *knew* who you guys were, who thanked you for "the amazing, courageous work you guys are doing"—when you could see the prospect of a big federal or pharmaceutical job in your future, *after* the coming protease revolution. Already, Hector could see certain folks from the movement—the more complaisant ones, those who'd always half granted the feds and the drugmakers the benefit of the doubt—going in that direction, into their cushy jobs as community liaisons or marketing consultants in the bright-eyed new landscape of the chronic manageable illness, supposedly no more menacing or stigmatized or weird than high blood pressure or diabetes.

Lying in the hotel bed, Hector conceded that, all through '93, '94, and '95, an ever-widening river of good data, mixed with a steady ambient wash of self-importance, had anesthetized his grief. He'd needed that. But now a maw of emptiness and rage was opening beneath him. Idly, he rubbed his bare, trimmed chest beneath the sheets. He'd faithfully hit the gym through these past years of high-level consultancy, grunting out his misery over barbells and machines. His chest was broad and he wished beyond anything that the arm caressing it at this moment was Ricky's, not his own. But that sunny, silly cutie, like a blond sliver of sunshine on the timeline that Hector envisioned as his life, had missed the drawbridge, along with Issy and Korie and a baleful lot of others. It had all happened in the very, very worst years of sickness and death, Clinton's first term, overwhelming loss mingled confusingly with tidings of the coming respite.

Hector wished he could cry, but he could not. He wrapped both arms around a giant, nearly human-size pillow and said, again, "I wish you were here." He lay there in his strange hollowness and emotional muteness for several more minutes, thinking about the queen's expensive, legendary palm on his face. He hoped Ricky had seen that! Double snap! *That* would've signaled triumph to Ricky—not the data, not the outcomes, not the plunging viral loads and soaring CD4 counts, but the diva idol's $30,000 hand on Hector's cheek. Well, Hector thought, we all measure success differently.

The melatonin made him feel funky, cotton headed, but he forced himself to rise, dress, reapply gel to his hair, and go meet Maira, Chris, and the others in the lobby to catch a cab to Davie Village. There were thirteen of them at dinner—from New York and D.C., some Vancouver locals, David and Ed from Chicago, even Paisan from Thailand—convivial, some toasting with beer, some with ginger ale, everyone's bowels holding out through the spicy food, everyone talking about the Internet and AOL. Hector got mildly drunk and, at one point, put his arms around Chris and Maira, on either side of him, smiling goofily.

"Someone's cheering up finally?" Maira asked.

"I'm allowing myself a very small window of self-congratulation," he replied.

She leaned in closer to him, kissed him on the cheek—a rare show of tenderness from somewhat-severe Maira. "It's about time," she said.

They had a plane to catch home early the next day. As soon as he was in his room, he plugged the phone cord into his laptop, heard that satisfying dial-up crackle and wheeze. Mentions of AOL at dinner had made his insides flicker delicately; it had become his great pleasure, his balm, his late-night, soft-digital-glow Shangri-la the past eight months. Shortly, Hector—no, make that RicanTopStud57—found the room he'd been setting aside for himself until the end of the conference: "Vancouver M4M4now."

CouverPrtyBud: Wassup rican?
RicanTopStud57: Wassup?
CouverPrtyBud: You go out tonight?
RicanTopStud57: Just dinner. In town for work. At the Hyatt.
CouverPrtyBud: Nice. Want company?
RicanTopStud57: Swap pics?

A minute or two later, he got mail. Color pic of a late twentysomething sandy blond, dancer's body, naked on his stomach on the bed, throwing a smile over his shoulder, a butt Hector knew he could easily make himself at home in for an hour. Certainly, yes, he wanted company. Thirty minutes later, the front desk rang up his company, who stood before him in a Bjork T-shirt with the sleeves ripped off, cargo shorts, and flip-flops, backpack hung over one shoulder.

"I'm Nick," he said, slipping inside, sliding his backpack onto a chair.

"I'm Hector."

Nick wasted no time, pulled off his tank top and dropped to his knees in front of Hector's fly, which he quickly unzipped. "Where are you visiting from?"

"New York. I'm here for the big conference."

"What conference?" Nick was caressing Hector's briefs now.

"The big world AIDS conference."

"Mmm," went Nick, as though he'd hardly heard.

Okay, thought Hector as Nick got busy on him. *He's focused on one thing. Okay, no problem.* Hector, by rote, started saying the usual bullying, encouraging things he'd said to the endless succession of boys who'd knelt before him like this, all too eager to service RicanTopStud57. Hector obliged him with the reacharound, the digital probing that elicited bass-deep moans of expectation from CouverPrtyBud . . .

. . . who looked up for a minute. "You wanna smoke?"

"I don't smoke," Hector said. "This is a nonsmoking room, too."

"I don't mean cigarettes." Nick walked on all fours to his backpack and pulled out a red velvet box, which he carried to the bedside and opened, revealing a scarred, clouded glass pipe with a small globe head.

"You're gonna smoke crack?" Hector exclaimed. He'd once hooked up with a guy who'd pulled out a crack pipe, disgusting Hector, who'd left immediately in a huff.

"Ew," said Nick, reaching into the box for a glassine baggie. "I don't do crack. It's chrissy."

"What?" Hector had never heard of that.

Nick looked up at him, sighed slightly as though such pedagoguery was beneath him. "It's crystal meth," he said. "You don't have it in New York?"

They did, of course. Hector had done a bump or two at dance clubs, astonished and a bit frightened by the searing burn in his nose and throat, enlivened but alarmed by the jagged, jaw-grinding high it provided, which had been great for dancing till seven A.M. but not so great for trying to get to sleep later, which had necessitated a Klonopin.

"You do bumps of that," Hector said feebly, feeling as though he'd quickly lost all his RicanTopStud authority.

Nick smiled at him affectionately. "Come here." He patted the bed. "This is much better and much more mellow. It's almost like smoking pot."

"How can crystal meth be like pot?"

"You'll see."

"Will it last long? I have a flight in the morning."

Nick shook his head. "You'll be fine." He'd lightly tapped a few tiny white rocks into the glass globe. He pulled a small lighter from the box, clicking it to produce a fierce blue flame, like a tiny blowtorch.

"Come closer," Nick instructed Hector.

Hector sidled closer, curious, and Nick put the pipe end between his lips. "Hold it here," Nick said. "Now wait until you see smoke coming out of the hole in the globe, then inhale, but *lightly*, not like a bong."

Hector did as he was told. As he inhaled, he felt every hair on his body stand on end and tiny electric currents rush to the tip of his penis and nipples, his scrotum and his rectum. His belly crumpled inside into a gorgeous velvety rosebud, and the dim room seemed to become three shades brighter.

"Now come here," instructed Nick, pulling Hector close. "Blow it to me, then we go back and forth. Hold it, then blow it back, and don't pull away."

Again, Hector complied. It felt immensely freeing to take orders. As they blew the smoke back and forth, Hector's arms found their way around Nick. *This is it*, Hector's deep-down voice said. *This is how it felt. This* was his memory of holding Ricky, the I-need-nothing-else-ever perfection of that moment, or the fetish his memory had made of that moment. How strange to feel it again after four years!

Nick sparked the pipe for a few more rounds. Finally, when he put the pipe down, Hector looked at him with large, happy eyes. "Oh, *papi*,"

Hector said, breathless, one hand tugging madly at his shrunken dick. "This is fucking amazing."

"I told you it was better than bumps."

"Thank you," said Hector, pushing Nick up onto the bed, toward the luxurious bank of pillows. "Thank you so much."

Nick giggled. "It's just some hits of chrissy."

But Hector wanted to tell CouverPrtyBud that it was so much more than that. He wanted to say, *You just helped me figure out how I'm going to cope with the rest of my life.*

PART III

GROWN-UPS
(1992–2021)

FIFTEEN
TOGETHER AGAIN
(2012)

Four months after Mateo went briefly to L.A. County Jail, then into a prison-diversion residential program for first-time drug offenders, Milly sat in Terminal 5 at JFK Airport waiting for a plane to L.A., an unread copy of the Friday *New York Times* by her side. It was November, right after Obama's reelection, which had been a mild source of happiness for Milly. There she sat, nearly forty-three years old, hair in a loose ponytail, wearing a leather car coat, skinny jeans, and old suede cowboy boots and sipping coffee out of a white-and-red Illy cup, occasionally fussing with her iPhone. Most people still found her a beautiful woman—slim, her face a bit leaner and harder than it had been when she was twenty-four, but her hair was still a gentle mess of loose curls, espresso brown as ever thanks to a color job, which concealed the dozens of wiry gray rebels that had sprung forth.

Sometimes these days, when friends and colleagues engaged Milly for long periods in conversation, they would notice a tic she had, even while she was being perfectly polite and still often very warm and kind. Her eyes would repeatedly glass over, as though she were about to cry, then they would dart away as she fussed with a lock of hair or with her iPhone, emitting a slightly peremptory "Mm-hmm, mm-hmm, ahh, hmm," to whatever someone was saying to her, as though she were trying to take it in faster, hurry them along a bit, and wrap up the conversation. It was as though, underneath her measured surface, she was saying, *Leave me alone, let me be alone again,* even if she had no particular reason at that moment to want to be alone. She was still teaching at the arts high school, and on weekends, she would trudge to her little studio and plunk away at her own art, as someone unpracticed plunks at piano keys. But the truth was she had not engaged in her art with true satisfaction in about two years—about as much time as she'd known that Mateo had a drug problem.

And as for her life mate, Jared . . . Well, in her most unguarded moments—with herself, that is, not with others, for she would never admit this to others—she would feel a stab of blinding rage toward Jared, her husband of nearly fifteen years and her partner for more than twenty, that startled her because she couldn't fully account for it. It was something similar to the rage she had felt back in those early years before she'd broken it off briefly with him: a panicked, hysterical feeling that, underneath his ministrations, affection, and stabilizing demeanor, he was holding her back from something big and important that she couldn't quite put her finger on.

It had become strained between them. They flat-out hadn't had sex in four months, not that that was any surprise given that they'd been in a state of trauma over Mateo's freshest tumble into disaster. Drew gave reports from L.A. while they went about their lives in New York, amid a version of empty-nest syndrome they hadn't envisioned while they were raising Mateo: their son across the country, not in some MFA program at, say, CalArts or UCLA, but in a halfway house for drug offenders. Several times a day, Milly would remember this fact and feel a stab of self-recrimination. Where had they gone wrong? Had she overloved him, overneeded him, overtolerated his adolescent aggression because he wasn't her born child, because she'd felt badly for him? Milly turned over these questions in her head constantly, all the while imperceptibly drifting from things that had long defined her—her painting, her teaching, her friends, her marriage. Then she would remember the incident with the sculpture and shudder and half wonder if perhaps Jared wasn't right.

Milly picked up the *Times*, halfheartedly attempted to absorb the front page, then put it down again with a sigh. The truth was, if she were being honest with herself, that even prior to the last few months—that is, in the fairly calm period after Mateo's first L.A. rehab, when he was cleaning up his act and living with Drew, when everything seemed to be finally going okay, until it no longer was—even in this period of relative calm, Milly and Jared had barely had sex. Sitting there in the JetBlue terminal, she almost winced remembering one Saturday morning when they actually were having it but she mentally checked out from beginning to end—organizing her coming day, shuffling around the timing for various things she wanted to accomplish, like visiting her mother and buying a new, better vacuum—while Jared humped away at her. She made a few obligatory noises to make Jared think that she was coming, or at least engaged, but really she was just bearing up, relieved that he was climaxing. When he finished, he stayed inside her, his heaves subsiding, and they held each other without saying a word, Milly overcome with the deadness she felt.

"I love you so much, Millipede," Jared finally said.

She smoothed his hair. "I love you, too," she said back. Which only increased her dead feeling. Not that she didn't mean it, she was fairly certain. Just that it stirred no warmth in her to say it.

"You got therapy today?" he asked.

"Mm-hmm."

"I'm gonna hit the studio then shoot hoops with Asa. But walk up and down the river after? Burgers and beer?"

"Mmm," she said, wondering if she sounded as flat as she felt when she was saying it.

Therapy was where she'd come up with her best understanding of the cold rage she felt toward Jared a great deal of the time. It was, she determined, because of Mateo. Because they'd always had a split on Mateo. Jared had basically agreed to adopt Mateo in the first place because Milly had wanted to. And Jared had actually turned out to be a very good father, and back in what they could consider the "good years," Jared and the boy developed what appeared to be something approaching companionability, taking their bikes on Metro-North upstate to Beacon to visit the Dia museum and ride along the Hudson, sometimes with Asa and his two daughters, that sort of thing.

But it was in the recent, truly hellish years—especially, curiously, after Mateo turned eighteen—that Jared detached. Not to say Jared wasn't dismayed when they learned of Mateo's latest relapse or hospitalization, but it consumed Milly in a way it didn't with Jared. In fact, stunningly to Milly, in the very years when Mateo was really declining, Jared went deeper into his own art than he had in years—more time in the studio, more time with art people, then his first solo show in years, in a small but well-regarded Williamsburg gallery.

That first rehab in Connecticut hadn't stuck for Mateo. He stayed three weeks there, complaisantly enough, but when he returned home, in time to hop onto the new semester at Pratt, he seemed to be doing nothing to preserve his clean status. Prompted by Drew, Milly asked him if he was going to meetings for Narcotics Anonymous, to which he replied, "The counselors at Silver Hill said that's not the only way to stay clean."

"How are you going to stay clean, then?" Milly had asked him.

"Focus on my work," he'd said.

Then, walking home in the neighborhood one evening, she came across him having beers and smoking cigarettes outside Sidewalk Café with Fenimore and Keiko, who urged her to join them, but she demurred. When Mateo returned home, drunk enough to stumble a bit en route to his room, she called out, "I thought you were supposed to be clean and *sober*."

"Dude, I didn't have a *drinking* problem," he called back, mimicking her cadence, before slamming the door behind him and blasting hip-hop.

Did they know when he picked up heroin again? Milly figured it was sometime in late September a year prior, 2011, when his comings and goings became more erratic. More than once in those weeks, Milly woke in the middle of the night to the sound of the front door unlocking and Mateo's uncertain steps in the dark to the bathroom, then his room.

One of those nights, right after four A.M., she woke to the sound of a giant crash in the kitchen. Jared, typically, kept snoring.

"Wake up," she said, shaking his shoulder. "Someone's in the kitchen."

Jared lifted his head, his eyes sticky with sleep. "Are you sure?"

"I just heard a giant crash."

They went into the kitchen, Milly in a long T-shirt over her underpants and Jared in his boxers, and snapped on the light to find Mateo on his knees in jeans and a camouflage hoodie, picking quarters out of a huge mound of loose change they kept in a blue ceramic vase, which had shattered everywhere.

"What are you doing?" Milly cried.

Mateo looked up. "I didn't think I'd wake you," he said.

Jared bent down, grabbed Mateo's arm. "I can't see your pupils, Mateo," he said. "Jesus Christ. Not even home six weeks." He roughly lifted Mateo by the arm into a standing position, then reached for the pockets of Mateo's jeans. "Come on, buddy, you gotta give us the house keys and go. I can't go through this again."

Milly felt a lump in her throat. "Wait!" she said, grabbing Mateo by the other arm. "Mateo, just be honest with us, did you use again?"

"Milly, look at him!" Jared cried. "He's high as a kite."

"I didn't use," Mateo said, his words a slurry. "I wanted change for a juice."

"But you don't look right," Milly said. "Have you been up working all night?"

"Milly, give it a rest," Jared said, dragging Mateo by the arm through the dim living room toward Mateo's bedroom. "Grab some clothes and give us the keys and get out of here. Enough is enough."

Mateo shuffled forward alongside Jared. But suddenly he broke away from him and picked up Jared's three-foot weathered steel sculpture, of a kind of wolf creature with jagged edges all around, and threw it through the glass top of the coffee table. Mateo then stepped back from the wreckage and stood there, shaking wildly. "Don't you fucking touch me!" he screamed at Jared, his eyes now wide open. "You fucking fraud mediocre rich piece of shit."

Jared stepped back now toward Milly, fury and fear warring in his eyes. "Milly, call the cops on the kitchen phone," he said, steeling his voice. "Mateo, drop your keys on the floor and get out."

"I didn't work out so great for you guys, did I?" Mateo sneered, still shaking.

"Mateo," Milly pleaded, "just sit down and try to breathe and let me call an ambulance, okay?"

But Jared took the phone out of her hand. "We are calling the police, Milly. This ends tonight. Get out, Mateo."

Mateo pulled his keys out of his hoodie pocket and flung them at Jared, hitting his knee. He stormed out of the apartment, his back pocket heavy with change he'd collected, and slammed the door behind him.

Milly just stood in the kitchen, her hands over her mouth, trembling, Jared breathing hard beside her. Neither of them said anything for nearly a minute. Then Jared turned to her and said, "This is over, Milly. He's eighteen. We are done."

"Jared—" Milly began.

"Done!" shouted Jared, raising a hand to stop Milly from saying more. He turned into the living room, carefully extracted his intact sculpture from the glass wreckage and set it on an end table, and retreated to the bedroom, closing the door behind him. Milly sat at the kitchen table and stared into space.

Drew had stepped in the next day in response to Milly's despairing phone call. "There is such an excellent, affordable rehab here in Pasadena called Gooden that's just for men and that does really intensive, deep work," she'd told Milly.

"But he's already been to rehab," Milly said.

"But maybe a reset outside of New York and all that context will be really good for him. I know so many guys who've gone there and say it turned things around for them. Believe me, Millipede, he's not the first to go to rehab more than once."

"I'm not sure he'll go again."

So it was Drew, in fact, who reached out to Mateo—"one addict to another," as she put it to both Milly and Mateo—and got him to agree to come out, on a ticket that Milly surreptitiously paid for. But it was Milly who pulled some of Mateo's things together, including new toiletries and underwear and his iPod and some of his cherished Frank Miller graphic novels, and then, unbeknownst to Jared, met Mateo at the airport to see him off. To her colossal relief, he actually showed up—his handsome face blotchy and sallow, that same camouflage hoodie smeared with faint stains, his eyes unable to meet hers for more than a moment. His whole presentation wrapped itself around her heart and twisted it.

"I tried to think of everything you might need out there," she said, handing him the bag.

"Thanks."

Please make it work this time, she wanted to say. But she knew she wasn't allowed to say that.

"I'm rooting for you, honey," she said instead.

He seemed to roll his eyes and scowl. "Thanks," he said again, before turning and walking away, leaving Milly standing in the terminal, bereft, wanting to reach out, pull him back, put him back together, turn back the clock, fix everything.

That had all been seven months ago. In the coming weeks, her heart swelled when she received reports from Drew that Mateo seemed to be thriving at Gooden, embracing the process, the group therapy, even the self-examination workbooks. She worried slightly when Drew said that Mateo had taken her and Christian up on their offer to come stay with them and continue going to outpatient sessions and AA meetings in L.A. What if Mateo failed them like he'd failed her and Jared? But, based on calls and texts from Drew, that's not how it seemed to play out.

"He's finding himself," Drew had texted her after Mateo had been with them for nearly a month. He even had a part-time job at a coffee shop.

"Can I finally exhale?!??!" Milly had texted back alongside a smiley emoji. And she thought: *He'll show you, Jared!*

Then she got a distressed voice mail from Drew and learned that the story had changed.

Drew picked her up at the airport. They hadn't seen each other in over a year, since well before Drew had drawn Mateo out to California. Milly stepped into Drew's Prius and the two hugged wordlessly for a good long time.

"You look really good," she told Drew, half-consciously inspecting Drew's peasant blouse, her armful of pearly bangles, her big, slouchy leather bag. She always thought Drew looked good when she saw her, and the next thing she thought of was Drew walking at an effortful clip around that reservoir near her house with her dog, which Drew did religiously every morning before she went to her meeting.

"So do you, Millipede," Drew said in the kind of supportive tone where she may as well have just appended *in spite of everything*.

As Drew drove, they made small, inconsequential chatter about work until they got to Drew's house in Silver Lake. Drew brought out lunch—a huge salad of greens, roasted squash, farro, and pomegranate seeds in a big bright yellow enamel bowl—and Christian joined them in the sunroom.

"My dear Millicent," Christian said, hugging and kissing Milly. "Haven't we all been through it with that kid?"

Milly was relieved that Christian had finally thrown it on the table. "I don't think Jared even wanted me to come out here—well, to see Mateo, I mean," she said. "I don't mean seeing you two. How do I even thank you for dealing with the arrest and all that? I barely left the house for four days after you told me."

"We think he may finally be licked," said Christian. "In a good way. Like, the addiction has finally kicked his ass enough for him to know he's powerless over it."

Even hearing *kicked his ass* in reference to her son was a bit too much for Milly, who found herself tensing.

"He's horrified—no, I think he's terrified—by what happened," added Drew.

Milly nodded slowly. The news of what had happened had sent Milly into utter bewilderment, then fury at her mother's old colleague Hector, whom she'd come to see as the absolute worst person who had ever wandered into her family history, especially when she learned that he and Mateo had been getting high together all along in New York, just blocks from the Christodora.

And apparently there had been two other people, including a young woman who'd died of either overdose or cardiac arrest, or both. Milly had barely been able to believe the whole horrific story when she'd heard it. But after Drew told her about Mateo's taking off with the credit cards and his massive second relapse with a girl dying and then his ending up in jail, Milly began thinking maybe Jared was right: that Mateo was beyond hope.

Milly finally picked her fork back up and ate a few bites. "What's up with Hector Villanueva, anyway?" she asked, grimacing as she said his name.

"He's in jail here still as far as I know," said Drew. "Some AA folks are checking in on him. Nobody put up his bail. And nor should they. It probably makes sense that he just sit there and start getting sober until they mandate him into a rehab program, which I'm sure they will. His charges weren't that major."

"He can stay in jail for the rest of his life, for all I care," Milly snapped. "He's bad news."

Drew and Christian glanced at each other. Then Christian shrugged. "He's an addict," he said. "Just like Mateo. They both need help."

Milly said nothing. She felt guilty that she couldn't see the situation as dispassionately as Drew and Christian. But she also didn't like hearing her son called an addict, even if it was true.

So instead, she finally said what had been nagging at her the whole flight to L.A.: "Jared wouldn't come with me. He said if I wanted to come, it was my choice, but he was in a work cycle and he couldn't afford to break it off."

Drew and Christian once again gave each other that minute, what-should-we-say? glance. Drew reached over and put a hand on Milly's arm.

"Sweetie," she said, "I'm just glad you came out here to see us. And I know you want to see Mateo because you love him, and I know not seeing him is eating away at you. But you also have to know there is nothing—*nothing*—you can do at this point to make Mateo stop if he doesn't want to stop."

"And also that it's not your fault," Christian broke in.

"That's right," Drew said. "If there was damage there that led to this, it happened before you adopted him. All you and Jared ever gave him was love and safety. And frankly," Drew added, her voice rising a bit, "at a certain point, with addiction, you have to stop mulling over what caused it and just decide what you're going to do going forward."

"That's right," Christian said firmly.

Milly nodded obligatorily. She felt a bit cowed into silence, hearing this from the source, as it were. Then they all just sat there for several seconds, saying nothing, picking at their food.

"Milly?" Drew finally said gently. "Can I ask you something?"

Milly nodded.

"Have you been able to paint the past year or two with all this?"

"Oh, yes," Milly said. "I mean, I go to my studio. I have a few things cooking."

On the surface, this was true. There were two or three half-finished canvases in her studio right now. But she didn't particularly like them. They were sort of ugly and dark and gunkily painted and she didn't really know where they were coming from. But in the hours here or there, usually on weekends, when she went into her quiet Chinatown studio and listened to Beck or Radiohead or Moby through speakers hooked up to her iPod while she worked, she would feel like she was attaching to something that felt blank and wide and open.

Then, after she'd painted for a few hours, after a mild sense of panic and doom started to overtake her as the night deepened, she would sneak a cigarette out of the pack that she kept in a file cabinet and swing open the industrial window that faced the Manhattan Bridge. She would sit in the window and smoke, flicking the ashes down five stories, getting dizzy in a half-awful, half-pleasant way because she so seldom smoked, looking out at the city and thinking about flying, as she'd once done often in her dreams. This was a longtime favorite thought of hers; the ease and lightness with which she could get around the city if she could fly absolutely exhilarated her. What if she could walk out the door of the Christodora every morning, turn on her jet pack, waft upward until she was hovering just over the rooftops of the East Village, and then fly—arms outstretched, feet sailing behind her, a bit like swimming—at a northwest diagonal across Manhattan, gracefully slaloming through the skyscrapers of midtown, to Columbus Circle, where her school was? And better: What if, at night, unable to sleep and oppressed by Jared's snoring, his smell, his spasms where he would kick her, she could put on sweatpants and a sweatshirt against the wind, take off from her own window, and tour the city at night? Just for a half hour or so, when she couldn't sleep? The thought thrilled her.

"—call Mateo later?"

Milly came to from her reverie. "Hmm?"

Drew was speaking. "We'll call Mateo later and see about a visit on Sunday?"

Milly nodded and went back to her salad.

The next day, after she and Drew had passed the morning in a vigorous walk around the reservoir, which made Milly feel about as good as she'd felt in a long time, Drew came into the sunroom, where Milly was reading Drew's copy of Tina Fey's book *Bossypants*, and sat down beside her. She sighed and put a hand on Milly's knee.

"What is it?" Milly asked warily.

"I talked to Mateo. I don't know if he's ready for a visit this Sunday."

"But you said you've already visited him twice," Milly said, then, "Oh." She winced. "You mean he's not ready to see *me*."

Drew sighed again. "He seemed fine with it when I mentioned you were coming two weeks ago."

Milly put down the book and crossed her arms. She could feel the Melancholy Demon bearing down.

"Listen," said Drew. "I told him you were here and I asked him to think about it and talk to me again tomorrow. He probably just needs a night to adjust to the idea." Drew paused. "He's humiliated, Millipede. You put him on a plane, sent him out here to an expensive rehab, and he blew it, and now he's in a halfway house with a bunch of ex-cons."

"Wait," Milly interrupted, startled. "There's a bunch of *ex-cons* in this house?"

"It's a very good program," Drew said. "It's a nonprofit. I know many people who've done it. It was also the only place for him to go because nobody was paying for him to go somewhere fancy a third time around."

This much was true; when Jared had heard Mateo was in jail, he'd instantly said that Mateo would never receive a dollar of support from them again.

Drew stood up. "Just give it a little time, okay, Mills?"

She went back to her office down the hall, but when Milly picked up her book again, she couldn't concentrate. After a few minutes, she padded down the hall and tapped on Drew's office door. Drew turned around in her chair.

"Can I ask you something?" Milly began.

"Ask."

"Do you even remember this drug time in your life anymore? When you first tried to stop, from that night you came to my place and then, I guess, the following year in rehab and all that?"

Drew smiled. "I remember it vividly."

"What do you remember about it?"

"It was like—" Drew searched for the words. "It was like being born again."

A memory flashed through Milly's mind: Drew wearing that ankh pendant! Which, as it turned out, she had abandoned a year or two down the line, much to Milly's private relief.

"I don't mean that in a Jesus-y evangelical way," Drew said. "But it was like—every day those first few months were so *hard*. But everything was so vivid. Colors, interactions I had with people, emotions, thoughts, things I noticed on the street. Daily epiphanies. Everything was so raw. I wouldn't want to go through it again. But I think that was the best year of my life."

Milly mulled over this a long time. "Do you think maybe Mateo's finally having that now?" she finally asked.

"I hope so. But maybe you should try to have a year like that, too."

SIXTEEN

WEST ADAMS

(2012)

Mateo is on his hands and knees, cleaning the second-floor bathroom. This is his job every morning after breakfast, at least for this week's work cycle in the house. By far, it's the gnarliest job here. With cooking duties, there's the social element, goofing with the other guys in the house, putting a bit of creativity into the chopping of vegetables, listening to cheesy Top 40-hip-hop on Power 106 on the old boom box in the kitchen. Vacuuming and dusting, there's still an element of remove from the gnarly factor; at least you're standing up, Mateo figures. But when you're on your knees because you've got to spray and wipe down the floor where two dozen guys have planted their feet while they took a dump over the past twenty-four hours, then have to wipe down the shower where they've probably jerked off, savoring that brief moment of privacy in a house where privacy is hard to come by, there's no getting around the fact that all your choices have led you here, to where you're living under court mandate in a house with a bunch of other court-mandated dudes, who were actually lucky that alcohol or drugs were part of their records, because it gave them this option of choosing a halfway house over more jail time.

And the funny thing is Mateo doesn't even really mind. While he's working, guys in the house are singing that schmaltzy half-rap, half-ballad "Lotus Flower Bomb," by that guy Wale, and he finds himself lifting up his head and joining in, cracking himself up as he cleans. And when he's done, he stands up in the doorway of the bathroom and takes a moment to admire his work before he puts away the spray cleaner and the paper-towel roll in the cleaning closet before he heads back to his room, which he shares with three other guys, to grab a towel and hit the shower himself. He has seven minutes to report downstairs. On today's morning docket: acupuncture, a bunch of tiny needles in his ear to reduce anxiety and cravings, at some nonprofit clinic nearby.

Every morning he wakes up in that room, where three other guys are snoring and mumbling in their sleep, and he looks around and his first thought is *How the fuck did I get here?* Then, every morning, whether he likes it or not, it all comes rushing back to him: that moment when five EMTs came rushing at him down the hall as he stared dumbly at them, naked, paralyzed from what turned out to be the combined effects of heroin, crystal meth, ketamine, and MDMA. There he was, looking up at the squad in a narcotic haze. Instantly, two of them threw one of those silvery thermal blankets around him, pulled him onto a stretcher, and started taking his vitals. A cacophony all around. The other EMTs blew open the door to the apartment, where he could vaguely remember hearing the music and assorted moans and exclamations of the porn video.

The EMTs coalescing in the apartment around *her*. Carrie. (A woman at the nonprofit yoga-like clinic they go to taught him how to do a breathing exercise, after he confided to the woman that every time he thought of Carrie—and it was usually several times a day, starting with shortly after he woke—he wanted to hurt, or kill, himself. He clings to that breathing exercise now like a madman.)

Anyway, Mateo remembers that much. He doesn't remember much more. Well, he vaguely remembers lying on a bed that was only half concealed by a curtain on a ceiling runner, shouting things, and people holding him down. And that's about the last thing he remembers until he came to in a hospital room. Then there was a period in a detox unit he can vaguely recall, shuffling awake a few times a day to go eat some bad food with a bunch of freaks, sitting there in a half-coma with a social worker talking to him about his options, then, at night, a makeshift AA meeting with some outside people brought in, mumbling out his dank thoughts.

It had all led to an inpatient rehab center for a month, some place that accepted Medi-Cal, which apparently they had put him on. He barely remembered anything from that month. He didn't remember much until he was discharged and a minivan drove him here, to this not-so-pristinely maintained fourteen-room Craftsman home, called Triumph House, in a run-down, poverty-stricken neighborhood full of beautiful old houses called West Adams.

At this point, he finally started coming to, distinguishing one day from another, becoming aware of the guys around him—mostly black and Mexican guys coming out of prison for some addiction-related crime, usually dealing, sometimes assault or burglary. There is one guy he really loves, a funny, crusty old white geezer named Bobby G. who just got out of prison after serving twenty-two years for a crack-fueled murder. He and Bobby play poker every night after dinner, for pennies, along with a hugely fat Mexican dude named Santi, a former dealer a few years older than Mateo, who calls his mother "sweetheart" over the phone, which everyone in the house gives him a hard time for.

The funny thing is, in many ways, Mateo is the happiest he's ever been. He feels like he's with the right people for the first time in his life. Cleaning up the kitchen one night with Bobby G., he asked, "So what were all those years locked up like?"

And Bobby G. just turned and looked at him—a pissed-off look, Mateo thought. "How old are you?" Bobby G. asked him.

"Nineteen."

"You have no fucking idea how lucky you are not to be in prison," Bobby G. said.

Mateo laughed. "This is fucking prison!"

"This is fucking nothing," said Bobby G. "This is a fucking picnic. Look at me. I can barely walk, my joints are so fucked up. I'll never get those twenty-two years back. Go in at forty, come out at sixty-two."

Bobby G. dragged out the trash, leaving Mateo standing there in the kitchen with Wiz Khalifa on the radio.

Today, when Mateo and the other guys are in the minivan on the way to the acupuncture clinic, Mateo sees him again: the tagger working on his wall, the sidewall of a building fronting an abandoned lot. The tagger's been working on this wall the past week, and Mateo's never seen anything like it. His work is so beautiful, abstract, all pale greens and blues, none of the fat black outer lines of traditional Pop graffiti, and it almost looks like he's rubbing it out, or wiping it away, as he paints, like he's leaving behind ghost colors. Every few days, Mateo's noticed, in various trips here and there in the group minivan, the tagger makes progress on it, just this short figure with a baseball cap and his back to the street, working away. Mateo's started becoming obsessed with the wall, wondering at random hours of the day if the tagger is there, dying for when he's no longer on restriction and can come and go freely from the house.

As the van drives away from the corner, Mateo suddenly feels the saddest pang he's felt in a long time—and, remarkably, he can identify it. It's that he hasn't painted. With the exception of some doodling he's done here and there in rehab and in the house to pass the time, he hasn't made a thing in over a year now, since well before coming to L.A. Can he even remember the last canvas? Oh God, that's right. It was that black impasto—the leaves, the sad, foreboding tumble of dead leaves in the corner of the canvas, exactly what that last fall in New York had felt like, chilly death creeping in.

When he gets back to the house, feeling light as air from the acupuncture session, there's a message on the chalkboard for him to call Drew. He feels the usual mix of shame and heaviness that comes over him when he thinks about her or talks to her. And, of course,

Drew is the link back to her—Millimom. He says the Serenity Prayer to himself—he can't believe he actually does this now, but actually he finds himself doing it a lot, whenever he feels the least bit stressed over something—and he calls Drew.

"Are you doing okay, hon?" she asks.

"Yeah, I'm okay." He still can't believe Drew is so kind to him after what he did to her and Christian. "How are you?"

"We're good. So—" She pauses. "You know, your mom's just here till Monday. You think we could come see you Sunday? I don't want to push, but I know you said you'd think about it a few days ago when you didn't feel ready."

Mateo knew this follow-up call was coming. And he isn't sure how he can put Millimom off again, her having come all this way just for him to rebuff her.

"Sure," he says. "You guys can come on Sunday."

Oh, shit, he immediately thinks. He can already see it—Millimom's stricken mask of pain. That's all he basically can remember about her during his fucked-up last year in New York. He'd practically stopped coming home; she never knew where he was. And he was barely at Pratt anymore. He was going anywhere he could to cop and use, sometimes to freaky Hector's, only a few blocks away from the Christodora; sometimes to the filthy holes of various "friends" in Williamsburg or Bushwick or Bed-Stuy; sometimes to shit-traps that passed as after-hours clubs. He avoided having to be face to face with Jared-dad and Millimom as much as he could. But once a week or so, he had to come home, for clothes or a shower or because he was so dopesick he just didn't care, and always—always—it was her stricken face, the sadness and fear etched into her face until she looked like a hollow-eyed Munch phantom.

That was the period, he remembers, when he and Millimom had nothing to say to each other. There would just be his mumbles, her mutters, a flash of her face, crestfallen anew when she realized that, yes, he'd been out there yet again, then her retreating into her room. Behind the door, he could hear the murmurs between her and Jared-dad, trying to figure out what was to be done with him. Then came the sculpture-throwing finale and his last look at Millimom's drained face before he got on the plane.

Mateo didn't give a shit what Jared-dad thought of him. Mateo wasn't a fool; he could always sense Jared's fundamental equanimity about him, that Mateo would someday be eighteen and no longer Jared's problem. Mateo knew that it was psychotic of him to have thrown the sculpture, that he'd done it in a jittery panic as he faced a new wave of dopesickness, but he also couldn't help quietly reveling in the fact that he'd let Jared know exactly what he thought of his stupid, macho metal art. He knew that spite and revenge weren't good for his sobriety, but he couldn't let that go.

Yet Millimom—she wasn't so easy to write off. The sick shame he felt when he knew that she'd heard about the whole EMT incident and jail and Carrie—

And then, oh God, Carrie! He'd sought her out that day, lured her in—he was so hungry to use and to take someone there with him. His AA sponsor told him he had to pray for her spirit but otherwise "put the Carrie self-hatred on the shelf"; he'd figure out down the line how to make amends to Carrie's survivors and, in some spiritual way, to her, but it was too soon to deal with.

That's about the only thought that keeps Mateo from blowing his brains out over the thought of Carrie, because basically he feels like he killed her.

It's always hard for him to get his bearings when Carrie thoughts come up. And from Carrie back to Millimom—Jesus Christ. And now Millimom will be here on Sunday.

Two days later, his initial thirty-day probation period is up; he's no longer housebound except for supervised group outings. He can come and go as he pleases when he doesn't need to be in the house for chores or groups, and moreover he needs to leave the house to find a job; it's mandated. So he's leaving the house after his cereal at nine A.M., thinking he'll catch the bus to Silver Lake, catch an NA meeting, then skulk back into Intelligentsia, the coffee shop, and see if they'll take his skanky ass back. It's just then that he passes the tagger, his back to Mateo across the empty lot, working on his exquisite, intricate, dreamlike flurry of pale blue and green tattered flags.

Mateo stops and watches him work, up on an eight-foot ladder, spray-painting through a handful of different stencils. Obviously the tagger's got to be working legally; no way he could undertake such a long, complex project otherwise. How old is this compact little dude? Mateo can't tell. He's never seen his face.

Mateo knows he should walk on, but he keeps watching the tagger work—so methodically, so unself-consciously. This has to be his seventh or eighth morning out here by now. An ache opens up inside Mateo and grows, overwhelming him, filling his glands and then his eyes with tears. *What have I done? What have I done? What have I done?* he frantically asks himself. Then, just as frantically, he collects himself, blinks and brushes away the tears, and walks forward. On one hand, he doesn't want to disturb the tagger, but—

"Excuse me," Mateo calls up to him, his voice still full of burrs, "I don't wanna disturb you, but I just wanted to say your work is really beautiful."

"Thank you," the tagger calls down, not turning away from the wall. But wait—something about the voice catches Mateo. Finally, the tagger turns to look at Mateo, then leaves his sprays and stencils at the top and climbs down. "Hold on a second," he says.

Once he gets down to Mateo's level, rubbing sweat from his dark brown forehead with the sleeve of his massive, old, pilly Wu-Tang T-shirt, Mateo realizes—he is a she. He is actually a little black baby dyke with a nose ring and a bandanna tied up under her flat-brimmed baseball cap.

"Hey, brother." She offers a sweaty palm, which he takes.

"Hey," he says, processing.

"I know." She smiles. "You thought I was a guy, right? I know that look. It's all good; I don't care."

Mateo hadn't expected being called out like that. "Well, no," he says. "I mean, I don't care—I mean, I came over to tell you your wall is dope. It's—" He struggles for the words. "It's really beautiful. It's like a dreamscape."

"Thank you, brother. Yeah, a dream. I want it to be a place where the eye catches it, where the eye and the mind can rest and fly away for a few seconds. Just walking or driving by."

"It's all done with stencils?" Mateo asks.

"All done with stencils," she says. "That and about, fuck, twenty different shades of blue and green and yellow. Some I had to mix myself."

"It's really dope," Mateo says again. Then he just stands there. *What the fuck is your problem?* he asks himself.

She looks at him funny. "You one of the new guys at Triumph House?" she finally asks.

He can feel himself blushing in embarrassment. "How'd you know?" he asks.

She shrugs. "I just figured 'cause you're a new face on the block. I love those guys. They put up half the money for me to do this wall."

Mateo nods. There's something he desperately has to tell her. "I'm an artist, too," he says.

Her face brightens. "Oh, yeah? What kind?"

"Painter. I go to Pratt in Brooklyn."

"Shit, man! You're for reals," she says. "I go to CalArts."

He nods. "I mean, I used to go to Pratt." He kicks the dirt with his sneaker. "I kind of fucked that up."

She smiles again. She's got the most adorable smile. "Aw, brother, come on, we all make mistakes. You'll get back there."

"Maybe."

She picks up a bottle of water and swigs from it.

"I'll let you get back," Mateo says.

She offers her hand again. "I'm Charlice."

"Mateo. See you around here later." He starts to walk off the lot.

"Hey," she calls back to him. "You got spare time to come by and help me out?"

He smiles. "I might."

"Come back when you can." Then Charlice climbs back up the ladder.

Mateo picks up a bus heading toward Silver Lake. He feels light and sparkly after staring at the paint for so long; when he closes his eyes, he can see the maritime-hued flurry of paper shreds exploding on the wall. He tries to take the colors in with him to Intelligentsia, where he works up the gumption to go up to his old manager, a pretty blonde yoga-type girl named Kayla, and see if she can give him some hours.

"Mateo, you just didn't show up for work one day and never came back," Kayla reminds him flatly.

He's steeled himself for this. He and the guys in the house have had a lot of group sessions about how to face people they've let down and hurt.

"I know," he says. "And I'm sorry. But now I'm in a rehab house, I've got four months clean and sober, and I have to have a part-time job to stay in the house. I can take any shift except the last one because there's a curfew."

"Oh, Mateo." Kayla laughs lightly and a bit sadly; he's not quite sure why. Then she sighs, peering at the schedule on the wall. "Can you come in and help Kevyon open Mondays through Thursdays? Can you really be here at six thirty in the morning?"

"Yep," he says before he can talk himself out of it. Do the buses even run that early? He'll figure it out, he decides. The good thing, it occurs to him, is that he'll be done by noon. He can catch an NA meeting and then go back and help—who's the baby dyke? Charlice.

"You can start on Monday," Kayla says.

"Thanks, Kayla."

"Mateo, please don't fuck me over again, okay?"

Kayla's words ring in his head all the way to the meeting he catches on the other side of the reservoir, then all the way back to West Adams on the bus. He starts getting that bad feeling, starts rubbing his arms. The house doesn't allow him to have a cell phone until he's a month out of house confinement—under the theory that it's too easy to use it to find drugs when someone's in early sobriety—so he can't call his sponsor. The feeling is the hot rush that convulses his whole body and makes his brain go scalding white with senselessness when he thinks about that moment—that nano-moment—when the needle slips under his skin and he pulls back blood in the syringe. That final moment before he free falls off the top of a building, going "Whooooaaaaaa!" Funny thing is, first time around getting sober out here, before the Carrie incident, he used to love nursing that memory—it was his private balm, his secret treat. Now when the thought slips into his head, it fills him with terror and panic, a new raw horror at what total physiological control it has over him. He starts taking deep breaths, saying the Serenity Prayer in rhythm to his breaths.

He does this all the way back to West Adams, more or less, by which time the episode has subsided. It had come on because Kayla's parting remark had pushed him down another psychic wormhole: the wormhole of everyone he's fucked over. Deep in that wormhole, he'd ask himself why he even thought he deserved to go on with a good, happy life. How could he even show his face to anyone? A fucking needle in his arm was all he deserved. The wormhole was a very bad and scary place to be.

When he gets back to the hood, Charlice is still working. He walks on over to her. "Hey," he calls up.

"Hey," she calls right back down without looking. She's made considerable progress in the past few hours, advancing about three feet to the right of where she was before Mateo left. Her work is so dense, Mateo marvels; she moves across the wall so slowly, and the layers of shredded paper, or leaves, or whatever her forms are just keep getting thicker and more interlocked.

"How'd your day go?" she asks.

"I got my old job back."

"That's sweet," she says. "You wanna help me with something? Hand me that can down there with the greens called Satin Italian Olive."

He finds the can of Krylon and passes it up to Charlice. "Satin Italian Olive," he says. "Sweet."

"I know, right? And you can pick up that can of Peekaboo Blue and you can deepen the center of those pollywogs right down by your knee."

So that's what she calls her shapes. Pollywogs. They really don't look like pollywogs to Mateo. But more to the point: he's never tagged before. Or "written"—that's what the taggers call it. He grew up with a brush in his hand. So he tells her so.

"It's okay," she says. "The can's already got the right tip on. Just shake it, hold it about eight inches, and deepen the centers."

So he does it, shaking the can, feeling the ball bearing inside rattle around. He presses the nozzle and the spray of baby blue hits the center, deepening the existing hue.

"You're a toy, man!" Charlice laughs. "Don't fuck up my piece."

He knows what a toy is, in tagger parlance. It's an absolute beginner.

He's back there the whole next day, Friday, then Saturday, too. He's feeling so light, so happy. Then Sunday morning comes. He's queasy as he eats his cereal down in the kitchen with the guys. He's waiting for them to show up. He told Drew he'd rather just meet them at the Beverly Center, but Millimom really wanted to see where he was living. So he goes outside and waits on the front porch for them to pull up in Drew's Prius. Finally, around eleven A.M., they do. And here they are, two rich, skinny white women looking totally out of place in the neighborhood, walking up the pathway, Drew with a bag from Trader Joe's in one arm. From twenty-five feet away, he can see Millimom smiling toward him already, but he can already feel her strain, her sadness, burning through the smile, so obvious in the eyes. His heart is pounding out of his chest and he frantically starts saying the Serenity Prayer to himself. *Please, please, please*, he's praying, *just get me through this in a chill way. Just let me do this right.* He stands up and takes a few steps forward, forcing on a smile.

"We come bearing gifts," calls Drew cheerily.

"Hey!" Mateo calls back, pushing out the cheer. "Thank you!"

Suddenly they're there right before him. For the first time in months, he locks eyes with Millimom, but what he sees there—the hurt, the fear, etched so much deeper than the last time he saw her—instantly diverts his eyes away toward—what? Anything. Drew will do.

"Heyyy," he says again, stepping down. "Hey, Mom." He embraces her. God, she feels so tiny, so thin, just a bag of bones.

"Hi, sweetheart!" She embraces him and won't let go. Drew gives him a look behind her back that says, *Please, honey, just be gentle with her.*

Finally, Millimom pulls back. "Let me look at you . . . You look okay," she says, as though her worst fears have been allayed. "You look good. They feed you well here, right?"

"They do, they do!" he assures. He's all sorts of smiling and nodding and even laughing, a bit maniacally. "I even cook. It's part of my tasks."

"You even cook?" Millimom echoes him. "Wow, I'd like to sample that."

"Hey," he says, "I make some mean burritos."

"Mmm," Drew says. "That sounds good."

There, he thinks, his heart rate subsiding a bit. Maybe the worst is already over. In a second, they're all inside and he's giving them a tour of the first floor—the front TV parlor, the kitchen, the screened-in back porch, the rooms where they have meetings and groups. He introduces Drew and Millimom to the various guys in the house as he bumps into them, and it's just as he expected, all warmth and cordiality.

"This old house is gorgeous, isn't it, Mills?" Drew says. Mateo knew that was coming, he chuckles to himself. Drew and Milly have never seen a charming vintage anything they didn't want to rehab, edit down, and curate.

After the house tour, after he's stored away the bag of snacks they brought him under his bed, because he knows they'll disappear in fifteen minutes if he leaves them in the kitchen, they load into the Prius and head off to the Pacific Design Center, that huge, chunky blue glass building designed by César Pelli, to see the solo show of an artist named Amanda Ross-Ho. That was Drew's idea, that they all go and see some art, and he'd said he'd read about this show and wanted to catch it. Drew and Millimom are in the front and Mateo's in the back as they head north on La Cienega. Drew's got KPCC on the radio and is telling Millimom about some actor friend of theirs from a million years ago who moved to L.A. from New York recently, and in that moment, with the pressure off, Mateo thinks that he just might make it through this afternoon.

When they get to the Design Center, it occurs to him that this is virtually his first time in months being surrounded by art people, almost all of them white, including Drew and Millimom, instead of the ex-cons he now lives with. The sheer tone of the voices he hears around him—hushed, serious, considered, using vocabulary he usually only sees in print—feels a bit bizarre and off-putting. But even harder, perhaps what he hadn't accounted for, is to be standing in the middle of an artist's expensively produced solo show and to be reminded of the whole art-world machinery he'd once had at his fingertips, the world he'd thrown a bomb at and run away from. He keeps telling himself that, yes, Amanda Ross-Ho is nearly forty and he's nineteen, but still, the exhibit starts to burn him up—a slow burn he can't even fully put a name to—until his hands are fists shoved down deep in his jeans pockets. What's frustrating is that it's hard even to see the artist's true hand in the work—it's all installations and pastiches and collages of a bunch of random, everyday shit; half of it looks like something some crazy schizo guy in a cabin off the grid would spend days feverishly putting together. But then again, maybe that's the point.

Drew, walking a few paces beside him while Millimom peruses the other side of the room, seems to sense this from him. "I admire the constructions but still I'm strangely underwhelmed, you know what I mean?" she asks.

Mateo sort of half nods.

"I mean, where's the beauty?"

"It doesn't look like she cares about beauty," he says. "It's all think-y."

"Mmm," goes Drew. "All think-y." She and Mateo lock eyes for a second. Drew smirks, puts her hand on the back of his neck for a moment, and says, "Don't be so think-y, ya hear me?"

Mateo's caught off guard. "How can you be nice to me?" he asks her, looking down.

She puts her arm around him. "Because I've known you since you were a little boy and I love you," she says. "And because I've been there, Mateo." Her eyes flash with mischief. "I was a devious pathological little user when I was your age, too, you know."

They laugh together, attracting a curious look across the room from Millimom. "You know who else loves you, Mateo?" Drew asks.

Mateo knows whom Drew's referring to. He lowers his voice: "I just don't know why she took me in," he says. "Why didn't she have her own kid?"

"What does it matter?" Drew asks, also sotto voce. "Stay clean," she says. "You'll get your answers."

Mateo looks down, digs at one sneaker with the toe of the other. Drew is always saying slightly Yoda-ish stuff like that. She rubs his neck again and saunters across the room toward Millimom, whom Mateo watches. She's standing in front of the one piece he really likes, which is a massive wall assemblage of white cutout shapes divided into nine square panels and anchored by a bunch of black bottles on the floor. It's monumental and intricate and, if not exactly beautiful, certainly able to engage the eye for a long period of time. And it looks like it's engaged Millimom, who's standing before it.

Watching her from afar—her arms folded, rocking ever so slightly on her heels—Mateo can't get over how small she seems. How old is she now? Almost forty-five? What is she thinking about? Her own art? For the first time, it seems, he wonders if, or how, his whole mess of the past few years has affected her own art-making. Did it set her back? There's yet another thought, in what seems to be an ever-increasing pile of thoughts related to the repercussions of his life, that he just can't deal with.

They all end up eating panini in the Design Center café. After Drew's last bite, she asks if Milly and Mateo mind if she goes and checks out a few of the interior-design showrooms in the building; there's a room in her house she wants to do over and she wants to get some ideas. Mateo can feel his heart quickening; he feared this moment was coming. But of course what can he and Millimom say? Drew picks up her bag and darts away, saying she'll be back in twenty, twenty-five minutes. Mateo and Millimom watch her go.

"She has such a beautiful home here, doesn't she?" Millimom finally says.

"She does."

"It's so crazy how people have actual homes here, isn't it? You can have a front yard and a porch and a backyard. For the price of a studio in New York! I've always wondered how Drew could stand it out here all these years after living in New York. I mean, most people I know eventually move back to New York. But, hey, what can I say, when I woke up this morning and smelled the bougainvillea outside my window, it kind of got me thinking, you know?"

"Yeah," he says, "there are some good smells out here, it's true." He can sense she's prattling because she's nervous. It's such an old, familiar sound track, Millimom's self-soothing ramblings, her little debates with herself.

She sighs, picks up the crust of her sandwich, puts it down. She smiles at Mateo, looks around the whole café, then smiles at him again. He half smiles at her, too, then looks down at his crotch, picking at a loose thread in his jeans.

"Dad's sorry he couldn't come," Milly finally says. "He's been feeling super under the gun getting ready for a show."

Mateo shrugs. He almost wishes she hadn't mentioned him. "He's got his own life," he says. He feels a little sulky and passive-aggressive saying it, even though what he sort of meant to say is *I didn't expect you guys to get on a plane and fly across the country to come see me in a rehab house.*

"Well, no, no, it's not that," she says hurriedly. "He wanted to come. He just really—he just feels like every moment that he's not in school teaching counts until this show goes up. He told me—"

"I told you it's okay," Mateo slightly snaps. Instantly, he feels badly about it. But damn, doesn't she know to leave something alone?

But it's too late. He sees that all-too-familiar look on her face, as though he just swatted her back. She puts her index finger up to her teeth and sort of bites it.

"I just meant—" he says. Oh God, he can feel himself going down one of those bad, bad wormholes. Fuck! He needs to call his sponsor. What would his sponsor say to him right now? What is the right thing to do? He takes a breath. "I just meant it's okay," he says in a softer voice. "He didn't need to come out. I'm really, really doing okay. I feel really good, like I'm on a good track."

But it's really too late now. She's crying. Quietly, but he can see the tears. Then she grimaces in self-disgust as she smudges them away with the knuckle of her index finger.

"Mateo," she says, "I tried to do the right thing. I—when I started visiting you, I—I guess I just came to love you over time and I—I mean we—we wanted you to have a better chance. I don't know where I went wrong, honest, I don't. We just sort of—we were winging it. We did the best we could. We—" She stops, then says, more quietly, "I just, visiting you in the boys' home, I just really fell in love with that five-year-old face."

Oh God, he realizes. She's going all the way back to *that*? Holy shit. Oh, shit. He knows he must look absolutely like a deer in the headlights right now. He prays to say the right thing.

"I don't think you did anything wrong," he finally says. "I'm grateful for what you did for me. I don't think you had anything to do with the whole drug thing. But I gotta tell you something." And now—oh, holy shit, he can feel tears coming on, too, but he swallows them back because he doesn't want to lose his ground on this. "I wanna be an adult now and find out who I am. I lost enough time to this drug bullshit and now I wanna be someone."

Milly's face lights up. "Of course," she says. "Of course! I was hoping for that. And we don't expect you to live with us when you come back to New York. We'll understand if you want to get your own place in Brooklyn or live with friends or—"

"No, naw, you don't understand," he says. "I don't think I wanna come back to New York. I think I wanna stay here."

And the funny thing is he didn't even know that's what he wanted until he said it. But suddenly it all comes crashing down on him—New York. Those East Village and Lower East Side streets, every block crawling with drug memories. And her. Her, her, her. The 04/14/1984 photo, presumably tucked back behind his bed at the Christodora where he'd left it, but which he thinks about every few days. Where she was from and where she died. He wants to feel like he doesn't come from anybody. That he's not Mateo Heyman-Traum, but just Mateo, nineteen years old, artist, adult. It all clicks into place before his eyes with stunning clarity. He doesn't want to go back to New York.

Milly sits before him, blank faced, taking it in, her mouth literally an O as she absorbs this. She looks like she's casting about for a reply. "What about Pratt?" she finally asks.

"I don't want to go back." Even as Mateo says it, he realizes: it's true. He'll reenroll out here, or maybe he won't go back to school at all. He'll figure it out. But he doesn't want to go back there. He can suddenly feel that in his gut as clear as day.

Millimom doesn't say anything. She just licks her lips slowly and sits back in her chair and folds her arms. She looks down into her arms and then latches some hair back behind her ear. She glances up at him once—a flash of a look that he doesn't know whether to read as shock, rage, or a challenge—and then looks back down again. He feels like he's sinking down, down the wormhole, into sadness and betrayal. But. Well, but. There's something else. Half of him feels like he's coasting above those feelings, like he knows he'll come out the other end. He feels . . . very light. Untethered.

Finally, she looks up again, rather steely. "Don't worry, Mateo, I'm leaving tomorrow," she says.

He remembers Drew's exhortation to treat Milly well. "It really means a lot to me that you came out," he says.

She says nothing. The two of them just sit there over their sandwich crumbs. A part of Mateo is telling him to just bolt, just leave. But another part of him tells him to just breathe, that this will pass, that—for once, finally—he's done nothing wrong. Soon he'll be back in West Adams where he feels okay, with the guys, with the blue and green leaves flying off the wall just paces away. Just keep picturing the blue and green leaves, he tells himself. Keep picturing Charlice up on her ladder, you down below.

Drew finally comes back, bearing samples and brochures. "Hiii," she says breezily, plopping down. She's going on and on about what she saw, but it doesn't annoy Mateo. He knows Drew is sharp enough to have sensed the nanosecond she saw him and Millimom sitting here in this posture that the best thing for her to do was swoop down and take the pressure off either of them to say anything by running on about her interior-design adventure.

"Well, shall we bolt?" Drew finally says.

"Sure," Millimom says, gathering the plates.

Everybody's quiet on the way back to West Adams, the radio filling in the silence. Driving by the lot, he takes in his long afternoon look at the wall. When Drew pulls up to Triumph House, there are guys on the front porch playing cards.

"I gotta get back in and start dinner prep," Mateo says. That's a lie. He had dinner prep last night. He could conceivably spend another hour with Drew and Millimom, but he doesn't think he has it in him. "Thanks for coming to see me and thanks for taking me out," he says. He leans forward in the car to kiss Drew on the cheek.

"Bye-bye, honeybunch," Drew says. "I'll call you this week."

He leans right and kisses Millimom's cheek. "Thank you again for coming out to see me." *Say hi to Dad for me* is what he should say right now, he knows, but he doesn't.

"Bye-bye," Milly says to him flatly.

He hops out of the car. He squares his shoulders and walks up the path to the house, waving hello to his house buddies as he does. He resolutely does not look back at the Prius. He listens and waits until he hears it recede down the street. Bobby G. is sitting on the porch steps reading a battered old James Patterson paperback, probably from the house "library."

"Mr. Mateo," he says, "how was your day with the ladies?"

Mateo sits down next to him and puts his head in his hands. "Sometimes I fucking hate myself," he says.

Bobby G. puts a hand on his shoulder. "Welcome to my world, little man!" He laughs. "The Try-Not-to-Hate-Yourself-Too-Much-Today Club! We're all VIP members here!"

SEVENTEEN

REVELATIONS

(2017)

Asa Heath, Jared Traum's buddy dating all the way back to St. Bernard's School in the early 1980s, hauled his forty-seven years of girth down East Seventh Street. He was sweating in his haste, late to meet Jared at some new bar, and preoccupied, his head still pounding with a day's worth of data from the office. He'd briefly set aside his tablet while in the subway to rest his eyes but was still seeing algorithms in front of him. Yet he was not too much in his own head to suddenly stop and gape in front of the humble, rickety-awninged redbrick entrance to the Blue and Gold Tavern.

"The Blue and Gold is still here!" he blurted out, aloud, to himself. A lifelong Upper East Sider, he was always elated to discover, when he visited other neighborhoods, anything that still existed from his school days, back when they all had high hopes, say, that Mayor David Dinkins would hold on to a second term. And so this: the Blue and Gold! This was the very bar where he, Jared, Milly, and their other friends—that pretty, crazy Drew, who'd gotten her act together out in L.A. and become a big writer—had drunk away so many nights, shoveling quarters into the jukebox to hear more Guns N' Roses.

"Twenty-five years!" exclaimed Asa—again, aloud. He often talked aloud when walking alone. That, he thought, was something you could still do in New York without attracting so much as a raised eyebrow. And yet pretty much every other memory seemed like an unreliable old dream of an analog New York, when you promised friends you would leave them Friday-night messages on their work voice mails that they might call into from a payphone to find out where to meet you.

Meanwhile, the stores, restaurants, bars, and coffee shops began looking more and more like it was ninety years ago. Of course, in these shops would be the gleaming transparent plastic devices that did the business and the math, but as the future took hold, nobody wanted it to look like the future anymore.

So it was that evening that Asa found himself walking into one of those very throwback, let's-pretend-it's-Prohibition bars a block past the good old Blue and Gold, which would've suited him just fine. A perfectly scratched, repurposed old mirror ran the length of the bar, surrounded by fake vintage white-and-black subway tiling. At the end of the bar, nursing a pint, sat Jared, his still-full head of honey-colored curls dusted through with white, his hands very calloused and his waist trim, thanks to the vegan diet that virtually everyone seemed to eat now, plus three mornings a week in a concrete-walled gym, tossing heavy balls at a $200-an-hour trainer. Jared, everyone told him, looked far better at forty-seven than he'd looked at forty.

The two men exchanged a rough hug. Asa called for his pint.

"How you been?" he asked.

Jared smiled slyly. "Pretty good."

"Oh, yeah?"

"In fact," Jared said, running his thumb cleanly around the rim of his glass, "she may come by in a bit and join us."

"Sweet!"

Jared smiled and fondly shoulder-bumped his friend. Asa was *that* friend, the one some people have, if they're lucky, who hears out decades of highs and lows and only passes judgment if he thinks major self-sabotage is looming. Asa had never played that card with Jared.

Certainly not when Milly and Jared adopted Mateo, even though Asa had still been single at the time and, truth be told, viewed the kid at first as a menace to their drinking schedule. But then Asa grew pretty crazy about Mateo. Two years later, when the woman he'd been dating asked him if he wanted kids, he thought about a particular afternoon in Tompkins Square Park kicking around a soccer ball with Jared and Mateo, then about a certain pizza they'd shared at Two Boots afterward—an afternoon that had felt to him like a perfect embodiment of bare-bones male happiness—and he said to his girlfriend, "Very much so." Together, they then had two daughters.

Still, Asa wasn't too dim to understand that, for Jared, agreeing to adopt Mateo, just when he had started wanting his own kid, was his concession to Milly, to his love for her. And once they adopted him—well, whoa. They had no idea how hard that would be. Not that there wasn't a window of about seven years, when Mateo was between ten and fifteen, when the three of them seemed to find their groove. They had some good times in those years together, Jared and Asa with their new families, in Montauk each summer, once or twice in Europe. But then, around fifteen, Mateo, suddenly so full of himself and conscious of his coolness, "turned," as Milly and Jared would say. A few years later, his drug thing started. And it was around that point Asa started meeting up more and more with just Jared, for a beer or an art crawl.

Those were the years their marriage disintegrated, Jared told Asa. With Mateo's drug thing at first, when he started failing out of Pratt, there was a feeling that of course he's doing this, he's acting out all those childhood feelings of loss and rage and grief, they're just catching up to him now. Milly and Jared were on the same page at that point, for a moment.

But Jared's resentment was already starting to show. "I wonder if the zombie will come home tonight," Jared said one night to Asa.

"Say what?"

"When Mateo first came to live with us, I used to think of him—I mean, I never said this to Milly—as a kind of zombie, because he was so . . . flat. So shut down. Zombie kid from the land of the dead. Then, you know, once he hit nine, ten, he started coming to life. Sweet kid, showing enthusiasm, learning to show affection, really into his art. That's why, when the dope started, I remember thinking: *The zombie's back*. He wasn't there behind the eyes anymore."

Asa was the first person Jared had told about the sculpture incident, minus Mateo calling him a "fraud mediocre rich piece of shit." If Mateo had meant to gut-punch a fortysomething artist who'd not yet attained the status he'd blithely considered his birthright in his early twenties, he'd succeeded, and Jared had too much pride to repeat those damning words.

"He's become aggressive," was what Asa had said after hearing the tale. "Like the junkies on the train begging for money."

Jared nodded. "That's why I had to ban him from the house."

Once Mateo went to California and Milly started receiving good news from Drew, a small window of renewed happiness opened for her and Jared, Asa knew that much. Jared and Milly told each other that what Mateo had needed all along was simply to get away from New York, the scene of his crimes, for a while. Some normality returned for them. They'd have dinner in the neighborhood after work, talk about their students and their own art, walk home together through Tompkins Square Park, curl up and watch a movie in bed, fall asleep to it. Milly slept without the dread fear of waking to Mateo coming home in the wee hours, shuffling through the apartment like a ghost.

"I know this might sound cold," Jared told Asa one night on the way into a movie, "but it's so nice just to be alone in the house with Mills again and not have Mateo to worry about."

"He's an adult now," Asa said.

"He's an adult," Jared echoed, as though trying to convince himself.

But out in L.A. the adult didn't last. When Milly gave Jared the news about jail and the girl who'd OD'd, Jared merely rubbed his temple and said nothing. His dismay at the news, and at Milly's fresh wave of grief, trumped any desire on his part to pull a *told you so* on Milly. But privately, the news confirmed his belief that Mateo was a lost cause. If he thought about the situation for longer than he cared to, he would peer into a window of a whole sector of New Yorkers whose lives, going back generations, were infinitely more scarred and beset with challenges than his own, and he would feel uncomfortable stirrings of guilt, pity, and helplessness. So he'd return to the more conclusive thought that Mateo was, as he suspected, a lost cause—and thankfully one that was no longer his legal responsibility. Their work was done.

But Milly. "She can't fucking let go," Jared complained. "Even at this point. She's fucking in L.A. right now trying to see him. She's become, like, a masochist to his drama." The trip of Milly's galled him. Why would she go across the country to see someone who'd made it clear he didn't want to be seen, when he—Jared—yearned for more time alone with her? For the first time in their marriage, doubts rumbled darkly within him.

"It would be nice for once to just see Milly happy," Asa offered.

Jared snorted in derisive laughter. "Milly won't let herself be happy. She's afraid that if she lets herself be happy, her mother will go manic again and ruin the seventh-grade dance for her. She needs a disaster to feel normal."

As for Milly, she'd not felt remotely normal since that moment Mateo had more or less told her he wanted to be left alone, then left her in the Prius with Drew as he walked back up to his halfway house. Drew had driven for several minutes before she asked: "So can I ask what you guys talked about in the café?"

Milly continued to stare out the window. "He said he didn't want to come back to New York."

Drew drove on in silence. "You know," she finally said, "he's just trying to find himself apart from his parents like any kid his age."

"I think he wants to cut me out of the picture," Milly added.

Back home, in the driveway, Drew hesitated before opening the car door. "Millipede," she said softly, "can I tell you something? You and Jared did an amazing job with Mateo. Whatever you may think based on the past few years, you did. You helped your mother fulfill a promise to his mother, and you took him out of a group home and gave him an amazing education and an amazing life and gave him lots of love. But he's nineteen now. You know what it's time for now?"

Milly smirked slightly. "What is it time for now?" she said.

"It's Milly Time."

Milly laughed. "And what does Milly Time look like to you?"

"That's for Milly to find out."

Milly tried to take this idea back to New York with her and her broken heart. She kept reiterating it in her head as: *work and Jared, work and Jared.* The work part, actually, was not so hard. She had her students she cared about, and on weekends, she was happy to go to her studio and lose herself in paints and canvases for several hours, to the point where, after about six weeks, coming into the holidays of 2012, she was growing a significant new body of work and having one or two of the new Lower East Side gallerists up for studio visits. The works were studies in whites and grays—how many shades of white and gray could she glob and spackle onto a canvas and still create the illusion of a monochrome if you stepped back ten paces? On breaks, she'd sneak her cigarette and sit in the big, open warehouse window, looking at the Manhattan Bridge and wondering what Mateo was doing at that moment. Would he make it this time? Would he survive the night? Would he ever come home?

The Jared part, however, didn't go so well, to her frustration. Some nagging, quintessentially Milly, to-do-list part of her brain kept telling her that she had to put the magic back into her marriage, and she would pay lip service to this idea by, say, texting Jared midday and asking if he wanted to meet after work to see a movie. But then, before he could even answer, feelings of rage toward Jared would overwhelm her. Years ago, those feelings of rage, if they had any coherence at all, might have said something like *He's stopping me from making art*; now they were more like *He doesn't give a damn if he sees Mateo ever again. He just doesn't care!* And Milly, in a paroxysm of conflicted feelings, would text Jared again: "Sorry have to nix that. Forgot faculty meeting. See you home later." Then she'd go to a movie alone.

"She's so brittle at home," Jared told Asa over a pint. "She can barely look me in the eyes anymore. We haven't had sex in over a month. Well, anything approaching real sex, I mean."

"You guys should probably go to couples therapy," Asa said.

Jared mustered up the nerve to say as much to Milly.

"I already go to therapy!" Milly protested. "I've spent my life in therapy."

"We need to go to therapy," Jared said. "Mills, come on. We're growing apart. We have to talk out what happened with Mateo. You know it."

She could hardly bear to hear Mateo's name. When Jared wasn't home, she'd go in Mateo's room and lie down on his bed and stare at his posters of rap artists she couldn't identify, save one that was clearly labeled TYLER, THE CREATOR. This young man, with his rubber-faced grimaces and baseball cap askew on his head, terrified her. She would stare at his image and, over time, started irrationally blaming him for Mateo's downfall, even though she'd never heard any of his lyrics. She supposed she could go on the Internet and listen, but that prospect terrified her more.

She and Jared actually ended up going to couples therapy at the office of Richard Gallegos, MSW, the same guy Mateo had gone to when he was in high school. Going to him had been Milly's idea. She knew that saying no to couples therapy was all but saying she was through with the marriage, so at least she seemed proactive, being the one to suggest a therapist. Jared actually agreed with Milly's rationale that at least Gallegos would have some context for them. Really, though, Milly wanted to see someone who, when she said "Mateo," would see Mateo's face and know whom she was talking about.

And so, on a Tuesday night, they walked the few blocks to the still-beige office of Richard Gallegos, now a bit stouter. They told him that, now that it was just the two of them in the house again after fifteen years, they had lost "it"—the marriage, the two-ness, whatever had existed before the Mateo years.

It seemed like they were getting off to a good start over the first few weeks. Then came a certain Wednesday night that Jared and Asa met up, Jared looking ashen and stunned.

"What's up?" Asa asked, ordering their usual twin pints.

Jared closed his eyes, shook his head, put his head in his left hand with an elbow propped on the bar. "I almost texted you to tell you I couldn't make it," he said. "But I figured I better talk. Because I'm about to start hitting people on the street."

"What the fuck?" Asa put a hand on his back. "What the fuck is up?"

What was up was, the prior night in therapy, Jared had figured it out.

Finally, that night, finally, finally, Jared had found the courage to say what he'd wanted to say the past several weeks—no, really, the past many, many years. Something that a certain icy intransigence on Milly's part had laid to rest even before Mateo had come into their lives. And certainly something that fifteen hectic years of Mateo had all but frozen out as a topic.

"Milly," Jared had said, taking her hand in his before Richard Gallegos as though the therapist were remarrying them, "before it's too late . . . I really, really want to have a child with you."

Just so Milly couldn't reply with *We've had a child . . . we have a child*, he added, to be utterly clear, "I want to *bear* a child with you. I want to *make* a child with you." He did not make the dread mistake of saying *our own child*. He'd learned his lesson several years ago about using that phrase.

The beige room plunged into silence. Milly looked at him blankly, then looked away, blinking several times. Richard Gallegos said nothing.

"Are you going to say anything?" Jared finally asked Milly. Already, he was tumbling into regret that he had even asked.

"It's too late," Milly finally said. "I think—I think it's too late."

"It's not too late," Jared shot back. "Look around at people we know. You know it's not too late. Especially with medicine. We've never even really tried."

But Milly was crumpling under his campaign. She began crying.

Richard Gallegos said not a word for several more seconds—a bit perversely, Jared thought. At length, Gallegos asked, "Milly, what are you feeling? Why are you crying?"

Milly suddenly drew herself up very straight and gave Jared one—one—prolonged look, full of despair and apology. Then she looked away, wiping away tears.

"And then it hit me," Jared told Asa. "It hit me like a smack in the face, it was so clear. So I said, 'Milly, were you pregnant once?' And she nodded. And then I couldn't even ask the next question."

"She had a miscarriage?" Asa asked.

Jared smirked bitterly. "She didn't have any miscarriage." He held Asa's stare. "She didn't have any fucking miscarriage."

"Oh, shit," Asa finally said. "She had an abortion?"

Jared looked down dully into his drink.

"Oh, shit, man. When?"

"*Before* we took in Mateo," Jared said. "She said she didn't want to have a mentally ill child." His eyes locked with Asa's, then watered over. His jaw trembled. Asa rubbed Jared's back while Jared blinked rapidly, then smudged away tears with the back of his hand. "I can't believe she did it," Jared said, his voice an octave higher than usual. "It was our baby and she just terminated it. She didn't even tell me."

"Oh my fucking God, man," Asa said quietly. "I'm so fucking sorry." He was at a loss. He thought about his own daughters, if they had simply . . . never been. Carolina's bizarre little made-up songs she hummed under her breath all day, which made him dizzy with love, and the turndown in Alice's mouth when she encountered even a tiny cruelty, like a lady pulling a little dog too harshly on a leash. Asa believed Alice would one day become a human-rights lawyer, or the president. His stomach churned in a sickening void. "I'm so sorry, man."

"She had an abortion and then pressured me to adopt Mateo," Jared said. "Can you believe that? We could have had our own child."

After Milly's revelation, she and Jared went into free fall. Jared would express rage and grief while at therapy each week, and Milly would silently sit there and absorb it, rubbing her arms, feeling as though this excoriation was her due. In all the days in between, they lived separate lives and avoided each other. Milly slept in Mateo's room. She started spending more time than usual with her mother and father. After Milly finished teaching, she would go to her parents' house on the Upper East Side, the house she'd grown up in, and make dinner for Ava and Sam.

"Where's Jared tonight?" Ava would ask. That was Ava's way of saying, *Why aren't you with your husband tonight?*

"He's in the studio," Milly would answer.

"Does he ever come *out* of the studio?" Sam would ask.

"Why don't you call and ask him that, Daddy?" But then she regretted the bite in her tone, especially when her parents exchanged their signature glance that said, *Well, well, well.*

The truth was she didn't really know where Jared was most of the time. She'd told her parents that she and Jared were in therapy, that they were having trouble after the traumatic Mateo years, but she didn't tell them the abortion revelation that had sent everything over the edge. If she had, if she'd been honest about why she'd done it, it would have been a direct affront to her mother—a manic-depressive woman who'd borne a depressive daughter. Of course, Milly told herself, Ava hadn't borne her thoughtlessly. Ava hadn't even had any symptoms when she got pregnant with Milly at twenty-six. But it didn't matter. Milly knew her mother would still take the news as an affront. So she said nothing and was grateful for the book- and art-lined haven of her parents' home to crawl back into in this most unhappy period.

Somewhere around this time, Jared and Asa were prowling galleries in Chelsea on a Saturday afternoon. "So I think I'm gonna bring it up at therapy this Thursday," Jared told Asa. "I want to separate."

Asa turned away from a shag-rug sculpture and looked at his friend. "For real?" he asked. Asa truly hadn't known if this was coming. Everything had been in limbo for six weeks after Milly's revelation, and Asa had doubted his friend's ability to walk away from the woman he'd been crazy over for the better part of thirty years.

Jared nodded and said nothing. An hour later, over a turkey burger and a beer, while the two men were idly discussing the shows they'd just seen, Jared crumpled in his chair and put down his burger and stared into space.

"You okay?" Asa asked.

Jared finally looked up. "How could I ever possibly stay with someone who did that?"

"You're having a whole debate with yourself in your head, right?" Asa asked. Jared didn't reply. "Look, why don't you just say you need some space alone right now and not make it out like it's permanent?"

Jared's eyes flicked back toward his friend. "That's probably a smart idea," he said.

That Thursday night in therapy, having met Milly there to find she had a miserable cold, Jared pitied her and almost went back on his promise to himself. But then he decided that the moment had come when he simply had to push this thing through or it would never happen. Jared let Richard Gallegos take him and Milly through their routine "check-in," which meant saying where they were immediately coming from and what state of mind they were in. With each passing week, Jared had grown more tired of this ritual. Tonight, he had to breathe deeply to keep from telling Gallegos to take his $250-a-week check-in and go fuck himself.

"I feel like shit," Milly said flatly, wiping her nose with a tissue. "I only finished out the afternoon at school because my students had final-term crits." She looked at Jared, lightly reached for and then briefly took his hand. "I missed you today," she said.

Jared tried to smile warmly but it probably just appeared wan. Could she sense what was coming? he wondered.

"I feel sort of sick to my stomach tonight," he said.

"Why so?" asked Gallegos. Milly's eyes flashed back toward him.

"I decided after last week's session," Jared pushed on, making himself meet Milly's narrowed eyes. "I need to move out for a while. I need to be with myself."

Slowly, Milly recoiled on the couch, her mouth opening. She raised her eyebrows several times as though to speak, but said nothing. Finally, she said, "That wasn't the plan. The plan when we came here was to work this thing out."

"I didn't know then what I know now," Jared said.

"Oh, great!" Milly said. "So now you're punishing me for that."

"Punishing you?" Jared yelled. "Punishing you? You fucking aborted my child because of your own fucking fears and you never even discussed it with me. How *selfish* is that?"

"Oh my God," Milly said, bursting into tears. "Oh my God!"

"Hold up, guys," Richard Gallegos said. "Hold up. Let's take a minute of silence, okay?"

Grudgingly, Jared took a breath. Milly kept on crying and shaking her head. Jared fixed on her for a moment, watching her cry, and suddenly a tidal wave of fury—far deeper than anything he'd felt so far, something that truly scared him—began creeping over him from behind his shoulders. *I've lived twenty years with someone who doesn't really love me*, was the thought he had. Total panic, madness, coursed through his entire body. Yet he steeled himself to stand up and grab his coat.

"I'm not staying for this," he announced. "I don't have to stay for this."

"Jared, can you just sit through the minute of silence with us?" Gallegos asked.

"He doesn't even want to," Milly jeered.

That just about did it. "I fucking hate you, Milly," Jared said.

In a moment, he was down on the street, his heart pounding, the world spinning before his eyes. He walked eight blocks up First Avenue in a blind fugue, with no destination whatsoever, then rounded a block and walked eight blocks back down. He stood outside Lucy's bar for a moment and contemplated downing several whiskeys in a series of smooth, uninterrupted arm motions until he was completely obliterated and beyond responsibility for something like starting a street fight, because he suddenly wanted to beat the shit out of the male half of every happy couple he passed. He just stood there and stared through the dirty window at the bar, lasering in on what stool he'd choose.

And as he did that, boring down pitilessly with his eyes on one stool, his heart rate slowed. The world stopped spinning. He took an extremely deep breath. He ran his palms over his sweaty forehead, the angry parallel creases above his nose, and then his fingers through his salt-and-honey curls. Then he calmly got on the L train, went to his studio, opened the window, plugged his iPhone into his speakers and cued it up to Radiohead. With a calm and a cold resolve sinking ever deeper into his gut, he blowtorched a six-foot column of metal until two A.M. Then he shut off the lights in the studio, took off his belt and boots, and curled up under a blanket on a couch in the corner. *It's just me now*, he whispered to himself, over and over. *Just me.*

Jared never looked back. In the circle of friends around him and Milly, people would marvel about the cool, clean precision with which Jared had left her, how he seemed to pour all his cold rage and shock and despair into his work, so that in a year he had a solo show at a gallery on Orchard Street that the *New York Times* praised for its "unadorned Rust Belt materiality." After that, his work started selling and he wasn't in his high-school teaching job but six more months. In the following four years, he became that rare figure in an art world that fetishizes the young and the new: a longtime midlevel artist who becomes a collector's darling around the age of fifty.

For Asa, it was a point of glamour and pride to have a boyhood friend who was now an artist who was out of town half the time supervising the construction of crazy-ass metal hulks on public lawns or in wealthy private yards. And this night, walking a bit reluctantly past the Blue and Gold and on to the bar whose address Jared had voiced to Asa's tablet a few hours ago, Asa wondered who might be the mysterious third Jared had hinted might later join them.

In the old-timey Prohibition-type bar, after Asa and Jared had shot the shit for an hour or so, Asa finally saw her: a mid-thirtysomething cocoa-skinned beauty with voluminous, curly hair and chunky cobalt earrings, wearing a long swath of iridescent slate-gray fabric that Asa could only identify, inwardly to himself, as "Japanese."

She entered the bar, Jared's back to her. Putting a finger to her smiling lips in Asa's direction, she slipped up behind Jared and lightly kissed his neck.

Jared spun around. "Hey!" he boomed. He planted a happy-puppy kiss on her lips. "You made it!" Then he introduced Asa to Tonya Gomez, an associate curator at the Whitney Museum. Jared had met her at an opening there three weeks before.

Tonya wedged in a stool between Jared and Asa. "This is the third place I've been this week that makes me feel like I'm in some old-time gangster movie," she said.

"You're right," Asa enthused. "It's, like, Prohibition chic."

"Right?" she said. "I don't get why we—I mean, why America—why we're so obsessed with that archetype. Do you? We can't get enough of it!"

"We love our old-school rogues, I guess," Asa said.

Tonya lightly put a hand on Asa's arm in acknowledgment. "I know, right?"

Asa glanced at Jared, who'd pivoted slightly away, smiling placidly into his own reflection in the long antique mirror over the bar.

After Jared left Milly, he'd sublet an apartment in Carroll Gardens for a year. The apartment in the Christodora was his—it was his family's, fully paid-for long ago. But telling Milly to leave immediately strained the limits of his cool, clean secession. Through a lawyer—because, he quickly realized, he could hardly bear to e-mail her, and certainly couldn't bear seeing an e-mail from her in his queue—he told her she could stay indefinitely as long as she paid the monthly maintenance. He knew that someday he should reclaim the apartment, either to live there or to sell it—in fact, he knew he probably should get off his butt and talk to a divorce lawyer—but for the moment, he just wanted to be away from the Christodora, from every room and every book and every painting and every kitchen utensil—not to mention every Alphabet City block, café, denizen, dog, and junkie—that reminded him of his life the past twenty years. His therapist—a new one, not Gallegos, to whom he never returned after that night—spent a great deal of time trying to get him to see that those prior twenty years had not been a complete waste and a lie.

As for Milly, she'd sat there on the couch in Gallegos's office alone, speechless, for several moments after Jared had said, "I fucking hate you, Milly!" and stormed out.

"Let's just give it a minute," Gallegos had murmured.

Milly drew her knees up to her chest on the couch. Turning away from Gallegos, she rested her head on the back of the couch and closed her eyes. Finally she said, "I knew it'd end up like this. I knew everybody would leave."

"Can you just sit in this moment for a minute, Milly?" Gallegos asked.

She turned to him with a corrosive smile. "I've been sitting in this moment my whole life. It doesn't get any better."

"Yes, but you know that's depression talking, right, Milly? You know that moments vary and change. You know you've been happy before and you'll be happy again."

She unleashed a laugh that sounded unhinged to her. "I'm tired of trying so hard to be fucking happy!"

Sitting up that night at the Christodora, at the dining-room table with the crossword puzzle mostly blank in front of her, Milly waited for Jared to come home. Certainly he'd come home at least to sleep. But, by two A.M., he'd not. In the morning, she had a text from him: "Staying elsewhere for a while. Will be by apt during work hours to pick up some things." *In other words*, thought Milly, *I'll be by when you're not there*.

It all felt very inevitable to Milly. She was torn between thinking that Jared should forgive her and the truer feeling that she'd had this coming all these years. Even Mateo's flight—she'd had it coming. *You can't adopt a child to fill an inner void*, she'd tell herself. *You have to do it out of some detached, selfless impulse to put good out into the world. You can't expect a motherless kid to fulfill your own need to be someone's mother because you're afraid of having your own kid.* And yet, Milly would think, it had sort of worked for a while, hadn't it?

She sleepwalked through her days, telling only Gallegos and Drew out in L.A. all that had happened, and at the end of the day, she'd come home to the large, empty apartment at the Christodora. She would sit in the window and stare down at the bare treetops in the park and think, *Well, it's come to this. And I'm not surprised at all.*

EIGHTEEN
NO MEANING
(1993)

The middle-aged, heavyset woman coming up out of the train station at Fourteenth Street from Queens on a chilly November night had to orient herself, as she wasn't normally in downtown Manhattan, and then she had to ask a passerby to point her in the direction of St. Vincent's, the entrance of which she stood in front of for several seconds, frozen in distress, before she thought to reach into her pocketbook for her rosary. She pulled it out, kissed it, and prayed to the Virgin Mother for strength, resolve, and compassion, and then she entered. At the front desk, reassured by the large crucifix hanging on the opposing wall, she asked for directions to the room of Ysabel Mendes.

Walking down the hallway, she glanced into rooms where extremely frail young men lay, their faces sunken, often with people at their sides holding their bony hands. She heard a fragment of a song that was always on the radio at the bank where she worked, that "Dreamlover" song, float out of one room. As she approached the room she was looking for, she found a woman sitting in a chair just outside, a pile of paperwork in her lap.

The woman looked up and rose. "Mrs. Mendes?"

Gladys Mendes nodded, peered into the face of this woman she'd never seen before and determined that her face looked kind and trustworthy. "Are you Ava?" she asked.

"I am," Ava said. "I'm the one who called you. I'm so glad you're here. I think it's going to mean so much to Issy that you came."

Gladys's eyes filled with tears. "I didn't tell her father I was coming. But I couldn't not come. It would haunt me for the rest of my life."

"It's good you came. Will you sit with me for just a minute before you go in?"

Gladys sat down, looked beseechingly into Ava's face.

"It doesn't look good," Ava said, putting her hand on the woman's arm. "This was the second time this year that Issy had pneumonia and this time the drugs haven't been able to beat it. She went into acute respiratory failure four days ago and this afternoon she went into multisystem organ failure and septic shock. She's on a lot of pain medication right now and she's on a ventilator to lessen the pain of breathing. She's going in and out of consciousness but I think she's called for you a few times."

Gladys averted her eyes, overwhelmed with the terminology and that final piece of news. "She's gonna pass?" she finally asked.

"The doctors think she'll pass tonight. It's just about making her as comfortable as she can be now. I'm so sorry, Mrs. Mendes."

But Gladys was sitting up straighter in her chair. "Is a priest here?"

Ava took a breath. "Issy didn't want a priest."

"But she has to." Gladys's voice rose, alarmed. "She can't die without a priest."

"She's in there with Shirley, her best friend from the house. She wanted me and Shirley here at the end. Some of the other girls from the house and a few friends have already come by to say good-bye. Mrs. Mendes, we have to respect her wishes."

But now Gladys was upset, restive. "I have to talk to her. She can't do this."

She began to rise, but Ava gently pressed her back down. "You can't go in there and upset her, please, Mrs. Mendes. She is at the very end and the best thing you can do is go in there and hold her hand and smile at her and tell her that you and her whole family love her and send her off with peace in her heart. Please promise me you can do that."

But Gladys was now crying freely, shaking her head and twisting her rosary in her hand. "She didn't get married, she didn't have children, and now she's going to die without last rites. Her life had no meaning."

Listening, Ava remembered the promise Issy had extracted from her when Issy made her Mateo's legal standby guardian: that Ava would not tell her family about Mateo, that Ava would find a truly extraordinary home for him—educated people, open-minded people. So instead, all Ava said was: "Her life certainly had meaning. She's done incredible work the past four years fighting this disease. She's been incredibly brave telling her story. And she's been a part of our family at the house and she is very loved. So she is *certainly* not dying without meaning. You *cannot* go in there and make her feel badly. It's better you just leave if you're going to do that."

That caught Gladys up short, stifling her tears. She had a painful realization, which was that other people—including this Ava woman, apparently—had been taking care of her daughter these past years, had come to consider her their family, and that her own maternal right to intervene in her daughter's life had withered in the interim. She had forfeited it when she submitted to her husband's order that Issy was too much a source of anguish and hence no longer welcome in the house. She'd always submitted to her husband's orders, and in the wake of that bitter edict, she'd contented herself with stealth phone calls to Issy—calls that often ended badly, anyway, in sighing fits of recrimination on both ends. Gladys loved her daughter and prayed daily for her health, yet she hadn't understood why Issy felt the need to parade around so publicly with her disease in front of the police and TV cameras—especially when Issy knew how much it upset and embarrassed her father!

Yet for Gladys, being reminded by this woman that she was no longer the first authority in Issy's life was a shameful and humbling feeling. She regretted her outburst of a few moments prior, even as the matter of the priest still nagged at her.

"I don't want to upset her," she said. "I just want to tell her I love her."

"That's the best thing you can do at this point," Ava said.

Gladys steeled herself and walked into the room—filled with flowers and, on a wall facing the bed where Issy could see it, a blown-up photo of Issy shouting into a megaphone, surrounded by other women—to find her daughter—her lifelong borderline *gordita* of a daughter, that childhood lover of whole plates of *tostones* with garlic sauce—to find her a wraith, a third her former size, her damp black hair pulled back from her face, a ventilator across her nose, her eyes remote and half shut, her thin hand being held by a tall, skinny black woman with a long, aquiline nose who sat by her bed, gently dabbing her forehead with a damp washcloth.

"*Dios mío,*" Gladys said quietly to herself, which made the black woman turn to her.

"You're Issy's mom?" she asked.

Gladys nodded, unable to take her eyes off Issy, who didn't seem to have noticed her yet.

"I'm Shirley," said the woman. "I'm her roommate at the house. She's like my sister." The woman turned back to Issy. "Isn't that right, Issyboo? You're my sister, right?"

This elicited a shadow of a smile and a nod from Issy.

"Look who's here, baby. Your mom." Shirley turned to Gladys. "Come sit here."

Gladys approached and sat in Issy's line of sight, took her hand. "*Hola, cariño,*" she whispered. "*Es Mami. Te amo, cariño. Mi nena hermosa.*"

Gladys couldn't read the look in her daughter's eyes. It seemed far away, aloof even. Issy did not smile, weakly but clearly, as she'd just smiled for this Shirley woman. But Issy still pressed her mother's hand, barely perceptibly, and whispered, "Mami."

At that moment, three years of remorse flooded over Gladys, forcing tears to her eyes. How wrong they had been to push Issy away! How could they have let shame conquer their own blood? How weak had she been not to stand up to her own husband? How much time had they lost? But Gladys made herself withhold these thoughts and only cried and continued to hold her daughter's hand and say, again and again, *"Mija, te quiero mucho, mucho."*

"You should," Shirley said. "Issy's done some amazing things. You know she got the definition of AIDS changed."

Gladys had no idea what that meant, but it sounded important. So she turned back to Issy and said, *"Estoy orgullosa de ti, Issy."*

Finally Issy smiled vaguely, her eyes darting about. She mouthed something.

Shirley leaned in. "What is it, honey? What you trying to say?"

Issy looked aggrieved, her breathing more labored than a moment before. She began mouthing something again.

Shirley darted out, returned with Ava, who stood over the bed, taking Issy's hand.

"What is it, sweetheart?"

Issy mouthed the word clearly this time: "Hector."

Ava's eyes widened. "You want Hector? You said you just wanted the girls, sweetheart."

"I want Hector," Issy mouthed, a mere whisper.

"Who's Hector?" Gladys asked.

"That's her friend," Ava said. "He brought her into the activist group." Then, back to Issy: "You want me to call Hector and see if he can come here, Issy?"

Issy nodded once, slowly, her eyes widening.

Ava pulled her battered Filofax from her bag, found Hector's number, dialed it on the hospital phone. As she listened, she fumbled for a pen in her bag. "It's his machine," she said. "He's in D.C. right now and he left a number there." She scrawled the number into her Filofax, then dialed it.

"Hector? It's Ava." She paused. "I'm at St. Vincent's with Issy and her mother." She paused, then soberly: "Yes." She paused again. "I know. But she just called for you, she said your name." She paused again, sitting by the bed in the chair Shirley had relinquished, once again taking Issy's hand in her own and rubbing it gently with her thumb. "No, I don't think so." She paused. "Yes, of course."

Ava put the phone close to Issy's ear. "He wants to talk to you, Issy. Go ahead, Hector."

Faintly, the women in the hospital room could hear Hector's voice: "Issy? It's Hector. I love you, Issy. I'll never, ever forget you. Okay, do you understand that? I love you so much. I'm so glad you came into my life, *chica*."

Tears rose in Issy's eyes, then one raced down her cheek. She made a low, guttural, urgent sound. "Hector," she said. "Hector." More tears came and her fingers gripped Ava's as hard as they could.

"What do you wanna tell him, honey?" Ava asked. "You wanna say you love him, right?"

Issy made another guttural sound, her hand breaking free and reaching feebly for the phone.

But Ava gently shushed her and placed her hand back down. "She wants to say she loves you, too, Hector," she said back into the phone. "That's what you want to tell Hector, Issy, right?"

Issy raised her head slightly and looked at Ava, Shirley, and her mother beseechingly, unable to say more.

Ava concluded her call with Hector. Then the three women took turns sitting by Issy until 1:46 A.M., the Monday before Thanksgiving, when Issy made the sound that Ava knew too well, that final horrible rattling sound in the throat, and then lay there, her mouth and eyes open and immobile.

"She's gone," Ava said. "Our beloved Issy is gone."

The three women prayed and cried and said their good-byes until 2:05 A.M., when Ava stood up to go find a nurse. Before she did, she gave Shirley cab money to get back to Judith House, where an eleven-month-old baby boy named Mateo, his silky cap of hair just as dark as his mother's had been, was sound asleep.

NINETEEN
PRODIGAL
(2021)

The twisting in Mateo's stomach starts subtly, when the plane is probably somewhere over Pennsylvania or eastern New Jersey, then intensifies when he first catches a glimpse of the skyline, glittering amid the black, even higher reaching and more crowded than it was in his youth. That familiar parabola: the peaks in midtown, then the dip through Chelsea, the Villages, SoHo, Chinatown, Tribeca, then the jagged ascent at the island's tip—once again with a pinnacle, the past ten years now, much as there'd been a staggering pinnacle before a day he vaguely remembers from childhood, when he was eight, nine, back in the days of *frites* on Avenue A and his first East Village friends. But today, the pinnacle is one tower, not two, and its summit is a spiky radio spear, not twin flattops. There will never be a drug that hits him as hard and as fast as New York City, the first sight of which, swallowed whole from above, seizes him with dizzying waves of exhilaration, nostalgia, and panic. And unlike a drug, it's real, it's all real. Everything that happened down there is real, real, real.

On his little tablet, he pings Gary, his AA sponsor: "looking down on ny now from plane, freaking out a little." How long before he pings back? What will he say? "You're gonna be fine." "Breathe and pray through it." "Hit a meeting ASAP." Or: "You've done this before, not your first time."

True, that. Mateo's been here before, several times the past few years. Less than he might've, given all the professional invitations he's gotten. And never for more than a few days, a week, where he stayed in Brooklyn, well away from the old neighborhood. But this, now: at least six months! And smack-dab in the old hood, on a big job no less. It's almost more full circle than he can deal with.

Next, he pings Dani: "Landing soon. You home?" She'd come here a month in advance, for various design jobs, and she'd moved into the loft they'd subletted in Chinatown, set it up all cozy for them.

Now he just sits back and breathes, wondering who'll thumb him back first. But soon he's landing at LaGuardia, soon he's picking up his huge duffel at the baggage claim, soon he's in a cab speeding through Queens toward midtown, soon—oh God!—he's cabbing it down Second Avenue on a Thursday night, his mind a patchwork of memory-stabs of storefronts that have remained and of marvels of those that have changed. It seems like everyone bikes now, it feels like Copenhagen or something. The newer buses are so streamlined, streaking up and down their designated lanes, and more and more of the cars are so small, electric. What's changed and what's remained? Do the kids on the street look the same? On not one wall but two he sees ads for liquors or clothes that have been done in a cheap, knockoff version of the style of him and Charlice—ah, ah, he means Charlie. He keeps forgetting the subtle change and he feels like, in his head, she—uh, fuck, no, he, Charlie—keeps rolling his eyes at Mateo in disapproval. *Well, she always basically was a he to me, anyway*, Mateo thinks, *it shouldn't be that hard*. But yeah, it's just like L.A., he can see people have been ripping off his and Char's style, and that both annoys him and makes him privately proud.

A message flashes on his tablet from Gary: "Pray to be protected. Then go to a meeting and get your hand up, idiot." Mateo laughs. Fucking Gary. How many times has this AARP balding dude, who's basically been living off rerun checks from his 1980s sitcoms the past thirty-one years, talked him off the ledge and set him back on course over the past decade? Many, in a word. Because there were so many times when Mateo's daymares and nightmares about Carrie felt like they were going to get him, too. *You didn't deliberately kill her,* Gary would tell him, *you were just two addicts and sometimes there are casualties—that's the way it goes. Just pay it forward, pay it forward.* So he had, hours and hours doing art projects with unlucky L.A. kids who reminded him of how he'd been born an unlucky New York kid, helping them get into programs and schools, wondering when, *when,* he would crawl out from under the shadow of hell and into redemption.

Now the taxi is crossing Houston Street, which after decades of work almost looks like some kind of fucking Paris boulevard with its lush, manicured strip of green running down the middle and more glass towers on either side than he wants to count. A message flashes from Dani: "You on your way?"

"Xing Houston in cab," he thumbs back. *Oh, shit,* he thinks, *these streets! Wasn't that stoop . . . or didn't it look like that stoop? No, wait, that stoop was on Orchard, right?* The stoop where he and Oscar had nodded that Christmas night when the snow fell, leaning against each other in their black puffy coats and black caps, barely able to keep their heads up to look at the swirling wonder, and the feeling that the sky was infinite, that the sky spun counterclockwise to the snow.

His stomach twitches—his first anticipatory junkie twitching in a long, long time. *Oh, shit,* he thinks. *Gary's right.* He really does need a meeting. Maybe later tonight.

The cab pulls up in front of a blue glass sliver on East Broadway. All these fucking tinted glass slivers and shards that have shot up everywhere amid the dirty, old, stone street walls—it's surreal! There'll be one, two, three, four old tenements, brick and fire escapes and the like, then suddenly a glass shard, whose street-facing apartments are utterly transparent, like looking in a glass box at someone's life. They're either like that or they're opaque, a milky glowing white or a shimmery onyx. These new apartments never have curtains or blinds anymore, Mateo notes. It's all this fucking window technology, making the windows go opaque white or black or red or jade.

Coming off the elevator, Dani's there in the open door to greet him. Mateo's heart bursts open; he hasn't seen her in eleven days, since she left L.A., and whenever he sees her after a separation like that, he can't control his desire. He drops his bags in the hallway and swallows her up, backing her into the apartment.

"Oh, damn!" she exclaims, pealing laughter.

Ignoring the apartment he's never seen before, ignoring the twinkling outside the infinity windows, he finds the bedroom. They get each other naked, begin.

"Oh thank God, thank God, thank God," he keeps saying the whole time, bucking his ass back and forth atop Dani, who's clutching him with both her arms and legs, her head thrown back. And he means it—he's so giddy with thankfulness to be entwined in her body again that he wants to cry.

Then it's over and they lie there, clutching each other. Mateo runs his lips from her neck over her breasts, down the side of her belly, down her leg, up her leg, and back up her belly, where he just holds her and buries his lips in her hair.

"Missed you so much, Neenee," he mutters. "Love you so much."

"Missed you and love you so much, too, Taytay," she says.

They both fall asleep for twenty minutes. Mateo wakes up before her and lies there holding her, thinking about next steps. First would be to pull his bags out of the hallway and close the door behind him. Second would be to inspect the art on the walls he caught out of the corner of his eye while he was bum-rushing Dani into the bedroom. Yep, he thinks, that's what it was: a tiny Kara Walker cutout and two or three of McGinley's Morrissey photos. He takes a shower. When he comes back in the bedroom, Dani's awake.

"Do you mind if Char comes over?" she asks. "He didn't know if you'd be up for it or not tonight."

"Are *you* okay if he comes over?" Mateo asks back. *There*, he thinks, *I said* he *without a hiccup first. Progress!* "We can order up some food."

"Okay, well, ping him and let him know. I'll order food. You want Malaysian? There's a really good place downstairs I can ping."

"Yeah, that sounds good." He's in the living room now, fishing jeans and a T-shirt out of his bags, wondering if he can still make the midnight meeting on the other end of Houston Street.

"So what do you think of this place?" Dani calls from the bedroom.

"Just how you described it to me," he says. "Very downtown person-with-money aesthetically correct." And it is: mostly white space with a massive gray couch system facing the infinity window and lots of chunky dark wood, including the requisite kitchen farm table, for the old-timey contrast.

"Complete with a Kara Walker and a few Ryan McGinleys," Dani says, and laughs.

"Yep," Mateo says, coming back in the bedroom and flopping himself down again near her. "Very correct. But it'll be comfortable for the next six months." He kisses her. "Thanks for finding it while I was crazy in London."

She strokes his hair. "Are you happy to be here? You feeling weird?"

"The cab went straight through the East Village tonight. I got a hot flash when we crossed Ninth Street."

"Why?"

"That's the street the Christodora's on."

"You mean you passed it?"

"No, we were going down Second Avenue and it's on Avenue B. But I could feel it when we crossed Ninth Street."

Dani pauses. "Well, I didn't grow up here so I don't exactly know what that means."

"It just means I could feel its latitude. Or longitude or whatever."

"Ohh," says Dani. Then: "Milly still lives there?"

"I think so. I think Jared basically let her have it as a mercy gift when he left her, so the whole thing wouldn't drag into court. That's kind of what Drew told me once."

"The same talk when she told you that your grandmother died?"

Mateo winces slightly. He's mentioned this to Dani in the past, confided that he felt shitty that he didn't reach out to Milly, never mind that he hadn't gotten on a plane to New York for Ava's funeral and shivah. He'd felt the instinct to do it, felt the loss of that indomitable woman who'd been sweet to him as a kid when she had the time to spare, but the thought of actually doing it—and having to see Milly amid her grief—was more than he could bear. Shamefully, he'd shunted the news aside in his head.

"She wasn't really my grandmother," he says to Dani.

She laughs, mildly reproving. "You called her your *bubbe*, Mateo."

He raises a hand to his forehead and turns away, at a loss for a response. He flat-out doesn't like talking about the Heyman-Traums—it sparks remorse and regret in the pit of his stomach, a distinctly unpleasant feeling that threatens to throw him off his confident, present-day linear course.

Dani senses his displeasure. "Okay," she says, gently pulling his hand away from his forehead. "I'm sorry I pushed it."

He sighs, rubs her wrist with his thumb. "It's just I get sad and bad feelings when I think about them."

"I know, sweetie, I know. But while we're in the sad and bad zone, there is just one more thing I want to mention, to head it off down the line. You know that Jared has a show opening here in a few weeks."

Mateo's hand flies back to his brow. "Yeah, jeez, I know," he says. "What, you're saying I should go?"

Her face goes all innocent and know-nothing. "I'm not saying anything. Did I say anything?"

"Well, then, why'd you bring it up?"

She strokes his hair again. "I just wanted to make sure you knew, because somebody else is probably going to bring it up with you." She gets up and heads to the shower. "You know I have no opinion about your relationship with Jared and Milly."

Mateo laughs sharply. "We have no relationship."

Dani turns slowly in the door and looks back at him meaningfully. Then they both laugh.

"Yeah, right, you have no opinion," Mateo calls as she closes the bathroom door.

Twenty minutes later, he buzzes up Char, who got here two weeks ahead of him. Char's been down at the site and looks tired, bits of paint on his face and T-shirt. Char basically looks like the same baby dyke he met ten years ago doing that mural in L.A., if he added some scruff and a little bit of age to the face, then subtracted boobs.

Mateo and Char lock fists, hug. "Welcome, brother," Char says. "Thanks. Good to be here."

Char gives him a funny double take. "For real?"

"For real," he assures. "It's amazing. It's exciting. We're doing public art in New York City! Underground art. Literally underground art. It's all good."

"You better be ready for a full plate this week," Char says. "You have no fucking idea how difficult it is to paint on scaffolds on curved white tile above your head."

"Michelangelo did something like that," Mateo says. "And he didn't even have six MFA students working for him."

Char looks at Mateo skeptically. "Dude, Michelangelo definitely had assistants. The pope or the king or whatever probably gave him slaves or something."

Dani walks in from the bedroom, her hair still wet, gives Char a hug and a hello.

"Neenee, did Michelangelo have assistants?" Mateo asks.

She looks up from her tablet, where she's ordering food. "He had to," she says. "I mean, right?"

"He probably had fucking slaves," Char reiterates. "Everybody had slaves then."

"MFA students are the new slaves," Mateo says.

Later that night, after the food's come and after Char's shown him about a thousand pictures and videos of the project on his tablet, Mateo walks Char down to the street. They pull bikes out of a bike station.

"See you at the UnderPark at nine tomorrow," Mateo says.

"You off to a meeting now?" Char asks, to which Mateo nods. "How you doing, being here?"

"Four hours in, I still don't have a needle in my arm."

Char frown-smiles. "Oh, come on, man, don't say fucked up shit like that," he says. "Go to your fucking meeting." He bikes off toward the Williamsburg Bridge.

Mateo bikes the opposite way, west and then up to Houston. It's a mild Sunday night in May, nearly midnight, and the streets are quiet, the faint chlorine smell from white pear-tree blossoms in the air. There's so much fucking glass everywhere! Some of the glass has been opaqued for the night, but some of it's clear and he can look right in and up to some of the world's richest people amid their humdrum Sunday-night routines, sprawling in front of fifteen-foot-wide screens that dance with images and light. But between the glass spires and wedges there are the old stoops, fire escapes, cornices, and witch-hatted water towers he still sees in his dreams.

On West Houston, near to the river, he comes to the black door with MIDNITE stenciled in white paint on it. He finds a station to dock his bike about a hundred feet away, retraces his steps, nods at a few guys sucking on their vape-sticks outside, and then he walks through the door and up the steep, narrow steps. The last time he was here, four years ago for a show, this place saved his ass. He walks in the candlelit room, where some dude with a bolt through his nose is already telling his tale to the group, and takes the first empty seat he sees, next to a dirty-blond girl with cutely sardonic lips who looks not a day over twenty-five. She glances at him, looks away, then glances back. He catches her glance and smiles.

When the sharing starts, the girl raises her hand. "Sophie, addict."

"Hi, Sophie," everyone says.

"I have twenty-nine days today," she says. The room applauds. Then her tale about how her parents want her to move back to Santa Barbara but she wants to stay in New York but she can barely pay her rent now that she's lost her job, and does anyone have any advice after the meeting?

"Thanks, Sophie."

Mateo really doesn't want to get his hand up and share; he feels bleary-eyed and out of it from the flight, but he knows he better. So up goes the hand, which catches the eye of the dude with the nose bolt.

"Mateo, addick," he says. Ten years on, he still won't pronounce the *t*.

"Hi, Mateo."

"Unnnnnhh, now what did I want to say?" he thinks aloud. A few people chuckle, including Sophie.

"I wanted to sayyyy," he continues, "that I'm very glad I'm here. I just got into town from L.A. tonight and this is where I needed to be, and even my girlfriend and my work partner said as much and kicked me the fuck out of the house after dinner." More chuckles.

"I can remember when I would raise my hand in meetings and talk bullshit," he says. "And I'd leave the meeting and go cop, or spend the meeting thinking about what girl I wanted to cop with." More chuckles, maybe a tiny bit of slightly uncomfortable seat adjustment around the room.

"So, unnnnhh, I'm truly glad I don't put my hand up in that bullshit spirit anymore, but more like something I'm able to make myself do when I know I need to. Like I've got smart arm nerves or reflexes or something that take over for me. But, unnnnhh, I just wanna say it's good to be here in a safe place because New York is a very hard place for me to be. I mean, don't get me wrong, I fucking love this city, but this is where it got really sketchy and sad for me about ten years ago and where I really left some scorched earth behind me. And when I hit the streets here—" and here, he surprises himself, his voice catches hoarsely and he can feel tears welling up in his eyes, and then Sophie's gentle hand on his back.

He catches his breath and swallows it back. "When I hit the streets here, it hits me so hard. It's, like, visceral; it's, like, uh, cellular memory. And the thing was, it was ten, eleven, twelve years ago. I was a fucking kid—I didn't even know what the fuck I was doing or why I was so angry. And even now, after being sober almost ten years, therapy and all that shit, talking it through and the Steps and all that, I can just hit the streets here and it's like the first smell, some particles in the air, bring it back to me. The fucking way the streets are here and the stoops and the doorways. And I can feel my whole body turning to jelly, and that fucking scares me. And it's not just remembering the needle, it's—"

The guy with the bolt through his nose lightly holds up a warning palm to Mateo.

"Oh, hey," Mateo continues, "I'm sorry, I didn't mean to trigger folks. What I meant was it's not just the, unh, the using, it's—" He pauses. "It's the people. It's all the fucking loose strings. I have not tied up my loose strings and made some key amends and stuff like that."

Half the room nods with him. He feels a bit back in their good graces after his slight gaffe. "But hey," he says, "I'm getting ahead of myself. I'm here, and I'm sober. I mean, I am in fucking New York City and I am sober, and that's truly a miracle. And I am here on a fucking amazing project with amazing people and I'm psyched about that. And, hey, I just hope I can get here most nights, 'cause it's gonna be a crazy few months here."

After the meeting, after everyone's said the Serenity Prayer together and unjoined hands, Sophie turns to him. "You're here to work on the UnderPark, right?" she asks. "You and Charlie Gauthier?"

Mateo nods. He's a little taken aback but not really surprised; the news has been all over art verticals the past six months. "That's why we're here," he says.

"That's so cool," she says. "I actually used to be Ruby Levin's assistant."

"Oh, yeah?" he asks. Ruby Levin is the head of Creative Production Fund, a nonprofit that usually has a hand in the biggest public-art projects in the city; in twenty years, she's kind of become the town's fairy godmother of popular art, and, no surprise, she's playing a big role in the art for the UnderPark. "What are you doing now?" Mateo asks her.

"Well," says Sophie, pulling back her lank blond hair, "not much. Going to meetings and looking for a job. Ruby fired me for being an alcoholic fuckup." She laughs, but her face flushes with shame as she says it.

"And knowing Ruby, she probably gave you about five chances first, right?"

"Yeah." Sophie laughs again. "She told me to go to AA about five times before firing me."

They laugh together, and Mateo feels that spark. This, he realizes, has become a recurring minor problem. The fucked-up pretty girl, the art groupie, the AA new arrival, and the sudden confusing stabs of empathy and desire he feels for her; the pretty girl who reflects him back to himself and who is so unlike Dani and Char in their stolid, competent, crisp non-fucked-up-ness. He's learned it's simply better to let other folks exchange pings with such girls; he can always provide real-time support when he sees them at meetings, but he doesn't need to have their data. He did that once, a long time ago, and where that led . . .

So Mateo says, "I guess she finally did what she had to do to get you here, right?"

Sophie shrugs, sheepish. "I guess she did."

He offers her a fist bump, and she accepts. "You're gonna be okay," he says. "I remember the crummy loser feeling. It goes away."

"Does it really?"

Oh God, he thinks, *she's breaking my heart with those eyes.* "It seriously diminishes," he says. "If you keep coming here."

He walks out of the building and down the treacherous narrow staircase, exchanging hellos and fist bumps with a few familiar faces he knows from when they drop in on meetings in L.A. His gut instinct tells him to hop on a bike and hightail it home to Dani. But God, those quiet, dark post-midnight streets below Houston call him back. Can he do it? Can he walk those streets and face down memories? Hating himself for being the weak addict he is, he buys a nineteen-dollar pack of cigarettes at a bodega, lights one, ducks a block below Houston and swings left on Prince. Scarcely a soul passes him. Eventually, Prince gives out onto the Bowery and he's standing in front of the Chinatown YMCA, where they took him Saturday mornings for swim lessons. She would take her coffee and a magazine into the little glassed-in room overlooking the pool while he would take Mateo into the men's locker room and help him get into his bathing suit and goggles. He'd put Mateo under the shower and point him toward the instructor and the other kids with their inflatable doughnuts on their arms. And from time to time, Mateo would look up and see them behind the glass, watching him, giving him a thumbs-up, and Mateo would wave back at them, feeling the good feeling of being watched over.

The next morning, Mateo's at the site at nine A.M. in a ratty old T-shirt and jeans, ready to make things happen. Char's already there, a dozen scruffy assistants swarming around him. This is the first time Mateo's been at the site since a brief initial visit six months ago, and he marvels at the progress. Here's a huge, dank underground space, a former hideaway for subway cars, that a massive infusion of new-style private New York mega-money is transforming into a subterranean park with a high-tech lighting system that collects sunlight up on the street and then funnels and diffuses it below. The interior envelope is nearly complete; the ceiling is countless square feet of undulating silvery reflective material.

His and Char's project, the biggest public project they've ever been commissioned for, is to paint the entryway corner ceiling in a twinkling profusion of greens, blues, and yellows so that, once trees are planted, their leafy tops will disappear into the work. For the past two days, Char's been supervising assistants to paint the ceiling in a kind of high-tech primer that will hold their paints; they've long since abandoned working with spray cans, precluding anyone from ever again putting the word *graffiti* anywhere in a description of their art. Besides, the whole point of Mateo and Char, the whole reason for their explosion of highbrow success the past seven years, is that the two of them "revolutionized" street art, transformed it from something that, however artful, always looked like graffiti into something that took an existing wall or surface and made people feel their eyes were playing tricks on them—that, say, an old brick wall was oozing black tar from the center outward, or that the concrete parabolas of a skate park were breaking open with a lacy neon moss.

The original idea, street art that looked like something in a dream, was, of course, Char's—that much is certain, from that very first piece Mateo saw him (well, then, her) doing on the wall in West Adams, back almost ten years ago at Mateo's lowest point. But Mateo feels confident he's brought something to the collaboration, to the style they both take the credit for today.

"Let's make it less," he would always say to Char once the two of them started working together in earnest. That was 2013, 2014, those years after Mateo left the halfway house and bunked in that shithole in downtown L.A. and actually learned, for once, how to live a life and not blow it up with needles every few months.

"Like," he'd say to Char, "less form, less form, less like we were even there. Let's make it like you just look at the surface and the first thing you think is something's wrong, what the fuck is happening to that wall, it's, like, melting or frying or transforming itself or something." He loved this kind of stealth approach, it felt so sneaky, and Char, after a moment's pause, liked it too, and that's how the two of them bonded. Even as they got more and more attention, they felt like two sneaks, ever so delicately fucking with the existing surface and making people do a double take.

Now, Char hustles over to Mateo, wiping his hands on a rag. "You ready to do this?" he bellows, a big grin on his face.

Suddenly, Mateo crests with excitement and happiness. The space is so strange, so different, so—so strangely filled with light! "I'm so fucking ready," he says, and the two of them bear-hug. "Let's paint the shit out of the place."

Everyone's turned to watch the two of them embrace, including Ruby Levin.

"Woo-hoo!" she finally calls. "We're doing it! Guys, we're doing it! We're putting art in the UnderPark!"

This leads to a big round of applause and more woo-hoos. Soon, Mateo, Char, Ruby, and the assistants are standing in front of the awaiting corner and tracing their fingers over images on their tablets. Two assistants are warming paints on hot plates hooked up to a generator— these special paints they're using have to be heated to a certain warm-but-not-hot temperature in order to molecularly bond with the primer and with the high-tech reflective surface of the park's inner walls.

Char asks Mateo, "Do you want to start tracing in B7?" He means the B7 section of the grid they've superimposed on their tablet images of the wall.

"The primer's dry?" Mateo asks.

"We tested it this morning. They heat-sealed it last night."

"Okay, let's do it then," Mateo says. "Let's set up the scaffolding."

And it begins. Once the scaffold is set up, he installs himself up there with a stack of stencils and a charcoal pencil. He sketches in the very first stencil of an abstract leaf pattern he and Char have designed.

"Nicely done," Char calls, climbing up the adjoining scaffold. "You gonna work toward me in a spiral pattern?"

"You like spirals, not me," he says. "I'm gonna slice down into C6 in a sort of wiggly diagonal."

"Ah, a wiggly diagonal!" Char echoes, teasing him. "Very high-concept, Mendes."

He blows Char a kiss off the top of his middle finger, turns back to his work. He's very happy, lost in the patterns, just where he likes to be.

Sixty minutes later, he climbs down to stretch, pee, have a smoke, grab a bagel from the craft table Creative Production Fund's set up. Talking to Char and Ruby and some of the interns, he notices a pretty late-twentysomething brunette standing off to the side, smiling his way. He nods in her direction, and once he's broken off from Char and Ruby to spread some cream cheese on a bagel, the brunette walks up to him.

"Mateo?" she asks.

"Yeah, what's up?"

"Hi. I'm Tanzina Parcero. I'm an arts writer for the *Times*'s art vertical."

"Ah!" Mateo says. "Ah, okay. Well, hi there, Tanzina." He offers a hand. "Nice to meet you."

"This is super-exciting, isn't it?" she says, pointing to the wall and the scaffolding.

"Uh—" he says. "Well, yeah, it is!" He's a bit mesmerized by her glossy brown hair and massive brown eyes. She's definitely in that same category of pretty light-brown girl with glossy hair that Dani falls in for him. "We just started this morning and I'm super-excited."

"Yeah, I know," she says. "People are very intrigued about this. Can I talk to you for a little write-up about the project?" She's already pulling her tablet out of her bag.

"Uhh—" he says uncertainly.

Ruby's hustling over. "Hi there, Tanzina!" she says brightly.

"Hi, Ruby!" The two share a little hug. Tanzina asks, "You don't mind if I get a little something from Mateo for a post for the vertical, do you?"

"Umm," Ruby says slowly. "It's really up to Mateo and Char if they want to talk about the project at this point. They literally just started this morning."

"Char!" Mateo calls. Char turns away from the scaffolding, hustles over. "Do we want to talk to Tanzina? She's a writer for the *Times* art vertical."

Mateo catches a little sparkle in Char's eyes; he figures Char's as attracted to Tanzina as he is. Char shrugs. "Sure," he says. "Thanks for coming down."

"Okay, great," Tanzina says, tapping the "record" button on her tablet screen. "Okay, wow, guys. So, here we are, day one. So what is the process going to be?"

"Uhh—" Mateo and Char say, nearly in unison. Then Char picks up: "Well, I think the general idea is, you see, there will be a, um, a copse of baby silver maple trees in that corner. So, um, our idea is we are going to do a kind of wall of, like, well, I like to call them space leaves—"

Tanzina laughs, delighted. "Space leaves?"

"Yeah," Char says, laughing. "Like, leaves that if you found trees on Mars or Neptune or something, they'd have these kind of leaves. Like, you'd recognize them as leaves, but there'd be something weird, like, mutant, about them. A little creepy, maybe, even."

"Char's not totally from the planet Earth," Mateo jokes. "He's part Vulcan."

It goes on like this for a while, Mateo and Char enjoying this banter and describing the process. Then, without changing a note, Tanzina asks, "Okay, cool. And, Mateo, are you going to the opening of your father's show at Blum-36 a week from Friday?"

Mateo, Char, and Ruby all do a start. "Huh?" Mateo finally says. "My father?" He starts getting a crummy betrayed feeling that all Tanzina's questions about their project were just a ramp-up to this.

"Well, yes, your father Jared Traum's new show at Blum-36 a week from Friday," Tanzina repeats. Mateo can see a certain something harden around those big brown eyes of hers, as much as she's still smiling. He supposes it was foolish of him, or naive or wishful thinking, to imagine that nobody was going to bring up this connection at some point.

"I mean," Mateo says, "he's not really my father."

"He's your adoptive father, right?" Tanzina asks.

"I think Mateo and Char want to keep the focus on this project," Ruby says firmly. "I mean, they just started this morning."

"We got a shitload of work to do," adds Char. It's clear they're both backing up behind Mateo now, protective.

"No, no," Mateo says, flustered. "I mean, it's okay." He turns to Tanzina, whose eyes are intense, gleeful that he's engaging her on this, as she holds her tablet toward him. "I mean, yes, he's my adoptive father. But we're not really in touch. I've been living in L.A. the past ten years or so and—I mean, I was a wild child growing up here. Ten, fifteen years ago, I mean, the Lower East Side isn't what it is today, I mean, it was rougher. Like, not as rough as, like, the eighties or whatever, but, uh, way more drugs, and . . ."

He loses his train of thought, then regains it. "I mean, I think they needed a break from me. My adoptive parents. I really put them through it."

"Mmm," says Tanzina, as though she's gravely absorbing his words. "Well, you think you'll see your adoptive mom while you're here? She still lives here, right?" She's holding that damn tablet toward him.

"This feels like it's getting far too personal," Ruby says. This time Mateo can hear the indignation breaking through her usually flawlessly bright and diplomatic demeanor. "I thought you said you were just writing a post about the project getting under way."

Tanzina widens her eyes, all innocent. "This is part of the story!" she says. "A New York art family."

"Oh, Jesus," Mateo says, before he can stop himself. "That is so not the story."

Tanzina's lovely eyes dance with drunken delight at his small explosion. Oh God, now he's fucked. "I mean," Mateo says, "the story is—that we have a shitload of work to do. So I'm gonna eat my bagel and get back to work. Take care."

He simply walks away, back toward the craft table. When he reaches for the knife to scoop out some cream cheese and put it on half of a poppyseed bagel, his hand is shaking.

A hand lands on his shoulder. It's Char. "Hey," he says. "Brush your shoulders off, bro. That was sick stupid."

"I guess I've been fucking naive," Mateo says. Out of the corner of his eye, he sees Ruby giving Tanzina a polite but firm talking-to, Tanzina holding her tablet at her side, as Ruby's obviously taken her off the record.

"I guess I really should've been ready with something a little smarter than that," he says. "'I wish Jared Traum the best, I really respect his work,' and all that kind of stuff."

"Fuck it," says Char. "You don't have to be ready with anything. You're here to make a piece."

"I'm fucking terrified of making contact with them, Char," he says. "I haven't talked to them in, like, ten years."

"Dude, you don't have to deal with that now," Char says. "You're here to make work."

Mateo watches Tanzina bop away, putting her tablet back into her bag, ready to go back to the office and package up her piece of bounty.

"What a pretty little sneak, huh?" he says to Char, nodding with his chin toward Tanzina.

"Why the fuck'd you think I came over?" Char asks. "I wasn't gonna let you have all of that!"

Mateo and Char crack up a little. Ruby walks over to join them, frowning.

"I am sorry about that," she says. "I didn't see that coming. I was caught off guard because usually she's a very work-focused writer."

"I was naive," Mateo says.

"No, no," she says, putting a hand on his shoulder. "That's not your job, it's mine. Do you want me to keep them away from now on?"

"I mean . . ." Mateo starts, then gives up, exasperated. "I mean, whatever," he says. "I don't have anything to hide. The situation is what it is."

Everyone just stands there for a minute. "I just want you guys to be able to enjoy the project," Ruby says. "It's special."

Over the next few days, they do, in fact, manage to enjoy the project. Char starts adding color even before Mateo's finished stenciling. He begins to be able to visualize how the wall is going to explode like delicate fireworks behind the silver maples. He's feeling good, he's having good dinners in Brooklyn and Queens every night with Dani and Char and, eventually, some cute redheaded jewelry-maker girl named Becky whom Char starts bringing around. He's managing to make a few AA or NA meetings here and there, he's holding it together.

Then on Thursday morning, he and Dani wake up to pounding rain against the infinity windows of their rental. Mateo calls Char.

"Has Ruby called you yet?" Char asks.

"No, why?"

"Shit, man." Char half laughs, so exasperated. "Rain is fucking leaking into our corner at the site."

"Fuck, what?"

"Fuck yes, man! Fucking leaking into the project."

"Fuck, fuck, fuck!" Mateo exclaims. Dani looks up at him from the bed, alarmed. "I thought that wasn't supposed to happen. There was all that high-tech sealant."

"Yeah, so they thought it wasn't supposed to happen, either, but—"

"But—"

"So let's get down there, we're gonna patch it up."

He throws on some clothes, grabs an umbrella, hails a cab, and still arrives at the site half drenched, the rain is coming down so hard. Char and Ruby and two of the guys from the UnderPark Foundation office are directing a bunch of interns and technicians, covering the existing work on the project with clear tarp and sealing it up a hundred times over with industrial duct tape.

"Where's the leak coming from?" Mateo asks the UnderPark guys.

"We've got the contractor and the architects down here all day today," one of them, James, says. "Do not worry, we are going to remediate and you guys will be back to work as soon as the rain stops. So I say go home and take a breather while we remediate."

Remediate. Mateo, Char, Ruby, and a few of the interns laugh about the word twenty minutes later when, all still damp, they're sitting in a nearby restaurant, some cute Israeli place with whitewashed clapboard walls, having coffee and shakshuka. After that, at a loss for what else to do amid the downpour, Mateo goes back to his chic infinity-windowed sublet and takes a hot shower. Poor Dani's out in this devil rain on a design job, sourcing carpets, so he's got the place to himself. He flops down with his tablet, cranks up some Odd Future for old time's sake, answers e-mails. But after a while, the loneliness and the rain shattering over the Lower East Side start creeping into his bones. These are always the most dangerous moments: when the noise of the present clears and he finds himself alone, unoccupied, staring into the abyss of the past with all its broken objects and shameful acts.

And then he tries something that's never occurred to him to try before: instead of typing "Ysabel Mendes" and "AIDS" into his tablet, which has never yielded anything the past many times he's done it— usually late at night, when he sometimes slips into just such a wormhole of the past as the one he's in now—he types "Isabel Mendes" and "AIDS," just to see. Thoughts of her come rushing back to him sometimes, in rare, lonely, unguarded moments like this. He left that photo of her behind at the Christodora, tucked inside his boyhood bed, and often he thought he'd like to have it back, which would require communication he couldn't bring himself to initiate. But still, he spent so much time looking at it growing up, he doesn't need to fetch it. His brain just calls it up. The leather jacket, the denim mini, the moussed-up head cocked to one side, the elbow propped up on that gay *moreno*'s shoulder, the sassy smirk on her face.

And there it is. Oh God. He catches his breath. There's a link to a site called "AIDS Warriors Speak" and a bit of text underneath it, which reads: " . . . and a year later, also died, a woman named Isabel Mendes, who played a very big role in . . ."

Mateo looks out at the sheet of rain. He clicks the link. It's from the transcript of a video interview from 2004, also posted, with a guy named Karl Cheling, who looks like a lefty radical version of Charlton Heston's Moses, with a prominent forehead and a white beard and ponytail. So he clicks on the video and sits through several minutes of this Karl Cheling talking about all this old shit, about the AIDS days in New York in the late 1980s and early 1990s and the various surprise demonstrations and takeovers he and his buddies pulled on city hall and the Department of Health and Human Services in D.C. and various other bureaucratic places. And Mateo looks up and thinks for a moment how crazy it is that there is no more AIDS anymore—well, he knows, he's read, that there are still people in Africa who haven't gotten the cure therapy yet, but even there it's being done, and some expert he read said that it would be eradicated off the globe by 2030, just like polio was. The disease that killed his mother, Mateo thinks. Wiped out.

He looks back at his tablet. The interviewer behind the camera, a woman whose voice has a thick, old-fashioned New York accent like his *bubbe* had, says, "And you're obviously talking about a lot of activists who died before the emergence of Internet archives in, say, the late 1990s, so there's very little record of them, correct?"

"Yes, correct," says the white-ponytailed guy. He reels off a long list of people and things they did. "Particularly women and people of color," he says, "they've not been archived as properly and made into heroes in documentaries and such. There were some especially amazing women. There was a black woman named Katrina Haslip who played a very big role in getting the federal definition of AIDS expanded to include more symptoms held by women, then she died very shortly thereafter in 1992. And a year later, also died, a woman named Ysabel Mendes, who played a very big role in working with Katrina. She was on the Latino committee, putting a lot of the literature into Spanish translation. And she worked very closely alongside a very, very smart treatment activist named Hector Villanueva who is still alive and actually very active with ShelterHelps—very much a part of the ShelterHelps family and a link from the past to the present. Katrina and, uh, Ysabel were very vocal, fierce activists at a time when it was still widely considered that women were not as susceptible to AIDS, when they were undercounted and under-included in research, and routine testing for them was still rare and not widely urged."

"And what were the primary goals, the agenda, going into 1993, '94?" the interviewer asked.

Mateo listens through the rest of the interview, but Ysabel Mendes isn't mentioned again. Then, for the umpteenth time, he searches "Hector Villanueva" and "AIDS" and "drugs," and all the usual old links and stories come up.

But the links on Hector Villanueva seem to drop off after the early to mid-2000s. No mentions of his arrest in L.A. in 2012. Mateo goes back to the link of the interview with the Cheling guy and sees that it's dated only two years ago. *Still alive and actually very active with ShelterHelps*, the Cheling guy had said. Mateo searches for "Hector Villanueva" and "ShelterHelps" and finds a pdf of a newsletter from this ShelterHelps, which seems to be some kind of nonprofit housing group for AIDS people or homeless people—he can't quite tell if it's either or both—and, pulled up from the newsletter, he reads: " . . . included Trayvon Spratt, Hector Villanueva, Eduardo Salazar, and Melvin Robinson, residents of SH's newly opened Brownsville home. Heading up Christmas tree duties . . ."

The newsletter dates back only four months.

Mateo looks up from his tablet at the sheets of rain pounding the Lower East Side. *Oh, shit*, he thinks. *You've really gone down a wormhole now.* He knows he should call Gary, his sponsor, or at least ping him a message: *I've gone down the wormhole again.*

But he doesn't. Zombielike, he looks up the address for this ShelterHelps Brownsville residence, and before he can even let himself think about it too much, he's grabbing his keys and an umbrella. He's down on the street holding the umbrella in front of him like a shield, fending off the rain, until he's inside a half-flooded subway station, fingering the digital map on the wall to figure out the best way to Brownsville.

Once he's on the 3 train, he has nothing to do but sit there in a car with about six or seven other rain-bedraggled passengers, various dirty puddles of water on the train floor, and think about what a fool thing he's doing, walking like a, yes, well, a zombie, right back into the belly of the beast. *Fucking Brownsville? Where the fuck are you going?* he thinks.

When he steps out onto the elevated platform at the Rockaway Avenue station, the rain is still driving down hard. He pushes open the umbrella and makes his way through what, even amid the torrent, he can see is maybe the last ungentrified neighborhood in New York City—a warren of behemoth brick towers that make the projects of the Lower East Side look positively quaint. He pushes his way along, adrenaline charging through his whole body like before a drug rush, getting soaked by the diagonal sheets of rain, his umbrella offering little protection. Finally he finds the house, walks up its sad three-step brick stoop, and rings the bell, flattening himself out under the door's narrow ledge to beat the rain.

A skinny, short bald man, probably in his late forties and of Latin background, opens the door, wearing a Yankees cap and a faded Lady Gaga concert T-shirt from 2014. "This is a private residence!" he says.

"I know, I know," Mateo says. "Um, I'm here to see a resident. Hector Villanueva."

The guy's face brightens, amused. "You here to see Hector?" He cackles. "He never gets visitors!"

That stabs Mateo's pounding heart a little. "Well," he says. "I'm one."

The guy ushers Mateo inside to a little sitting room with black-and-white political demonstration photos on the wall and about three other guys, two chubby black men and a skinny queeny-looking old white dude, watching one of last year's intergalactic blockbuster movies on the big, family-room-size tablet affixed to the wall, a keyboard and console beneath it.

"Sit down," the short Dominican guy says. "You want coffee?"

Mateo declines, shaking rain from his head.

"I'll go up and tell him you're here," the guy says. "What's your name?"

"Mateo," he says. "Mateo Mendes."

He trudges up the stairs. Sitting there half soaked, Mateo notices that the other three guys keep glancing at him. Finally, one of them, the chunkier of the two chunky black guys, says, "You Hector's nephew or something?"

"Hunh?" Mateo asks. "Unh, no. A friend. An old friend."

"You look like him!" the white guy exclaims.

"Oh, really?"

The less chunky black guy points a finger at the white guy. "You think all brown people look the same."

"That's offensive," the white guy counters.

Then everyone settles back into awkward silence. Mateo sits there and stares dumbly at the cosmic shoot-'em-up unfolding on the tablet screen. He thinks about Dani, Char, Ruby, and the project, all back in Manhattan, which suddenly seems so very, very far away, as though he may never get back. It's not too late for him to ping Gary, he thinks. He begins to pull out his tablet to do so, but then the short guy hurries back down the stairs.

"What's your name again?" he asks Mateo. "I forgot."

This sends the other three guys into cackles. "You don't got AIDS no more but you still got AIDS dementia!" the chunkier black guy crows.

"Shut up, queens," the short guy says, unfazed. He turns back to Mateo.

"Mateo," he says clearly. "Mendes. I haven't seen Hector in, like, ten years. I grew up in his building in the East Village."

The chunky black guy points at the little Dominican guy. "She can't remember all that!"

"I'ma cut you in your sleep tonight," the little guy says. Then back to Mateo: "Hold on."

Mateo and the three guys settle back into their mute watching of the movie. Finally, the less chunky black guy turns to Mateo with what looks like a newfound suspicion. "Are you here to sell Hector pills or drugs?"

"What?" Mateo says, startled. "No! Of course not."

"You better not be," the guy says. "We are so damn sick of her little binges and her little crashes and all the tiptoe, tiptoe we have to do, bringing food to her room and all that."

The chunkier one turns from the screen. "Yeah, but she's been pretty steady lately."

"She finally found marijuana maintenance, thank goddess," the white one says.

This last bit of news brings Mateo an internal heave of profound relief. In fact, now he notes that the whole house smells faintly of marijuana. Not that that's any big deal—it's pretty much legal everywhere. He wouldn't be surprised if the house grows its own supply. Everybody else does.

The short guy comes down again. "He says come on up," he announces, plopping next to the white guy on the couch. "Second floor at the end of the hall. The door's open."

"Thanks," Mateo says. Out of the corner of his eye, he sees the four of them watch him as he gets up to leave. Halfway up the flight of stairs, it occurs to him that he could simply leave now. He still has that choice. He knows this is not the way Sponsor Gary would have him do this: impulsively, without consultation, seeking out his former number one using companion. But beneath that mild panic, a quieter voice tells him to go ahead, and he does.

He comes to the second floor, where the smell of pot has grown thicker. He walks down the hallway. He hears old R&B, maybe Mary J. Blige, coming from one of the rooms behind a closed door. The last door down, with a big Puerto Rico flag pinned on it, he peers in.

And there he is, lying barefoot in bed with his back to Mateo, reading a tablet, rain pounding on his closed window. Mateo's heart throbs, his head spins. He tries to make out the old smell, which was always so rank and earthy yet strangely comforting. He glances around the room—it's plastered in posters and photos that are, variously, of near-naked musclemen, Puerto Rico, and the old demonstration days, all the shots with the hand-lettered posters and the cops and the handcuffs and the megaphones. The room looks like how Mateo remembers his derelict basement apartment: a mess. Clothes, magazines, and books everywhere, sprawled out on an old-fashioned woven carpet. A pot haze hangs over the room.

Mateo knocks on the open door lightly, and Hector twists around in bed, looks at him. Oh God, Mateo thinks. His face is so, so worn, so much more creased and hollow, than the last time they saw each other, that nightmare in the L.A. apartment. Hector looks about half his former size, swimming a bit in his old jeans and a faded, pilly T-shirt that says, in black block letters on a white background, STOP THE CHURCH. Mateo notices two crutches propped against the bed. He must be, what, now—Mateo roughly calculates—sixty-five? Older?

The two men just stare at each other. Mateo can feel his eyes filling with tears, which he blinks back firmly. "Do you remember me?" he finally asks.

"*Negrito*, right?" Hector says. Oh God, that voice. It is all hurtling back to Mateo now so fast, so fast. That last psychotic night. Oh, shit. "Yeah, I remember you, kid. From the Christodora."

"Right," Mateo says. He realizes his right hand is trembling, so he shoves it in his coat pocket.

With great difficulty, Hector sits up in bed, swings his feet around. "Come in," he says.

So Mateo does. He steps into the small room with its sink and mirror in the corner, his eyes blinking a bit from the pot haze. He spies a Siamese cat curled up in the corner of the bed. The cat raises herself, stares at Mateo evenly.

"That's Dulce," Hector says, reaching over to stroke away her concern. "She's everybody's here."

Mateo nods.

"You can close the door," Hector says.

Mateo does, then just stands there by it.

"You can sit there," Hector says. He points to an old armchair by the window that Mateo hadn't noticed, it's so covered in clothes. "Just throw those clothes on the floor," Hector says. "I'd help you but I can't get up fast. I just had back surgery."

"It's okay," Mateo says, pulling clothes off the chair. As he does, that scent—leather, sweat, cigarette smoke, an outdated cologne—comes unmistakably back to him, sends him reeling into those days and nights nodding in the basement apartment, strangers' feet passing by the window.

Finally, Mateo sits. "I wanted to come see you," he manages to say.

Hector sits up in bed. "Why's that? Do you wanna talk to me about some information you got?" He looks at Mateo narrowly, which unnerves Mateo, until he realizes it might be partly because he's stoned, with heavy-lidded eyes.

"Actually, there is some information I got," Mateo begins.

Hector holds out a flat palm to stop him. "I gotta tell you something first. I didn't know, okay? I didn't know until the very last minute."

Mateo frowns in confusion. "Didn't know what?"

Now Hector withdraws his hand. He looks at Mateo for a long moment, searchingly. Then his shoulders droop. "Don't fucking listen to me," he finally says. "My head's fried. What did you wanna ask me?"

"I wanted to talk to you about my mother," Mateo says. "Ysabel Mendes. You knew her, right?" He's surprised to find that his voice is getting hoarse, that he feels like he's going to cry, but he gulps and carries on. "From the AIDS movement, right? You guys were friends, right? I found it online today. Why'd you never tell me?"

Hector's eyes have grown wide. "*Negrito*, I didn't know she was your mother," he says. He seems agitated despite his pot haze. "I didn't even know she had a baby. She stopped coming around to the meetings. Then I was in D.C. all the time. We lost touch before she died."

Mateo sits there, staring at him, absorbing all this. "I always knew her name growing up," he says. "I knew she died of AIDS and I knew she did stuff for AIDS. But I never tried to look that shit up until just recently. I didn't want to know. But then I found this stuff online, this interview with this guy that runs this place—"

"You mean Karl?" Hector asks.

"Yeah, yeah, Karl. And he said in this interview—he said you and my mother were close, you worked on stuff together. Like, on the Latino committee?"

Hector leans back again in bed, closes his eyes, and sighs. "We did," he says.

"But just like that you broke off with her and didn't see her when she was dying?"

Hector opens his eyes, looks at Mateo with a face full of shame, then looks away, saying nothing.

Now Mateo's crying quietly and wiping away tears. "Hector," he says. He realizes it might be the first time he's ever called him by his real name instead of Fagfunk or Freakshow or something. "Can you do something for me?"

Hector doesn't look up at him, but manages to say, "What is it?"

"Can you just—tell me about my mother? Tell me what you remember about her?"

Hector doesn't look up. Mateo wonders if he's fallen asleep. But then Hector makes a snuffly, creaking sound, and Mateo realizes that he's crying as well, his creased face balled up tight.

Mateo watches him, paralyzed. He's scared the guys downstairs are going to hear Hector and come running up and accuse him of harassing their housemate. Eventually, Mateo gets up and goes to sit down next to Hector on the bed. He puts a hand gently on Hector's knee.

"Hey," Mateo says. "Hey, I'm sorry. I didn't mean to upset you. I'll go, okay? I'll go."

But as Mateo is about to stand up, Hector reaches out and pulls him back down. "No, no, don't go," Hector says. He draws in a deep breath and sits up straighter. "I'll tell you about Issy."

Mateo's eyes widen. "Issy?" he says. "That's what you called her?"

Hector nods. "That's what everyone called her." Then, with Mateo sitting close by him on the bed, the cat climbing up between them, Hector tells Mateo about a night in, oh, he thinks it was 1988, 1989, a typical Monday night at a meeting of the movement, and Hector had just given a presentation, and he was out in the lobby having a breather when a woman, a short Dominicana with a huge head of hair, crept in and asked him, *Is this the AIDS meeting?* And Hector said yes, and said, *Why?* and she broke down and said she had AIDS and thought she was dying, and she was so scared, so scared, nobody knew, her family would turn her out if they knew, and she was going to die just like her friend Tavi had just died.

And then he, Hector, remembered that, yes, he had met the woman, Tavi's best friend, at a club, oh, say, five years before when it was only first breaking out that there was an illness going around. And how relieved this woman, Issy, was when she realized that, yes, they had met before. And how, he thinks, they all went out later that night, how it had felt good to dance together. And how this shy, awkward Issy did not know anything about the disease, but how she started coming to meetings, week after week, and how they formed a Latino caucus, and how she gained confidence that she was certainly not going to die any time soon, and maybe not die from this disease at all, because here they were working on new treatments—government-researched treatments, but also all sorts of experimental treatments, too—and it was very likely they would beat the clock. They—well, a lot of them— thought that, together, they would beat the clock. And he watched this insecure girl from Queens, a dental hygienist, become a very, very effective speaker and communicator and organizer and motivator of other women, Latinas, living with AIDS, and how, oh, she came to a very prominent place in the group going into 1990, 1991, along with a few other women.

And how, then, Hector's lover was dying, then died, and Hector cut everybody off and eventually split off into a group that all but moved to D.C. for three years, and how in that time, Hector got a call from the hospital that Issy was dying, she hadn't been able to beat pneumonia again, and Hector said good-bye to her over the phone even though she wasn't able to speak back to him.

"You didn't go to the funeral or anything?" Mateo asks.

"I couldn't leave D.C.," Hector says. "We were so busy that year."

Mateo looks at him skeptically. "You knew about treatments that could have saved her?"

Hector flashes an alarmed look at Mateo. "Oh, no, my friend, oh, no," he says. "You have no fucking idea, you need to read your history. Everybody who was looped in, who wanted it, got the best that New York had to give, but it didn't fucking matter until '96, '97, when the big guns came along."

Mateo is confused. His face must betray it, because now Hector says, "You need to read your history. We were rushing to get drugs made to save her. Everybody. But we couldn't get to everybody in time."

Mateo sits there silently, not knowing what else more to say or to ask. Hector strokes the cat with his large, brown-flecked hand.

"How've you been these past ten years?" Mateo finally asks.

Hector shrugs, gestures around the room. "I'm still here," he says.

"Me, too," Mateo says. "I'm still here."

Hector laughs quietly. "You're better than here," he says. "I read about you in the paper. You're a big-time artist now."

"Not big-time," Mateo says, embarrassed. "Like, small-time big-time."

"Small-time big-time," Hector echoes, laughing. "You finally got your shit together. Good for you. How's the lady from the Christodora who adopted you?"

This catches Mateo off guard. "Uh," he begins. "I don't know. I haven't really talked to her in a few years."

Hector's eyebrow cocks. "Why not?" he asks. "She was always looking out for you when you were a little *negrito*."

This line of questioning makes Mateo distinctly uncomfortable. "I dunno, uh. We just needed time apart, that's all."

"*We?* Both of you?"

Now Mateo sits up a bit, defensive. "Well," he says, "*me*. I needed some time out west to myself." Hector regards him skeptically. "What about you?" Mateo asks to change the subject. "How have you been?"

Hector looks down again. Finally he says, "What can I say? I don't have the energy I used to. Mostly now, I sleep."

They fall back into silence. Mateo glances at Hector, who's staring down into his lap, stroking the cat. Mateo realizes that the druggy, adrenaline-charged fear he felt on the way here, coming up the stairs, has passed. This is where, in the end, Hector's madness had left him: in a group home in outer Brooklyn, with a little room and a cat. And yet this man knew his mother, the woman he never knew, and that means something to Mateo, makes him feel differently about Hector than he did back when he never much thought about his mother's past as an activist.

"Anyway," Mateo says now, "thank you for taking care of her. I mean, when she first came to you when she was all scared." He stands up to leave. "I wish I'd known her. I've only had this one picture all these years. From, like, 1984. Which I don't have anymore." He laughs. "She looks, like, so eighties in it. Her hair is huge."

"Just like yours," says Hector. He braces his hands flat against the bed. "Hand me my crutches. I wanna take you down to Karl."

Mateo hands him his crutches, holds him up while he fits himself into them. "Why?" Mateo asks.

"I think we maybe have something to show you."

Hector instructs Mateo to go down the stairs ahead of him slowly, walking nearly backward, so that if Hector falls and tips forward, Mateo can break his fall. So Mateo does, all the way down the narrow flight, until they're in the hallway of the first floor. Mateo walks by the sitting room, where the fellows stare at him pitilessly through the doorway. Hector leads him back through the kitchen to a messy little office with a single window, where that guy in the video, Karl, the lefty-Moses white-beard-ponytail guy, is sitting before a tablet, tapping away furiously, sipping an espresso and listening to public radio through the tablet. Just like every other room in this house, his office seems to be a shrine to all the dead AIDS people, old photos and posters everywhere. *It looks like all those people ever did all day was get arrested,* Mateo thinks.

The Karl fellow looks up. "Hey there, Hector," he says. He sounds a bit professorial or preacherly, Mateo thinks. "Who's this?"

"You know who this is?" says Hector, out of breath. Now, to Mateo's surprise, he sees there's half a gleeful smile on Hector's crazy, craggy face. "This is Issy Mendes's son."

Karl fixes his eyes on Mateo, confused for a moment. Then his mouth pops open. "Issy Mendes's son?" he loudly drawls. "Good Lord, that's right. I'd heard somewhere she had a baby before— " He stood up. "And it's you?"

"It's me, sir," Mateo says.

Stunned, Karl looks Mateo up and down. "Well, holy fucking Jesus, no damn way!" He comes around from behind his desk. "Come here!" Mateo steps toward Karl, who embraces him passionately. Karl steps back, looks Mateo up and down again about three times, looks at Hector in wonder. "The grown-up son of Issy Mendes! My God, I hope she's witnessing this. Where have you been all these years?"

"I've been living in Los Angeles."

"He's an artist," Hector says.

"Do you know the role your mother played?" asks Karl.

"Not much," Mateo says. "I found something online, an interview you did. That's how I found you. And Hector was telling me a little."

"Oh my goodness," Karl suddenly says, idea-struck. "Esther's videos."

"That's why I brought him down to you," Hector says.

"There is a woman," Karl says. "She was in the movement, Esther Hurwitz. She put together that website that you found me on, the AIDS

Warriors website. She has thousands of hours of tapes, of interviews and demos, that she hasn't put online yet. She just got a Guggenheim grant for the project. And she was very good friends with your mother. So I'm voicing her, okay?" He motions for Mateo and Hector to sit down in chairs opposite his desk while he taps on his tablet. Mateo helps Hector down into a chair.

"Hello, Karl," comes an old-time New York voice, that now–nearly-vanished accent, out of the tablet speaker. "What's going on?"

"Esther," Karl booms into the tablet. "I have someone here I very much want you to meet."

"I was just about to go out."

"I'll be quick," Karl says. "This is too good to miss." He turns around his tablet and props it up on his desk so that it's facing Mateo and Hector. Mateo is staring at a sixtysomething woman with a steel-gray crew cut and black-framed reading glasses, shelves messily crammed with books and papers behind her. Karl comes around his desk to wedge himself between Mateo and Hector so that the three of them are facing her.

Esther finally cracks a smile, spying Hector. "Oh, hello, Hector," she says. "How are you, honey?".

"Hello, Esther," Hector says, grinning.

"Who's the handsome young man with you?" she asks. "Is that your new boyfriend?"

Karl and Hector both giggle. "No," Hector says. "That's Issy's son."

Esther pauses, looking blank. "What?" Then slowly her face blooms open. "Issy Mendes?"

"Issy Mendes," Karl repeats.

"My old friend Issy Mendes?" The woman is scrutinizing Mateo through the screen. "Well, oh my goodness," she says slowly, then she starts to cry. Mateo doesn't understand why his presence today is reducing everyone to tears.

"Oh my goodness, you're the baby she—oh my goodness, I have goose bumps all over!" Esther laughs. "What's your name?"

"Mateo," he says. "Mateo Mendes."

"You have her name!" Esther says delightedly.

"I took her last name later in life," he says. Shortly after he started working with Char, when he needed a professional name, he took it. "Mateo Heyman-Traum" no longer sat right with him.

"My God," she says, brushing tears from her cheeks. "I can see her now in your face. Guys, it's so strange, isn't it? It was thirty years ago!"

"We were just babies," Karl says.

"We were babies!" Esther echoes. "We'd never get away today with what we did then. We live in a fucking police state now. Three people can barely ding each other before the fucking NYPD-slash-FBI is shutting you down."

"Ping, Esther. Ping," Karl says. "Get with the program."

"Right, ping, ping!" She looks back at Mateo. "You don't know what it was like back then," she says.

"I don't," Mateo says.

"You must have no memories of your mother," she says.

"I don't."

"Well, let me tell you. Wow. She was a scared little girl from Queens, where nobody knew she had HIV, when she first came tiptoeing into the meetings. But she kept coming. And within about a year or two—wow, Mateo. She blossomed. That was the thing about the movement, wasn't it? People came thinking they were dying but they ended up finding out how powerful they really were."

Karl nods soberly. "It's true."

"So your mother—" Esther continues, then: "Oh, wait! Oh my God, you guys, I have the tape!"

Karl and Hector start laughing. "That's why we voiced you, Esther," Karl says.

"Hold on, Mateo, I wanna show you something," Esther says. The tablet screen goes green but she keeps talking through it. "The winter of 1990, Mateo, there was a very, very important demonstration at the Centers for Disease Control in Atlanta to get the government to expand the definition of AIDS so that women would be included in it, because they weren't. Because at the time the symptoms and illnesses the CDC used were mostly seen in men, so women weren't being counted and they weren't getting the money and attention and care they needed. And the people who led this particular demonstration were the women in the group, and especially the women with HIV. So watch this, okay?"

Mateo stares at the green screen, his heart beating fast. "This is when, again?" he asks.

"Nineteen-ninety," Esther says. "Thirty-one years ago. When were you born?"

"Nineteen-ninety-two."

"Well," she says, "this is your mom before she was pregnant with you and also before she got really sick."

Suddenly Mateo's watching old pre-digital video footage of a bumpy camera panning around some huge demonstration taking place, in pouring rain, outside the bland suburban offices of the Centers for Disease Control. Hundreds of men and women, some of them with their faces painted a ghostly white, most of them wrapped in black garbage bags to ward off the rain, are massed in front of the CDC's main entrance, blowing whistles and shouting, "Women don't get AIDS, they just die from it!" The camera pans upward to the office windows, where workers in shirts and ties are frowning at the demonstrators, then back down to a round-faced black woman with short bursts of dreadlocks on either side of her head, holding aloft a megaphone.

"My name is Katrina Haslip," the woman says. "I'm from New York City and I'm a woman living with AIDS." The crowd roars. The woman goes on to talk about the health problems she and other women have had that the government doesn't include as markers of AIDS that could help her get treatment or disability benefits. Then the woman says, "Now I want to introduce you to someone to tell you that it's not just white women or African American women who get AIDS, it's Latinas, too. And you do not mess with an angry Latina!"

The crowd laughs. As Katrina hands off the megaphone, the camera pans left to a woman—a short woman, also wearing a wet black garbage bag, her rain-bedraggled black hair pulled back under a black baseball cap with a pink triangle on its upturned rim.

"That's her, Mateo," Esther says. "That's your mom."

"That's her, for sure?" Mateo asks. He's craning forward, studying every detail of her face, trying to make matches with his own.

"That's her," Esther says again.

"Thank you, Katrina, my sister," the woman on the tape says with the same accent Mateo always used to hear around the Lower East Side growing up. "My name is Ysabel Mendes and I am a thirty-one-year-old Latina from Corona, Queens, living with HIV/AIDS!"

The crowd erupts, some people shouting, "We love you, Issy!"

A broad smile breaks out on her face. "Woooo!" she cries, holding the megaphone aloft.

"I'm here today," she continues, "because the CDC doesn't want to count me, even though I was diagnosed with this disease two years ago and my T cells are around one hundred when the average T cells are around one thousand. Even though I've had more small infections the past few years than you can count, including—and I'm sorry to maybe gross out the boys here—more vaginal yeast infections in a year than most women get in a lifetime. There!" She laughs. "I said it!"

The crowd laughs with her.

"The CDC doesn't want to count me, doesn't want to say that I have AIDS," she goes on, "and that goes for me and all my HIV-positive sisters here today. And if you don't count us, we can't get disability benefits, we can't get research, we can't get treatment—we can't get a chance to save our own lives!"

The crowd goes wild again. She looks so strong up there, Mateo thinks, soaked in rain but triumph and anger flashing in her eyes. Those eyes he keeps staring into, that voice he keeps parsing, trying to see and hear echoes of himself. But even as he listens to her, he's forced to admit—he talks mainly in the cadences of Milly and Jared, the people who raised him, not this woman's. She's from another world.

"So I want to say to you, Dr. Curran and Dr. Roper and all your staff," she continues. "I want to say to you, we've been trying since

1988 to get you to change the national AIDS definition to include us women. We've invited you to come meet with us. But you've ignored us. So that's why today, even in this downpour of a rain, we've come to you! And we're not going away until you hear us!"

She's drowned out by the crowd chanting, "ACT UP! Fight back! Fight AIDS!" but she's got her megaphone up in the air again, elated, that huge smile on her face, all her teeth showing.

"Woo-hoo!" she cries again, as though she's at the top of a roller coaster.

Esther stops the tape there, on that image of her. "So that's your mother, Mateo," Esther says, coming back on the screen. "A very courageous woman, you see. And you know something else?"

"What?" Mateo asks.

"She lived to see them expand the AIDS definition. It took until 1992, but they finally did it—they finally caved to all our research and all our protests and admitted we were right. They did it right before Katrina died in 1992, but your mother lived a whole 'nother year, and benefited from the change with her disability benefits, before she died."

"Which was when?" he asks.

"Late 1993."

Late 1993, he thinks. He was eleven months old; he doesn't have a single memory of being held in her arms. "You were really good friends with my mom?" he asks this woman, Esther.

She pauses, smiles. "We were, Mateo. We were. After she got pregnant with you, she stopped coming to the meetings. I wanted her to keep coming, but she didn't want anyone to know she was pregnant, she said. She was afraid they were going to judge her for having a baby when she had HIV. I told her that was ridiculous, that everyone knew she was protecting the baby by taking AZT. Still, she wouldn't come. I couldn't force her. So I would visit her because she was living in a group house for women, near me in the East Village, started by a lady named Ava Heyman—an amazing lady who died a few years ago."

"That was my *bubbe*," Mateo says. "I used to visit that place, Judith House."

Esther frowns in confusion. Then, "Oh my God," she says slowly. "Oh my God, that's right. I remember now Ava telling me that . . ." She draws a blank.

"That her daughter?" Mateo supplies.

"Right! That her daughter adopted Issy's kid." Then her voice drops, slows. "Oh my goodness, dark-eyed Milly Heyman." Then she stops. "Well, hmm, whatever. That's for another day. But, Mateo!" She tears up again. "I'm having some kind of time-travel cosmic moment!" She laughs, which makes Karl and Hector—and even Mateo—laugh, too. "How old are you now, Mateo? What do you do?"

"I'm twenty-eight," he says. "I'm an artist. I live in L.A. but I'm in New York right now to do some of the art for the UnderPark."

Esther just looks at him, shakes her head. "Mateo," she says. "If only Issy could see you. Mateo, I want you to know something very seriously. There's not a lot of documentation and I know everyone's forgotten about it, but your mother really was a hero."

Mateo feels as though the woman has just put a healing hand on a place inside him that's ached his entire life, at least since he'd learned about his mother. "Thank you," he says, wiping tears away. "All my life, I wondered. I never knew anything about her, where I came from. We didn't really talk about it in my family growing up."

"Well, honey, you come from strong stuff," Esther says.

"Thank you. Can I watch the tape again?"

"Of course you can. And I'll send you a digital package with the tape and all the photos and clippings I have of your mother. Actually, you come see me and I'll put them together for you here."

"Thank you so much," Mateo says, half embarrassed that he's crying, half not really caring. And she runs the video again. Oh God, there she is. Could he hold her? Could he only hold her? But she at least held him, he thinks. Years before he was old enough to remember. She'd held him.

The tape runs out and Esther says good-bye, signs off, leaving Mateo, Karl, and Hector sitting there, the rain still pounding against the windows. "I can't believe I finally saw her," Mateo says.

"You know," says Karl, leaning forward. "The work isn't done. AIDS isn't over. There are millions of people around the world who can't access cure therapy."

"I know," Mateo says, nodding respectfully. "I read that."

Then Hector says, "Let him go, Karl. He came here to find out about his mother, not to get recruited. And you don't wanna say it, but you know it. It's over. AIDS is over. You won. There's plenty else to do. But"—and here Hector goes into a sarcastic singsong—"fucking AIDS is over. We're the last fucking ghosts from the AIDS days. We won the war, Karl."

Karl's been half aloft in his seat the whole time during Hector's rant, but now, to Mateo's surprise, he just gives Hector a dirty look and sits back and folds his arms over his chest. He looks down, runs his finger sulkily over the glass of his tablet. "Why doesn't it feel like we won, then?" he asks quietly.

"Because you're tired, Karl," says Hector. "You're fucking pooped like the rest of us. But we still fucking won. So relax, you still got a bunch of old broke-down ghosts to take care of. We still need you, honey."

With difficulty, Hector makes to rise. Mateo stands, puts a hand behind his elbow, reaches for his crutches and hands them to him one by one, until he's upright.

Mateo turns to Karl, who's standing now, too, and offers him his hand. "Thank you so much," Mateo says.

Karl takes his hand. "Don't forget us," he says to Mateo. Karl's face brightens, then he looks sly. "How about an art fund-raiser? A ShelterHelps art fund-raiser? We had an art auction in the movement once that raised nearly half a million dollars. Nineteen-eighty-nine. Remember, Hector?"

"I do, babe," Hector says, making his way slowly out of the office in front of Mateo.

"We could do that again," Karl continues.

Mateo fixes his eyes on Karl. "Let me get through this project I'm on now," he says, "and then I'll get in touch with you."

"You promise? These folks may be cured, but they haven't got two nickels to rub together—the survivors, I mean. They need this home, they need services."

"I promise," Mateo says, before shuffling slowly out the office door and down the dim hallway with Hector.

Near the foyer, Hector mutters from ahead, "I'll walk you out. I want some air."

"It's still raining out, I think."

"I don't fucking care."

Mateo opens the front door and helps Hector down the step so that they're both out under the ledge in the rain, somewhat lighter now, the empty street silent before them with shuttered warehouses. They stand side by side, getting spattered. Mateo watches Hector fumble on his crutches for something in his pocket. Then Hector pulls out a half-smoked joint that he struggles to light with a book of matches.

"Here," says Mateo, taking the matches and lighting it for him. Mateo watches Hector close his eyes as he takes in the first hit, its cinders crackling on the end. Mateo is overcome with a flash of memory, all the times the two of them communed like this: the silences, one holding the flame for the other, the long indrawn breaths, the blissful exhalations, the crumpling together into one barely sentient being. His heart starts pounding and he balls up his fists in his pockets, fighting his instinct to flee.

Finally Hector releases his hit and hands it to Mateo.

"No thanks," Mateo says.

Hector looks at him, cackles. "You don't even smoke pot anymore?"

Mateo shakes his head sheepishly. "I've been reprogrammed," he jokes lamely.

Hector stares out into the rain, savoring his new high. "I never got that, why some people had to take it to extremes," he says. "I mean, fine, put down the needle, put down the pipe. But leave me something. You know, *negro*?"

Hector looks so comical suddenly, Mateo laughs, and Hector's eyes pop big and he laughs along. A truck roars down the street and nails a deep puddle in the road so hard that the backsplash nearly reaches the two of them over the sidewalk.

"Whoa," Mateo mutters—awkwardly, because he doesn't know what to say now.

"What day is it?" Hector finally asks.

"Thursday," Mateo says. "It's Thursday."

Hector gives him a sort of *for real?* look, and Mateo nods. Then the silence engulfs them again. Hector stares placidly forward, looking like he's content with his buzz despite the rain.

"I wanna say I'm sorry," Mateo finally hears himself saying.

"Sorry for what?"

Huh? Mateo hadn't expected he would say that. "For—" Well, for what? Using him for drugs and shelter? Mateo is not about to say that. That last time in L.A.? The truth was Mateo hadn't needed Hector that time for drugs or shelter. Why had he called Hector from that apartment, the very thought of which never failed to make Mateo shudder? Mateo figures it'll probably be like that for the rest of his life.

"If I hadn't called you that last time in L.A.—" Mateo begins.

But Hector puts a finger to Mateo's lips. "Shh," he goes. He shakes his head, slowly but firmly. "No, no," he says.

"But—"

"No, no," Hector says. "Not going back there."

Mateo is stumped. "Okay," he says. "Sorry."

"Stop saying sorry."

Mateo laughs bitterly, surprising himself. "You never stop saying sorry," he says.

"Now listen," Hector says decisively. He's still staring ahead, not meeting Mateo's eyes, but something authoritative in his tone disarms Mateo. "You go say you're sorry to the woman who raised you," he says. "That's what you should do."

Now Mateo is scrambled. "Say what?"

"You heard me," Hector says. "You know now about the woman who had you. Now you go to the woman who raised you."

Mateo looks down, kicks one sneaker with the other. "I told you, we haven't talked in, like, ten years."

"Okay, fine," says Hector. "So now you're in New York, so you can go pay her a visit."

Mateo says nothing.

Hector laughs. "There," he says. "Now you know why you came to see me today."

"You know why I came to see you," Mateo protests. "To ask you about my real mother."

Hector giggles now, like he's feeling the full ripeness of his buzz. "Well, *negrito*, I guess I had more to tell you," he says. "Because you may forget, but I watched you and that lady—your *other* mother. Every day, up Avenue A, holding your hand, you with the fucking backpack that was too big for *negrito*. Fucking nice lady showing everybody in the building somebody's drawings. Her husband, not so much. But the lady. Ava's daughter."

Hector shoots Mateo a look now. "That was one fucking nice lady," he continues. "She put a note under my door begging me to go to rehab to keep from getting kicked out of the building. She said she'd help me find one."

Mateo looks at him. "Are you serious?"

"Yep. I still have the note upstairs somewhere."

Mateo nearly squirms in discomfort. "She had a fucking guilt trip, that's all," he says. "She pitied me. That's the only reason she adopted me."

"No, *mijo*, I watched her. That wasn't pity. She needed you."

Mateo stuffs his hands in his pockets, tucks his head down. He stares down at the pattern the raindrops make in the puddles on the sidewalk. Then he feels Hector's hand on his back, right below his neck. Mateo glances sidelong, sees the effort Hector has expended to hold himself up on one crutch to put the other hand on Mateo's back. Something about the gesture unlocks a compartment deep in Mateo's chest.

"I can't," Mateo mutters, feeling tears rise behind his eyes. "I can't deal with it. It'll crush me."

Hector emits a short, sharp guffaw. "*Negrito*, take it from me. Just go see her," Hector says.

Neither of them speaks for a long time. Mateo starts to realize he feels a comfort he hasn't felt since those times he and Hector would nod out together. Except this time it's different. He's actually lucid enough to realize it, that he feels safe with him. *I miss this guy*, he thinks. Awkwardly, he puts an arm around Hector, careful not to hang on him too heavily.

Hector turns and looks at him a good long time. "I actually needed this joint to ask you something, *negrito.*"

Mateo laughs. "Really? What?"

"If I give you my e-mail, will you write to me? I get lonely here."

"Of course I'll write to you." Mateo pulls out his tablet as Hector recites his e-mail, with the prefix SonyaBrisa. "I'll come see you again before I leave."

"There might be more I wanna tell you eventually."

"Yeah, definitely," says Mateo. "When you remember things about my mother, will you tell me? Anything you can remember?"

Hector regards him keenly, emits a short laugh. "I remember a lot, *negrito*. I'll tell you little by little. Okay?"

Mateo gingerly puts an arm around him, draws closer until their heads are lightly touching. "Okay, brother."

Hector looks down at the ground. "Okay," he says again.

"I gotta go," Mateo finally says. "Let me help you back in the house."

"No, you go," Hector says. "I wanna stand here and watch you go."

"For real?"

"Jesus, I just wanna little more fresh air, okay?"

"Okay! Fine!"

Gently, still awkwardly, Mateo hugs him good-bye one more time.

"I can't hug you back with these crutches, *mijo*," Hector says.

"That's okay."

"If you promised to help Karl, you better do it," Hector says warningly. "He'll come find you otherwise."

"I will," Mateo says. "So I'll see you again."

Mateo starts off down the street, his hands thrust in his pockets and his head down against the rain. But after a few paces, he turns and walks backward, watching Hector recede on the cinder block stoop, smaller with every step away Mateo takes. Near the corner, Mateo raises his hand farewell before he turns.

Moments after he turns, Hector pivots carefully on his crutches and rings the doorbell. Melvin, the chunky black queen, answers the door.

"You gotta prop the door, ya damn pothead, so I don't have to keep coming to do this for you," Melvin whines.

"Just help me the fuck back inside," Hector says, handing off his crutches to Melvin.

"What a damn pain in the behind you are."

Hector looks up at Melvin with a stoned, elated grin. "I did something right, Melvin."

"What?"

Hector slowly brings up a right leg into the house, then the left, held up under one arm by Melvin. "I said I did something right in my life."

Melvin sighs. "That's right, girl, you did something right. You and Karl and you all else saved the day back about a hundred years ago and that's why we're all here in this mansion living the high life."

Hector lets out a high, ragged laugh. "Fuck you, Melvin."

"Come on now, get back on your crutches, Superwoman, and come get your dinner."

TWENTY
MILLICENT HEYMAN
(2021)

Her life had basically become all about her father. Good old Sam. That's what Milly said on the rare occasions now when she talked to people and they asked her what was going on. He'd become her organizing principle, in addition to the fact that she loved him deeply.

She'd wake up. She never got as much sleep as she wanted; she was perpetually tired. She'd sleep in the "small" (Mateo's old) room, not the "big" (her and Jared's) room. That started after he, meaning ex-husband *he*, moved out. She couldn't bring herself to use either of their names. As for that "other" room, she'd taken down the posters and all the other stuff a long time ago and put it all in a box in the closet, so she didn't think of it as sleeping in *his* room per se. It was just the "small room" now, and nobody had slept in the big room since the night she had to take her father to the ER at Beth Israel downtown because he had bronchitis, and by the time they got out of there, it just made more sense for Milly to bring him to the Christodora and put him to bed there. Often, Milly considered bringing her father there permanently for his final days, because she didn't know how much more of the constant back and forth to the Upper East Side she could take.

So, the small room. It was filled up with her books and magazines; she supposed she was one of the only people left on earth who still read that way, surrounded by paper clutter. And she stayed up far too late reading, but it didn't matter, she still seemed to pop awake around six A.M. and was impervious to all efforts to fall back asleep. Those were those ragged gray hours when she kept reminding herself that she should get a cat or a small dog, because those hours were the hardest for her: pulling on her robe, putting on the kettle, sitting at the table by the window that looks down on the slumbering park, tapping on her tablet and looking at the news, which made her sick. The New Reform Era. The whole thing was privatized! Health care was privatized, schools were becoming privatized, hurricane response was privatized. *This is what I've lived to see in my country*, she'd tell herself. Even her own father, who worked in business his whole life and certainly was no Trotskyite like some of his uncles, couldn't believe what had happened. She guessed it had worked out okay for New York and California and other states run by well-educated technocrats who actually knew how to get people housed and educated and fed. Not so good for the middle of the country and the South, though. It was more of an embarrassment than ever down there. But there you have it. That was the direction the country had gone in while she was creeping through her fifties. Not that she was surprised.

So, that's where her day began. Already, sitting there, she felt the crumbum lack of sleep, the matte-gray ordeal that the day was going to be. The e-mails were next. They were mostly spam and junk. Alerts from the different community action groups she'd gotten involved in over the past few years, but she really couldn't deal with them anymore. Yes, she hated privatization as much as the next person—on principle, she supposed, less so in practice—but she really couldn't go to any more meetings where a bunch of middle-aged women who reminded her of herself, frankly, stood up all night and keep yelling "Privatization! Privatization!" She just found it too depressing.

There weren't so many art e-mails anymore. Let that world slide, stop making stuff or showing up, and at first the notices keep coming.

But give it about three, four years, and the only e-mails you'll get are from people who don't really know who you are, for stuff you'd never go see anyway because you don't know who they are. Occasionally there was the e-mail like the one she got last week from Caroline Harrell. Caroline said she'd been at Chuck Pierson's opening the other week and she and Chuck and some others got to talking and wondering where Milly was. Caroline said she missed Milly and did Milly want to have lunch in the neighborhood or get a coffee?

Milly stared at the e-mail for a long time. She actually got a tight feeling in her throat. She thought about long-ago afternoons in the park with Caroline in her wheelchair on one side, and with *him* holding her hand on the other side, when he was the darling, adorable child of half the neighborhood, with his paper and box of crayons in his little bag. And Milly kept staring at that e-mail and wondering how Caroline was doing with her disease, her degenerative nerve disease that kept her in that wheelchair, the chair that people would help her out of when she did her performance art. And then Milly decided that she just couldn't see Caroline and she couldn't see anybody anymore except her father, and she deleted it and just made herself forget it had ever arrived.

And then there was a day staring her in the face. Up until about a year, maybe eighteen months ago, she'd still head down to the studio in the mornings. To so much as pick up a brush, she'd had to assiduously banish from her mind any thought of the two men who'd divorced her, her ex-husband and her ex-son. And frankly that wasn't so easy to do anymore, because it felt like she couldn't scroll the blogs or click on the arts vertical of the *Times* or *New York* anymore without seeing or reading about one or the other. She'd just be sitting there having her coffee and innocently reading the *Times* and there they were.

The worst was when there were pictures—especially with their girlfriends. Well, not M. so much. His girlfriend, an interior designer, was very pretty and looked like a nice person. Milly was glad he was being taken care of, and it appeared he was off the drugs, or if he wasn't, then he was doing a pretty good job of having a career alongside them, but she was pretty sure he was off them by this point. He'd alluded to being clean and sober in a few articles she'd read, against her own better judgment. She really hoped he was. He'd broken her heart but she still wanted him to be happy out there in the world. What had been the point of raising him all those years if he wasn't?

As for her real ex—forget it. God forbid she saw some party picture of him alongside that curator. It was like a slap in the face and always made her stomach turn. The final indignity had been two months ago when she saw that picture of them, her with her bump, and Milly knew she was pregnant. The huge smile on J.'s face, that stupid Japanese-type black Yohji Yamamoto asymmetrical suit thing she'd obviously dressed him in, that slim coupe of champagne in his hand!

I guess he's got absolutely everything he ever wanted now, Milly thought. *He's an art star, he's got a young art babe for a girlfriend, and he's finally having a baby. His own baby, as he'd put it.* Milly hoped that when his baby was up screaming all night and spitting up and peeing all over him, it didn't compromise his brilliant career. He'd always made it perfectly clear he couldn't really have that while playing dad, and he certainly didn't waste any time relieving himself of his paternal duties. They'd probably just hire a nanny. God forbid he'd let anything come between him and his work. When nobody knows your name until you're forty-seven, you really have to hustle!

Milly knew how bitter she sounded to herself. She talked a lot with Gallegos about the bitterness. He'd been her marriage therapist, true, but she kept going to him after. After he saw the way that J. went absolutely psychotic on her before he stormed out that night, she felt like Gallegos was the only person who could ever understand what she'd been through, having witnessed it, so she kept going to him.

There she was, one week after the big storming-out, sitting there all by herself. Weeks and weeks went by, and she kept saying to Gallegos, "What do you think? Is he ever going to come back around and see that he's been absolutely psychotic?"

And Gallegos kept saying to Milly, "Can we put a moratorium on trying to figure out Jared"—*Oh God, he said his name, and continued to, rather callously*, she thought, until she politely asked him if he would just refer to him as J.— "and talk about what's going on with you?"

"I'm fine," she said. "I raised a drug addict who turned his back on me and I spent the better part of my adult life with a man who told me he hated me and walked out on me. I'm fine. I would just like to find someone who doesn't walk out on me for a change! Who's next? My dad? Thank God my dad's too frail to abandon me, too! They always stick around until they don't need you anymore, so I guess I have my dad until he passes. Lucky me!"

Gallegos smiled and shook his head. "You do make me laugh, Milly, even when I'm trying to help you break patterns," he said.

The specific pattern was putting someone else's happiness before her own. Gallegos would always ask Milly if she'd made it into the studio that week, if she was keeping up with her art-world friendships. He'd even come to a little show of hers several years ago, which Milly thought was touching, because she didn't think therapists were supposed to do that sort of boundary-crossing thing. But she also thought he wanted to see her work to help him understand her better, or something, and the next week at his office he mentioned how he could see a lot of vulnerability in the work or putting herself on the line or something. She tried to explain to him that she was essentially a formalist and she wasn't thinking about her problems when she worked, but she supposed a therapist would see what he wanted to see. That was his job.

So Gallegos was trying to keep Milly in the studio. And for a few years she was. It wasn't easy for her, the more famous her two exes got. She talked about that a lot with Gallegos.

"When you go in there, it's your studio, it's your art," he'd say. "It's for you."

She tried to keep that in mind. Then she had a sort of epiphany. She was at the Armory Show at the Javits Center. She waited until nearly the end of the run to be as certain as possible she wouldn't run into either of *them*, and she also stayed about a mile away from their gallerists. Suddenly she was overwhelmed by the sheer volume of the art and all the rich jerks browsing it, and she wanted to throw up. She was looking at about the umpteenth stupid neon wall sign. It said in big swoopy pink neon script: MY PUSSY! Like that was some kind of revelation. And Milly thought, *That's it. I don't need to keep contributing to this pile of junk.*

She had probably been to her studio about twice since then, and that had been eighteen months ago. Often, she considered giving it up to no longer have to pay rent on it. The same canvas had been sitting there half-finished since last year. Whenever she thought of picking up the brush, she thought, *Here I am, another low- to no-name-recognition New York "artist" adding to the junk heap. We'll all die and only .00001 percent of this stuff will have any resonance beyond our own lifetimes.*

Of course she shared this with Gallegos. He'd once told her he liked to write a little fiction or poetry on the side himself. He shared these little bits of himself with her from time to time very offhandedly, which flattered Milly. She was fairly certain he didn't do that with all his patients.

Gallegos heard Milly out. Then he said, "But aside from all that, how do you feel when you're painting? Don't you feel good?"

And she said, "Honestly, Richard? I feel stupid. I feel silly. I feel there has to be something more productive I could be doing. Kids are growing up nearly illiterate right in my own neighborhood, right over in the projects on Avenue D, and I'm sitting here dabbing and daubing? I'm a joke."

"How did you feel when you were teaching kids to draw and paint?" he asked.

"That was different," she said. "That wasn't necessarily for them to grow up to be professional artists. It was to help them find a creative voice and to introduce them to art and the role it can play in their lives. Especially if they're from unstable homes. I mean, just to have craft paper and a box of crayons—that's such a balm."

Craft paper and a box of crayons. Her eyes welled up as she started to say it. She couldn't even think about craft paper and a box of crayons.

"What came up just then?" Gallegos asked her. "That affected you?"

Milly deflated in her chair and rubbed her eyes. "I can't think about craft paper and a box of crayons without thinking about the first time I saw him," she said. "M."

"You felt love and delight because you saw a kid being creative and you wanted to encourage it, right?"

"He was drawing scary, hairy monsters." Oh God, she would never forget him, lying on his stomach, kicking his little sneakers together in the air.

"You could have more of that feeling if you went back to work."

So that was why he'd brought that up? Milly felt a bit tricked and betrayed. "I don't have the time or the mental energy anymore to teach," she said. "I have to take care of my father. He just gets worse and worse."

"He's with his own nurse all day," Gallegos said. "He's with her right now, safe and sound. Here you are, here with me, and everything's okay."

Milly didn't like this conversation very much, frankly. She no longer liked leaving the house and avoided interacting with other people. The whole thing made her very uncomfortable and exhausted her. She made some exceptions. Groceries, obviously. Sometimes she went to see a movie. Taking the train back and forth to see her father. Even these things, though, she had to bear up for, and the whole time she was out there, she felt like a raw nerve being pummeled by other people. Loud young kids, for one thing, the N-word being every other word that flew out of their mouths. Couples who were too demonstrative. People whom she thought she knew, or had known. They were the worst of all. She literally crossed the street if she thought she saw up ahead someone who looked like someone she thought she once knew.

"I'm sure I'll go back to work part-time eventually," she finally said, to shut him down.

He gave her a skeptical look, like he was not very pleased with her.

At least, Milly thought, *we're not talking about* her *anymore*. She meant Drew. The issue with *her* had taken up sessions with Gallegos for months. How was Milly feeling about it, one week later? Had she and Drew communicated? And on and on and on.

Two years ago, Drew had left Milly a voice mail. For Milly, even just seeing Drew's name there in the queue on her tablet was a bit startling, because Milly felt she had barely heard from her in a year. But there was the message, all hushed with portent: "Millipede? It's Drew-pea. Millipede, I am freaking out, I'm having twins. Call me, please, I need to talk. I'm freaking out. Christian and I are both freaking out. Love you."

Milly calculated: You had to be several weeks into your pregnancy to find out you were having multiples. That meant Drew knew she was pregnant weeks before. A fact she hadn't shared with Milly. And then: *A voicemail. She tells me this news on a voicemail*, Milly thought.

Milly didn't call back right away. She actually put down the tablet and went to the window and finally sat and just stared out. Then she stood and picked up the tablet to call Drew. Then she put it down. The truth was she didn't know what to say to her. She didn't know if it was such a good idea that Drew was doing this at her age. Milly knew the treatment and technology had changed a lot in ten years, but no amount of technology could mitigate the fact that when your kid was ten you were going to be sixty and when they were twenty you were going to be seventy. Your kid was probably going to watch you die when they were thirty or thirty-five. So much for *their* kids having a grandma. Milly couldn't get past this, and in some ways, it just felt so completely Drew to her. Like there was nothing left for Drew to write about coupledom, or about the new urban couple communes, or about couples growing all their own food on their roof, so she was going to have kids to put herself into the next readership bracket. That didn't feel very fair to those kids, Milly thought.

So Milly simply didn't reply for five days. That felt like the decent thing to do because she just didn't know what to say.

"She's probably waiting to hear from you," Gallegos said when she told him about it the next day.

"I don't know if she's doing the right thing," Milly said.

"Can I ask you, Milly? Can I ask you how you really felt when you heard the news?"

"I felt: Don't tell me you're going to do that to those kids," she said to Gallegos. "Just for another book."

Gallegos challenged her on that. "Here's your best friend and it's always been a certain way between the two of you and now it's probably going to change. She's probably not going to be able to come to New York as much as she used to. You might need to go out there to see her, help her with the kids."

"Oh, I hate it out there. It's still so fake and plastic to me, even though it's all supposedly become like Brooklyn but with constant sunshine. But obviously some aspect of life out there appeals to her, because she's never come back to New York."

Gallegos rolled his eyes in that way that he did. "I'm asking if you're afraid you're going to lose the friendship."

Milly laughed a bit. "I think I've told you the friendship's already been fading the past few years," she said. "She's allergic to sadness. If you can't just make lemons into lemonade and be *grateful* for whatever happens to you, Drew doesn't have a lot of patience for you. It's all about being *grateful* with Drew. Grateful, grateful! I'm sure she's just grateful she's having these kids, she's thanking the universe, and she's not thinking about these kids when they're twenty or thirty."

"Listen carefully to yourself," Gallegos said. "You're starting to cut the cord with your best friend of thirty years."

For better or worse, that thought stuck with Milly over the next several days. She felt quite chastised by Gallegos. Finally, she picked up the tablet. But she could not figure out how she wanted her own voice to sound when Drew picked up or if it went to voice mail. So she pulled up a text box. "Oh my God!" she pinged. "Awesome news! Keep me posted! xo Mills." And she sent it.

Five minutes later, Drew pinged back: "Uh . . . that's it? No call after six days? :("

Oh, shit, thought Milly. "I was digesting," she pinged back. Well, that was honest, right? Should she have to be fake?

Drew didn't ping back, which Milly thought was pretty rude. She was probably too busy, Milly thought. She'd probably interrupted Drew while she was blogging to all the people who hung on her every word. And basically because Drew blogged or tweeted or CoffeeDated every single moment of her life, it was hard for Milly to avoid following the pregnancy in excruciating detail. It was so obvious she was building up content for a book. What Drew was eating and what special yoga Drew was doing to aid the pregnancy, how the pregnancy was affecting her and Christian's sex life, and then, of course, every minute aspect of how she felt when they learned they were going to have twins. "Twice Blessed, Twice Yikes" that post was called. *Yikes?* Milly thought. *Yuck.*

This went on for months without Drew responding to Milly's text. Milly thought Drew would break down and ask her to come out to L.A. for the delivery, but Drew didn't. Suddenly Drew was blogging and tweeting pictures of her, Christian, and two baby girls named Erika and Fiona. The first picture of the four of them she posted, all huddled together like four peas in a pod, Milly just stared at, dumbfounded, for about fifteen minutes. Drew had had children. They were the two who'd never been through pregnancy when everyone else had, and now Drew had gone ahead and done it.

Milly told her dad about it over dinner uptown that night. "Drew had babies this week," she said. "She had twins. Two girls."

Sam nodded his head sagely, as though he had something to say about that. "That makes three kids for her now?" he asked.

"She's never had kids before, Daddy. These are her first." Milly pushed her father's water glass away from the edge of the table, where it was sitting perilously near his elbow.

"No, no," he said. *Here we go,* Milly thought. Her father was always doing this these days. "She's got the kid who won the science award in Boston."

"That's Liesl," Milly said. He was thinking about another old friend of hers from college. "Liesl had that kid sixteen years ago. This is Drew. Remember Drew, the writer Drew? She lives in Los Angeles."

"The one that had the drug problem."

"Right. The drug problem was twenty-five years ago, though."

He looked at Milly like she was crazy. "She just went to rehab!" he insisted.

"She went to rehab twenty-five years ago, Daddy."

Her father looked annoyed. He resumed eating the pasta she'd made him. "I hope she stays off that junk," he said. "She's a smart girl."

Milly just smiled and shook her head. This was her dinner company these days. She loved her dad. Since Ava, her mother, had died of ovarian cancer two years ago, at only seventy-four, it was like a hush had fallen over her and her father. She and Sam could sit at the dinner table together most of the night, watch TV together later, and not say a word, and it was okay. There was a hush in her parents' busy house after all those years.

And there was a bond. Because Milly and Sam were both empty vessels now. Ava had consumed their lives so completely. Milly had lived most of her life defining herself against someone she didn't want to become, trying to be the un-her, only to find she had nothing left to work with once Ava was gone. Then came the identity void. The weirdest thing had been sitting with Sam at the memorial service that a bunch of the old downtown AIDS people had organized. Someone would get up to speak and Milly would whisper to her dad, *Oh, so that's the So-and-So she was always complaining about!* And then Milly and her dad had heard all the tales. Like when Ava planned a "ceremony" to "honor" the city council speaker, but it was really just to get the speaker to come to Judith House and to trap her in the sitting room with all the clients, all the residents, and say, "Actually the reason we asked you here today was to show you what we'll lose if you really cut the housing budget 30 percent in fiscal 2015."

The whole memorial had cracked up when someone, a former Judith House resident who was now a social worker, told this story. "That was Ava!" people were cackling. "That was Ava! You didn't fuck with her!"

Amid the laughter, Milly and her dad had looked at each other. Her dad shrugged, as though to say, *I never knew that*, and Milly put her arm around him. There were stories they never knew, or maybe stories they'd only half listened to, and they all belonged to a woman who was larger than the two of them, larger than her own family, who sucked it up and demonstrated heroism every day, and then often came home and had little left for her husband and daughter except perhaps to charm her husband into giving her a foot rub.

"She loved those foot rubs," Milly's dad said over dinner. "That's why she needed me to stick around. I was the foot rub at the end of the day."

"You were more than a foot rub, Daddy."

"She was very proud of you," her dad said.

"I don't think that's really true, Daddy."

"Oh, no, she was. She was just too busy to tell you."

She and her dad both laughed heartily over this.

Then he'd ask: "How's the kid?"

This line of questioning never stopped. "Dad, I've told you a million times he's out in Los Angeles and we're not really in touch."

"He's your son. You need to get on the goddamned phone and call him."

"He doesn't want to be in touch," Milly said, too sharply. "I'm sorry." She put her hand on his. "But I've told you that he told me he wanted to live his own life now. Our work is done."

Her dad shook his head. "I don't understand that situation one bit."

"Neither do I."

But as for Drew? So, the twins came. Milly saw the constant pictures of the twins. She watched the twins grow up in pictures. And one day when Milly was looking at a picture of the two of them in matching striped onesies, in a moment of softness, she typed, "Adorable!" A few hours later, Milly noticed that Drew had put a smiley emoji next to her comment. A week later, when Drew posted a family Halloween picture, Milly wrote, "Boo-dorable!" A few hours later, Drew posted back, "They're still so small I almost wanted to pose them inside the pumpkins!" To which Milly posted back her own smiley emoji. Six weeks later came the inevitable holiday Santa-hat pictures.

"First visit from Santa coming up!" Milly posted.

"I know," Drew posted back, "Santa better get crackin'!"

This is how they started communicating again. Pathetic, Milly knew, but that was what the world had come to, just these little pleasantries or silly faces people tapped out underneath one another's pictures. Then one day Milly was on the tablet and Drew popped up in a chatbox:

"Hi millipede."

Milly heard the little ping and then just stared at it for about thirty seconds.

"Hi drewpea."

As soon as she wrote that her gut twisted in an unexpected pang of yearning.

Drew: Long time no see.
Milly: I know. Well, you've been busy.
Drew: It's been crazy. Didn't know what I was getting myself into.
Milly: Well, you all look pretty happy in the pics.
Drew: It's wonderful. It's a blessing beyond blessings. Grateful doesn't even describe. [*Here we go with the whole grateful thing*, Milly thought.] But it's still exhausting!
Milly: But you have help, right?
Drew: Yeah, a great girl. But still!
Milly: I'm sure. Well, but wonderful you did it.

Quite a long pause there. Then:
Drew: I would love for you to meet them. I tell them about you all the time.
[*Tell them about me?* Milly thought. *They're six months old!*]
Milly: I'm sure that holds their interest.

Drew: It's mostly just me rambling to them during feedings or rocking the cradle. Rambling on like a crazy mother.

This was almost too twee for Milly to take. Finally she wrote, feeling lame:

Milly: You sure sound busy with them.
Drew: Do you think you could make it out here to visit?

Suddenly Milly had to go to the bathroom. She went and came back, and then she wrote:

Milly: My dad takes up a lot of my time now.
Drew: I meant to ask you. How are you both doing? [*She means since my mom's death, obviously*, Milly thought.]
Milly: He's a bit addled but he's doing okay. He has his Rachel Maddow. He's had a crush on her for ten years now. He thinks she's going to come around for him.
Drew: Haha! What about you?
Milly: Nothing to report.
Drew: Making work?
Milly: Been too busy with Dad.
Drew: Mmm. That's gotta be tough.

Quite a pause passed.

Drew: We might all make it out to New York next spring to see Xtian's sister.
Milly: That sounds fun. First time on the plane with the kids?
Drew: It would be, yeah. Would be so great to see you!

Milly pictured the four of them just coming at her.

Milly: Of course. Let me know if you come.

Drew: It's pretty definite. I miss you Millipede!

[*No, you don't*, Milly thought. *You're too busy, too full. You don't know what it means to miss someone. It's not a warm, fuzzy feeling. It's a cold void.*]

Milly: Well, hang in there with the kids!

A pause.

Drew: OK, I will. Take care.

Then: "xoxo." As far as Milly was concerned, "xoxo" was the end of a conversation, so she left it at that. She and Drew went back to their usual one-word exclamatory comments and smiley-cons. The winter that followed was the warmest in New York ever. On January 6, the temperature hit seventy-one degrees, a record breaker, and it never really got properly cold for three months. Milly couldn't take it. When she went out, people were frolicking in the park, throwing around a football in shorts or with their shirts off, and she would wrap an unnecessary midweight coat around herself just to feel some semblance of normalcy. Everybody else loved the warm weather, it seemed, while to her it just felt like the end of the world.

She left the house to do whatever she had to do as quickly as she could, then came home and made hot tea just to pretend it was an old-fashioned January. If it wasn't for the thought of her father alone at night, fumbling to put his dinner together, she probably wouldn't have left the house that winter. Half the time, she ended up staying uptown with her father. Once she stayed up there for a week. She would be lying around reading her tablet regardless of where she was, so it made little difference to her whether she was uptown or down. She slept in her childhood room and read old papers from high school. She found letters from J. from the summers of '89, '90, '91. "I got a house off campus with Jon and Lew for next year," read one. "There's a huge kitchen where I'll make you dinner every night—penne with broccoli rabe, Cajun salmon, all your favorites, sweet Milly."

He was going to leave me someday, Milly thought, reading the letters. *He just didn't know it yet.*

In March, Drew pinged her: "Hey! So like I said, we'll all be at Xtian's sister's place in Brooklyn the second week in April. Would LOVE to see you. Please let me know how that week looks for you. xoxo."

They would *all* be here. Not just her. All.

Milly got that message on a Saturday. She had the wherewithal not to reply until she could talk about it with Gallegos the following Monday.

"It sounds like she misses you and she really wants to see you," he said after she told him.

"How can I make it clear to her I don't want to end up in one of her chapters as the childless single friend she goes to visit in New York?"

He laughed. "Is she working on something?"

"She's always working on something."

"If you're really worried about that, you could wait to bring that up until after you've seen her and you know for sure she's working on something."

Milly crossed her arms in her chair. "I just don't want to feel like I'm being used as fodder."

"Has she ever written about you before?"

"A little bit, in her first book. She was sweet about me."

"Then why are you worried about it?"

Milly thought about this on the way home. She thought that she would definitely not go out to Brooklyn to see them. It didn't seem fair that she'd have to be the one doing the traveling just because they had strollers and bags of diapers and that sort of thing. So instead she did some research online and found a brunch spot in the East Village that was right off the F train for them.

"Hi," she wrote back. "Would love to see you guys. How about Four Figs Sunday at noon? Right off the F train in the old hood. I'll make a reservation."

A few hours later Drew pinged back: "Restaurant in Manhattan a bit tough for us with the kids. But we'll rally! It'll be an adventure. See you there. Can't WAIT to see you! xxoo Drewpea."

From that moment on, Milly was pretty much sick whenever she thought about it. She saw Drew's post when they arrived in New York: "Grime! Shoving! Assholes! New York, I'm back and I'm loving it!" Oh, jeez. The pic of the four of them on the stoop outside Christian's sister's brownstone in Brooklyn. Saturday night at dinner, Milly told her dad she was meeting them the next day.

He looked vague, like he couldn't remember from their last conversation exactly who Drew was, never mind that she'd had twins. "That sounds jolly," he finally said.

"I don't wanna go," Milly told him flatly. "I'm sick about it."

Her dad seemed to truly look at her for the first time in a long time. "Come here," he said, beckoning Milly to lower her head toward him.

"What?"

"Lemme see that forehead."

She bent forward and he kissed her there.

"What was that for?" she asked him.

"For being here for me," he said. "And for what a beauty you are."

Milly looked at her dad's face. His nose had to have grown about twice its size in the past ten years. *That's what happens when you age*, Milly thought. *Your nose grows.* She was disgusted at the thought of that happening to her, though unfortunately it was already happening. For the first time in a while, she let herself cry a little, her hand on her dad's.

"Everyone's gone, Dad," she said.

He started in with his head nod, vaguely side to side, like his brain was going ticktock as he weighed that idea. "A lot of people are gone," he finally said.

Milly stayed up reading dumb mysteries at her dad's that night till three A.M. Finally she took half a pill to get to sleep. She woke up, feeling crappy, to the sound of the day nurse coming.

Back downtown, she showered and tried to put together something upbeat to wear. It was so rare when she cared that she hadn't bought new clothes in about four years, but this particular morning, her choices seemed truly grim. She finally put on some jeans that once fit her like a glove but now actually were a bit slack around the waist, plus a red-and-yellow Mondrian-type blouse, the brightest thing she had, and some midnight-blue leather boots she once thought of as her "fun shoes." She applied some eyeliner and lipstick for the first time since maybe her mother's funeral and tried to do something presentable with her hair and a hairband.

Then she started walking toward the brunch spot, feeling increasingly nauseated. Truly nauseated. She thought it was the lack of sleep and the pill. It was an eighty-one-degree early April day and she started sweating, feeling the blouse stick to her back. She never walked across the neighborhood during Sunday brunch hours anymore. There was too much life, too much romance, too many couples, too much Sunday-morning post-sex dewiness and arm clutching going on, too many babies, and way, way too many loud teens talking that outer-space hip-hop talk that was completely indecipherable to her. At a certain corner she just stopped and put a hand to her forehead, and a gentleman behind her slammed into her and scowled at her irritably before hurrying on his way. She had pills in her bag but she'd be damned if she was going to take one.

She was barely lucid by the time she crossed the street and, through the big, old-timey front glass window of the restaurant, she saw them. The four of them. Christian, his hair half gray now, appearing to try to talk down the manager. And her, in her big dark L.A. sunglasses, soothing one of the babies in her arms as it—*she*, meaning the baby—wailed.

Milly put both hands to her lips. She hunched her shoulders very small. Then, slowly, she started backing up, then quickly turned, walking rigid and compact in the hopes that if she made herself very, very small, she could get away.

"Milly!"

It sounded like her, but Milly kept walking. *Just get home*, she told herself. *Get back home*.

"Milly! I saw you! Where are you going?"

Drew was going to catch right up to her; she wasn't letting her off the hook. Milly just stopped in place without turning. And then suddenly there she was in front of Milly, out of breath. Milly hadn't seen her in a few years. Sure, she had aged. She had some lines around the eyes that seemed deeper than the last time Milly saw her. And Milly noticed that Drew had a stain on the chest of her Pucci-type silk blouse, probably where one of the babies had been drooling on her. But otherwise she looked great. She looked like she still managed to do yoga every day, even if she didn't. She had huge Dior sunglasses propped up on her head, and her toenails were painted a deep, velvety red against her raffia wedge sandals.

Drew took Milly by both arms. "Where are you going?" she asked, laughing, confused. "You saw us in the window, right? I mean," and she laughed again, then pulled Milly close and kissed her. "Hello! It's so good to see you!"

Milly just stared at her, blank, at a loss for what to say. Over Drew's shoulder, Milly could see Christian stepping out of the restaurant with one of the wailing girls in his arms, walking her back and forth, trying to calm her.

"I suddenly felt so ill walking over here," Milly finally said, "I thought I'd just better get home and text you I couldn't come."

Drew's brow furrowed. "What?" she asked.

"I didn't want to give one of the girls a bug. I haven't felt well all weekend."

"But we're together now," Drew said. "Don't worry about the girls. Just come sit with us at least a half an hour and have a juice. I want you to see them. I've waited so long for you to see them."

The brunchy-shoppy types were rushing past them, to and fro, through the bright, fake world of Sunday morning. "I don't think it's a good idea," Milly said. Then, shocked to hear herself, she said: "I've really struggled with your having decided to do this in the first place."

Drew started back. "Do what?" she asked. "You mean have kids?"

"You can't undo it now," Milly said.

Drew opened her mouth to speak, but said nothing. She took a step back from Milly and just looked at her, as though something was slowly dawning on her. "Oh my God," she finally said. "Christian was right."

This caught Milly off guard. "What do you mean, Christian was right?" she asked. "About what?"

Drew continued to look at Milly, as though she were staring deeper and deeper into her soul. Milly didn't like what she was feeling. She kept searching Drew's face for clues to the Drew she had known. But all she could see was a glossy, superior stranger—the kind of woman, the kind of entitled mother, taking up too much space, whom she would resent if she passed on the street.

Drew's face softened and she took Milly's hand. "Come inside and sit with us, Millipede," she said softly. "Please."

It made Milly profoundly uncomfortable to be pleaded with like that. "I really don't feel well. I haven't—I haven't been feeling well."

"I know," Drew said, still holding her hand. "Please come and sit with us."

Milly let Drew lead her forward. They were still holding hands. They walked a few paces, but a tidal wave of ooze was engulfing Milly. She stopped on the sidewalk and wept. She found her way into Drew's arms and wept on the shoulder of her silk blouse.

"It's all gone wrong," Milly said.

"Oh, sweetie," Drew said over and over, stroking her hair. Milly could hear street conversations swirling around them, then that pocket of silence as passersby realized something was amiss. It was one thing for a woman to cry on the street late on a drunken Saturday night, Milly knew, but she wasn't supposed to cry on a bright and cheery Sunday morning.

"Is she okay?" Milly heard a woman's voice.

"It's okay," Drew said. "I'm with her."

Milly kept on crying. She was horrified at herself, but she also didn't really care anymore.

Finally, Milly laughed. "Okay, all done!" she said.

"Come sit with us, Mills. Have something to eat. Have you eaten yet?"

Milly shook her head no. Drew led her into the restaurant. There was such a high-pitched, desperate din in the crowded room: mimosa-swilling youth and frantic waiters, everyone's shouts clanging off the pressed-tin ceiling and brasserie mirrors that lined the walls. Like a little girl, Milly let Drew pull her across the room toward the table where

Christian was daubing mushy food into the tiny, pursed mouths of two baby girls, one of them wailing away, who sat side by side in high chairs wearing tiny calico pinafore dresses that Milly guessed cost $300 each.

"I caught her!" Drew exclaimed triumphantly.

Christian stood up and took Milly in a long, tight hug. "You are a sight for sore eyes," he said. "And never, never again do we go this long apart. Deal?"

Milly laughed, self-conscious about looking like a holy freak from her crying jag. "You've obviously been busy," she said, gesturing at the little wriggly calico bundles, one's hair tuft slightly darker than the other's.

Christian picked up the one who was wailing. "This," he said, handing her to Milly, "is Erika. And Erika, this is your Auntie Milly."

"Auntie Milly, oh, no!" Milly exclaimed, trying to settle the baby in her arms comfortably. "That's a spinster if ever there was one."

"Sexy, fabulous, brilliant Auntie Mills," Drew corrected. "A New York bohemian and a painter. Like Auntie Mame!"

"Now you're setting the bar too high," Milly said, sitting down. Erika kept on wailing. "Oh, come on now, shh, shh," she said, smoothing back her tuft, "come on now, it's okay." Milly rocked her a bit until she quieted down. Her adorable face—like a ball of dough with two eyes, a nose, and a mouth pressed into it—went slack, dreamlike.

"Now you know why I dragged you in here!" Drew exclaimed.

So there it was, thought Milly. She and Drew were back on. After brunch and a walk, Drew sent Christian back to Brooklyn with the girls in a double stroller and she and Milly sat in a café to have a tea. There was a moment when Drew was looking up at the waitress to order her tea, one leg crossed over the other, and it occurred to Milly that she hadn't seen Drew in so long, she'd forgotten how beautiful she was.

When the waitress left, Drew leaned forward, crossing her arms on the table. "So you're still at the Christodora? It's yours?"

"It's not mine," Milly said. "Two years ago, his lawyer told me I had the option of staying there indefinitely, at least for the coming year or two, as long as I paid the maintenance. But it's getting hard to pay. I think I'll be moving into my parents' place soon."

"Would you ever consider moving to L.A.?" Drew asked. "Even just for half the year? Nobody should have to live through winter here."

Milly laughed. "The winters here now are practically as warm as in L.A.!"

Drew's eyes widened. "Everybody tells me that," she says. "I guess I just haven't really experienced it. That must be awfully weird, right?"

"It's beyond weird. It's so creepy. The world is falling apart. I'm glad we're not long for it."

"Millipede!" Drew exclaimed. "You are fifty, not eighty. Please take a break from here and come to L.A. and stay with us so I can introduce you to some guys. Or some girls. Just some fun dates for you!"

Milly recoiled. "Oh God, no, please!"

"Boaz!" Drew persisted. "You have to meet a guy named Boaz. Please, please come."

"What about my father?"

"Can't you leave him with a nurse for even a week?"

Milly didn't like that idea. No doubt the minute she landed in L.A., the nurse would ping her to say that her father was back in the hospital. "I don't know," she said.

Drew just shrugged. "The invite's open," she said.

"Thank you," Milly said before falling silent a moment. She was itching to ask Drew something but trying to hold on to enough pride not to ask her. Finally she couldn't stand it anymore. "Have you seen Mateo?"

"Umm," Drew began, as though she were slowly turning to acknowledge the elephant in the room. "No, in fact. He knows he's always welcome—he and his girlfriend. But other than a smiley face online once in a while, nothing." Her mouth twisted ironically. "Mateo's far too big for all of us now anyway. What about you?"

"Nothing," Milly said quietly. "No contact."

Drew absorbed this. "You do know . . . ?" she finally began.

"Know what?"

"That he's going to be here in a few weeks? In New York. Working on a project for an underground park."

This startled Milly. "No, I did not know that. How do you know it?"

"He posts it all over his feeds. He's looking for a place to stay in New York."

"Oh," Milly said. "We're not connected on there. All I see are a few pictures that aren't private."

The tea came, two separate little pots. Drew lightly traced the teapot handle with her finger. "Maybe now's a good time to reach out to him."

Even the thought of doing that filled Milly with humiliation. "I most certainly will not," she said. "I vowed that day in L.A. he'd never hear from me again, if that's what he wanted."

Drew pursed her lips, looked down. "That kid pisses me off, Milly. Wait! Don't get me started. It's not my business."

"It's okay," Milly said. "I know you know I've got a broken heart. That's enough."

Drew took Milly's hand across the table.

Walking home, Milly felt lighter than she'd felt in a while. She wondered how she'd come to tell herself a bitter story about Drew in her head and let the past few years between them slip away. In the grocery, picking up a few things, she chatted longer than usual with the cashier lady before leaving.

Up in the apartment, she pulled up the vertical posts. Sure enough, she saw, he'd be working on the UnderPark, not ten minutes away from the Christodora. In the very same neighborhood he'd grown up in. After a week or two, Milly started wondering if he was in town yet. Then she read something on a vertical that made it clear he was in town. It appeared a reporter had actually gone up to him and asked him about his parents. And he'd said, "I think they needed a break from me." And: "I really put them through it."

You're right about that last line, bud, she thought ruefully. But as for the needing-a-break line, she wanted to shout back: You *needed the break from* me. *At least be honest with yourself.*

Still, Milly couldn't get it out of her head that he was so nearby. When she ran errands in the neighborhood, she was terrified she'd somehow run into him. Then the day came when she put on her floppy-brimmed hat and large sunglasses and walked down to the site for the UnderPark. Of course the entrance was guarded and cordoned off to the public. Inside a deli across the street, she sat on a stool near the window, nursing an iced tea and feeling like a fool. She scrutinized every person who came and went past the guards.

Finally, she saw the guy, Char, the transgender black man whom she knew he worked with, come out, wiping his hands on a rag. Char turned back around, said something, and a moment later, right behind Char, there he was. Oh my goodness, Milly thought, there he was. Twenty-eight years old now! Oh, look at him! So lean and fit, his arms covered in tattoos. So he worked out now. Not that skinny dopesick kid she remembered, the kid she used to lose sleep over. So handsome, so healthy! With a red bandanna tied around his head, just like how he wore it the year he finally became a skater boy. Her hands flew to her lips watching him.

Then she realized, with horror, they were coming her way—they were taking a deli break. She fled the deli, twisting her head and neck to the left under her glasses and hat as she hurried down the street. Only at the end of the block did she dare glance back. They were out of view. Milly walked home stunned that she'd seen him, relieved to know he looked healthy, desperately hoping he hadn't recognized her.

"Why didn't you say something to him?" Gallegos asked her two days later.

"Are you kidding?" she said. "I'm not a glutton for punishment. I don't need to debase myself."

A couple days later, there was a horrible early-summer rainstorm that caused flooding all over the city. Milly rode it out uptown with her father and didn't come back downtown for two nights. But when she finally did, she woke up again in the Christodora to the familiar morning sounds of dogs barking and children playing down in the park. She walked to the window. It was late May and the temperature was already up in the high eighties at—what time was it?

She peered at her tablet. Ten A.M. *Good Lord*, she thought, *I can feel the heat already*. She idly watched people dart through the park on their way to work. The usual neighborhood bums were already gathering, paper coffee cups in hand. A young, dark-haired man on a bench, wearing a T-shirt, jeans, and white sneakers, was reading a tablet.

Then he raised his head and looked straight up at Milly's window.

She stood up and stepped back, her heart pounding, hand over her mouth. Was that him? Was she crazy? She turned, walked slowly back to the window, peeked out from the side. The young man was gone.

Then her buzzer buzzed.

She just stood there with her hand over her mouth. It buzzed again. She walked toward the door, pressed a button. "Who is this?" she asked.

"It's Mateo," a voice said. "I just saw you."

She put her hand on the wall. Then, finally, a hand on the "talk" button. "What do you want?" she asked.

"Can I come up and talk to you?"

"Just give me a few minutes," she said.

She walked away from the buzzer, sat down on the couch. Suddenly, the past bitter, lonely decade of her life broke over her like a giant wave. *Lost years, lost years!* she thought, balling her hands into fists. Why should she talk to him now?

Finally she managed to go to the window again. Mateo was sitting there on the bench again, his back to the Christodora.

Milly opened the window and stuck out her head. "I'll be down in a minute," she called to him. He turned around and held up a hand in recognition.

She washed her face, brushed her teeth, combed her hair and pulled it back in an elastic. She put on some jeans and a T-shirt and flats, took the elevator down the six flights, walked out the door of the building, across Avenue B, into the park and toward the bench Mateo was sitting on.

Mateo stared at her inscrutably as she approached. The first thing she thought was *What a handsome man I raised*. The second thing she noticed was that he had some gray flecks by his temples and furrows in his brow. And finally, she was just so relieved that he wasn't a scarecrow anymore.

She sat down on the bench a few feet away from him. "You look just like you look in all the tablet photos," she said. It was about all she could think of to say.

Mateo smiled dutifully and looked down again. Milly made idle patterns with her index finger on the leg of her jeans. Occasionally, she glanced at him. He was looking down in his lap, at his tablet screen, which had reverted to swirly sleep-mode patterns.

Milly noticed Ardit, the super, sweeping the sidewalk across the street in front of the building. He kept glancing their way, trying to be subtle. "Ardit's watching us," she finally said.

Mateo laughed a little, the way someone in an uncomfortable situation might allow a distracted laugh. Then the two of them continued to sit there in silence.

"Thanks for coming down," Mateo finally said, his voice scratchy.

"For some reason it was easier for me to come down than to have you come up," Milly said.

"That's okay." Mateo made another scratchy, scraping sound in his throat. "I wasn't going to just buzz you by surprise," he said. "I was getting ready to call you on this"—he pointed toward his tablet—"to see if you were okay with talking."

"It's okay."

"But then I saw you in the window and I just got up and buzzed. That was kind of stupid." He looked away again. *He's barely been able to make eye contact with me*, Milly thought.

"No, no, it's fine," she said. "I mean, here we are now. It's all fine."

But Mateo just kept looking down, paining Milly. "You look good," she continued, trying to brighten her tone. "You look healthy. You're healthy, right?"

"Yeah, I'm pretty healthy," he said, still looking away. "I've been clean ten years now."

"I know," she said. "Drew told me. That's wonderful. And you've done really well for yourself."

Finally, he looked at her with stricken eyes. "You look good, too," he said.

"Oh, please!" She laughed. "I'm an old lady. Withered on the vine!"

"No," he said. "You look good. Maybe like you need to eat a little more, though."

Milly laughed again. "Well, now you know what I used to think every time I looked at you."

At last Mateo laughed softly. "Okay," he said. "Fair enough." He flashed her an amused look, then turned away again.

They fell back into silence. "How's the UnderPark going?" Milly finally asked.

That earned her another glance. "Pretty good," he replied. "We had a setback with the rain. We had to vacate the site for four days while they remediated."

"Remediated! Wow. Is that the word they used?"

"That's the word they used."

"Very high-tech," she said.

He laughed again. "Yeah. It's a very high-tech, high-grade, high-stakes operation, painting leaves on a wall."

"Oh, I'm sure it's more than that. I've seen your work with your partner. It's beautiful."

"Char?" he asked. "Yeah, well, it all started with her. I mean with him. I'm always slipping on the pronouns."

"That must be hard to keep straight," Milly said, "after knowing someone for so long."

"Just the pronoun thing, mostly," he said. "Char was basically always a man, from the day I met her. Him."

More silence. Ardit sure seemed to be taking his time sweeping the sidewalk today, Milly thought. It was a very funny thing to live in a doorman building. They didn't need to see much to put things together.

"How about you?" Mateo finally asked. "You doing okay?"

Milly sighed. "The last few years haven't been the best. Bubbe died."

"Yeah, I know," he muttered. He was ashamed, Milly could tell, because he hadn't gotten in touch when it happened.

"That was an awful, drawn-out thing," Milly continued. "And Zayde's going senile now. He takes up a lot of time."

He glanced at her, shook his head.

"So no, I can't lie to you. The past few years haven't been great. Past many years, actually. Life's just kind of . . . emptied out." Milly didn't mean to make him feel overly bad, but she didn't feel like putting a fake smiley face on things, either.

Suddenly Mateo pivoted toward her, his eyes glassy. "Can you accept an apology from me?"

That came so suddenly to Milly! She caught her breath, then sighed and looked down. If only he realized it was about so much more than an apology, she thought. It was about everything; it was about all those years together and why the void that followed walloped her.

"You want me to just shut up and go?" he asked.

"No, no," she said. "It's just—I have been hurting for so long, Mateo. Really, really hurting."

"I know, I know," he said, all in a rush. "I know, and I didn't mean to hurt you. I just—I never knew. I never really understood why you adopted me, why you wanted me, and why you kept taking me back. I fucked up so many times, it got to the point I couldn't look you in the face. I didn't know what to do but to be alone. Every time you looked at me, all I can remember is I saw disappointment, I saw pity."

"*Pity?*" Milly interjected. "You saw pity? Is that why you think we adopted you?"

"Why else would you adopt a fucking AIDS orphan when you could have your own kid? Bubbe brought you to the boys' home in Brooklyn one day and you saw me and you ended up taking me home out of pity."

"I fell in *love* with you, Mateo," Milly snapped back, quite peeved to have had her intentions mistaken. "I fell in love with a little boy with a big bushel of hair and a bunch of Crayolas and craft paper in front of him. And I didn't want to give birth to a kid because I didn't want to watch my kid go through what I went through and what my mother went through with mental *illness*. So you're where I put that love instead, okay?" Milly took a breath, winded from the sheer volume of her revelation.

Mateo was silent, tracing finger patterns on his tablet. "So why'd you never tell me that?"

"I thought it was obvious. I thought it was obvious every single day I held your hand and walked you through this park. Mateo, those first years with you were the happiest years of my life."

He looked up. "They were?"

"Yes, they were. But then you hit a certain age and I think suddenly you started asking yourself all these questions—"

"I did! I did!" he said, worked up. "That's when it started, when I was fourteen or fifteen."

"Yes," Milly continued, "and you know? You know what? We should have sensed it; we should have gone to therapy with you instead of sending you yourself and putting it all on you. We should have talked this all out then. But—" Milly was smudging away tears now; she felt rather overwhelmed from suddenly putting words to something she hadn't fully understood at the time. "I guess I was just scared of you and I stepped back. It was wrong, it was wrong. Then the drugs started, and then I was really scared."

Mateo looked at Milly, eyes wide. "Those years are, like, such a blur to me," he said. "Just, like, years lost."

"And then suddenly you were in the sober house in California and you said you weren't coming back. And when a boy grows up and says he wants to be set free, what can a mother do?"

Mateo snapped his mouth shut, considered. "You really thought of yourself as my mother?"

"You are absolutely thickheaded!" she exclaimed.

Mateo laughed. "Well, I don't know if Jared saw it that way."

Oh God, thought Milly. Now he'd gone and said the dreaded J-word. "Well, I'm not speaking for him," she said firmly. "I'm speaking for me. Millimom. The bleeding heart."

Mateo looked at her sidelong. "You do have a bleeding heart, you know. It used to drive me fucking crazy."

"Well, it drove—" Milly caught herself before saying the J-name herself. "It drove him crazy, too. He used to mock me for it and tell me I was a pushover."

"Do you talk to him?"

"No," she said. "Well, through lawyers."

"Can I go back to my original question?"

"What was that? I can't even remember at this point. My head is swimming."

"Can you forgive me for being a fuckup and wrecking ten years of your life?"

She looked at him again. *I can't believe I raised this man* is all she kept thinking. *This is the boy who elaborately matched his* frites *to his condiments? Who kicked his feet against his butt while he drew? My God*, she thought, with a catch of fear in her throat. *Life is zooming by, slipping out of my fingers like salt, more than halfway gone.*

"I'm just glad it's over," she said. "It's really over?"

"It's really over. I mean—"

"I know, I know," Milly stopped him. "One day at a time, that's how it goes. Drew's told me that a million times. Just for today." She said it in kind of a singsong, and he laughed. "But it's still really over, right?" she asked again.

"Yes." He shrugged. "It's over."

"Well," she began, "then I forgive you." She paused. "I can't believe you thought all those years we took you in out of *pity*. If that's what you were really thinking, then it explains a lot."

He looked at her keenly. "There wasn't just a little bit of pity in there?"

She opened her mouth, about to protest. Then she considered. She held her open hands aloft. "Mateo, what can I say? I am a middle-class, old-school-liberal Jewish New York woman. A dying breed. Look at my mother!" she pleaded.

"That's exactly what I mean!" he said.

"I know what you mean. But I don't think *pity* is quite the word I'd agree with. I visited you with Bubbe and I saw a little boy without a home, who'd lost his mother, with a lot of talent. And it just so happened that I needed you and I didn't know it yet. And the more I came back, the more I fell in love with you."

Finally, Mateo managed to look at her with a yielding softness in his face. He made a fist and held it toward her.

"What's that?" Milly asked.

He frowned. "It's a fist bump. Remember the Obamas and the fist bump?"

"No one's ever offered me a fist bump before."

"Well, here you go."

Milly made a fist and bumped it against Mateo's.

He smiled. "Not bad. That's a start."

"Not a bad start?" Milly asked.

"Not a bad start."

They sat there silently for a moment. Milly felt at once deeply contented and wiped out, like she'd just run a marathon. There were a million other things she wanted to say, to ask him about, swimming in her head, but somehow she couldn't grasp onto one of them. Then something occurred to her.

"I have something upstairs I need to give you," she said.

Wariness flashed in his eyes. "I don't think I'm ready yet to see the apartment after all these years."

She raised an eyebrow. "You mean the scene of your sculpture demolition?"

He held a hand up to his forehead. "Oh, shit, please not that."

Milly erupted in laughter. "You don't know what perverse joy that memory has given me these past few years. Once I got over the initial horror."

But her remark seemed to discomfit him. "I owe him an apology," Mateo said.

Milly regarded him keenly. Then she sighed. "Sometimes I think I do, too," she said.

"For what?"

But she shook her head. "It's too much to go into now. And suffice to say, sometimes I think I don't, so . . ." She trailed off. "Anyway, just wait here a second."

In the lobby, she smiled sheepishly at Ardit while she waited for the elevator.

"Reunion," he said.

"Ish," she replied.

Upstairs, she pulled the Polaroid from between the pages of a book on a shelf where she'd safe-kept it, then tucked it in a small manila envelope from her desk. Back outside, she sat down beside him again and handed it to him.

"You've gone a long time without this," she said.

He glanced at her, then opened the envelope. He looked at the Polaroid, then buried his face in his hand. Then, only then, she noticed the small letters tattooed on his fingers. *I, S, S,* and *Y.*

"Issy Mendes," he said, his face still buried away.

She sat closer to him, put an arm around him, and nestled his head on her shoulder. "Yes indeed," she said. "Thank you, Issy Mendes."

Three days later, Milly walked down to the UnderPark. "I'm Mateo Mendes's mother," she told the security guard.

"Yeah," said the security guard, waving her through. "He told me to look for you today."

Milly walked down a sloping old concrete passage that slipped suddenly underground into musty darkness, old wood and stone on both sides of her and above. Then the passage opened into a garden the size of a parking lot, full of an eerie sunlight filtered down from above.

There were workers everywhere, laying down paving, carrying greenery, hoisting beds of tile up onto scaffolding.

"This is unreal," she exclaimed to the guard. "Whatever happened to the old, abandoned Lower East Side that nobody cared about?"

"That place is long gone," he said. He led her to a far corner of the garden, which had been cordoned off with sawhorses. Half of one wall shimmered with tens of thousands of tiny silvery-blue-and-green painted leaves.

Mateo was up on a scaffold, his back to her.

"Mateo, your mom's here," the guard called.

Mateo turned. "Hey!" he shouted down, waving. He and Char climbed down, wiped their hands on rags, walked over to Milly. Mateo pulled back a sawhorse so that she could enter their workspace.

"Milly, this is Charlie Gauthier. Char, this is Milly Heyman, my mom."

From afar, a woman who'd been conferring with two assistants walked forward. "Millicent Heyman!" the woman exclaimed, her arms open. "Where have you been?"

Milly flushed in pleasure and shame. It was Ruby Levin, the head of Creative Production Fund. She was one of so many people Milly had dropped contact with over the past few years. Events not attended, e-mails not replied to, friendships not maintained.

Milly took her hug. "I've been a total disaster," she said. "Can you forgive me?"

"Shut up!" Ruby crowed. "Forgive you? I'm just thrilled to see you. I'm going to pimp you out for our fall fund-raiser."

"I'm useless!" Milly cried.

"Oh, shut up," Ruby clucked. She stepped back, held both arms wide in her mama-bear manner. "Mother and son artists at the same project site!" she declared. "I am loving this moment!"

Embarrassed, Milly turned to Charlie. "It's so great to meet you," she said. "I think you're so fantastically talented."

Charlie shook her hand and lightly hugged her simultaneously. "It's great to meet you, too," he said. "I've been waiting to."

Mateo looked down, blushing. Everyone was quiet a moment.

Ruby, reliably, broke the silence. "What do you think of this gorgeousness?" she asked, pointing at the shimmering leaves.

"They're stunning," Milly said. She stared at them, squinting, blinking, as they twinkled before her eyes. "They look like they're dancing off the wall."

"It's the paint we're using," said Char. "It's superspecial."

"It's the most expensive paint ever created in the history of humankind," said Ruby.

"But how—" Milly began. She couldn't stop staring at the forest of shimmering, tiny leaves. "How do you get—"

"Show her, Mateo," Char boomed. "Take her up and show her."

"Go look at the paint up close, Milly," Ruby joined on.

"Well—"

"Come on." It was Mateo. He grabbed Milly's hand, led her over to the scaffolding.

"This is, what?" Milly asked. "Thirty feet high?"

"Thirty-two exactly," he said. "Go up the ladder first. I'll come up behind you."

"This is crazy!" she cried, giggling. She felt a little dizzy, a little crazy.

But Milly climbed all the way up to the platform, then slowly dared to turn and look around. "Oh my goodness, it looks out over the treetops! It's so beautiful."

Mateo climbed up on the platform next to her. "Wave to the people," he said, and they waved down to Char and Ruby and the rest.

"Isn't it amazing?" Ruby called up. "Soon, this whole area"—she gestured with a sweep around her—"will all be trees. Gorgeous subterranean trees."

Milly spied the paint in a bucket, full of rich, iridescent streaks of green, blue, and gold. "That is really some wonder-paint," she marveled.

"So," Mateo said, picking up a stencil with an array of leaves cut into it, "I just sort of place a stencil halfway over what I did last. Like this—" He held the stencil over a blank area where he'd left off. "And then—well, here, I'll hold the stencil. Pick up the brush and try this one."

"I'll mess it up," Milly said.

"You can't mess it up. It's stencils; it's like kids' play."

Milly dipped the wide brush into the bucket and stirred it around in the paint, which glistened to life when disturbed. Briefly, it mesmerized her. *Oh, paints!* she thought. *Oh, the beauty of paints in their jars.* "It looks like there's diamond dust in there," she said. The paint shimmered on the edge of the brush.

"Now come here," Mateo said.

Milly put the brush against the stencil, began to draw it downward as streams of luminous paint trickled beneath the brush.

"No, no," Mateo said, "watch this stroke." He put his hand over hers on the brush and flicked it quickly left to right, as though he were spackling something. "You see how the colors in the paint open up now? Watch the blue start to emerge."

He was right. Blue and green bloomed out of the silver, so that when he pulled away the stencil, new leaves twinkled before Milly's eyes.

"I've never seen anything like that," she said.

Mateo stepped back a pace, handed her the stencil and the heavy brush. "Here you go," he said. "Your turn."

ACKNOWLEDGMENTS

Susan Golomb and Scott Cohen at Writers House and Morgan Entrekin and Peter Blackstock at Grove Atlantic all saw something in *Christodora* and helped me make it a better book. Also at Grove Atlantic, Deb Seager, John Mark Boling, Judy Hottensen, Elisabeth Schmitz, and Becca Putman were a joy to work alongside in putting this book out into the world. Also, Charles Rue Woods and Roberto de Vicq de Cumptich created a beautiful cover.

Several brilliant magazine editors gave me work prior to and while I was writing this book, and I count many of them as friends: Walter Armstrong, Laura Whitehorn, Jennifer Morton, Oriol Gutierrez, Carl Swanson, Jesse Oxfeld, Aileen Gallagher, Jebediah Reed, Noreen Malone, Denny Lee, Aaron Hicklin, Jeffries Blackerby, Jesse Ashlock, Maura Egan, Kai Wright, and Sally Chew.

Christodora is a work of fiction obviously inspired by the history of AIDS activism in America, particularly New York, and in my efforts to cleave to the bones, if not the fine points, of what really happened, I am indebted to the amazing documentaries *How to Survive a Plague* by David France and *United in Anger* by Jim Hubbard, as well as Sarah Schulman's invaluable online ACT UP Oral History Project. And also to more than twenty years of in-depth coverage from the folks at *POZ* magazine, the closest thing to a work family this freelancer has ever had.

I am so grateful to the generous-hearted Sarah Burnes, an early reader of this book, who told me what to lose, expand on, and modulate. Other first readers were Mark Leydorf, Maria Striar, Jeffrey Golick, and James Hannaham—all members of my beloved urban family, which also includes Clint Ramos and Jason Moff, Cathay Che, Cara Buckley, Stephen Best, John Polly, Christian Del Moral, Mike Ackil, and Diana Scholl. My love and gratitude for all of you are woven into these pages. Thanks as well to Noel Alicea, Michael Alicea, Maggie Malina and Tim Horn for their reads and feedback. And to Nancy Tan for an impeccable copyedit.

In the past twenty years, I have met and interviewed so many people living with and/or fighting against the epidemic of HIV/AIDS, which has colored my entire adult life as an urban gay man. Many of them are no longer alive and many of those who are have had a rough go. Those conversations live in my heart and moved me to write this book, which I hope in part is about what people are capable of, individually and collectively, when pushed to the wall.

CREDITS

picador.com

blog
videos
interviews
extracts